THE KNIGHTS ETERNAL

VOWBREAKER

BOOK TWO

Robert J. Duperre

Published by Outland Entertainment LLC
3119 Gillham Road
Kansas City, MO 64109

Founder/Creative Director: Jeremy D. Mohler
Editor-in-Chief: Alana Joli Abbott

ISBN: 978-1-947659-74-2
EBOOK ISBN: 978-1-947659-78-0
Worldwide Rights
Created in the United States of America

Editor: Alana Joli Abbott
Copy editor: Lorraine Savage
Cover Illustration: Tomasz Chistowski
Cover Design: Shawn King
Interior Layout: Mikael Brodu

Printed and bound in the United States of America.

Visit **outlandentertainment.com** to see more, or follow us on our Facebook Page **facebook.com/outlandentertainment/**

For Beverly Jenkins,
whose influence forms the emotional core of this book.

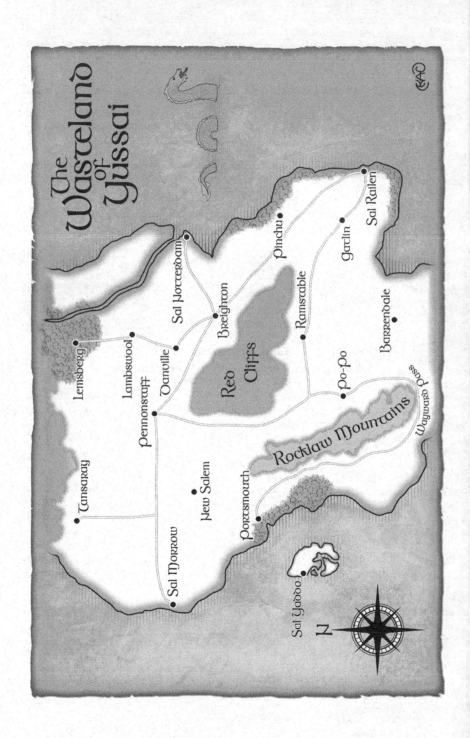

Should one sheep in one hundred turn up missing, it would be irresponsible of the shepherd to abandon the loyal in service of the lost. It is the obligation of the sinner to discover why they went astray. Celebrate the faithful, for they have not left your side.
—**Book of the Pentus, Allegories 6:12**

A s he took one laborious step after another, Shade concluded that there was nothing in the world worse than the cold. Not demons from the Nine Hells, not morally bankrupt brigands, not immortal undead-controlling fiends with visions of grandeur. He had survived all of those. The cold, on the other hand, was about to do him in.

Snow billowed all around, and flecks of sleet assaulted his face like a million wasp stings. His thick beard had frozen solid, becoming a weight that pulled down his chin. Fully buttoning his duster and pulling it up over his nose did no good because the stiff leather chafed his flesh just as badly as the ice and wind.

After clawing at another rocky ledge with bone-numb fingers, Shade pulled himself upright. He turned around, staring at the downward expanse of never-ending white. It was like Lemsburg and the outer Wasteland had ceased to exist. He didn't know how far up the mountain he had climbed, nor how long he had been moving. It seemed like days. It could have been longer. And yet he still struggled ever upward, seeking passage to a land that he was not sure existed.

Why?

Because his dying brother had told him to, and his dead lover had confirmed it.

I've made worse decisions based on less, he thought, and laughed through his shivers. Meesh would have been proud.

Thinking of his brother brought his laughter to a sputtering end. Meesh, who never met a joke he wouldn't tell, no matter how stupid. Meesh, whose zest for simply *living* used to be enough to break Shade from his doldrums. Meesh, who would eventually hunt him down and end his life.

Shade slumped down into a mound of snow, sinking in up to his chest. His head drooped, his eyes fluttered closed, and he debated whether he should go on. What good was this quest if his own brother would eventually come to kill him? And it wasn't as if he could blame Meesh for that. The Pentus had brought him and his brothers into the world for a reason—to protect the innocent, to spread joy through music, and to send demons back to the Nine Hells. Meesh and the new Abednego would simply be doing what they were supposed to in hunting him. Shade, and Shade alone, was the one who had broken his sacred vows.

"Stop it," he muttered into the wind. "The Pentus isn't real."

He was stalling again, ruminating—his constant pattern ever since he lost Vera. He could not do that any longer. He owed it to her, and to Abe, and even to Meesh, to do everything he could to find the truth.

With that thought, he forced himself to renew his upward trek. The wind continued its assault, fluttering his duster and trying to force him back. It was only when he reached a natural channel bordered by two jagged stone walls that he was able to regain his footing. He felt his heartbeat through his fingertips as he used the rock face to steady himself. His feet ached. His usually dark skin was ashen and felt like crinkled paper. He slid his hand across a sharp wedge of stone and a cut opened on his palm. Blood trickled out, thick as syrup.

Shade tucked his hands into the sleeves of his duster and cursed the fact he hadn't brought gloves. Truth be told, there were many things he wished he'd had the foresight to obtain before this journey. A pair of heavy undergarments would have helped, along with a woolen cap and boots that wouldn't fray from the constant moisture and cold. When exhaustion struck him and his eyes drifted half-mast, he thought that perhaps it hadn't been the brightest move to discard his Eldersword at the Hallowed Stones. Sure, he'd tossed aside the ancient weapon out of principle—he had abandoned his sacred duty as a knight, why should he continue carrying a knight's weapon?—but he sure could use the healing energy of the Rush right about now. The torrent of energy that surged through him when holding his old Eldersword would've dulled the worst of his pain, at least for a little while. The deceased Ronan Cooper's saber, which hung from his hip and thwacked painfully against his knee with every other step, was useless by comparison. As was the guitar strapped across his back, which made it difficult to keep his balance.

His foot struck something beneath the snow, and he fell like a toppled monument. The guitar case flipped up, whacking the back of his head hard enough to bring stars. Intense, hard coldness slipped upward against his side, then disappeared. Rising onto his knees, Shade patted himself down. The revolver he'd stolen from Meesh was no longer tucked in his belt. He thrust his hands into the snow, searching until his numb fingertips thwacked against a wedge of cold steel. He lifted the gun, swept ice from the barrel, jammed it back into his belt. This wasn't the first time he had dropped the burner. Add *holster* to the ever-growing list of things he should have taken with him.

What made it all worse was that Lupe, his Warhorse, had mentioned all of this to him before he started the trek. The tinny voice coming out of the hovering machine had berated him constantly after he abandoned his brothers. *"You really should gather some things to protect yourself from the elements,"* it had said. *"You don't know where you're going. Only an idiot would start a journey blind to the path,"* it had scoffed. *"Please think about what you're doing before you leave,"* it had finally pleaded. But of course, Shade hadn't listened. He was too desperate to get the hell out of the Wasteland and find answers. So he'd stowed Lupe in a trench halfway up the mountain—the Warhorse had been adamant it would not be any help to him when the ground pitched at an angle greater than forty degrees—and went off on his own.

Lupe was right, he thought. *A freaking machine has more sense than me.*

He rolled his eyes, stretched his unsteady legs, and kept moving. Onward and upward. Ever upward.

The channel ended, exposing him fully to nature's wrath once more. Shade hobbled out in the open, his muscles screaming, his head spinning. It was getting much darker now than it had been when he'd entered the channel. He wondered whether the sun was setting or if his eyes were starting to fail him.

Either option would be disastrous. He'd already spent multiple nights out in the open. Just the thought of another few hours spent tucked under the snow trying to keep warm filled him with dread. He considered the weight of the guitar on his back. Perhaps if he could find some shelter, he could put the instrument to good use. Playing it might not be an option, but it *was* made mostly of wood, and he had a pair of flintstones in his pocket...

No. He gripped the part of the case that protruded over his shoulder with one freezing hand. The only shelter he had found during this futile journey was the partially concealed channel he just exited. Even if he could shield himself from the wind and snow enough to get a fire going, the meager fuel the guitar provided wouldn't last long. Was he really willing to burn his most prized possession for a few fleeting moments of warmth?

The survivor in him said *yes.* The musician said *hell no.*

The musician won.

As he trudged along, the steadying darkness turned his surroundings gray. The falling snow now resembled blowing ash. He reached a formidable wall of bleak stone that stretched out as far as he could see in either direction. His already sunken spirits dropped even further. He lifted his head—his neck creaked like a rusty hinge—and realized he stood at the base of another cliff. He brought his freezing hands to his mouth, blew on them, and pondered his next step. He could walk the length of the cliff to see if he could find a way around, or he could climb. The rock face seemed to have plenty of handholds and it was only thirty feet tall. Perhaps forty. It was hard to tell with the dim light and billowing snow.

"I've climbed steeper," he said, thinking of the times he and Meesh had raced up the face of the largest crag in the Red Cliffs. The sorrow of betrayal squeezed in on him again. He put it out of his mind.

And he climbed.

Not yet halfway up, Shade regretted his choice. His fingers bled from jabbing them into gaps in the stone, and his toes screamed in pain when they bent backward while trying to gain footholds. Every part of him ached and his breath came out ragged. He paused for a moment to get his bearings, feeling the full weight of all the useless junk he carried, and then reached his right hand up for another weight-bearing protrusion. His fingertips, now painted with red crystals, jammed into the gap. He forced his arm to flex, pulling himself upward. His right foot slid up as well, the toe of his boot coming to rest against an outcropping. After another deep breath, he shoved off as hard as he could, trying to take the pressure off his arm.

Another gust of wind blew, carrying with it a thunderous howl as loud as a hellbeast's bleating. The sound rattled Shade as he pressed too hard against the stone ledge beneath his right foot. The rock crumbled and both his legs lost purchase, sending him into a series of spastic windmill kicks. The added weight, combined with his fatigue, made him lose his grip with his less-dominant right hand. He hung there by four numb and aching fingerbones, flopping like a fish out of water, crying out into the wind.

That howl pierced his eardrums again, and Shade lost his grip entirely. He flipped head over heels as he plummeted. Time seemed to slow. For a split second, he could see the white, snowy ground he careened toward, only fifteen or twenty feet away at most. *That's not too far*, he thought during the moment of calm that comes before tragedy. *I survived a fight with the master of the dead. This should be a piece of ca—*

He fell into the snow back-first. His guitar case took the brunt of the blow when he struck bedrock, jerking his spine severely, knocking the air from his lungs and causing his extremities to explode with white-hot fire. His head struck the ground with such force that the world around him went black, then blinding white, then black again. That strange howl washed over him like a harbinger from the Nine Hells come to claim his soul.

It's over, he thought meekly. His body wouldn't obey him when he tried to move. Likely his back was broken. If that were true, he knew his fate would be to simply lie out here in the elements, waiting to either freeze to death or for whatever beast made that horrific sound to rip him limb from limb. He would never be a knight again. Never honor Abe. Never find the truth. Never get the chance to plead with Meesh to spare his life.

Oddly, none of that really bothered him. Wondering if his brothers would ever find his body, did.

That ominous howl continued. Using the last of his strength, Shade succeeded in pivoting his head. His vision was half obstructed by both agony and a layer of snow, but he was able to see something out there in the burgeoning darkness that caused his heart to thump and the breath to wheeze in his throat.

A pair of figures cloaked in shadow approached through the dim void. One walked on two legs, the other on four. Shade knew who they were: Hadden, the guardian of the Nine Hells, and his faithful hound Sereberus, come to claim his soul and deliver it to Fawkes the Sorter, who would then decide what kind of torment a blasphemous monster such as Shadrach the Twentieth deserved to suffer for the rest of eternity.

"I'm sorry," Shade whispered. His eyes, rimmed with frozen tears, squeezed shut. The outside world went dark and soon his inner world did too. In the moment when he greeted oblivion, he found relief in the fact that he wasn't cold anymore.

As Abe would have said, it's the little things that matter most.

The sight of gawking masses sent waves of giddiness through his body. He stared out at the crowd—faces as far as he could see, gathered beneath an overcast sky, silent in their reverence—and lifted his guitar. The feedback from the amplifiers buzzed in his ears.

As the moment captured him, he did what he did best. He picked note after note with his capable left hand, while his right danced between frets. The sounds he created were jarring, a spiraling cacophony of off-key tones that transformed a once beloved hymn into the celebration of chaotic violence he always believed it to be.

The crowd ate it up. They grew steadily more agitated, until the very end, when he threw back his head and let loose with the frenzied climax. The sounds infused him with vigor, with desire, with *purpose*.

This was what he was always meant to do, to blend all his life's doubts and fears and hardships into this one pure moment of abstract art. It was only in times like these that he felt truly free.

Shade's eyes fluttered open and the song faded away. His ears stopped ringing and his fingers stopped tingling. When his vision cleared, he found himself sprawled out on his back on a slatted wood floor. A musty blanket covered him and a fire crackled in a large stone hearth a few feet away. He smiled at the marvelous warmth, but that smile disappeared when he realized he didn't know where he was or how he had gotten here.

He stretched his arms and legs tentatively and arched his back. There was pain, but a bearable amount. *No broken bones. Lucky.* He pushed the blankets off his body and inched himself to sitting. Glancing around, he saw that he was in what looked to be a log cabin consisting of a single large room. The cabin had many windows looking out onto a brightening but still snowy world. Combined with the fireplace, those windows allowed enough light in that he could see the rest of his surroundings clearly.

There was a couch behind Shade, serving to section off a portion of the vast space. Propped on the center cushion was his unbroken guitar case, the neck rising above the cushions like a beacon of hope. A short table stood against the couch, atop which Shade's neatly-folded duster, Cooper's saber, and Meesh's pistol was stacked. Someone had definitely taken pride in their presentation; it looked like a shrine. He cocked his head and listened but no sound came to him other than the crackle of flames.

His knees creaked when he stood up, and he groaned at the soreness running up and down his spine. He limped to the table and snatched up the saber—it hurt to bend to the side like that—and slid the blade free from its scabbard. When no demons appeared to flay him, he went about searching the rest of the room.

The place was filled with oddities that would have been a rarity in the Wasteland. Tables and chairs with hollow aluminum legs; books with glossy covers reflecting the firelight; panels with switches embedded in the walls; a mounted black mirror similar to the ones in the Heartcube chamber of the Cooper Station; a couple of darkened globes hanging from the ceiling indicating electric lighting. The room was divided into sections—the den around the hearth, a sleeping nook with a large four-poster bed, a dining space with a small table with two chairs, and even a kitchen, complete with an oven and a large white refrigeration unit that constantly hummed. The only door into or out of the cabin was to the right of the unit. A placard stating *Keep Calm Shit Happens* was nailed on the door.

All of it, baffling. Shade rubbed his eyes and re-sheathed his saber.

He wandered back to the warmth of the hearth, held his hands out, and rubbed them together. None of this made any sense. One minute he was on the mountain, near death after falling from the cliff, and the next he was here. Perhaps he really *had* died, and this was where he had to wait for the Ferrymaster to row him to the Crystalline Hall. *No, that's not right.* He had seen the shadows approaching. If this was a waystation, it belonged to the forces of darkness, not the Pentus.

The Pentus doesn't exist.

The blasphemous thought made him shudder. He turned away from the fire, approached the bookshelf beside the hearth, and ran his calloused fingertips along the spines. So many strange books with nonsensical titles, written by authors whose names seemed foreign yet somehow familiar. *Babel-17* by Samuel R. Delaney, *The Penguin Science Fiction Omnibus* by Brian Wilson Aldiss, *Winnie-the-Pooh* by A.

A. Milne, *Imperium and Imperio* by Sutton E. Griggs, *Blonde on Blonde Songbook* by Bob Dylan. He paused at that last one.

His eyes drifted closed, and he found himself back in the dream that he had nearly forgotten after waking up.

The scene shifted. No longer did he hold a guitar in his hands, but a rifle. His clothes were thick and uncomfortable and patterned in shifting greens and browns. He soared in a steel bird high in the air, something heavy and ungainly strapped to his back. Someone shoved him, and he screamed as he plummeted, falling much too quickly toward the earth below, surrounded on all sides by men who shared his fate...

A *clank*, followed by the scrape of wood sliding over wood, broke him out of the untimely hallucination. Shade spun around, hunkering down in a defensive pose. He grabbed the handle of the saber and kept his breath steady. If this unknown fiend decided to test his mettle, Shade would be prepared.

Only it wasn't a fiend that entered the cabin, but a man dressed head-to-toe in heavy garb. A large dog hustled in after him. The man shoved the door closed, sealing out the wind and cold, and audibly sighed when he leaned against it.

The dog spotted Shade first. It took a few pattering steps forward, bright hazel eyes that seemed far too intelligent for a canine taking in seemingly every inch of him. It had a long snout, short black hair, large floppy ears, and a long whipping tail. The dog barked at its master. The man's shoulders tensed. Eyes hidden by draped fabric stared Shade's way.

"You're awake. Cool. Sorry I wasn't here for it. Sucks when your only bathroom's outside."

The man kicked himself off the door, patted the dog with a gloved hand, and began to remove his clothing. He did all of this, as if having a Knight Eternal standing fifteen feet away was the most normal thing in the world.

"Who are you?" Shade growled.

The stranger unwound the scarf from around his neck and pulled off his woolen hat, revealing a middle-aged man with pale skin, dark eyes, and a head of moppish dark hair gone gray at the temples. He gave Shade a sideways smirk. "I have been called many names," he said as he unbuttoned his jacket. "Only a few of which are pronounceable by the human tongue."

"Such as?" He pulled the saber a few inches out of the scabbard. "Are you a demon?"

The man hung his jacket on a hook and winced. "Shit. Idiot. Yeah, no demon here. Sorry 'bout that. Feeling my oats a bit, and a little nervous. It's not everyday someone famous literally falls out of the sky right in front of you."

Shade glared.

"Jesus, you're serious," the man said, sounding disappointed. "The name's Ken. Ken Lowery." He pointed at the black dog, who'd joined his side once again. "And that's Silas."

"Ken. Silas." Shade relaxed ever so slightly. "Where are we?"

"Everywhere. Nowhere. On the top of a goddamn mountain." He sighed. "You thirsty? Beer okay?"

When Shade didn't answer, Ken muttered something under his breath and approached the refrigeration unit. He grabbed a handle hidden on the side, and the front facing swung open.

"Lager's all I got," Ken said, snatching a pair of glass bottles. "Hope that's okay. I don't really got a choice. I just drink and eat whatever they give me."

Moving with the nonchalance of someone without an ounce of fear for his life, Ken approached him and held out the bottle. Shade took it mindlessly.

"Cheers," Ken said and took a swig.

Something bumped against Shade's leg. He glanced down to see the dog, Silas, sitting at his feet, mouth opened wide, tongue flapping. He patted the dog's head. It was an automatic action, done without thinking. Silas, panting, seemed to smile. Shade's tension eased even more.

"Yeah, he's a great boy," Ken said as he wandered to one of the wall panels and flicked a switch. The electric lights hanging from the ceiling came on, brightening the cabin. "The best."

"How did I get here?" Shade asked. He couldn't stop looking into Silas's far-too-intelligent eyes.

Ken pulled the table away from the couch and plopped down onto it. "Si and me were out in the blizzard looking for you. Si howled when he caught your scent, but we didn't get to you until you'd already fallen off the cliff. We dragged you back here on a sled."

"You were looking for me?" Shade froze in place, blinking rapidly. "You knew I'd be here?"

"Well, yeah."

"Who *are* you?"

Again, Ken shrugged. "Just a guy who got held up on the way to seeing his wife. Which sucks, but hey, the universe works in mysterious ways, right?" He laughed; it was a sad sound. "Anyway, I'm a sorta lighthouse keeper, I guess. Put here to greet travelers when they've lost their way and put them back on the right path. So they don't die out there in the snow and low oxygen. You know, the usual."

"You get a lot of people wandering up onto the mountain?"

"Nope," Ken said with a chuckle. "You're the first."

"How long have you been here?"

"Too long."

Shade sipped the surprisingly tasty beer while he mulled it over. None of this made any sense. It hurt his brain thinking about it. Silas nudged him, demanding his attention. Shade lowered himself to the floor and allowed the dog to lick his bearded face. A genuine smile creased his chapped lips.

"How'd you know I'd be coming?" he asked when Silas finally stopped licking him and curled his large canine body into his lap.

"Someone left instructions," said Ken.

"Instructions?"

Ken pointed toward a hefty wooden chest that Shade hadn't thought twice about when he first explored the room. "Every seven days I get supplies. I empty that chest there and leave it outside. When I get up in the morning, it's filled with everything I'll need to survive all by my lonesome up here. Well, this week's delivery came with lotsa stuff I wasn't expecting, including a letter telling me I'd have my first visitor." He spread his hands out wide. "And here you are."

"I'd like to see this letter."

"Sure." He reached into his shirt, pulled out a folded piece of paper, and slid it across the floor to where Shade sat.

The paper was crisp and sturdy, unlike any paper Shade had seen before, even in Sal Yaddo. It felt... new. He opened the letter. The message was short and nonsensical: *Your favorite guitarist is coming. You'll find him out by the northwestern cliff. Don't let him die. He's important.*

"That's all?" Shade asked, letting the paper dangle between his pinched thumb and forefinger.

"That's all."

His eyes narrowed. "Your favorite guitarist? You know of me?"

"Sure."

"How?"

"Dude, I've loved you since I was a kid. First tape I ever owned was one of yours. My dad and I would rock out in the car to it all the time." When Shade gave him a disparaging look, Ken shook his head. "Okay, so it wasn't *you* you, but that's beside the point, so just forget I said anything. Because I know who you are *now*. I know you're Shadrach, twentieth Knight Eternal of your name, and that you prefer to be called Shade. I know about Abe and Meesh, too, how you all came to be, what happened to Vera, Ronan Cooper, the Heartcubes, Asaph the Collector, everything. I know you hopped dimensions fighting Asaph, and I know you think Vera brought you back. But she didn't. Someone else did. Someone who appreciates everything you did to protect those who couldn't protect themselves."

Shade wanted to laugh aloud at the ridiculousness of it all. But there was something about Ken's tone that gave him pause. Or perhaps it was the comfort of the dog breathing deeply in his lap. Either way, he did not scoff, or turn away, or storm out of the cabin in frustration. Instead, he gave the man the sincerest look he could and asked, "Was it you? Are you a god?"

"Me? Oh, that's rich." The laugh that vibrated from Ken's throat was earnest enough to be disarming. "If I was, you think I'd be hanging out *here*? I'm just a guy. Wrong place, right time. Or something like that. I just *know things*. Don't know how, but I know why. Because I unwittingly connected to everything that's happened here, in this world and the next. I was here before this place technically existed. My actions allowed it to be created." He paused, tapped a finger against his lip. "Y'know, now that I say it out loud, maybe that *does* make me a god. Wow. Go me."

"You, my friend, are an odd one," Shade said.

Ken grinned. "You called me friend. Now I can die in peace. Again."

Before Shade could ask what that meant, Ken rose off the table, went to the chest, and knelt before it. With a flick of his wrist, the lock popped open, and he flipped up the heavy lid. Silas gave Shade another knowing look before doing another adorable canine stretch and getting onto his four feet. He pattered to his master, glancing back as if beckoning Shade to come over as well.

So he did. Sometimes it was best not to question impossible happenings too deeply, especially knowing that most of the outlandish things the bastard Asaph had told him and his brothers had turned out to be true.

"Here's the deal," Ken said, looting through the contents of the chest while Shade hovered over him. "I'm not here to guide you or tell you what to do. Just to help you along your journey, maybe point you in the right direction."

"Understood," Shade answered, though of course he didn't.

"Awesome. So, first thing's first. Your Shotstrate 1250 over there is useless without ammo. And you're not gonna find any of it where you're going. So here." He lifted a stack of six boxes, pivoted on his knees, and offered them up. Shade took the heavy stack. "**9MM–50CT**" had been printed on each of the boxes. He braced the stack on his forearm and slid free a sleeve. The brass heads of fifty pristine bullets pointed up at him. He whistled between his teeth, shoved the sleeve back in, and placed the stack down on the table, too shocked to say thank you.

"Oh, then there's these," Ken said, tossing over a spare burner cylinder and a shoulder holster, both of which Shade instinctively caught. "There's also this, and this, and these. Whichever way you go with this, they'll be important. Even your accelerated healing won't fix you if you lose fingers and toes to frostbite."

Ken piled a heap of clothes on the floor. Heavy undergarments, a scarf, thick gloves, a sweater, a new pair of wool-lined boots—everything he would need to survive out in the elements.

Lastly, Ken lifted out a length of wrapped fabric. "And here's the most important part," he said, peeling the bundle open to reveal a foot-long golden cylinder with notches cut all along its length.

"What is it?" Shade asked.

Ken shrugged. "Dunno. And that's not an 'I can't tell you' type thing. I just...really don't know anything about it other than it's some sort of artifact and you're supposed to take with you."

Shade took the rod from him, then ran the pad of his thumb along the notches. "Why?"

"Like I said, I dunno. Guess you just gotta take it on faith that when you need it, you'll know what it's for."

Shade frowned. Faith was one thing he seemed to have a limited supply of lately.

"And...that's about it," Ken said. He slammed the lid of the chest, used it to help him stand. "And as much as it hurts to say, that's almost the end of our, um, friendship."

"Why is that?"

"Because you gotta go. This mountain's gonna get hit with a massive storm just after the sun sets tonight. So if you wanna make good time going wherever it is you're going, you're gonna have to leave in five hours at most."

Shade glanced toward one of the windows. The sun shone brightly, turning the snowflakes into sparkling crystals as they blew past the glass. The pull of forward momentum gripped him. Whether Ken was telling him the truth or just trying to get rid of him, he knew he had to leave soon.

A hand fell on his shoulder. "My man," Ken said, smiling. "Before you go, let's eat."

It was midday when Shade stepped out of the cabin, bundled up against the cold, with a loaded burner holstered beneath his armpit and a belly full of something that Ken called "caribou stew." Excitement made his muscles twitch. For the first time in a long while, he felt something akin to optimism. Someone or something out there was watching out for him. Ken and Silas had proved it.

"Shade, one more thing," Ken said. The man stepped toward him, one hand held behind his back.

"What's up?" Shade asked.

"I know you lost your hat. Figured you might like a new one, and I think this'll suit you."

He whipped out his hand, which held something that looked similar to Shade's beloved wide-brim hat. This one was deep brown, with one side of the brim folded up to create an asymmetrical appearance. It was certainly handsome, and he grinned beneath his scarf as he placed it atop his head and adjusted the stampede string below his chin so it wouldn't fall off.

"It's called a slouch," Ken said, grinning. "Australian. Looks good on you."

As if to back up his master's words, Silas barked from the doorway.

"Thanks, both of you," Shade said, holding out a hand that Ken shook. "Your help was much appreciated, whether it was preordained by some higher power or not."

"Even then, I think it has meaning," the man answered. "After all, it's always possible that deities are a lot like you. Always going forward but trapped in the past, looking for a way to either rediscover or avenge a lost love."

Vera's face swam into his vision. "Maybe so, my friend. Maybe so."

Shade turned to the oppressive white world before him. The cabin rested on a peak so high that clouds obscured the downward slopes below. He started in the direction Ken had pointed him toward, only to stop when his new friend called out one last time.

"Got some parting words," Ken said, kneeling beside Silas and stroking his fur. "A great man once said, 'Oppressed people cannot remain oppressed forever. The yearning for freedom eventually manifests itself.'"

Those words struck Shade as if he had heard them before, and he screwed up his face. "Why would you tell me that?"

"Just something to keep in mind, dude," Ken said. "Now get outta here before you get stuck out in the cold with nowhere to go. And if you ever find yourself in my neck of the proverbial woods again, don't try to find me. I'll find you."

Ken punctuated his remark with a wink. He gave Shade a wave, and then he and Silas disappeared into the cabin. Shade shrugged, adjusted the pack of gear on his back, and went on his way down the steep mountain trail.

The going was difficult but endurable, and he made excellent time. The trail led through natural gullies and trenches that could become avenues for massive snow drifts if he were to get trapped in a storm, which made him thankful for Ken's warning. He walked for a long time, as day passed into night, and took shelter in a hanging crag when the trailing storm finally caught up. At night, he curled up in his borrowed blankets and fell asleep easily, despite the storm raging only a few feet away.

Just after sunrise the next day, the air began to warm. Shade stripped off his extra layers. Sweat beaded on his brow. His surroundings gradually changed. Tufts of grass sprouted from gaps in snow-dappled rocks, and a few mountain vermin showed their faces—the first life other than Ken and Silas he had encountered since leaving the forest of Lemsburg behind.

Small trees began to pepper the landscape, growing larger the farther down the mountain he trekked. Eventually, they grew tall enough to create a canopy overhead where birds sang, critters scurried, and insects chirped.

A forest on the other side of the world. He had to laugh.

When the sun emerged fully from behind the mountains, he came upon a break in the trees to his right. The view was breathtaking—a sea of lush, endless green that sloped downward from the cliff face where he stood, ending at a wide valley of still more green. There were buildings down there, too far away for him to make out clearly. But closer to him was something that caught his attention even more:

a white spire breached the top of the trees, beckoning him onward. It oddly resembled the spire at the top of the Scourger's temple of worship, only this one had a star at the top instead of a cross.

Civilization.

Shade removed the rest of his heavy clothing and packed them away, continuing his journey wearing nothing but the clothes he'd started with. He walked easily, a growing sense of cautious excitement brewing within him as the sounds of nature grew louder.

The steep pitch of the land gradually lessened until Shade was treading easily on flat ground. The path curved, and around the bend he came upon a signpost on the side of the path that made him stop short. The sign was as tall as he was and made out of a thick, five-foot wide plank. He considered the words written on it in blocky, accusatory script:

Darkenwood

Only the Righteous May Enter

He continued briskly along the dirt path, his guard up, ready to dash into the woods at the first sign of trouble. But nothing jumped out at him; nothing blocked his way. His only companions were the insects and whatever scurrying creatures called the suddenly hot woods home.

After another slight downward slope, an unnatural spot of color drew his eye through a slight gap in the foliage. Shade halted and stooped down, shoving aside a low-hanging evergreen branch. It didn't reveal much, as the forest was dense and the trees formed a spidery maze over ground covered with vines and brambles, but he could tell by the way the sun shone down in a huge bright splotch that there was a clearing on the other side.

Shade tilted his head to the left and stared down the path. "Who knows where that leads?" he whispered with a shrug.

He squeezed through the tightly-packed woods, his face constantly whipped by branches and his duster snagged by hundreds of thorns. By the time he emerged into the clearing, he felt like a victim of an elderly woman he and his brothers had encountered a few years back. Living just outside Sal Railen, she had a penchant for poisoning thieves, binding them, and then subjecting them to death by a thousand cuts from a homemade razor.

What he saw before him now stole away the whimsical memory of listening to the old woman's stubborn insistence that she'd been in the right. He stared at the large, rectangular building before him, its windowless exterior walls painted such a vivid shade of purple that Shade had a hard time looking at it directly. Given the white spire that rose from the roof, this was certainly the same place of worship he'd seen on his way down the mountain.

Intrigued, he held his breath and listened. A dull *thud* sounded from somewhere off in the distance, but other than that, all he heard was the scurrying of tiny paws over dead foliage and leaves rustling in the slight breeze. He crept around the left side of the structure, marveling how pristine the grounds were. The grass was lush and green and kept short, as if an army of goats trimmed it every day. A fifteen-foot-tall hedgerow, itself maintained to blocky precision, obstructed his view of the forest to the left. The hedgerow created a border that wasn't strictly impassable, but was restricting nonetheless, stretching to the front courtyard Shade approached and taking a hard ninety-degree turn. He imagined the same obstructive shrubbery would be mirrored on the other side of the structure, bordering it on three sides, with unfettered woods behind.

These people like their privacy, he thought.

Shade had reached the front corner of the building when creaking hinges whined through the humid early-morning air. He leapt to the side, pressed his back against the wall, and waited for a parade of worshippers to storm out. Only instead of numerous footfalls, he heard what sounded like a single pair of heavily booted feet.

Shade reckoned that as many people frequented this place as the various temples dedicated to the Pentus that had been erected throughout the wasteland. In other words, not many.

Peeking around the corner, he watched a man with pale, milky-white skin and wearing a pair of thick trousers, stumble down the concrete front steps of the temple, his footsteps clacking. Shade kept as still as he could as he watched the man totter and sway onto the walkway at the base of the stairs. He had a wild look about him, his body language bringing to mind a man named Bishop, whom Shade and his brothers had met in Pennonstaff. Bishop had suffered a debilitating stroke, and his staggering gait as he tried to teach himself to walk again was mirrored by the man who staggered toward a gap in the hedgerow.

Only that wasn't truly correct, because there was something else wrong with this man that Shade couldn't quite understand. The knight stepped away from the wall for a better look, and his mouth screwed up in confusion. It was the man's legs. They were all wrong, bending at an awkward backward angle, as if they'd been broken at the knees. After inching a little closer, Shade realized the man wasn't wearing trousers; his muscular legs were covered in fur from his lower back on down to his feet—which weren't feet at all, but thick black hooves.

This doddering stranger had the lower body of a goat.

"Impossible," Shade whispered. He stepped into the open when the not-man exited the temple grounds, gazing at the trail between the hedgerows that led through the woods. The man was still visible, wobbling along the path, his shoulders rising and falling rapidly.

Baffled and growing concerned, Shade turned to consider the front of the temple. From what he could tell, it had a single way in—an oaken door festooned with carved symbols. The billboard above the door read, "Tro Choi." He wondered what god these people prayed to. He wondered if they were friendly.

The sign stating *Only the Righteous May Enter* that he had seen along the path through the woods entered his thoughts. He questioned for a moment if the sign was an invitation or a warning. Would the people who called this place home find him righteous? Would they have any of the answers he sought? Were any of them human, or were they all mishmashed creatures like the one who had just exited the temple?

At that moment, he realized it didn't matter.

He followed the stumbling half-man's path through the gap in the hedgerow, walking into the unknown with his head held high and a hand on his gun.

— 2 —

To withhold from desire is to know true suffering,
for you have denied the gifts which He has given.
—Book of the Pentus, Havacana 14:77

The landscape sped by in a blur. Desert sand gave way to short prairie grasses, which in turn became fields of corn and twisted, sickly trees. Meesh barely registered the changes. From the vantage point of someone riding on a Warhorse careening at full speed, all that existed was where you sat and where you were going. No sight remained in the eye's view for long, which meant no landmark could be properly appreciated.

That was perfectly fine with him. If he had time to properly observe his surroundings, he also had the time to reflect on the events of the past week. That being the *last* thing he wanted to do, he leaned forward in the saddle and sped faster.

"We're nearing population centers," his Warhorse announced from below his chest.

"Yeah, I know, Tito," Meesh grumbled.

He hadn't raised his voice enough to hear his own words over the rush of wind past his ears, but it was loud enough for the oblong machine he rode atop. "Then you would like me to slow down, yes?"

"Hells no," Meesh said. "We kick it full throttle 'til we reach the gate."

"Are you sure about that?" the Warhorse questioned. "Ivan has told me that your brother is afraid we might startle those who don't expect our arrival."

Meesh glanced to his left, toward the second Warhorse that zipped along beside him. The new Abednego stooped in the saddle-like driver's compartment, wearing a look of grim determination. His pale, sculpted face stared straight ahead. Long hair the color of stained rawhide whipped around eyes that squinted with worry. That was a part of his new brother that Meesh was growing to loathe—his tendency toward uneasiness and indecision. Abe may have been a pedant and a rule-stickler, but at least he'd always seemed confident in his convictions, even when they were failing him.

Give him time, Meesh thought. *He's only been alive a week. He'll get into the swing of things. Maybe.*

"Fine," he muttered, as much to himself as to Tito.

"Excellent. Reducing velocity now."

The whirring gears hidden beneath the Warhorse's steel shell wound down slightly, decelerating to a speed that Meesh's old mare Pam could only reach when at a full gallop. Now that he'd ridden Tito from coast to coast, he found the slower pace disappointing. This seemed outlandish, since nine days ago he wouldn't have believed such feats of speed were possible.

The first signs of civilization appeared. People tilled the fields bordering both sides of this outbranch of the Wayward Pass. The workers turned from their duties, eyes wide and jaws hanging open, tools held limply in their hands. Meesh appreciated that most folks could still experience a sense of wonder. Then Abe's dead face entered his mind, and that appreciation disappeared.

The field workers' huts sped on by, and the twenty-foot-tall wall surrounding the seaport town of Portsmouth came into view. Portsmouth was the only township to have built such defensive measures—accomplished with the help of Yaddo, of course. Portsmouth was one of two Wasteland settlements, along with Lemsburg, to be surrounded by fertile ground that didn't cause mutations in wildlife, as well as being the primary gateway between the island kingdom and the mainland. This fact led to Leadership giving quite a lot of gold over the last three-hundred years to make sure the place was well protected. Yaddo's survival depended on it.

Meesh and Abednego brought their Warhorses to a gliding halt in front of the reinforced entrance gate. Guards looked down at them from atop the wall, astonishment on their faces. Meesh jerked his chin in a way he hoped said, *Get down here now.* Meanwhile, Abednego waved up at them, earning a glare from Meesh.

That was the other thing about his new brother that he couldn't stand. He was *so damn nice.*

Chains rattled; the gate lifted. A squat man in his mid-fifties stepped out, moving in a coiled and defensive way. Winston Bennett had been guard captain for all of Meesh's six years of life, and he looked just as formidable as ever, though his hair showed more silver than Meesh remembered.

The man led five sentries toward the knights, smiling with half his mouth. "Hey there, Meesh."

"Winston," Meesh replied.

The guard captain inclined his head toward the new Abednego. "Where're the others? Who's that."

"Abe's dead," Meesh said, pointing at his new brother. "He's Abednego now."

"Rodney," said Abednego with a sheepish grin. "I would rather be called Rodney, please."

"Sorry to hear that." Winston offered Meesh a look that was both conciliatory and baffled. "And what of Shade?"

"Run off. Deserted."

"Oh." The guard captain shook his head, his eyes locked on the two oblong steel machines the knights straddled. "I'm not even gonna ask about those."

"Probably for the best, brah. I wouldn't even know how to explain 'em to you."

"Yeah. Probably right." Winston took a step back, waved for his subordinates to move aside, which they did.

Meesh kept his gaze locked straight ahead as he rode Tito through the streets of Portsmouth. He didn't want to see the locals ogling him. But more than that, he didn't want to know how Rodney reacted. He probably had his head on a swivel, offering timid waves and a pinched expression to everyone.

Rodney. What a stupid name. For the past seven days, Meesh had tried to convince his new brother to call himself something, anything, other than that, so long as it wasn't Abe. Abel would've worked. But no, he insisted on being called Rodney for some insane reason.

"Abe and Shade're gone, and I'm left with a moron," he muttered.

"That isn't nice," his Warhorse said.

"Shut the hell up, Tito."

"Sorry."

When they arrived at the wharf at last, Meesh finally let his eyes wander. He took in the mucky gray ocean, the numerous stone jetties, the docks reaching out into the rippling water. Countless fishing vessels floated listlessly back and forth beside the piers, their crews hustling to and fro. Bloodworms were far less plentiful off the Wasteland's western coast, which meant trawling for fish was actually possible. The boats didn't have to be the thick hulled, armored behemoths used in Sal Notterdam, built to defend against the vicious worms, the apex predator of the eastern sea.

He led Rodney toward a secluded port farther north of the busy fishing hub, allowing himself to smile when he spotted the flag of the five-pointed star flapping at the top of the port's outbuilding. That flag meant *home*, which he hadn't seen in far too long.

A large galley, the *Ocean Child*, waited at the end of the landing, long and lean with a hull painted gold. A figure cloaked all in black stood beside the gangplank, beckoning the knights forward with sleeve-covered hands. Meesh eased his Warhorse along the planks, up the ramp, and over. The deck of the *Ocean Child* was spacious, one hundred feet long and forty feet wide, with rows of seating surrounding the staircase to the unused belowdecks cabins. Meesh had never understood why there were so many amenities on this boat. It was only ever used to ferry the knights back and forth, which took at most three hours, and that's when the waters were rough. Four people traveling such a relatively short distance didn't need such a big boat.

But hey, at least it was comfortable.

He brought Tito over to the open-air section where he had hobbled Pam during their journey here two months ago. A brief stroke of sadness gripped Meesh's heart. He sighed and strapped the Warhorse down to the deck.

"Shutting down," the Warhorse said.

"You do that."

"Mate, this is where the, um, bikes go?"

Meesh glanced over his shoulder. Rodney was sitting awkwardly in the saddle of his metal steed, a grimace on his annoyingly chiseled mug.

"Nah, brah," he snipped. "We're supposed to hang 'em over the side. Like decorations."

Rodney gave him a funny sideways glance. Meesh shook his head and walked away.

It took a little while for the helmsman to undo the moorings and set the *Ocean Child* adrift. Meesh used that time to pace the fringes of the ship, keeping as much distance between himself and Rodney as possible. He even went so far as to help the helmsman wind the ropes before departure.

"So, Char, what'd you do while we were gone?" Meesh asked as he worked.

The helmsman didn't react to the question, nor to Meesh's pet name for him. Meesh expected that. He didn't know what the guy's real name was or what he looked like, given that he was always dressed in that hooded getup. He didn't even know if it was the same man every time. The helmsman was merely silent and broody, as someone decked out like the Ferrymaster was destined to be.

Unlike the fishing boats in the wharf, the *Ocean Child* had no masts or sails. Wind didn't power Yaddo's prized vessel; magic did. Or what Meesh had passed off as magic before the whole escapade with Ronan Cooper and his Outriders. Now, he understood that machinery powered by Heartcubes hid inside the hull. While the helmsman climbed the platform at the rear of the ship and worked the levers that propelled the boat out toward the sea, Meesh wondered about all those inventions of the Ancients that Ronan had discovered in the mountains. Horseless carriages, Warhorses, and hundreds of Elderswords! Did Reverend Garron know about them? Had he hidden their existence from everyone to build his own power? Would he—

"Shut up," Meesh told himself. Those weren't thoughts he wanted in his head. They were blasphemous.

Abe would've been proud of his restraint.

The sea calmed once the *Ocean Child* pushed into open water. The boat glided gently above the waves while the apparatus that impelled it hummed beneath Meesh's feet.

Rodney approached him warily, asking, "Wanna talk, mate?" in an irritatingly tender voice.

Again, Meesh scowled and walked away.

For a while, he reclined on one of the benches in the center of the deck, pencil and notebook in hand. He tried to jot down a set of catchy lyrics to describe the knights' latest adventure, as tradition dictated. But he only tapped the sharpened charcoal tip against the page, over and over again. The words wouldn't come, and he was wracked with depression and anxiety. For the first time since his creation, Meesh was a man with nothing to say.

"Ain't that a bitch."

Frustration made him slap his notebook against his knee and stand up. The sudden movement, coupled with the boat's gentle swaying, made him dizzy. His stomach lurched; his head swam. He grabbed the Eldersword on his belt and the Rush immediately took those feelings away. Meesh looked down at the weapon, snug on its clip.

"What would I do without you?"

He released the handle, and the Rush faded. When his nausea didn't return, Meesh stuffed his hands in his pockets and strolled across the deck. Clouds parted overhead, revealing the red-tinged sun in all its glory. He stepped up to the railing, gripped it tightly, and looked out over the water. Everything seemed still, even with the gently lapping waves and the wind that fluttered his hair. There was calm here. Peace, even.

Kamini would've loved it, he thought with a grin. *Or would she? She was kinda hard. And grumpy. But lightning in the sack.*

He saw her face, caved in by his own Eldersword.

His good feelings disappeared.

Quiet singing reached his ears. Meesh turned to see Rodney on the opposite side of the boat, standing in a position similar to his own, gazing out at the ocean. Like Meesh, Rodney had a wonderful voice, only his was quiet whereas Meesh's was bombastic, full of heart and sorrow while Meesh embodied aggression and sexual energy. He wouldn't soon forget the first time he'd heard Rodney sing at a pub in New Salem two days ago, because he felt something he'd never felt in his short life.

Envy.

It was also, he realized, the moment his new brother started to annoy him.

Meesh spent the first few days after Rodney's creation trying to show his new brother the ropes while they zipped from settlement to settlement, returning the Heartcubes that Ronan Cooper had stolen. Rodney had been awkward and hesitant early on, as befitting a newly-formed adult. Standing five inches taller than Meesh, he carried his gangly frame as if his height made him uncomfortable, whereas Meesh's confident strut made him seem bigger than he was. Rodney's features were long, his chin cleft, unlike Meesh's rounder facial structure. They were both certainly handsome, but Rodney didn't seem to realize it. At each of the populated hamlets they visited over those first five days, from Lambswool to Danville to Sal Railen and Ramstable, the local girls (and even some men) would fawn all over him. Rodney passed off their advances with a withdrawn shrug, as if trying to fold his tall frame in half while shrinking from their gazes.

Meesh had found his behavior understandable at the time, even adorable. But after arriving in New Salem, his viewpoint shifted. He hadn't wanted to visit Fatisha Dorl's autocratic colony in the first place. The old city was like the now-deserted Breighton on a smaller scale, built around its own Sacred Tree and expanding outward. The buildings were shorter than the impossibly high towers of Breighton, and not nearly as decrepit. The center of the city even had a functioning greenhouse, a quarter-mile-wide dome set up in the shadow of the Great Elm that provided fresh fruits and vegetables to its citizenry.

But it was that citizenry which made New Salem a place better left alone. As that monster Asaph had said, "in the Wasteland, like sticks with like." Fatisha Dorl, a warlord who had come to power twenty years ago after a border war with Pennonstaff left the settlement in near-ruins, had taken that notion to the extreme. It'd long been understood that if an unwitting traveler came within a mile of New Salem, they'd be run down and executed if their ethnic makeup didn't match those who called the city home.

That was true for the Knights Eternal, as well, even if they were given more leeway than others. Over Meesh's lifetime, whenever Old Crone predicted a blight in that area, Abe and Shade would go on ahead, leaving him to camp by the Wayward Pass. He was only to enter if one of them came to retrieve him, which never happened.

But this time, in order to return the six Heartcubes the Outriders had managed to lift from the city, it had to be him and Rodney who did it.

Meesh's nerves had been on edge the whole time, while Rodney seemed oblivious to everything. Even when they encountered a squad of New Salem's brutal lawmen called the Black Masks, Rodney didn't seem to recognize that he should be afraid. Meesh had tried the confident approach, demanding to see Fatisha and making sure to ominously display his Eldersword. The Black Masks quickly got over their confusion from seeing the floating Warhorses and drew their battle axes in reply.

That was when Rodney politely asked to see "Miss Dorl." He told the intimidating men, in that soft, offhand way of his, that he understood their concerns. That they were the ones with numbers and control. That he and Meesh would bow to their wishes and be grateful for their tolerance.

Much to Meesh's surprise, it worked. They were led into the city, paraded around on their Warhorses, and even had a sit-down with Fatisha. The leader was shockingly generous, going so far as to offer her sympathies for Abe's death. Then—again startlingly—the two knights were invited to sup with Dorl's closest family and friends.

It was during that dinner when Meesh discovered the extent of Rodney's talents. Given the new knight's reluctance to talk about himself, it came out of nowhere when he admitted to Fatisha that he played guitar. As Abe's six-string had been destroyed during the undead attack on the Cooper station, the partygoers supplied a raggedy one of their own for Rodney to use.

For the next half-hour, his new brother had hypnotized the New Salemites with his gentle strumming and soulful crooning. The whole scene stupefied Meesh for a couple reasons, the first being that Rodney was good. *Damn* good. Second, he somehow knew a whole set of songs right off the top of his head, which shouldn't have been possible. Knights were supposed to come into being only with the innate knowledge of only how to play to their given talents, a knowledge that the elder brothers would then nourish. The songs of the Knights Eternal were communal creations that came about through shared experiences and passed down the line. As far as Meesh knew, not one of their order had come to being understanding how to create wonder from nothing.

The fact that Rodney apparently could made him special. This annoyed Meesh more than just about anything. He could accept Abe and Shade being better than him. They were his elders, after all, even if Shade only had a few months on him. But this tall and timid simpleton coming to life with such an awesome gift, one that none had ever been blessed with before, seemed entirely unfair.

Quite frankly, it pissed him off even now, standing on the deck of the *Ocean Child*, so close to home.

Meesh shook his head, squeezing the rail until his knuckles turned white while Rodney continued to sing to himself on the other side of the boat. He spun around. "Shut *up* already!" he screamed, then stormed to the staircase leading belowdecks without once looking to see his new brother's reaction.

He hoped he was crying or something similarly unmanly.

For the rest of the trip, Meesh kept himself out of sight in one of the comfortable cabins, sipping on bottles of Ministry-distilled whiskey. His mood went from pissed at Rodney to pissed at the Pentus to pissed with himself for acting like a petulant child. Finally, he reclined on the cabin's plush mattress and allowed the purr of the *Ocean Child's* machinery to help him drift into a semi-drunken sleep.

The insanely loud foghorn that greeted the return of the knights woke him a short time later. Meesh sat up and cracked his neck. He couldn't have slept for more than twenty minutes, but the short nap seemed to have improved both his mood and his state of mind. His guilt over how harshly he'd reacted to his new brother seemed lesser now, or at least compartmentalized. He could push it to the back of his mind and let Reverend Garron help him come to grips with his feelings later. The great man had helped ease his inner turmoil after he'd put a bullet in the head of an unarmed teenager during his first-ever mission as a knight. Meesh had hidden the incident from his brothers, and the Reverend had kept the knowledge to himself when Meesh came to him seeking forgiveness. *As the Pentus says, "If one's heart is righteous, one's actions hold no weight."* Even if those words had made little sense to Meesh at the time—still didn't, actually—the remembrance of them eased his nerves.

The Reverend had his back. Screw Abe, screw Shade, screw goddamn Asaph. Reverend Garron was holy. No way in the Nine Hells could the leader of the last bastion of free thought in all the world be a traitor to his own teachings.

By the time Meesh returned to the upper deck, the *Ocean Child* was sliding sideways toward a dock crammed with people. Yaddo's seacoast cliffs rose behind it in a solid wall of rock. Meesh grinned at the cluster of delegates awaiting them. Other than the usual marina workers, there were three minerabis dressed in fine suits and velvet hats; seven bikkus with flowing robes and shaved heads; nine jaris, their baggy pants rippling in the stiff ocean breeze; and fifteen or twenty imas, the lowest order, all women with faces wrapped so entirely in headscarves called *kimis* that only their eyes showed.

They were representatives from each branch of the religion, save one—Reverend Garron himself.

After the boat docked, Meesh nodded to Rodney, who nodded back solemnly. They unhitched their Warhorses while the black-clad helmsman prepared the ramp. Meesh climbed into the saddle and Tito came to life beneath him.

"We're here?" the machine asked.

"Yup. Home at last."

Meesh took the lead, guiding Tito over the ramp and toward the waiting envoys. They had obviously received the letter he'd sent via courier while in Lemsburg after bringing Rodney into being. Though how they knew the two of them would arrive today, at this time, was a mystery.

That was Yaddo for you. Always one mystery after another.

The delegation took a long time inspecting the knights and their Warhorses. Meesh and Rodney were left to sit idle in their saddles and allow the examination to happen. They were scrutinized up and down by important men who held their chins like they were doing import things, nary a word spoken between them. They checked the knights' Elderswords (which Rodney held as if it were made from spiders), and even tested Meesh's remaining empty burner. After a while, Rodney straightened his tall frame in his saddle, staring at Meesh over the inspectors' heads. The confused look on his face was beyond comical. Meesh shrugged. Rodney *harrumphed* under his breath and hunched back over.

Finally, the one in charge of the delegation, a tall, slender man with bronzed flesh who wore a finely tailored white suit threaded with gold, lifted his gaze to Meesh. "It is wonderful to have you back, Sir Meshach. Much has changed since your departure." He peered at Rodney. "And Sir Abednego, welcome to your home. I am Minerabi Bartholomew, Keeper of the First Gospel."

"That...is a long title," Rodney said hesitantly.

"As the Pentus says, it is only through the full disclosure of one's purpose that one can fulfill said purpose."

"Oh. Okay."

"Yo, Bart," Meesh interrupted. "Can we, like, go now?"

"You are not in the badlands any longer, Sir Meshach," Bartholomew said with a passive smile. "Proper decorum is the law."

Meesh sighed. "I can call you whatever the hell I want, and you know it. Let's get going already. It's been a long few months. I kinda wanna get this over with and sleep naked in my own goddamn bed for once."

Bartholomew winced, but his face returned to passivity in a blink. He folded his hands behind his back. "Please, Sirs, step off your new mounts."

"Why?" Meesh snarled.

"You know the rules, Sir Meshach. No artifacts of unknown origin are allowed into this great kingdom until they have been vetted. And as another point of fact, there is the death and rebirth of one of our knights to consider, as well as the desertion of another." He shrugged in Meesh's direction. "There could perhaps be questions about your role in both tragedies. Though your birth is not to be considered thusly, Sir Abednego."

"Please, call me Rodney."

"I will not," Bartholomew said, looking like he'd just sucked a lemon.

The bevy of imas with covered faces began to circle the two knights. Meesh looked into each of their exposed eyes as they passed, wondering if he knew any of them. Finally, he found a pair that were brown with flecks of green that shone with a little more fire than the others. *Octavia*, he mouthed. The ima gave him a surreptitious nod and followed after her sisters. He grinned. Octavia was one of three within the order whom he had seen without her *kimi*. She'd also been the first woman he'd slept with after his creation, her caramel flesh beading with sweat as she rode him, her long hair smelling like tobacco smoke when it brushed against his cheek...

The memory got his gut churning. Until he thought of Kamini again, and the smirk melted from his face.

"Meesh, what's happening?" Tito asked through his speaker.

"Shut it, brah," Meesh whispered.

The imas stopped their circling, staring at the machines with eyes that floated in seas of black fabric. The seven bikkus approached, led by the second-most powerful minerabi, Cassius.

"They speak," the short, unhealthy-looking man said. He ran smooth pudgy fingers that had likely never seen a day of physical labor over Tito's smooth metal hide.

"They do," Meesh grumbled.

"Interesting."

Meesh knew what came next. He shot Rodney a look, and miraculously his brother understood. They slipped out of their saddles at nearly the same time and allowed the delegation to come in for an even closer look. Countless hands touched and prodded the Warhorses; Cassius tried many times to get both to speak. Meesh chuckled, remembering when he and his brothers had presented the priests with a black orb they'd cut from the chest of an arwassa demon. The bikkus and jaris had spent hours examining the find right here on the docks, only to discover that the object was nothing but a clump of demon shit.

At least the Warhorses would give them something interesting to investigate. Hopefully, Tito would behave and keep his mechanical trap shut. The last thing Meesh needed was for the leadership to discover some of the blasphemous things he and his brothers had said about them.

If they didn't already know. In Yaddo, you never could tell.

The third minerabi—and by far Meesh's favorite—approached the two knights. He offered them both a kind smile, his unnaturally tanned skin, the result of constantly slathering himself in coconut oil, shimmering under the light of the early evening sun.

"Meesh, it is good to see you," he said.

"You, too, Frankie," Meesh replied. "Been gone too long."

"You have, you have." The religious scholar turned, lifting a hand. "And it is an honor to meet you as well, Abednego the Sixteenth. You said you prefer Rodney though, yes?"

Rodney hesitantly shook his outstretched hand. "Um, yes. Rodney's great."

"Fantastic." Francis retreated a step and considered them both, still smiling. "I will not ask you of your adventures. That which we do not already know is none of our concern. I am sure the scars are still fresh on each of your souls." He glanced at the hubbub behind him. "And your continued presence here is unnecessary. Why don't we get on our way, yes? I am sure you wish to speak with the Reverend and put this matter—and your bodies—to rest."

"Yeah, that'd be nice," said Meesh.

Francis clapped him on the shoulder. "I have always found you to be a fascinating man, Meesh. I'm glad to have known you, and I am sorry for your losses. Now come, both of you. The Reverend awaits."

Five of the imas—Octavia wasn't one of them, sadly—joined Francis in leading the two knights off the docks. They headed toward a large hole cut in the side of the cliff face, which led to a tunnel lined with smooth steel. The tunnel ended at a wide platform completely enclosed in rock.

Their transportation waited at the edge of that platform—a stunted, pill-shaped contraption hovering above a vibrating steel rail, positioned in front of another tunnel that disappeared into the bedrock below the island. The doors to the transport slid open. Francis gestured for everyone to step inside.

The doors glided shut, sealing them in with no windows to the outside world. With a sound barely above a whisper, the machine began to move. It surged forward, slowly at first, until they entered the tunnel before them and picked up speed. Not that he could see the tunnel without windows; he simply knew by the way the air constricted and the low hum of the machine rose a few notches. The transport rocked gently from side to side. Meesh watched with amusement as Rodney held one of the poles in the middle of the cabin with both hands, fear and uncertainty sparkling in his eyes.

He scoffed inwardly at his new brother's anxiety. While it was true that Meesh himself had never gotten used to this ride, the fact of the matter was that both he and Rodney had ridden flying metal horses around the Wasteland for a week. That should've been far stranger than zipping around in a train that he once considered magical.

While the transport careened on, Meesh stared at the bland white ceiling and glowing strips that ran along the sides. Intriguing, but in the most boring way. A part of him wished they'd gotten horses in Port Smedly and ridden the whole way north, an impulse quashed by his overriding desire to just get home already. It took a minimum of five hours to traverse the full forty-six miles between Port Smedly and Sal Yaddo on horseback, yet only a half-hour to get there via the underground transport. At this point, he preferred a quick journey over sightseeing.

There would be plenty of time to reorient himself with Yaddo's wonders later.

In no time, the train exited its earthen tunnel and skated to a halt. The doors opened, letting in yellow rays of sunset. Rodney finally released the pole, shuddering as he hobbled out the door after Francis and the imas.

The Sal Yaddo terminal exited onto a road flourished with statues, benign stone conquerors that seemed to step out of the brush of the bordering hillsides. They represented the most important figures of Yaddo's history: its first Knight Eternal, greatest musicians, most inspirational poets, and most inspiring artists.

The largest statue was the last. Thirty feet tall, the effigy stood with one marble foot on each side of the road, guarding the passage into the holy land of Sal Yaddo. It depicted the great Reverend Hampton Garron the First, the man who had led his followers out of the Wasteland and across the Western Sea three hundred and seven years ago.

Meesh blew a kiss up at the statue's crotch as he walked underneath. And he didn't feel weird about it, either.

Unlike the rest of Yaddo, the capital was all peaks and valleys with few wide-open spaces. Trees cluttered the numerous hills, creating a sense that if you were to wander into those forests, you would become lost in another place and time. All of Yaddo's leadership lived here, as did the most talented artisans. The neighborhoods were more organized than those on the rest of the island, and older too. *Much* older. According to Abe, many of the homes here, both quaint and grand, had been built before the Rising, and then reinforced and rebuilt by the culture that came after. A way to remember the mistakes of the past and prove that not only could people learn from them, they could create the proper infrastructure to make those mistakes unrepeatable.

Or something like that.

Meesh crested one of the steep hills, the setting sun casting the sky in hues of violet and burgundy overhead. Down below, nestled in a valley, lay the beating heart of Sal Yaddo—the Hall of Lucidity, the hub of Pentmatarianism and Reverend Garron's seat of power. The Hall stood in the center of a sprawling concrete grayscape, the buildings around it erected using ancient techniques, blending steelwork and glass to create what looked from above to be a sea of huge, sparkling crystals.

The Hall itself was the most unusual construction Meesh had ever seen, with towering red pillars and twin spires that rose on either side of a grand central keep. The whole building had an otherworldly look, all angles and inward-sloping shingles. Looking down on it were huge letters **H-O-L**, built into on the facing hillside, representing the three maxims that the Pentus preached more than any—hope, observance, and love.

"Do I know this place?" Rodney asked from behind him. "Looks familiar."

"No chance," Meesh scoffed and followed Minerabi Francis down the hill.

Guards, in the form of another bevy of imas, greeted them at the front of the Hall. These were younger members of the order. Meesh could tell by the light tint of their headscarves and the strands of hair sticking out on a few of the women, a big no-no that would eventually be cured by time and repetition. The imas parted, and Meesh gave Rodney a quick glance before they both stomped up the stairs, through the ornate double doors, and into the building.

The interior of the Hall was huge, with still more red pillars on the boundary. The floor was pink marble. And this was only the ante-chamber. A pair of bikkus, wearing flowing frocks of orange silk, guarded the entrance to the Sanctum. They stood with hands clasped before them, eyes pointed at the luxuriant golden ceiling while they hummed a delicate melody.

Meesh and Rodney's entourage stepped aside, allowing the two knights to approach on their own. Meesh lifted his arms, and the bikkus finally looked down, examining him and Rodney before letting them into the great room. They never stopped humming, even as they closed the doors.

The antechamber might have been large, but the Sanctum made it look like a wading pool beside an ocean. Meesh had seen more than three thousand people fit easily inside, all standing beneath the palatial domed ceiling, eyes glued to the altar as Reverend Garron spouted words of wisdom, the jaris danced, and the Knights Eternal played their songs of worship.

Presently, they were alone with the great man himself. The Reverend sat behind his desk on the altar, busily writing whatever it was that prophets wrote. Rodney went to take a step, but Meesh grabbed his sleeve, stilling him. His new brother raised a curious eyebrow.

"Just wait," Meesh said out the side of his mouth.

Finally, Reverend Garron dropped his quill into an inkwell and beckoned his knights to approach. Meesh lowered his head and strode forward, making sure to keep his gaze locked on the sea of burgundy carpet. Rodney's tentative steps made rustling *swoosh-swoosh* sounds behind him.

They both stopped in front of the dais, heads still bowed. It wasn't until the Reverend cleared his throat that Meesh looked up.

Like always, Meesh couldn't get over how beautiful Reverend Hampton Garron the Seventh was. He had narrow eyes that teemed with intelligence and compassion behind round-rimmed glasses, perched on a long and slender nose. His cheeks and chin were rounded and smooth, imparting a sort of youthful feminine authority that Meesh had always been drawn to. The absence of marks on his skin belied his age, whatever that age was. Abe had once told him that Reverend Garron looked the same now as when Abe came into being, which, if true, was impressive. Even the prophet's shoulder-length brown hair showed no hint of gray. Meesh wondered if the previous six men who'd held that title were equally striking. It was hard to tell from the statue that guarded the entrance to the holy city, weather-beaten as it was.

"Reverend," Meesh said with a slight bow that Rodney awkwardly mimicked.

A sad smiled bloomed on Garron's lips. "Meesh, it's good to see you. It truly is."

"Back at ya," said Meesh. He fidgeted, realizing that his leader's accent, which sounded so unlike everyone in Yaddo, was the same as Rodney's. His fingers inched toward the sack tied to his belt. "I have news..."

"Yes, I know," the Reverend said. "I've heard all about it. A tragedy, a great tragedy. Abednego was the best of us."

"Sure was." He opened the sack and touched the hilt within, which shuddered against his fingers.

Reverend Garron glided down the staircase at the side of the dais and approached Rodney. "Every tragedy brings with it a blessing. You, Abednego the Sixteenth, are that blessing. It is wonderful to make your acquaintance."

"Um, that's certainly the bee's knees," said Rodney, casting furtive glances first at Meesh, then the Reverend. His face screwed up, his head tilted to the side. "Do I know you?"

"I'm sure you do," Reverend Garron said with a lighthearted chuckle. "You likely saw me in your dreams, so as the Pentus gives."

"I suppose. But I mean, do I *know you* know you?"

The Reverend blinked saying nothing.

"Sorry," Rodney said, nervously staring down at his feet. "You just seem quite familiar."

Silence reigned for a beat, until Reverend Garron flipped a strand of hair off his face. Any uncertainty he might've shown disappeared in an instant. "You both must be quite tired."

"I could certainly use a kip," said Rodney.

"What about the other matter?" Meesh said. He removed the Eldersword from the sack, holding it out toward his leader with reverence.

"That is Shade's," Reverend Garron said.

"It is."

His expression turned sour. "What do you want *me* to do with it, Meesh? You know I cannot touch it. Those blades are for you and you alone."

"Well, I just thought—"

The Reverend spun toward Rodney. "Abednego, would you do the honor of giving me a moment alone with your brother? It won't take long, and he'll meet you out front shortly."

"Sure thing, mate," the new Knight Eternal said. He spun around and loped on his long legs toward the exit.

It was only after Rodney left the Sanctum that the Reverend considered Meesh again. His perfect eyebrows arched up at the corners. His mouth twisted into a frown.

"Sorry, sorry," Meesh said, tucking the Eldersword away. "I, like, wasn't thinking."

He'd expected a reprimand, but instead the Reverend placed a calming hand on his shoulder. "There is no need to apologize, my son. You did nothing wrong. I simply didn't want to broach a sensitive subject with such a fresh soul lingering about."

"I can see that."

The Reverend stared at the doors Rodney had just exited. "He's an odd one, no?"

"Yeah, can be. Bit of a moron actually. No offense."

Garron displayed a cockeyed look. "I assume you mean he has certain idiosyncrasies that belie understanding?"

"Well, sure. I mean, he's hesitant as all get-out, he don't talk much, and he, um, says he wants to be called Rodney."

"Rodney?"

"Uh-huh."

"That *is* quite odd." The Reverend's intelligent eyes once more traced toward the Sanctum doors. "Then again," he said in the introspective tone Meesh knew so well, "you are all odd birds. Each with your own set of eccentricities and opinions. No man is created from a mold, not even those such as you. As the Pentus has decreed, in all of his mysterious ways. Praise be."

"Praise be," Meesh answered.

Garron hopped up on the dais and planted his butt on the edge. His legs swung while he considered Meesh. "We need to talk about Abe and Shade. What happened there?"

"You don't know?" Meesh asked, surprised.

"If I did, there would be no reason to ask," his leader said, not unkindly.

"But I sent notice back while we were doing the stuff with the Heartcubes. That should've told you—"

"Their ultimate fates? Yes. You spoke of Ronan Cooper and his Outriders, the holy relic called a 'nuclear station,' the army of the dead and their supposed leader. But as for the why and how, alas..."

The last word dangled in the air, until Meesh did what he was supposed to and plucked the loose thread as best he could.

"To be totally honest, Reverend, I'm not entirely sure *how* it all happened. I was fighting a few thousand corpses with Cooper's followers when it all went down in the huge chamber I told you about, the underground one. All I know's what I told you—that the dude Asaph killed Abe, Shade sent Asaph to another dimension or something, and then all the dead collapsed. Other than that... I don't really know much."

"Do you know what made Shade break his vows?"

Meesh shook his head, trying to decide whether he should reveal his brother's blasphemous words. "Not really," he finally said. "He said something about this girl named Vera, but other than that he wouldn't talk about it. I couldn't pry it outta him." He looked down at his feet. "And after we brought Rodney—the new Abednego—into this world, he just…left."

"I see."

Reverend Garron took a deep breath and hopped back down off the dais. He gave Meesh's shoulder another squeeze, planted a fatherly kiss on his cheek.

"There is much I need to ponder, and I'm sure you're quite tired," he said, gesturing to the exit. "Take a few days to re-orient yourself. Grab a drink with mates. I hear an old flame is performing tonight. When I'm ready to give you my wisdom, I will let you know." He smiled, kindness in his eyes. "Hopefully that comes before the Crone has another of her visions."

"Yeah. Hopefully."

Meesh bowed to his leader and scuffled across the expanse of red carpet, hands in his pockets. His brain swirled with so many thoughts, he couldn't put a finger on exactly what they were.

"My son, one last thing," the Reverend called out.

Meesh paused and turned. Garron stood in front of the raised platform, a hand on his heart. "Try not to dwell on Shade," the man said. "Imagine a world in which he never left. A world where he remained at your side, his faith intact. And hold onto that imaginary world… until it's time to let it go. Glory to the Pentus. Praise be."

"Praise be," Meesh said, and out the door he went.

He found Rodney sitting on the front stoop of the Hall of Lucidity. His gangly legs were crossed, his eyes aimed at the burgeoning night sky. None of the entourage who'd joined them were anywhere to be seen, which was a relief. Meesh stopped beside his brother, looked down at him.

"It's beautiful here," said Rodney.

"It is," Meesh answered.

"But it doesn't feel right."

"How so?"

His shoulders went up and down once. "I don't rightly know. Just a feeling."

"Ah. Cool." Meesh huffed out his nose and mumbled, "Just a feeling. It's just a feeling," under his breath.

"What was that?"

"Nothing, brah. Let it be."

A few seconds later, a horse-drawn carriage trundled down the road. It came to a stop in front of the Hall. The driver hopped down from his seat, opened the door to the carriage, and waited.

"What's that?" Rodney asked.

"Our ride."

"Our ride? To where?"

"To the Temple. Our home."

"I've never been there. It isn't *my* home."

"Not yet. But it will be once you get there."

His new brother stared up at him quizzically.

Meesh offered an annoyed groan. "Just get your ass up and go already. You gotta fix up your room. It's kinda filled with a dead man's stuff. And maybe you can get a set of clothes that actually fits you now."

"What if I don't—"

"Just go!" Meesh yelled, flailing his arms. "Get the hell over there and see where we sleep. Do *something* other than pissing me off."

"Have I offended you?" Rodney looked so hurt, staring at him with those big puppy dog eyes, that Meesh felt instantly sorry for him.

"No. I just need a break. That's all. Go ahead. Get yourself situated. I'll see you in a bit." He sighed, taking both his and Shade's Elderswords off his belt and handing them to Rodney, along with his lone remaining burner. "Here, take these for me. Ask the Temple Keeper to show you my room and stick 'em in there. They're not necessary tonight."

Thankfully, Rodney didn't question him. His tall brother took the bundle, jerked himself to standing, and lumbered down the steps. Meesh shook his head at the driver after his brother disappeared inside the carriage. The man shut the door, resumed his perch, and urged the horses onward.

Once the carriage became nothing more than the echo of clomping hooves, Meesh shoved his hands in his pockets and walked. The streets around the Hall of Lucidity were empty. The quiet surrounded him, suffocated him. He picked up his pace. His heart beat a little more quickly with every step he took.

The street gradually brightened as he put the sacred ground of the Hall behind him and entered Sal Yaddo's residential district. Quaint homes and wide brick structures were built into the hillside on both sides of the road. The place teemed with life. Candlelight shone in open windows; children ran through the streets playing games in the dusk. Laughter filled the air.

He tied back his long hair and marched toward the one place he knew he'd be able to find solace. When he rounded the next bend, he saw his destination—a two-story building called Troubadours, whose simple design hid the most exciting atmosphere in all Yaddo.

Whenever Meesh wanted to escape when he was back home, this was where he went. Troubadours served as both Sal Yaddo's unofficial watering hole and the one place where artisans of all types and skill levels could ply their trades. Meesh had seen a great many plays and concerts there, though the Knights Eternal had never graced its stage. Troubadours was a place for the common people. Where they went to let loose, to *shine*.

I hear an old flame is performing.

He strode up to the swinging doors and burst on through. Inside, a group of musicians played loudly on stage while men and women laughed and danced with wild abandon. Meesh elbowed his way through the crush of people and ordered a drink at the bar. The bartender recognized him immediately, gave him a wide, adoring smile, and slid a bottle of whiskey across the counter. Meesh caught the bottle and took a long pull. The stuff was decent and burned going down. It wasn't as good as the stuff he drank with Kamini and Cooper on that fateful night, though.

"Nope," he said aloud, and took another swig. He wasn't going to feel sorry for himself. Not now.

From his vantage point at the end of the bar, he saw the full of the stage. The person he'd come to see was up there—a woman with curly blond hair who swayed in time with the music, her arms spread wide. When she sang, her high voice easily rose above the twanging guitars and thumping drums. Meesh wandered toward the stage, bottle still in hand, oblivious to the crowd.

Keedra was a vision in every way. Her singing was powerful and angelic, her body short and taut, her blue eyes alight with cold fire. He'd always felt drawn to her, though in truth it had more to do with her daring in the bedroom than anything else. They'd been together on a few occasions, most recently the night before he, Abe, and Shade had set off on their last fateful trip.

That memory steeled him. Picturing her naked performing a dance just for him combined with his continued pulls on the bottle brought his desire to a boil. He jumped onto the stage while the band's song reached its crescendo, grabbed Keedra from behind, and pulled her into him. She spun in his grip, shoved him away and slapped his face. Meesh stumbled a few steps cackling. He tripped over a guitar stand and fell into the percussionist. Bongos and symbols crashed.

The music descended into twangy silence.

"Meshach?" Keedra said. "Meesh?"

"It's me!" he exclaimed, raising his bottle triumphantly while still flat on his back.

Keedra wiped a sweat-soaked curl from her brow. She crossed her arms over her chest. One side of her mouth rose in a wry smile. Her head shook, and with a wiggle of her elegant fingers, the band started playing again. The percussionist picked up his drums and joined in. And Keedra *sang*. The sound pierced Meesh's eardrums, drove spikes of wantonness into his brain. He froze—all except for his right arm, which brought the whisky to his mouth at even intervals.

He watched the rest of the show while prone on stage, getting drunker by the second. Even when the crowd chanted his name, he refused to move. His eyes were locked on Keedra, on her every sway, shimmy, and shake. By the time the last note was strummed and the delicious woman crooned her final stanza, he was fully mesmerized.

Keedra approached him as the next act set up their instruments. She straddled him in front of everyone, let those golden curls drop like a curtain around his head. The same lust he felt shone in her eyes.

That was Keedra. Always ready to give him what he needed.

"You're drunk," she said.

"You're hot," he slurred.

"Were you a good boy while you were away?" she asked coyly.

"Always, Kee. Always."

"I don't believe it."

She lowered her face to his and their lips met. Their kiss was wet and sloppy, nothing but mad passion. The crowd behind them rose in volume, and Meesh, in his inebriation, didn't know whether they were cheering for the new performers or his and Keedra's show of unbridled desire. When Kamini's face briefly entered his thoughts, he tossed aside the whiskey bottle, grabbed a handful of Keedra's hair, and kissed her all the harder.

He didn't need any more liquor tonight. Keedra was all the drug he required.

Charity is best reserved for the affluent and efficacious,
for their wealth has been built on knowledge and strength, neither
of which those who live in bondage have the cleverness to reach.
—**Book of the Pentus, Platitudes 3:5**

There was no time of day that Indigo cherished more than the morning, just before dawn broke. The way the air held the fleeting crispness of nighttime. The way the light of the sun, still hidden behind the mountains, painted everything pastel. The smell of dew, the sound of birds chirping their greetings to the new day—all of it combined to create an aura of tranquility that made her think nowhere in creation was as inherently beautiful as Darkenwood.

She floated on the surface of Winninger Lake, eyes aimed skyward, and soaked it all in. The cool water tingled her bare flesh. The tiny fish that called the lake home gave her harmless nibbles as they zipped beneath her. The beating of her heart fell into rhythm with the gentle roll of the water's surface, and she swore she could feel the vibration of Wisteria's singing reaching her from somewhere in the depths. "Miss you, old friend," she whispered. She folded her arms over her chest and smiled. If only every moment of her life could be this peaceful.

Gleefully shouting voices shattered the mirage. Indigo sighed and swam for shore.

She had just dried herself off and slipped her plain shift over her head when a trio of individuals emerged from the forest on the other side of the lake. One man and two women stripped off their clothes and tumbled into the water, where they kicked and splashed and playfully wrestled one another. The three naked bodies intertwined in an intimate game that soon evolved into moans and caresses and sloppy kisses. Indigo pulled her cap down over the sensitive tips of her pointed ears. Conflicted feelings churned within her. She both loathed these people and wished she could be like them. That she could douse herself in sensuality, caring not for what came tomorrow, but for what pleasure she could bring herself *right now*.

Alas, she could not. For she was Ersatz, a people whose past sins were so hideous that they had been sentenced to many lifetimes of servitude. Those who churned the lake waters, on the other hand, were Righteous, beyond reproach. Her guests. She gritted her teeth, hefted her bag of picked mushrooms over her shoulder, and headed for home.

"As the overgod decrees, so it must be," she muttered.

Oh, how she hated them.

The path she took was well-traveled, cresting over a hillock and across a mile-wide clearing. It was beautiful, a sea of green grass spotted with patches of colorful wildflowers. She trundled onward, passing the fields where guests could practice skills such as swordplay or archery and the stable filled with horses. The stacked-stone firepit where bonfires were lit at night passed by on her right, the obstacle course to her left. The pavilion up ahead was being readied by her people for the afternoon entertainment, along with the neighboring gazebo in which Wisteria would play her harp on the rare occasions she left her watery home.

And finally, in the center of it all, was the place Indigo resided— Hickweis Tavern, the beating heart of Darkenwood.

The building was wide and imposing, all three stories made entirely from blocks of pink granite. The roof had been stained a dark mahogany that reflected the sunlight, giving the structure a sparkling appearance during the high point of the day, like a beacon. A beautiful, strong beacon.

Another lie, since what went on *inside* that wonderful structure was far from beautiful.

She breezed up the steps to the front porch of the tavern. Four of the five guests lazing about on rocking chairs ignored her; the fifth, Anthony, a handsome, lower-level Righteous with dark skin and close-cropped hair, smiled at her. Indigo smiled in return. Anthony seemed to be a genuinely nice man—much nicer than most of his ilk— and had taken a liking to her immediately upon arrival.

"Will you listen to my advances today, Miss Indigo?" he asked.

She paused with her fingers on the door handle. "Not right now, Mr. Bell."

"Maybe later, then?"

"We shall see," she said glumly. "Maybe later."

He grabbed her free hand and kissed the back of it. She held her breath; Anthony had not been this forward before.

"I hope so," he said, his voice a throaty growl, his breath already reeking of liquor. "I've heard it said that half-elves are the best lovers."

She forced herself to remain smiling. "We shall see, Mr. Bell," she said and slipped her hand out of his. Spinning on her heel, she pushed open the door and entered the building.

If she had it her way, there would be no requited advances later, so long as Anthony didn't force her. Which she would not put past him. No matter how kind he seemed, he had just proven to be as sanctimonious as the rest of the Righteous. He deserved her disgust, not only for his objectification of her, but for the fact that she walked away from him grinding her teeth, knowing that even if her obligation to her guests stopped at making sure they were sheltered, entertained, well-liquored, and well-fed, she would just as soon give herself to the man rather than allow him to take out his frustrations on those she was responsible for. With her status as house madame, that was both the most and the least she could do.

She paused when she entered the first floor of the building, which was mainly a single huge room—the tavern itself. Beside the entrance, a counter stretched from wall to wall, the shelves behind cluttered with all sorts of liquid concoctions in glass bottles. Tables and chairs filled the rest of the room, a quarter of them currently occupied by guests.

Indigo watched servers maneuver deftly through the space, trays held high, delivering morning meals to the guests. None of the Righteous paid the servers any mind, which was the whole point. The Ersatz who performed menial tasks around Hickweis Tavern were of the so-called "lesser" races—trolls, gnomes, halflings, and orcs. As long as a laborer was physically undesirable and generally unthreatening, they could slink into the background and become nearly invisible. All the best to not disturb the Righteous in the pursuit of their carnal desires.

"Feeling pensive today, huh boss?" asked a voice from her right.

"Every day, Macaro," she said, eyeing the dwarf standing on a stool behind the bar a few feet away, drying glasses. "Every godsforsaken day."

"It would concern me if you felt differently," he said with a shrug.

Indigo tilted her head toward the patrons. "Have they been behaving?"

"I assume you mean our guests."

"I do."

Macaro wiped stray water from his nose. Droplets beaded on his smooth cheeks. "As much as they can." He chuckled, though no amount of amusement reached his black eyes. "Not that there is anything we can do when they do not."

"From the mouths of dwarves," she muttered.

The hall remained less than half-full, which was not unusual for so early in the morning, since many of the guests were still off in their rooms, sleeping off their late-night dalliances. Busy but bearable—just how Indigo liked it. It was preferable to the dinner rush, when the tavern filled to capacity and events could become unpredictable.

Not that breakfast was a pantheon of predictability. As Indigo knew far too well, anything was possible with the Righteous. If they woke up in the morning with violence on their minds, violence occurred.

It was difficult living each day with the possibility of an unwanted ascension lurking like a phantom in every shadowy corner.

Presently, things seemed calm. She scrutinized the interactions between patrons closely—their mannerisms, their expressions, the speed at which they chewed their food—and noticed not a single nuanced action that forewarned of danger. This was good, since the courtesans were going from table to table, mingling with the guests, working the talents the overgod had given them.

Indigo felt her heart break as those she cared for defiled themselves.

The tavern hosted twenty-one Ersatz courtesans, each of them human, each with their own rooms on the upper floors. Indigo loved all of them dearly, but the six currently present had been around the longest, and hence were her favorites. There was Pipin, a solid brick of masculinity who stood six-and-a-half feet tall, with smooth brown skin and deep, soulful eyes. Bluebell oozed desirability with her flaming red hair and voluptuous curves. Vivo, a leanly muscular bronze sculpture of a man, captivated just as many male guests as women. Aqua, who had been tossed into Darkenwood not thirty seconds after Vivo, showed his sensitive nature by wrapping his massive arms around an orc who had broken a glass and placing a kiss on her forehead. Aspar, whose overly muscled chest could shake the knees of any Righteous woman, laughed hollowly at a joke told by a man with a scruffy beard and wild eyes. Finally, gliding between the tables was poor Mana, the most popular courtesan of them all, despite her waifish build, sad nature, and frequent crying fits. Or perhaps because of them.

Something touched Indigo in the small of her back, and memories of her own time as a courtesan spurred panic. She spun around. Her mouth scrunched when she saw no one standing behind her.

A high-pitched voice spoke, and Indigo lowered her gaze.

"Come on, Mum," said a halfling woman, all two-foot-five of her wrapped from neck to knees in gray burlap.

Indigo put a hand over her heart. "Orchid, you frightened me."

"Me?" The halfling rolled her huge eyes. "Did you get the mushrooms? Mita is waiting. You know how he gets when he cannot prep the stew."

"Ah. Yes. I nearly forgot. Apologies, sweetling."

Indigo slipped the sack filled with mushroom caps off her shoulder, pausing before she handed it over. A bit of impishness bubbled up inside her and she grinned.

"Sure you can carry it?" she asked, as sincerely as possible.

"Shut it, Mum." Orchid snatched the bundle with her slender, delicate fingers. "I am small, not helpless."

"I know." She leaned over, rustled the ungainly nest of black curly hair that Orchid could never tame. "But you are *so darn cute!*"

Orchid swatted her hand away and hustled toward the kitchen, balancing the bag of mushrooms awkwardly above her head. Indigo swore she noticed a grin on her face before she disappeared through the swinging door. It made her feel just a little bit lighter in the heart and slightly unworthy as well. Orchid had been cursed with such a disadvantageous form after her latest ascension, yet she never once complained about it, nor attempted to ascend again. She simply went on, working toward the day the overgod forgave her for her sins, hiding any misgivings inside a tiny package of adorableness, grit, and sarcasm.

Sometimes, Indigo wished she could be more like that.

No, she told herself. *Then I would not be* me.

One of the guests laughed heartily, making Indigo shudder. She glanced out the window where the upper arc of the sun had finally peeked over the mountains. It was past time she made herself presentable. She could not perform her duties as house madame while dressed in a simple beige shift.

The overgod would not approve.

Sighing, Indigo made her way to the staircase on the other side of the room. The clank of utensils on plates and the drone of conversation faded away once she reached the second level, replaced by muted grunts, moans, and thudding headboards that she couldn't ignore. She knew exactly what was going on behind some of the six doors on either side of the corridor. Her poor courtesans did not deserve to be used like this, no matter their past sins. *Especially* so early in the morning.

Up another floor she went until she reached the peak of Hickweis Tavern. The tapered third story contained a single dwelling—her own. She slipped into her three-room apartment, ripped the hat off her head, and went about preparing for her day.

Indigo indulged in a second bath, the feel of warmth against her skin combining with the sound of water rumbling through the tavern plumbing helping to soothe her damned soul. When she finally felt at ease—or at least as contented as she could feel in this life of servitude—she stepped out of the tub, toweled off, and powdered herself. The exhaust fan embedded in the ceiling whisked the steam away. She then went to her bedroom, where the large four-poster taunted her with promises of unconsciousness. Opening her wardrobe, she dawdled while deciding what outfit to wear. Did she want the red dress or the blue dress? The dress with yellow ribbing or the dress with the elaborate floral pattern across the chest? So many dresses. She hated all of them. She would have *killed* for the type of breeches and blouse that were popular among the more adventurous female Righteous. In an act of silent rebellion, she closed her eyes and picked an outfit at random.

The purple dress she landed on was a chore to pull up over her hips and chest. Layered skirts billowed around her feet. When she finally succeeded in tying the bodice strings, she looked into the mirror above her vanity to do her hair and face. She paused, staring at her reflection. Even without makeup, her gold-tinged skin nearly glowed and her green eyes sparkled. The pointed tips of her ears poked through layers of satiny black hair that tumbled in gentle waves over her shoulders. The image should have been perfection.

Instead, what she saw was a disgusting paradox.

Indigo possessed exquisite beauty coupled and a quick mind sharpened by two centuries of memories. If she had been Righteous, those traits would have blessed her with power. But for an Ersatz, they were disadvantages. She was always front and center, an object to be drooled over and taken advantage of. A whip-smart mediator whose only use for such abilities was to plan the workdays of her courtesans to avoid wearing them out. She was a matron with no control over any aspect of her life save whether she bathed in the lake, her own washroom, or both. A utilitarian fixture bolted to a single place, whose only chance at freedom relied on the whim of a callous deity deciding whether she had finally paid her dues, whenever that might be.

"Stop it," she told the gorgeous half-elf in the mirror. She had worn this face for so long; it would do her well to remember what had happened to the last one who wore it.

Before the sorrow of memory overwhelmed her, Indigo threw back her shoulders, swallowed her misgivings, and tried to remain calm. Thoughts such as these would do her no good. It was only after her fingers stopped shaking that she went about putting on her face.

This day went on just like so many thousands before. Guests woke up and came down for food. The courtesans who had been detained earlier in the morning appeared and socialized, the fakeness of their smiles invisible to everyone but Indigo. Some were brought back up to the rooms after guests bartered payment; others joined even more guests out in the courtyard; Indigo sent still others off for some much-needed rest.

The sun rose higher in the sky, reflecting off the snowcapped mountains to enhance the vivid colors of the wildflowers surrounding Hickweis Tavern. Yet another gorgeous day in the valley of lost dreams. Or was it the valley of dreams never dreamt? Indigo could never quite decide.

Just after noon, most guests made their way outside. Indigo and her courtesans followed them. She stepped up to the porch railing and observed. It was the time of day when the tavern staff were mostly offered a respite, though some—including Asper and Aqua—served their duties by remaining at the sides of the women who had purchased their services, lavishing them with compliments. Some of the Righteous practiced archery or fencing with Ersatz instructors; others stretched and performed calisthenics, preparing for an afternoon of physical activity.

There were still more who lazed about in the spacious courtyard, deep into their libations, intent on drinking themselves unconscious. These were the Righteous visiting Darkenwood for the first time, reveling in freedom from responsibility. Dangerous, yes, but danger of a mundane, idiotic fashion. Those who had frequented the valley many times over were the *true* danger, and it was on them Indigo focused her attention.

A large group of such guests, twelve in all, gathered around the stables waiting for their horses to be saddled. Indigo saw the ferocity in their eyes, even from two hundred feet away. They wore swords on their hips, daggers tucked in their boots, and bows slung over their shoulders. Indigo wondered if they were heading for The Path of the Hero or The Path of the Rogue. She hoped they chose the Rogue. Otherwise, she would find herself visiting Tro Choi tomorrow.

"What're you looking at?" a soft voice whispered in her ear.

Indigo peered over her shoulder. Anthony stood behind her, his off-kilter smile like a corkscrew on his handsome brown face. He grabbed her upper arm. His skin felt hot and clammy.

"Whatever do you mean?" Indigo asked with a smile.

"He means you're too busy staring."

Another man stepped up beside Anthony. This one had the thin build and sickly pale complexion of someone who had spent his life poisoning his body for pleasure. Tattoos of thorny vines wound their way up one side of his face, and his eyes gleamed with drunkenness and undeserved anger. "You been ignoring my boy, and now you give bedroom eyes to his boss. What's up with that?"

"Pete..." Anthony said.

The other man let out a hollow honking noise. "Ain't you tired of not getting any of the perks, Tony? I mean, all we've heard is how great this place is, and then we get here and we're stuck on the sidelines while Popp and the executives do all the fun shit."

"That's just the way it is, Pete," Anthony replied. He finally released Indigo's arm, but she forced herself not to back away. The two men were focused on each other; if she made a move, she might draw unwanted attention back to herself. "Popp only paid for the *rest and relaxation* package for us. You know that."

"Don't care. I'm bored. I want *action*."

"You've *had* action," said Anthony. "Like, twice a day, every day. And all that booze you didn't have to pay for."

"Glassy-eyed hookers don't do it for me, bro," Peter spat. His menacing gaze fell on Indigo. She sighed inwardly.

Anthony leaned closer to his friend. "You need to chill," he whispered, but still loud enough that Indigo could hear. "You know the deal, Pete. We're on a trial basis here. Prove-it-or-lose-it. Once we prove to Popp we're trustworthy, we'll become full associates and get full run of the place. Just gotta be patient."

That explained everything. Status and monetary gain meant everything to the Righteous, and no one had more of both than Jasper Popp, whose father operated a merchant guild that supposedly controlled the textile trade in the kingdom north of Darkenwood. She had seen it far too many times over two centuries—conflicts that arose between those of lower standing and those who had successfully climbed the social ladder. And because violence among guests was forbidden— it would be career suicide for a lesser Righteous to lash out at his betters—conflicts such as these were *always* taken out on the Ersatz.

Which meant she had to stifle this whole situation quickly.

"Mr. Ortiz, do not fret," Indigo said, pouring as much meaningless syrup into her voice as she could. She slithered up to Anthony and pressed her breasts against his shoulder while holding the gaze of the tattooed man. Anthony shuddered when she nipped his ear.

"What're you doing?" Peter snarled.

She died a little inside when she said, "What I have wanted to do ever since you and your friend arrived." She twirled around the front of Anthony and danced her fingers along his chest. "I care nothing for rank or prestige. Only passion."

She spun around and snatched Peter by the collar. Pulling his face up toward her, she aggressively kissed him. He tasted of alcohol and pity, which would have turned her stomach if she were not so used to it. When she pulled away, a string of saliva forming a bridge between his lips and hers.

"And you two have passion to spare."

"I do," Anthony stammered dumbly. Indigo turned back to him, placed a tantalizing finger on his mouth. Her fingertip pierced his lips, and he started smacking like a baby.

This was going to be horrible. Necessary to protect her courtesans, but horrible.

"I can please you both equally," she said while Anthony continued to suckle her finger. "It is true what you said earlier—half-elves *do* make the best lovers." She made a show of flipping her glossy black hair when she glanced at Peter and purred, "I can show you now, if you like."

The tattooed man glowered at her, wiping the spit from their kiss off his chin. "I didn't come here for pity," he growled. "And you don't do it for me, anyway."

He stomped a foot and put his back to Indigo and Anthony, just as someone stepped out of the tavern right in front of him. It was Mana, her sad eyes watering, her ankle-length dress with choker collar accentuating the frailness of her body. His rage palpable, Peter grabbed her around the throat. Indigo flung herself off of Anthony and reached out her arms. The sinking feeling of inevitability filled her chest.

Before she could do anything to stop it, Peter lifted Mana into the air and smashed her flat on her back on the porch. The girl cried out, her voice stifled when her head slammed against the solid boards. She sputtered, gasping for breath, until her attacker dropped an elbow into her face. Her blubbering stopped.

"Yah!" Peter bellowed. He raised his fist to smash into Mana again.

Indigo wanted to help, but Anthony grabbed her around her waist and pulled her backward. She kicked his shin, and a satisfying yelp of pain echoed in her ears. When he let go, she stumbled toward her felled courtesan, praying to the god that did not care if she could stop the inevitable.

She could not.

Pipin exploded out of the opened tavern door, all six-foot-five of him colliding with Peter and sending the Righteous man careening over the porch railing. Indigo fell to her knees, dejected, as Pipin gathered himself and helped a nearly-unconscious Mana to sitting. The side of her face was swollen with an ugly shade of purple with red veins, and her broken nose jutted off to the side. The girl blinked twice and looked up at her savior, eyes clouded over with dismay.

Out in the courtyard, Peter shouted, "I demand Right of Retribution!"

Indigo shook her head. Of course that was what the bastard had been after. She had seen it over and over again. Men—especially men—filled with the idea that they were owed success, sex, money, and power, indignant about anything that they could not simply reach up and pluck with no effort. Those sorts of Righteous lashed out at the world, demanding respect when they did not understand the meaning of the word. Indigo cursed herself for not seeing it sooner. Her overlong life had made her careless, and that momentary lack of attention to detail meant another of her charges was destined for pain, and likely an untimely ascension.

"Right of Retribution has been decreed," she said in a loud, warbling voice.

All eyes on the porch turned to her. The face of every Ersatz drooped with resignation. All but Pipin. The strapping courtesan gave Mana a kiss on her forehead, his face showing a hint of sorrow when he glanced at Indigo. That expression went to stone in seconds. He threw back his shoulders. With his light brown skin beading with sweat and his square jaw rigid, he was a vision of dignity and strength.

It would not be enough.

Macaro strolled out of the tavern, looking sorrowful. The dwarf raised a horn to his lips and blew. A low, tragic note sounded, stretching onward and outward. When finished, Macaro dropped the horn to his side, hung his head, and slowly walked back into the tavern.

"It is time," Indigo said. She grabbed the banister to help her stand and nodded to all those around her. Many individuals, Righteous and

Ersatz alike, had begun to form a circle out on the courtyard. With a heavy heart shared by the rest of her people, she threw back her head and marched down the porch steps. Pipin fell in behind her, a calf willingly being led to the slaughter.

The ring of flesh parted, and once she reached the front, Indigo moved aside so that her courtesan could take his rightful place. Pipin walked to the center of the circle, where Peter paced back and forth, spittle flying from his lips as he ranted incoherently. The man had stripped off his shirt, revealing a sick and wiry frame that was just as tattooed as his face. He glared at Pipin and nearly bit off his own tongue when he barked.

Indigo folded her arms over her chest, making sure to keep her air impartial as she took in the faces of everyone present. At least forty Ersatz had gathered—all those in the vicinity to hear the horn, per the rules of the Right of Retribution—along with half as many Righteous. She focused on the other side of the ring, where Jasper Popp and his band of merchants looked on impassively, as if there were other things they would rather be doing. Such a sight would have angered her, but she was taken aback by the sight of a man she did not recognize lingering just outside the circle. The stranger, his face bathed in shadow, quickly disappeared. Indigo felt a chill slither its way down her spine.

Anthony stepped up beside her, stealing her attention. The Righteous man seemed bewildered, yet excited. His eyes were wide, darting from side to side. He leaned in close. "I've heard of this," he whispered. "I thought it was just Jasper talking shit. I can't believe it's *real*." He swallowed, gnawed his lip. "But hey, after it's done, are we still...?"

Indigo wanted to roll her eyes. Instead, she asked loudly, "Has the challenger chosen a weapon?" She played the game as it was meant to be played.

"Labrys!" spat Peter.

Murmurs swelled through the crowd. They parted again, and Fol, the orc armorer, wheeled his cart into the ring. He reached his clawed gray hands into the stack of weapons, lifted a pair of double-sided battle axes, and tossed them onto the grass. His duty finished, he turned right around and pulled the cart back the way he had come.

"So it begins," Indigo decreed. "May the overgod watch over us all."

"And watch he will," answered the combined voices of the Ersatz.

The Righteous said nothing.

In the ring, Peter hastily scooped up his labrys and went on the attack. He swung a wild overhead chop at Pipin, who stepped easily out of the way. The tall, imposing Ersatz gave the Righteous man a hard elbow in the back, which combined with his already unstable momentum made Peter fall flat on his face.

The guests who looked on burst out laughing, which made the toppled man scrabble to his feet and heft the axe once more. Sweat beaded on Peter's brow and slicked his skinny frame. "Bugger off!" he screamed, his eyes tossing daggers at Pipin.

Pipin sighed, his chest rising and falling deliberately. He picked his labrys up off the grass and held it haphazardly. Indigo watched his body language—hunched and tense with a furrowed brow, like someone who knew the fight was hopeless and yet remained steadfast that he had made the correct choice—and her heart went out to him.

That was simply Pipin. Protective and quick to defend those he loved, no matter the cost to himself. Even suffering four ascensions in his scant two years of imprisonment had not succeeded in changing him.

The scrawny Righteous man went on the attack again, though not as frantically this time. He kept his feet a decent width apart and swung his labrys in measured arcs. Still, he was nowhere near the equal of Pipin. Every time Peter slashed, Pipin met the blow with a lazy parry, bringing a flurry of sparks.

The ease at which Pipin defended himself while never going on the offensive clearly frustrated the Righteous man. Peter was growing more unsettled, his grunts and howls when he swung becoming steadily louder. He was making no headway, a gnat trying to ram its way through solid brick.

Peter screamed at the sky. He dropped his obviously laboring arms and went for a sideways hack. This time, Pipin caught the shaft of the axe with his left hand, halting it in midair. He then bashed Peter in the face with the flat side of his axe. Head snapping back, Peter dropped like a rock onto his rump. Blood poured from his nose, cascaded over his chin and onto his bare chest. When he spun his upper body toward Jasper Popp and the other merchants, his eyes bulged with a combination of hatred and disbelief.

"I thought we couldn't lose!" he shrieked at his betters. Indigo took a perverse amount of pride in the fear trilling his voice.

The merchant leader stared down at him and smirked.

Peter twisted back to face Pipin, who stood with the axe resting on his shoulder as if he were not currently in the middle of a duel. "Screw this," Peter said. His upper lip curled, exposing his teeth. "You worthless bastard. Don't just stand there. Go ahead and kill me!"

Pipin laughed. It was a sweet yet scornful sound.

"What am I, a *joke*?" the tattooed man seethed. He struggled up to a kneeling position, gripping the labrys like a drunk gripped a toilet seat. "You have no idea who I am, do you? I could *own you* if I wanted! Because you're worthless. You can't even strike me down! So if you're gonna do nothing, maybe I'll go back over there and finish what I started with that sad waif. Sound good?"

Pipin stopped laughing. His lips pressed together so tightly they turned white. Any satisfaction Indigo had felt moments before dissolved to dust.

"Maybe I'll tie her to a bed," Peter went on. "Slowly cut her. Keep her alive the whole time. Tit to tit, neck to pelvis. Then maybe I'll take it a little lower, see how she likes it if I slice off her lab—"

Pipin let loose the most rageful roar Indigo had ever heard. Her courtesan took a menacing step toward his sitting prey and looped the axe above his head, his neck pulled taut. But when he reached the apex of his swing, his eyes went momentarily blank, the rippling muscles in his arms turned rigid.

That pause, however brief, gave the Righteous man the break he needed. He dropped onto his belly and spun to the side just as Pipin regained his functions and brought the labrys down. The blade sunk halfway into the ground with a dull *thud*. Pipin blinked in confusion.

Indigo knew this was where it ended.

Peter staggered to his feet along the side of his opponent. His arms shook when he hurriedly lifted the axe and drove it into Pipin's back. Flesh split, bone cracked, blood spurted. The Righteous man let go of the wedged labrys and stumbled back a few steps while Pipin writhed, still bent over. Indigo shook her head. The body of her courtesan trembled; a groan rumbled through his pinched lips. He toppled forward and landed on his face, the axe handle shuddering along with him.

All around, the gathered Ersatz whispered the required prayer to an overgod who obviously could not care less. Their words were drowned out by the cheering guests.

"I won," Peter said, standing there bewildered, blood continuing to flow out his ruined nose. The cheers grew more raucous as he gradually raised his hands above his head. "I won!"

The circle finally broke as the other guests mobbed the victorious man. Even more guests harangued the dying Pipin, nudging him, taunting him. One woman—the wife of the merchant leader, Kirsten Popp—went so far as to grab Pipin by the tight black curls atop his head, lift his face from the ground, and bizarrely lick his forehead.

Indigo bowed her head. She would never understand these people, or why the overgod favored them more than her.

A hand touched her shoulder. "Miss Indigo?" Anthony said.

She had forgotten he was there and wanted no part in even seeing his face. "Not now, Mr. Bell," she told him, unable to keep the dejection from her voice. "I will find you later, if you still desire my time."

"That...you don't gotta," he whispered, sounding conflicted. She saw him slink away in the periphery, heading off to rejoin the other guests in their celebration.

Good riddance.

The Ersatz slowly gathered around her, waiting for the moment when the throng cleared enough that they could go to the aid of their brother. Indigo glanced to the left and right. Aspar and Aqua stood beside her, diligent as ever.

"I hate this," Aqua said, his dark brown eyes brimming with held-back tears.

Aspar clenched his chiseled jaw, blowing a stream of air out his nose. "We all do. It is not fair."

"Not fair at all," Indigo told them both. "But it is simply the way it is."

The unruly guests eventually dispersed back toward Hickweis Tavern in a swarm, likely wanting to fill their heads with liquor to feed their new bloodlust. Indigo gestured to her people, telling them to go back to work. Their responsibilities needed to be fulfilled, even when one of their own was felled. *Especially* then.

Because that was what the overgod demanded.

When she was alone but for six tavern laborers and a few Righteous stragglers, Indigo approached Pipin, who still twitched where he lay. His blood had stained the grass around him a deep shade of purple, but Indigo slid down beside him nonetheless. The blood soaked her frilly dress, warm yet chilling against her flesh. She lifted Pipin by the chin and slipped her legs beneath, pulled on his shoulder until he rested on his side. The axe still buried in his back warbled, making him moan. His skin was clammy, his breathing shallow. When his eyes rolled in their sockets to meet hers, they looked glassy and so, so sad.

"Sorry... Mum..." he groaned.

"Shush now, my love," she said, tracing her fingers gently down his cheek. "Be still. It will all be over soon."

His eyes squeezed shut. "It... won't..."

His body convulsed one last time as he emitted a choking sound and fell still. Indigo kissed the pristine brown skin of his cheek. "Rest while you can," she told the empty vessel.

Rest. That was something she would not be getting much of today, given that she now had to prepare a pyre to burn the remains, along with managing the tavern staff and possibly giving in to Anthony's desires if he demanded it. Given that it was just past noon, it promised to be a very long day.

She lifted her gaze to Dur, the Hickweis Tavern landscaper. The flat nose of the troll twitched, her bulging red eyes dripping black tears over the cracked green flesh of her cheeks. Indigo raised a hand, intent on giving the signal that she was ready to remove the body, but something caught her eye that froze her in place.

It was *him* again. The dark figure who had observed from the rear of the throng during the fight, the one bathed in shadow. He lingered now just behind the house servants, hands in the pockets of the long leather jacket he wore despite the heat. His face hidden by the strange hat atop his head. A large case was slung over his shoulder. The dark stranger did not have an aura that pulsed like a Righteous, and he was definitely not one of her own.

Her heart raced; her skin broke out in a cold sweat. For the first time in her remembered lifetime, a random variable entered her world of constant and predictable pain. Whoever this man was, he did not belong here. An unknown. A deviation. An invader.

When he raised his head, and the whites of his eyes shone from beneath the brim of his hat, Indigo knew right away he would bring nothing but trouble. Oddly, part of her welcomed that.

— 4 —

*"This is no crime I am planning, O Lord.
A murder most hateful, a murder of strangers.
I am indeed avaricious for greatness, and that greatness is Yours."*
—**Book of the Pentus, Quotations 61:9**

The woman cradling the dead man's head in her lap was the most spectacular Shade had ever seen.

Her appearance combined the best features of every culture Shade knew, molded into a singularly perfect being. From her teardrop eyes, very similar to the shape of Mara Choon's people in Ramstable, to rounded cheeks much like the population of New Salem, to a delicately narrow chin common to those who called Breighton home. Her lips were like Vera's, a perfect rosebud, thin on top and plump on the bottom, and her black hair bounced over her shoulders in satiny ringlets, bringing to mind the residents of Pinchu. Her skin, however, held no ethnic standard. Equidistant between light and dark, her flesh possessed a golden hue and seemed to glow in the light of the early afternoon sun.

Her ears, which rose to gentle peaks that poked through that luscious hair, were her most alien feature. The only comparison Shade could associate were the stories of nymphs he'd heard about over his six years of life. A creature of fairy tales and legend made flesh.

That shouldn't have come as a surprise, since much like the goat-man who had exited the temple, the wildlife he'd encountered during his few hours wandering around Darkenwood reminded him of folklore. There were tall creatures and short creatures, fiends with squat faces and some with childlike visages, a few with wicked tusks and others with mouths so small they might not have been able to fit teeth. He'd seen monsters with green skin and gray skin and every shade in between, abominations that looked like birds or cats that walked upright.

What he found strangest of all were the few who appeared to be very much human. Their clothes were expertly made, and some of the women wore jewelry embossed with diamonds and jade, which Shade had never seen outside Yaddo. Although some walked around with wide-eyed expressions of wonder, no one seemed at all surprised to be surrounded by so many oddities.

None of that took into account the sudden outbreak of violence that had just occurred, leaving one man dead while the man who'd killed him was ushered into a large building by a wildly cheering crowd. The fight had been baffling. As the dead man, tall and muscular and agile, had seemingly toyed with the skinny tattooed one at every turn, he inexplicably faltered when it came time for the killing blow. To Shade, it looked like the loser had suffered a minor stroke just before he brought his double-bladed axe down, which allowed his opponent to come out victorious. The pause had been quick and subtle, but also obvious. Why the crowd cheered the winner so boisterously despite his obvious luck and lack of skill made no sense.

Shade shook his head and went back to staring at the gorgeous nymph in the courtyard. She stroked the dead man's face, her expression one of deep sadness, but her rigid posture seemed almost stoic. As one of the squat and ugly monsters approached the woman, she lifted her head. Her eyes, vibrant green and sparkling, met Shade's. Her eyebrows furrowed; her lips quirked. Shade felt like she wasn't looking at him, but *into* him, exposing all his treachery. He quickly tugged down the brim of his hat and averted his gaze.

He turned to find a looming presence blocking his way. The man before him was human, with dark skin mirroring his own, a handsome nose, and athletic build. Shade had seen him before—this same man had been standing beside the beautiful nymph during the fight. The stranger stared at him, gnawing on his lower lip as if nervous.

Shade went to step around, but the man grabbed his shoulder, stopping him. Shade tensed and dropped his left hand just inside the flap of his duster, fingers tapping against the handle of his stolen pistol.

"I don't wanna have a problem here," the man said in Straightspeak, his voice low and quivering.

Shade tilted his head but said nothing.

"Okay, not a talker then." The man tugged at his collar with his free hand. "I haven't seen you around, so you obviously just got here. My name's Tony. Second-level sales adjunct for Popp Mercantile. Not up there on the ladder, but my boss is, and he's here too. So, listen, I know this place is kinda a free-for-all and all that, but Miss Indigo's mine."

Confused, Shade tilted his head to the other side.

Tony's brow furrowed. "Miss Indigo? The half-elf you were just staring at?"

Shade reached further into his duster.

"Which party you with? What corp you work for?" When Shade remained silent and still, the man's grip on his shoulder tensed. He suddenly yanked Shade's collar down, briefly exposing his neck. Shade immediately knocked the invading hand away.

"Whoa, cool down," Tony said, backing away with both hands raised. "Sorry, didn't realize you were Ersatz. A new one, probably. Right? And a musician too." He pointed at the neck of the guitar case sticking up over Shade's other shoulder. "My bad. So...I'll just walk away now, okay?" He chuckled, shaking his head as he sauntered toward the building behind them. "Hope you make it through today. With your attitude, you're gonna get Right of Retribution called in no time."

Shade watched the man traipse up the staircase and disappear inside. "Hickweis Tavern," the swinging sign above the door said. Confusion washed over Shade. He had no clue what an Ersatz was, nor the meaning of Right of Retribution. The wiry tattooed lowlife had screamed those words before the fight began. Retribution? For what? None of it made any sense.

He scanned the courtyard once more, contemplating whether to approach this Miss Indigo that Tony was so keen on, but she was now heading away from him, surrounded by a phalanx of ugly creatures. The body of the slain man had been laid out on a cart that a gray-skinned monstrosity pushed. For a moment, he wondered if these beings had all waltzed into this world through a gateway, if his purpose in being here was to fulfill his duties as a knight of the Pentus and send them back to whatever hell they came from.

No, he told himself. He wasn't a knight any longer, and these odd creatures had not shown him an ounce of hostility. Rather, they all seemed despondent. Something itched at the back of his mind. What he really needed to do was settle down, get a drink, and get some answers.

A tavern was as good a place to accomplish that as any.

As soon as he slipped his way through the pack gathered on the porch and entered the establishment, Shade knew that *tavern* didn't describe the place's true purpose. He had been around the Wasteland enough to know a brothel when he saw one. The biggest difference was that every other brothel he had seen catered solely to the male gaze, whereas here the male prostitutes were as scantily clad as the women, both genders working the massive main room with clearly artificial enthusiasm.

He found an empty space at the long bar, propped his guitar case against it, and leaned back to keep watch. The congratulatory celebration went on as well-dressed people took turns pouring drinks down the throat of the skinny, tattooed man, oblivious to the demonic creatures that skittered around them, picking up their messes. Shade turned to see the bartender—a man with a baby-smooth face and button nose who could not be more than four feet tall—lug a crate around behind the bar. He was uncannily proficient at his job despite his diminutive stature, tossing down his crate and climbing atop it to prepare drinks from the vast collection of glass bottles against the wall. He somehow balanced the drinks on a wide circular tray while hopping off the crate, repositioning it at the bar, and climbing up once more to hand over his creations without spilling a drop. It was quite impressive.

Music began playing, a jaunty little ditty performed by a tall woman with red skin and black horns. The creature plucked an instrument that looked like the bastard child of a harp and ukulele. The reveling patrons stomped their feet and clapped.

A few of the beasts lugged tables and chairs from the center of the room. A male and female prostitute then entered the newly-created open space, performing a sultry dance full of twirls and dips and provocative gestures. Their sparse clothing was about to abandon their bodies, lace and leather whipping about. Shade's mouth twitched. He found the dance repulsive, not because it oozed sexuality, but because the performers looked like family. With their bronzed skin, thick black hair, lean builds, tender features, and dark brooding eyes, they appeared to be twins in every way save gender. The woman's face was covered with bruises.

"They are good, are they not?" a feminine voice asked.

Shade pivoted. A short, pretty redhead covered with freckles lingered beside him. Her attire of simply lacy green undergarments that showed off her wiles marked her as another prostitute. She stood almost perfectly still, her striking blue eyes brimming with tears as she took in the dance.

"It's sickening," Shade said.

"Not at all," the girl said. "Vivo and Mana move so easily together. As if they are two organisms trying to become one. It is wonderful."

"They're siblings, no?"

"Of course," said the girl. "We are all siblings here."

Shade's teeth grinded. "You're all related?"

"In many ways, yes." The girl laughed sweetly. "We are all children of the overgod, molded from the same stuff, with the same purpose in mind. In that way, yes, we are all siblings."

"So those two don't have the same parents, then?"

The prostitute glanced his way. Her lips pressed together, and she twirled a strand of her hair. The way she looked at him was odd, as if *he* was the strangest creature in the room. She breathed heavily, brought up a hand and touched his bearded face. Shade forced himself to remain still. The girl's eyes then widened in apparent fear, and she quickly hurried away without another word.

He watched her depart, and somewhere in the back of his confused mind he wondered what kind of comments Meesh would make at seeing her ample, barely-concealed rear end sway. His regret swelled up again, until someone tapped on his elbow from behind. He started, nearly knocking over his guitar case, and spun around to see the bartender standing there, fingers tapping on the counter.

"That was Bluebell," the bartender said. "The dreamer of the bunch."

Shade nodded, but kept his mouth shut.

"And I am Macaro," the short man continued. He pushed a mug filled with frothing liquid toward Shade. "This is on the house."

"Thank you," Shade said. He picked up the mug and took a sip. The concoction was unlike any beer he'd ever tasted, equally sweet and sour, with an undercurrent of honey.

Macaro made a show of drying off glasses while Shade drank. He waited until Shade swallowed before saying, "I have not seen you around before. Where are you from?"

"South," he said, remembering the old rule that if you wanted to get a head start on information gathering, you always started with the local tavern master. "*Far* south."

"Far south? I did not know anything existed south of here. Except for the mountains. They are haunted. Supposedly."

"You could say that, yeah. Though if you want *true* hauntings you have to get past them and into the Wasteland."

He thought of his own soul, haunted by Vera and Abe and his own sedition, and shivered.

"I have no reference for that," Macaro said with a laugh, setting aside one of the dried glasses and grabbing another. "But I believe you, since I would not know what exists outside Darkenwood. I have never left the valley."

"Never?"

"Never."

Shade squinted at him and turned back to the performance, where Vivo and Mana had heightened the passion of their dance. They were now locked together, arms and legs wrapped around each other as they spun, hands pulling and grabbing at every opportunity. Their lips were locked in the most passionate of kisses. Shade felt rumblings and turned away.

"When did *you* get here?" Macaro asked.

"A few hours ago. Early morning." Shade hesitated to go on, but decided that when trying to build trust, revealing not-asked-for truths was always the best practice. "I found a temple once I descended off the mountain. It had a strange name."

"Tro Choi," Macaro said.

"That's it, yeah. A man exited. A man with the legs of a goat. I followed him at a distance, until he arrived at a big settlement in the woods. Some folks greeted him." He nearly added something about how the vast majority of those he saw weren't human, but decided it best to keep that part out. "I wandered in. Looked around. Wound up here."

Something flashed across Macaro's black eyes. He leaned away from Shade, gestured to the ghastly smushed-face beast stacking soiled plates on the other end of the bar. "Find Indigo," he said. "Tell her the overgod finished with Truda. It seems she is a satyr now."

"Got it, boss," the creature said in a shockingly normal voice. It finished stacking its plates and shambled out the door.

Shade's interest piqued. "Overgod. The prostitute said something about that."

"Her name is Bluebell," Macaro corrected, though not unkindly. "I already told you that."

"That's right. I forgot. My apologies."

"And just so you know, we prefer *courtesan* here. Prostitute is such an ugly word."

"Understood, and again, I'm sorry." He tipped the brim of his hat toward the bartender in respect. "As for this overgod, is that the deity of worship here?"

"Worship? No," he replied with frown. "More like put up with, and curse over our undying days."

Weird. "How about the Queen of Snakes?"

"Who?"

"You've never heard of that one?"

"Not unless you mean Sienna when she plays with her pythons."

"I don't know who that is."

"You would not."

Shade picked at a splinter on the counter. "What god *is* worshipped here?"

"None," Macaro said. "Unless you count the Righteous. Then again, I am not sure being compelled to serve someone is the same as worshipping them."

"Righteous, eh?" Shade felt a twinge of excitement at the possibility of answers. The signpost on the path leading into the valley had mentioned something about the Righteous. "And where do I find this Righteous? Is the temple where he preaches? Are there priests I can question?"

Macaro seemed to find the questions hilarious, because he let out a hearty guffaw. "*Him* is *them*, and they are all around you." He pointed toward the fancily-dressed masses still clapping and stomping and watching the dance, then proffered both arms out wide. "*This* is their temple."

Shade sucked in his bottom lip. "Oh."

The riot in the tavern died down as the dancers finished their perverted display. Cheers were replaced with clinking silverware and the murmur of conversation. A man in a fancy top hat and a ratty beard grabbed the male dancer, gestured to the staircase a few feet away from Shade. The two of them headed for it, locked arm-in-arm. The female dancer with the bruised face hung her head and moved toward an empty chair in a lonely corner.

"Hold on a moment," Macaro said. "Business."

The bartender hopped off his crate, slid it a few feet to his right, and climbed back up in time to accept what appeared to be wooden coins from the patron, who then headed up the stairs with the male dancer in tow. Shade scowled in disapproval. He might have understood the necessity for this line of work, but that didn't mean he had to like it.

Macaro made his way back over, shooting a sudden glance at the tavern entrance before he stepped up on his crate. Shade took the last swig of the tasty beverage and slid it across the bar. "Another?" He rummaged in the pocket of his duster, where gold coins stamped with the symbol of the Pentus jangled. "I have payment."

"Out of the question," Macaro told him with a defiant shake of his head. "I have humored you so far, but the time is up. You cannot stay."

"Why?" Shade asked, baffled at the bartender's sudden change in attitude.

"Because you are not Righteous, and you are not Ersatz either. You do not belong here, and should never have been able to even *enter* here." He again glanced toward the entrance. "And Mum does not approve."

Shade followed the small man's gaze. His nerve endings buzzed when he saw the extraordinary woman from the courtyard standing there, framed by sunlight. Although Miss Indigo still wore the purple dress stained from toe to midriff with a dead man's blood, it did nothing to diminish her splendor. Not even the narrow-eyed distrust displayed on her face could make her look any less beautiful.

The woman started on her way through the room, only to be blocked by the same man who had confronted Shade outside. Tony, if he recalled correctly. The handsome young man shuffled when Indigo turned to go around him one way, then shuffled back when she turned the other way. Her sensuous lips mouthed the word *move*. Shade watched as Indigo tried to push him away, only for Tony to grab her wrists, lean over, and whisper something to her. Indigo visibly sighed and shook her head. She said something Shade couldn't hear, planted her hand on Tony's chest, and shoved him aside.

She didn't get far before voices were raised in anger. It wasn't Tony who shouted, but the tattoo-faced creep whose cheeks were red from what was likely a combination of leftover adrenaline from his fight and too much booze.

"Bitch, my bud *asked you for something!*" he shrieked, breaking away from his admirers.

Shade tensed. It looked like things were about to get out of hand, which made this place no different from any other watering hole he'd ever visited, no matter how strange its workforce might be.

Tattoo-Face stormed toward the gorgeous woman with hands balled into fists. Indigo took an unhurried step away, slowly raising her palms. The man threw a punch, his knuckles catching her under the chin, knocking her head back. Indigo stumbled. Those watching at the bar parted, allowing her to collide with a stool and fall over.

Everyone in the tavern, human and otherwise, became rapt. No one moved to help the struggling Indigo except for Tony of all people, but Indigo's attacker shoved him away violently. Tattoo-Face then raged over Indigo like an eagle about to spear a mouse. "You mean nothing, don't you understand that?" he bellowed, spit flying from his lips. With his insane grin and his shirt off, exposing the myriad ugly tattoos covering half his body, he looked far more like a monster than any of the inhuman creatures in the place. "It don't matter if you got work to do. You serve *him*. You serve *me*." He held his arms out to his sides. "You serve every one of us!"

Shade's neck grew hot, and he began to shake. He had seen too many men like this, belligerent lowlifes who demanded they be loved and respected, too stupid to understand that it was their attitudes that made them undesirable, and too lazy and self-absorbed to put forth any effort to change. He leaned forward, intent on intervening since no one else would, but a hand grabbed his sleeve, stopping him.

It was Macaro. "Don't," the barkeep said.

He stewed on it for the moment. Macaro was right; who was he to insert himself into the affairs of a culture he knew nothing about? Then again, who was he if he did nothing and let someone get hurt?

Before he could answer to those questions, Bluebell, the redheaded prostitute, came up behind the enraged man, grabbed his arm before he could drive another fist into Indigo's beautiful face. She used the man's momentum to spin him around and throw her arms around his neck. Shade thought she would drive a knee into his groin, but instead she did the unthinkable—she smooshed her face against his and kissed him. Tattoo-Face staggered against the weight hanging off his front, his eyes bulging.

Someone whooped, another person shouted, "Yeah, take her!" Tony moved to Indigo's side, attempted to help her stand up, an offer she refused. All the while, Bluebell continued to grind against the one who'd attacked her.

Tattoo-Face's hands squeezed the prostitute's ass, worked their way up her back, and disappeared into her nest of red curls. A sick feeling cramped Shade's stomach. Instead of matching Bluebell's sexual energy, the man grabbed fistfuls of her hair and yanked her head back with such force that she yelped. In one disgustingly violent motion, he drove his forehead into the middle of her face and released her. The *crack* of her nose snapping echoed through the room, harkening another round of cheers.

Bluebell quivered on her feet for a moment, blood pouring out her nose, until her legs gave out and she crumpled in a heap. The vile man began to kick her, viciously, his every strike against her side, back, arms, and face bringing gargled cries for help that went unanswered.

In Shade's mind, the prostitute became Vera. Helpless, struggling, pleading. He couldn't take it any longer.

With his whole body humming as fiercely as when he was consumed by the Rush, he shrugged out of Macaro's grasp and crossed the crowded tavern in less than five heartbeats. The barkeep shouted a warning to stop, but Shade barely heard him over the rush of blood in his ears. As Tattoo-Face bent over to deliver an elbow to the small of the prostitute's back, Shade grabbed him by the scruff of his neck, fingers digging into sweaty flesh, and flung him away.

"Leave the women be!" he hollered.

The man skittered backward, arms pinwheeling, eyes wide with shock, until he collided with a cluster of people wearing expensive clothes. One of their number, a nab who looked to be in his late thirties, with a well-manicured beard that formed a chin guard from sideburn to sideburn, caught the flailing man and tossed him forward once more. Tattoo-Face spun around to face Shade, but seemed to relent when their eyes met.

"Two in one day," Chin-Beard said with an evil smirk. "There's hope for you yet, Ortiz."

That got the tattooed man Ortiz grinning. He glared daggers at Shade, pointed a shaking finger at him.

"Retribution."

The tavern erupted in a roar so loud that it hurt Shade's ears. He noticed a woozy-looking Indigo waving her arms above her head and shouting, but her words were drowned out by the throng. A moment later, he found himself being shoved toward the exit by multiple patrons. He fought against them, but they were too many, their bloodlust too high. The most he could do was stop them from ripping his duster off his shoulders.

Eventually, he was impelled through the swinging door. The pulsing centipede of ferocious humanity shoved him down the steps and into the center of the courtyard, where the blood of the previous combatant still stained the grass purple. The hands on him retreated, leaving him to stand on his own.

A ring formed around him. Unlike the previous fight, there were fewer otherworldly fiends among the audience. If the spectators noticed, they didn't seem to care. They hooted and pumped their fists and shouted obscenities in Shade's direction.

Ortiz strutted into the center of the ring. He paced back and forth, shouting unintelligible words as if attempting to excite himself further. "Labrys, again!" he announced when his primal howl finished. "Let's do this!"

The cheers went on, but they grew restless when the armorer didn't come through with its cart of weapons. Ortiz looked all around, his rage mixing with confusion. "C'mon!" he yelled. "I'm enforcing my right! Give me my weapon!"

"He's got a sword!" someone exclaimed. Hands gripped the right side of Shade's duster and pulled it aside, exposing the saber dangling from his belt. Shade blindly shoved whoever had grabbed him, and his duster flapped back into place.

Chin-Beard stepped into the ring, drew the sword on his own hip, and handed it to Ortiz. "He is already armed, and now you are too," he said, seeming to be enjoying this whole charade. "Screw the Ersatz. Screw their rules. We don't need to follow them if we don't want to."

Ortiz nodded, took the sword, held it above his head like a captain readying the cavalry to charge. His tattooed face dripped sweat, his eyes burned with insanity. He bent his knees, brought the sword down, and gripped it in two hands, the tip of the blade pointing in Shade's direction. It was a good offensive stance, one Shade had been taught while sparring with Abe in the practice yard.

Ortiz might not have been good with an axe, but he obviously knew the basics of swordplay.

Great.

Shade considered trying to calm the situation down with words, like Abe would do. But Shade wasn't an orator. He wasn't a leader of men. Without a guitar in his hands, he held no sway over crowds. That meant the only choice was to fight, win, and get out of this bewildering hellhole.

Shade wasn't frightened of this man, but given that he wasn't the best swordsman and his opponent obviously knew what he was doing, victory wasn't necessarily guaranteed. Not odds Shade liked. Perhaps the best way to deal with this bastard was the same way he and his brothers dealt with bloodthirsty bandits back home.

"I don't got time for this shit," Shade muttered. He reached beneath his duster for his shoulder holster, grabbed the handle of Meesh's burner, and whipped out the gun. In one fluid motion he aimed, measured the distance, and squeezed the trigger. As the kickback brought his arm up ever so slightly, the explosive sound of the gunshot echoed off the mountains tenfold.

Ortiz's head snapped back, spraying blood, gray matter, and bone fragments on the people standing behind him. His chin slowly came back down, and he stared at Shade blankly as blood from the small hole in his forehead snaked between his eyes. His body shuddered, the sword fell from his grip, and he dropped to the grass.

The crowd went eerily quiet. Chin-Beard took a step forward, face splattered with the dead man's blood. He stared down at the corpse as if he expected it to stand back up again. Shade rolled his shoulders and swept the burner across the crowd. No one was paying him any mind whatsoever. Their attentions were on the man lying motionless in the grass with a gaping hole in the back of his head.

Indigo shoved her way into the center of the ring, her perfect golden face marred by a blooming dark spot on her chin. She raced to the fallen man, knelt down beside him, and pressed her fingers to his neck.

She did not look thankful. She not look relieved. Instead, when she brought her gaze up to Shade, her expression was both angry and very, very afraid.

"What have you done?" she demanded, her voice trilling beneath the still-echoing gunshot. *"What have you done?"*

Shade stared at her, his jaw working up and down. "What I had to."

5

He has told you, O servant of man, what is necessary.
And what does the Pentus require of you but to think and love freely,
and walk with pride knowing you are doing your Lord's duty?
—**Book of the Pentus, Platitudes 9:34**

J ust do it, you coward," Shade muttered. He knelt on the rocky ground a few feet away, head thrown back, burning eyes defiant.

Meesh drew back his Eldersword, which hummed with the sweet music of murder. His brother closed his eyes, awaiting his punishment. Meesh swung. His blade cut a star-filled gash through the air. *I don't wanna do this, don't wanna do this!* his mind shrieked. A lance of pain struck his temple, his sight blanked. The Eldersword lifted ever so slightly. He despaired, unseeing, knowing that when it connected with his brother, it would slice through his cheek instead of his neck, robbing a good man of the honorable death he deserved.

The blinding white intensified, then retreated. Meesh blinked to awareness. Sweat coated his naked body, tacky strands of hair clinging to his face. He groaned, staring up at a pale white ceiling dappled with bright yellow spots, the result of sunlight shining through the open windows and reflecting off the glass table beside the soft, downy bed he currently occupied.

A dream. Only a dream.

Meesh sat up with a groan. His head ached; his mouth tasted like ash. His surroundings were familiar, although he didn't remember arriving. Keedra's apartment was two streets over from Troubadours. The woman was sprawled out beside him, as naked as he was. The gentle curve of her spine flexed like a snake when she shifted position, and she murmured sweetly. He never stopped being amazed at how her voice sounded like sexualized honey even when she slept. Her blond curls, more extreme in the mugginess of the bedroom, formed a mane to the middle of her back. He knew what they had done that night, even if he didn't remember the act; the stickiness of the sheets told that story well enough.

Meesh grinned, his dream all but forgotten, and leaned forward to give one of her perfect ass cheeks a squeeze. Another spike of pain drove into his skull, and he recoiled. He groaned, curled his upper body inward, and massaged his temples.

"Hangovers. Ugh."

When the feeling subsided, he slipped out of bed. He shuffled through Keedra's four-room flat, went to the kitchen, and turned on the sink. Water poured with a flick of the handle, gurgling from the faucet and twanging softly in the steel basin. The sound was downright comforting. Add "running water" to the extensive list of things he missed when he and his brothers patrolled the Wasteland.

Brothers. The dream reentered his mind and made him grimace.

He splashed water on his face and gulped down mouthfuls to get rid of that hollow ashy taste. When he finished, the residual aches of the hangover were almost gone.

Almost.

Keedra had woken up by the time he meandered back to the bedroom. She was propped up on her elbows, soaking in the streaming sunlight, her back arched and breasts exposed. She turned Meesh's way, her blue eyes sparkling with mischievous energy. She obviously hadn't imbibed as zealously as he had last night.

"Morning, handsome," she purred, turning onto her side to face him. Her untamed hair flopped over half her face, and her delicate fingers traced a circle around one erect nipple. "Why aren't you in bed right now? You should be."

"You really want more? What, you didn't you get enough last night?" Meesh said with a chuckle.

She made a show of jutting out her bottom lip. "Not really. You were a little... quick."

"I was?"

"Yup. And you fell asleep right afterward."

"That's disappointing. So much for my legendary virility."

She patted the empty spot on the bed beside her. "You could fix that right now if you wanted." Her gaze lowered and she frowned. "Though it doesn't look like you're in the mood."

Meesh looked down at himself. Sure enough, he saw a flaccid noddle. What the hell was wrong with him? He was standing there naked with a beautiful, just-as-naked woman inviting him to take her, and his body wasn't reacting? He closed his eyes, but when he tried to force dirty thoughts to come, his abdomen remained irritatingly rumble-free. All he saw was the Shade from his dream, displayed against a backdrop of Kamini's caved-in face.

Great, I'm so damaged I can't perform unless I'm blackout drunk, he thought, sighing. Which wouldn't be the worst thing in the world, if only he *remembered* afterward.

"Gotta go," he muttered, scooping his discarded clothes off the floor and hastily throwing them on.

"Eh, that's all right," Keedra said. "I have my memories of last time to tide me over." She flattened out on the bed, stretched her arms over her head, and laughed. Meesh buttoned his wrinkled shirt, shaking his head as he walked away.

"See you later."

"If it's like usual, probably not for a while," her overly cheery voice answered.

He left the apartment, hopped down two flights of stairs, and exited the building. The sun beat down on him, intense and hot even in the early morning. His mind worked through his issues as he took stride after stride, ignoring greetings from the early-morning folks packing the street. Sweat beaded on his forehead, but he was too wrapped up in his own thoughts to care.

It took him a while to arrive at a disheartening realization: he hadn't actually *wanted* to have sex with Keedra. She'd been a salve, an added distraction to top off the booze. He didn't want her now, in his head-ache-heightened sobriety, because she didn't want *him*. Nowhere in her heart of hearts did Keedra desire anything from Meesh other than a few fleeting moments of carnal bliss. She liked the act, the release, the game. Keedra just wanted to have fun and move on, like the free spirit she was.

Nothing wrong with that. Never had been. Hell, Meesh had always thought he was the same.

But the events that had transpired when he and his brothers ran with Cooper had changed him. *Kamini* had changed him. He'd seen the pain and hatred and regret she carried, and he'd wanted to cure it all. Even though he'd known her only a couple of days, the depth he felt in their connection ran deeper than any he'd felt with anyone but his brothers. He wanted more of that, *longed* for it. But everyone who'd given it to him was either dead or gone. He had to start over. He didn't want to.

Brah, you're turning into a teenage girl.

By the time he tore himself out of his contemplations, he found that he'd walked all the way to the Hall of Lucidity. Two whole miles, gone without realizing it. He laughed to himself. Maybe he'd put off this contemplation thing for too long. Doing it more often when out in the Wasteland would make those long, boring trips go by far quicker. It was an almost perfect solution, if not for the pesky depression and self-hate that came with it.

Four imas in royal purple headwraps guarded the Hall entrance. Meesh stopped at the bottom of the staircase and waved up at them. "Hey, can I get a carriage?" he asked in the kindest voice he could manage, which in itself was strange, since Meesh always used to toss demands around like they were birdseed. He was a Knight Eternal, after all. He put his life on the line every time he left Yaddo's shores;

why didn't he deserve to be waited on hand and foot during those fleeting moments he was back at home?

Before he could correct himself and give a proper order, two of the imas rushed out of sight. Meesh sighed, plopped down on the bench next to the staircase, and waited.

It took a few minutes for a horse-drawn carriage to appear. When it stopped, Meesh slapped his knees and climbed inside. "Dakota Keep, now!" he shouted once he got situated, applying a little bit of the self he knew and liked to this new and not-necessarily-improved person he'd become. A warm feeling crept over him, stifled only slightly by fresh guilt.

While the carriage rumbled over the cobbled road, Meesh closed the window shades, rested his head against the back of the seat, and shut his eyes. He smiled, his mind drifting toward things that didn't involve death or change or this newfound sense of culpability. Mostly, he thought of how much he wanted to get a new horse and spend a few weeks reacquainting himself with Yaddo's wonders. He longed to bathe in the cool waters of Penny Lake or spend time with the free-love locals who frequented the hot springs of Northern Song. Hiking through the riding trails lined with coneflowers in the mountains of Clarabella would be nice, as would watching stallions run through fields of wheat on the island off the coast of Polythene Point. Before he left last time, he and Abe had gotten drunk on wine from the countless vineyards sprinkled throughout the twin regions of Sie Liebt and Savoy and followed that with a visit to the tar pits of Rigby. He'd like to do that again, but knew he couldn't, because Abe was gone. Maybe siting in an eatery on the coast of Port Smedley, watching the sun set over Jude's Bay while ogling the townsfolk who liked to bathe nude there was a better way to go.

The smile melted off Meesh's face when he realized that he was now imagining Kamini experiencing all of this with him. He spent the rest of the ride grumbling under his breath and mulling over how many demons he'd have to kill, how much blood he'd have to shed, to get the girl out of his head.

"Stop," Meesh said before the carriage could bring him all the way home. He exited without thanking the driver, shoved his hands in the pockets of his dirty, loose-fitting pants, and marched up the hill toward the northernmost point of the kingdom of Yaddo. Walking was better than riding in a carriage, especially when he had irritation to burn off.

The first thing he saw once he reached the top of the hill was the Temple of the Crone, jutting from the tree-covered mountainside like a huge, calcified tumor. The Temple consisted of a round black tower that rose a good hundred feet above the canopy. It sat on top of a thick concrete base five hundred feet wide, fronted by a door that resembled the one leading into the underground chamber at the Cooper Nuclear Station. The back of his neck tingled but he brushed the sensation aside.

Dakota Keep, the home of the Knights Eternal, lurked in the temple's shadow, dwarfed by the tower, even though the keep, a square, three-story edifice of pale red brick, was itself quite large. Meesh chuckled, thinking the building to be a huge waste of space. The knights' three flats were located on the top floor of the keep, with a huge kitchen and the Sacred Library on the second floor. The ground level consisted of a single room filled with training equipment, a shooting range, a workshop to create munitions, and the vault where countless weapons of the Elders were stored. All those amenities for three people who were away from home at least eighty percent of the time.

He wasn't sure if that really mattered. Yaddo might have had a booming population, but it wasn't like the three islands that made up the kingdom were overcrowded. *There're a buncha folks in the Wasteland who'd appreciate a life of comfort*, he thought, but quickly shoved away any more empathetic musings.

Meesh might have been changing, but he'd be damned if he'd allow himself to change *that* much.

Up the steps he went, humming a tune that he'd written with Shade during a quelling expedition in the cave system beneath Gatlin. It died in his throat when he pushed through the door to find Rodney sitting cross-legged on the floor in the middle of the exercise area, surrounded by the equipment the knights used to stay in top demon-fighting shape. He'd bathed, his long brown hair silken as it hung over his shoulders. A guitar rested in his lap, and his attention was so focused on the strings that he didn't look up when Meesh entered. The song he played was harsh and twangy and amateurish, far different from the complex, soulful ditties Rodney had strummed for Fatisha Dorl. A vile sort of satisfaction tickled Meesh's pleasure centers. *He's not so good after all. Ha!*

Rodney strummed another few off-kilter chords. He paused, turned the pegs on the headstock, and strummed again.

He wasn't playing, just tuning the instrument.

"Dammit," Meesh grumbled.

His new brother lifted his head with a sheepish smile. "Oh, hello," he said, sounding lethargic, per usual. "You didn't come home last night."

"No shit," Meesh said. He breathed deeply out his nose and headed for the stairs.

Rodney was up and striding toward him a second later. "Hey," he said when he caught up, sounding slightly out of breath. "Where did you go?"

"Out."

"I could have used your company."

"Too bad."

"What did you do?" Rodney asked innocently.

"Drank. Screwed. The usual."

"Ah." Rodney shrugged, matching Meesh's speed up the steps. "Sounds nice."

"Sure. Whatever."

"What was her name?"

"Whose name?"

"The lass you spent the night with."

"Oh. That'd be…"

Meesh stopped, leaned against the handrail, and stared his brother down. Rodney had never peppered him with questions like this, nor ever sounded this desperate. Not even when he was only a few hours old.

"You okay?" Meesh asked, cringing at the show of compassion.

"I suppose." Rodney shoved his hands in his pockets, averted his eyes. "Just lonely."

"You could've gone out and had fun too, y'know. We can do basically anything we want 'round here."

"I didn't know that." His gaze lifted again. He looked close to tears. "I don't know much of anything, really. Nor anyone. Anyone but you."

Meesh didn't want to admit it, but his heart broke a little. He sighed, rolled his eyes, and nudged his shoulder. "Sorry. Was in a bad place yesterday. For obvious reasons."

"Mm. I apologize too. I'm being a bit of a dolt. I don't mean to be." He winced. "Honestly? I'm scared. Very, very scared."

"Brah, no need. Nothing to be afraid of. Not when you got me around."

"I'll have you around?" Rodney asked softly.

Meesh considered his new brother, whose eyes were wide and sorrowful, and felt guilty once more. He remembered his own first few weeks of life. How off-kilter he'd been. How unsure he'd felt. How his thoughts were always filled with contradictions. To his brothers, he must've looked very much like Rodney did now. Yet Abe and Shade hadn't brushed him aside. They'd taken him under their tutelage, helped him cope, allowed his peculiar personality to form while showing him no judgment.

Didn't he owe that to Rodney too? After all, as the man himself said, Meesh was all he had.

"Yeah, I'll be around," he said with a half-smile, rapping his knuckles playfully against his brother's chest. "Just let me wash up. This afternoon, I'll show you around. We'll get drinks. We'll have *fun*."

The smile that lit Rodney's face could've melted glass. "Thank you, Meesh. Thank you very, very much."

"It's the least I can do, brah. Literally."

Meesh left his smiling brother behind, ascended the next two flights of stairs, and entered his flat. It looked just as he remembered it—crowded and homey. Paintings of beautiful women in provocative poses hung on his walls. The living area was stuffed with furniture upholstered with red velvet, display cases filled with mementos such as demon teeth and treasures taken from brigands, and exotic musical instruments that he had no clue how to play.

Truth was, the only items in the room that he considered his own were the paintings, which he'd purchased (or won) himself. Everything else had already been in the flat when he'd arrived; all that remained of the twenty-three of his name that came before. The Reverend had told him that the knights were free to decorate their living spaces as they so desired—something Shade had done, stripping his flat bare of anything save furniture—but Meesh chose to keep the place the way he'd found it. There was something poetic about being surrounded by evidence of lives lived and lost, as if being surrounded by history, and understanding it, could make him feel less alone in his plight.

And here he'd always thought he wasn't the sentimental type.

The flat was remarkably clean, as usual. While the knights were the only people to call the Dakota Keep home, it had a large staff that did the cooking, cleaning, and general maintenance. He glanced through his east-facing window and saw sunlight illumining the Temple of the Crone. The staff would be here soon, as they generally arrived mid-morning. Meesh decided to hurry. The help always treated the knights with reverence, as if looking them in the eyes or saying more than a single word to any one of them would bring down the wrath of the old gods. He had no desire to experience that, not with the way his moods were swinging lately like a spike-covered pendulum.

He was washed and dressed in no time, then hurried down to the second-story kitchen to get some breakfast, which consisted of a bowl of fruit and eggs that looked like they'd just been cooked, though there was no chef to be seen. When he finished, he felt better than he had since before he and his brothers followed Cooper to that damned sterile valley at the edge of the world. But thoughts of Cooper brought thoughts of his brothers, which reminded him that he had a duty to complete—one he wanted no part of, but needed doing nonetheless.

Gulping, Meesh wandered across the second-floor hallway and entered the Sacred Library. The room was dim, the only light coming from five artificial candles on pedestals placed throughout, four in the corners and one beside the table in the center. The air smelled musty, which was bound to happen when in a concealed space whose every wall was covered with shelves containing hundreds of books.

The tomes in the Library contained everything from the history of the known world to scientific journals to records of fissures and dimensional doorways. There were also volumes of fiction scattered throughout, and a whole collection on philosophy—three of which were penned by Reverend Garron himself. Or a few Reverend Garrons? Meesh wasn't entirely sure.

He'd read none of them, because nothing in them interested him. He wanted to *live*, not read about living, which to him equaled its own sort of slow, painful death.

He approached the central table, atop which lay a single gigantic book. Meesh ran his fingers over the cover of the *Chronicles of Eternity* and shuddered. Contained within that tattered leather binding was the complete history of the Knights Eternal—or, at least, as complete a history as the authors were willing to tell. It was a story of knights, written by knights. Meesh imagined the text held quite a few embellishments and fabrications. Some traumas were simply too painful to relive, even in writing.

With that in mind, he flipped to one of the bookmarks, two-thirds of the way through the thousand-some-odd pages. He read over words on the left side of the page, all written in Abe's meticulous penmanship. Each stanza told the last known words spoken by a knight before he died. By Meesh's count, Abe had lived long enough to eulogize eight of his brothers. It was Meesh's turn to do the same.

He grabbed the quill from the inkwell beside the book, let the narrow point hover over the next blank section of page. He didn't actually know the last thing Abe said—it was Shade who'd been there, and his irritable, vow-breaking brother hadn't been keen on discussing it afterward. Meesh flicked his tongue over his teeth, trying to think of something clever to say, something that captured Abe's essence.

In the end, he decided on the truth, or at least as close to the truth as he remembered:

"Go ahead, I'll be fine down here. I can take care of myself."

—Abednego the 15th

about twenty minutes before demise

Meesh looked down at the words he'd written and blew on the page, but he smeared the words a bit with his fingertips when checking if they were dry. Then he carefully closed the book and got the hell out of the library before his stupid emotions came back to bite him.

He found Rodney waiting for him in the common area, one leg propped up on the wall, grinning like a kid who'd just seen a woman topless for the first time. He held the guitar he'd been tuning earlier—a new one, Meesh realized, without a scratch on it.

"Hey, nice," Meesh said. "That's an Acclaim, ain't it?"

Rodney nodded, strummed the strings. "That Frank chap gave it to me last night. Said he made it." He held the instrument up and inspected the neck. "He does good work. *Great* work."

"Yeah, *Frank* is one hell of a craftsman," Meesh agreed. Shade had told him the story of how Minerabi Francis's grandfather, a minerabi himself, created the Acclaim line after all the older guitars began falling apart, as anything made from wood was bound to do after a couple centuries of being passed around. Shade had beamed at the telling, thankful that Francis had remembered to string the instrument for a lefty.

Dammit, don't go there.

"I wrote a song," Rodney said, saving him from sad thoughts.

"When? Just now?"

He shrugged. "Last night, this morning. It's an ongoing process. I only have a couple verses written. Not quite finished."

Meesh thought of his own poetry. "Trust me, I know how *that* goes."

"Would you like me to play it for you anyway?"

"Sure," Meesh said with a grin. "Why not?"

Rodney started to play before the last syllable had left Meesh's mouth. Meesh rocked slowly back and forth. His brother's right foot tapped the rhythm, while his hands created the most beautiful sounds. The tune was sorrowful, much like those he had played in New Salem, but this time the muted thrum of the lower strings formed a nearly hidden current that flowed beneath higher, much more lively and positive notes.

He began to sing, and Meesh became mesmerized. Rodney sang of hope, of being lost in the desert near death, only to be dragged from it by an angel in white. Meesh joined in the singing, his powerful baritone blending perfectly with Rodney's innocent-sounding falsetto.

And when Rodney reached the end of the second verse...that's when the fireworks *truly* began. All it took was a nod from the taller brother for Meesh to start improvising. He crooned words as they entered his head, forming a hodgepodge narrative of a man struggling to find his place in the world after losing both of his arms in battle. It began as a whimsical joke to offset Rodney's serious-sensitive lyrics, but with every line he crooned, he realized that the metaphorical person he was singing about was himself.

It was painful. It was heartbreaking. And, he had to admit, it felt pretty damn good to let it all out.

By the time Rodney let loose with a flurry of strumming to end the song, Meesh felt energized. His level of unease was the lowest it'd been since he found Shade lugging Abe's corpse out of the bunker. He smiled at his brother—sincere, understated, almost timid. For the first time, when he looked at Rodney, he saw the potential for connection. For companionship. For brotherly love.

"That was wonderful," Rodney said shyly.

Meesh just nodded. "It was, Rod. It really was."

"What do you want to do now?"

"Tell you what, brah." He slipped an arm over the taller man's shoulders. "Let's go have some fun. I know a great place where we can watch drunks stumble around."

"That...that sounds ideal," Rodney said, grinning so innocently it could've melted a heart of stone.

The moment the two of them stepped out of the keep, however, Meesh's good vibes disappeared. A carriage waited for them at the curb. Minerabis Bartholomew and Cassius flanked the carriage door in their pristine velvet suits, their expressions severe. Cassius ran a hand over his bald head and puffed out his fat cheeks. He opened the door.

Meesh's spirits dove even lower when Reverend Garron exited the carriage. The holy man wore his usual white frock, his hair tied back with a length of twine and his round glasses perched on the tip of his nose. He carried himself with his typical piety, hands clasped before him. He seemed uncommonly serene.

Never a good sign.

The brothers exchanged a look and went down to greet the convoy.

"What's up, Rev?" Meesh said, his voice sounding defeated to his own ears. "Just checking to see how the two of us're doing, right?"

"Alas, no," he replied.

"'Course not," Meesh grumbled.

"I'm afraid my presence here is more serious than that."

Rodney cringed. "Are we in trouble?"

"No, Abednego," the Reverend said. His eyebrows arched. A tiny reaction, but Meesh knew he was aghast at the suggestion. "If you had done wrong, I would have said so immediately. Being the voice of the Pentus on the mortal plain, I am not one for deception."

"Oh. Apologies." Rodney tugged on the collar of his clean shirt. "Then why are you here?"

"He's got a riddle," Meesh said.

Reverend Garron reached into his frock and pulled out a folded sheet of thick parchment. "Indeed, I do. The Old Crone sent word an hour ago, and I came as soon as I could."

"You read it?" Meesh asked.

"Yes. As will you."

The holy man held out the riddle.

Meesh sighed, took the paper from him, and unfolded it with resignation. He wasn't surprised that the Wasteland was in peril so soon after he'd arrived home. Pentus forbid he was given at least a week of rest and relaxation, let alone a chance to learn more about his new brother before they were cast out into the muck together.

As he read the words, dread overwhelmed him.

"No. Just no."

"What does it say?" asked Rodney, sidling up beside him.

With his brother reading alongside, Meesh went over the riddle again.

O'er mountains high and snow so bright,
dwell those made not to know,
steeped in shade the former knight
to match the righteous dread.

'A march to freedom!' So they sing.
'Unleash the ghastly clow!'
Yet when the next of bells do ring
their freedoms lie in death.

So find the sham of kingly past;
his conspiracy of crows.
To reach the passage, discontent,
through solid stone it weaves.

Let us lop the head of holy men
who abandoned duty crowns!
What once was pure, what once was grand:
Darkness now it feeds.

"It's a poem," Rodney said, confused.

"Yup. And a better one than usual." Meesh raised his eyes. "Please tell me this don't mean what I think it does."

Reverend Garron frowned. "Alas, there can be no doubt. The Crone is being more straightforward than usual, as she often does in situations such as these. The message is clear."

He stared at the riddle again, not wanting to believe the truth of it. Rodney broke the brief silence by asking, "Um, what message is that?"

"It is time to find your brother," Reverend Garron said.

"Shade?" asked Rodney. "The one who ran away?"

"Yes."

"And then what?"

Meesh sighed, thinking of his dream that morning. *Let us lop the head of holy men.*

"We kill him," he muttered.

Rodney tittered. "That seems rather harsh."

"Such is the price of desertion," the Reverend told him. "'*Have patience for the doubting flock, for they know not what they do; but for those who have been truly blessed, only death leads back to You.*' So says the Holy Book. Praise be."

"Praise be," echoed Bartholomew and Cassius, their heads bowed. Meesh stared at them, growing more despondent by the second.

Reverend Garron gestured for the two minerabis to enter the carriage, which they did without another word. He then clutched Meesh's arm. "May we speak in private?" he said, though it wasn't a question. If the leader of Pentmatarianism wanted to talk to you alone, you went with him. His asking was mere politeness.

"Sure," Meesh said.

"Abednego, please give us a few moments."

The newest knight grimaced, but he lifted his arms and backed away from the Reverend, nonetheless. Garron gently urged Meesh to turn around. The two of them walked farther down the road, until they were safely out of earshot from Rodney and the carriage.

"This is unfortunate timing," the Reverend said in a low voice.

"Yeah, it is," Meesh grumbled.

"As for the riddle, while it is obvious what Old Crone wishes of you, do you have any thoughts on how to find your lost brother?"

Meesh had his own ideas about that, but he kept them to himself. "Haven't had time to really think about it."

"I have," said the holy man. "While there are no directional clues in the wording, I take that to mean that Shade has done the same as every other knight to desert your order."

"Headed into the Unknown Lands to hide?"

"Aye."

"Awesome. So that's where we'll go."

The Reverend hummed a sympathetic note. "I truly am sorry for all this. I wish there were another way, but there is not. Our lives are guided by forces far greater than ourselves." He made the symbol of the five-pointed star on his chest. "It is simply our duty to comply."

"No shit," Meesh snipped. He eyed Garron warily, but the Reverend didn't seem offended by the outburst, only quietly contemplative. "I know it's my job. You didn't have to pull me aside to tell me that."

A faint smile formed on the Reverend's face. "I know."

"Then why?"

He halted, severity in his expression as he put his hands on both Meesh's arms and held him there, head bowed.

"You cannot trust your brother," he said finally.

"Who? Shade?"

"Yes, of course, but that isn't what I'm speaking of." His eyes drifted to the side. "I mean the new Abednego."

That wasn't expected.

"I fear he may be tainted," Reverend Garron went on in a hushed voice. "If Shade had already made his decision to abandon the Pentus before performing the ritual of creation, it is very possible that the same disease of the mind that infected him might well have infected Abednego while his body and mind were formed. He is…off, somehow. Fractured. Incomplete. *Dangerous.*"

Meesh's insides twisted. "You sure about that?"

"Sure? No." He sighed, releasing his hands from Meesh's arms. "But I have a dread feeling that I cannot shake. As if the Pentus is whispering words of warning into my head from his throne in the Crystalline Hall. He loves you more than most, you know. All of you that He created through divine power. And to see one of His creations perverted… I fear that He may decide to call you all back and remove His blessing from this world. Abandon us, recall what little of His light that we have left to see with."

Meesh stood there, conflicted. Sure, he'd had his reservations about Rodney, but for the Reverend to question his new brother's motivations was something else entirely. He didn't agree, but he couldn't deviate from the guidance of the mouthpiece of the deity who'd made him.

"That'd suck," he said by way of halfhearted agreement.

"Truly," the Reverend said. "Which is why I need you to be wary. Watch him, Meshach. Create a record of everything he does that seems strange. Every off-kilter word he speaks. Every tiny gesture that may speak to impurity of spirit."

Meesh sighed. "Seems totally reasonable."

"And after you fulfill your duty," Garron went on unabated, "you are to return straight here. Do not—*do not*—journey to the Hallowed Stones again until I have an opportunity to look over all the evidence you collected and decide if the new Abednego's existence threatens all our Lord has built. It may be time to start over. I will ask the Crone what she thinks. Is that understood?"

The look he gave Meesh, with eyebrows drawn and his normally compassionate eyes narrowed to threatening slits, seemed abruptly hostile. It was so unlike the Reverend Meesh knew that his breath stilled.

"Sure," he replied, feeling like a timid child in front of a coldly disapproving parent.

"Good. Very good." The man's face slackened, and the compassionate leader reemerged. "See me before you leave. You *and* Abednego. I will bless you before your journey. It may make things a bit easier for you."

"Yeah. Okay. Cool."

He accompanied the Reverend back to the carriage, held the door for him when he entered. The driver slapped the reins and the horses started trotting. Meesh gawked after the departing carriage, feeling hollow inside.

"Meesh?" Rodney asked, making him jump. He hadn't noticed his brother approach.

"Yeah?"

"What was that all about? Is everything okay?"

He looked up at his new brother, into soulful eyes that told the story of a spirit that couldn't hurt a fly, and his mind started reeling.

He didn't want to do any of this. He didn't want to wonder about Rodney's intentions or spy on his every move. And he *certainly* didn't want to kill Shade. The need to kill him was a fact he'd accepted when his brooding fellow knight left, but that acceptance relied on the preface that the chore would happen in some distant future.

The moment had come too soon.

"Why?" he whispered. "Freakin' *why?*"

"Why what?" his brother asked.

Meesh ignored him. He looked down at the riddle he still held. His eyes then traced up the hill across from him to the impossibly large tower that loomed overhead.

"Stay here," he told Rodney. He shoved the paper in his pocket and took off running.

Sweat poured down Meesh's face and stung his eyes by the time he reached the reinforced concrete entrance to the Temple of the Crone. He threw open the door and stormed into the antechamber. The space was huge—at least a hundred feet long and thirty feet deep, the ceiling so high that two Rodneys would have to stand on his shoulders to reach it. The walls were concrete, covered with countless images painted by those who pilgrimaged here. Artificial lighting hung high above, making the place look both inviting and intimidating.

He stormed toward the door leading deeper into the Temple, where Old Crone resided. Meesh had never met the Crone, didn't even know her true name. All he knew about her was that she'd supposedly been alive for over a thousand years, was cared for by the dedicated staff who hid their identities from even the Reverend, and her predictions always came true.

In a recessed shelf cut into the wall, a Heartcube glowed a deep amber color when Meesh approached. It cast flickering light that gave off the appearance of a roaring wildfire when reflected off the door. Meesh threw his fists against the seamless steel, demanding that he be allowed entrance.

"Talk to me, dammit!" he screamed. "Tell me why!"

After a while he stopped pounding and leaned his forehead against steel, breathing heavily with sodden hair plastering his face. He heard nothing beyond the hum of the lights above and a faint thumping sound from somewhere deeper in the temple. No one was going to come to answer him; there seemed to be no one there at all.

Frustrated, he punched the door one last time then skulked out of the bunker-like antechamber. The trees surrounding the path back to the road were dense, and in the cover of the shadows cast by the tower above, they seemed haunted. Something mewled, pausing him in the middle of the walkway. He stared at a spot of blackness where the sound originated. Meesh wondered if a fissure had ever opened on Yaddo. In that moment, as he watched branches sway and heard leaves rustle, he cursed himself for never reading any of the books stocked in the knights' Library.

A feminine shape emerged from the foliage, her long hair tied back in a ponytail that swung against soft caramel skin. Meesh recognized her immediately, even though she looked out of place wearing the blouse and slacks of a commoner instead of the baggy pants, form-fitting top, and *kimi* of her order.

"Octavia?"

The young woman put a finger to her lips. Her eyes darted for a moment before she bent over and placed something on the ground. Then she nodded once to Meesh and disappeared back into the trees.

"So…that's weird," he muttered, wandering over to where the third-to-last girl he'd slept with had just been.

Octavia had placed a rock the size of his fist on the ground. Just a rock, as brown and cracked and unimpressive as any other rock he'd ever seen. He squatted and picked it up.

A small scrap of folded paper lay hidden beneath it. Meesh plucked it between two fingers and pried it open. The words on the paper were few, written in hasty penmanship. Meesh read them once, twice, and then a few more times. His brow furrowed. He re-folded the small scrap and stuffed it into his pocket next to the Crone's riddle.

Rodney was still waiting for him by the steps of the keep when Meesh descended the hill. The tall man with the awkward gait and fidgety manner looked irresolute, as usual.

"Are you okay?" he asked.

"No, brah," Meesh said. "Not at all."

"I take it this means you aren't going to be showing me around today."

"Nope," he said. "We're gonna go back in there and get ready to go. You and me got a lost brother to find."

6

And tell the men to lift of their eyes and notice all beauty,
be it welcomed or no, so they may save the lonely woman from
chastity, and for one and all know the glory of their seed.
—Book of the Pentus, Havacana 53:2

An uncomfortable silence settled over the courtyard in front of Hickweis Tavern. The words Indigo had just shouted echoed in her ears.

What have you done?

What, indeed.

The stranger stood twenty feet away, smoke rising from the snout of his strange silver weapon. He stared at Indigo, his hat tipped back slightly to reveal a handsome, bearded face locked in a grimace. His expression was one of regret, but not seemingly for the man whose neck Indigo now pressed her fingers against in search of a pulse that was not there. No, this man with compassionate eyes and skin as dark as the sky on a cloudy evening appeared to be more ashamed of how *she* had reacted than the fact he had just killed a man.

Her heart thumped, either from fear or excitement. Perhaps both.

"Pete?" Anthony whispered. He slid down onto the grass beside Indigo, his eyes bulging while he examined the ragged crater in the back of the dead man's skull. Indigo watched him carefully, not sure what he would do next. The handful of Righteous to have died in

Darkenwood had fallen to physical ailments that precluded their entering the village, such as heart attacks after engaging in strenuous activity. None had ever been struck down in violence. Indigo would know, as she was among the first to be sentenced by the overgod.

Now, all that had changed.

Anthony lifted his gaze to the mass of bystanders who formed a wall behind them. "Popp?" he said, bewildered. "Popp, what the hell's going on?"

The textile merchant stepped forward, eyes narrowed as he looked first at the dead man, then the man in the long leather coat. Jasper Popp rubbed the clipped beard that traced below his chin. He hesitated to speak, as if he could not find the words. It made him look oafish, and Indigo would have laughed if the situation were not so dire.

At long last, Jasper was able to pry sounds from his throat. "This can't happen," he muttered. His attention focused on the armed stranger, and his cheeks flushed red. His voice pitched with anger when he repeated, "This. Can't. *Happen*."

The crowd grew unruly, spurned out of their stupor by the ire of the rich man. People tossed curses at the stranger, someone threw a rock at him, but none dared approach the one who had murdered a member of their party. The stranger spun in circles, those around him becoming more and more spiteful. Indigo feared that he would lose control and kill another Righteous. Or worse, ascend one of her Ersatz, who lurked behind the gathering, curious yet smart enough not to get involved.

Those worries fluttered away when hands grabbed her shoulders and lugged her to standing. Indigo was face-to-face with Jasper Popp. Above a clenched jaw, his dark gray eyes bore into hers.

"This is your fault," he seethed. "Guns aren't allowed here."

"I do not know what you are talking about," Indigo began, trying to stay calm amid the madness. "I have never seen this—"

Thick fingers wrapped around her chin and squeezed her cheeks together. A woman's pudgy face then forced its way into her vision. Kirsten Popp looked just as rageful as her husband. She spat a glob of snot and saliva that struck Indigo across her nose and cheek.

"Liar!" the woman shouted.

Something heavy struck Indigo in the back of her head, bringing stars to her vision. She dropped to her knees and brought her arms up, anticipating a further blow.

In the background, those who had been rebuking the stranger turned their vile insults on her.

"Wait, wait!" someone shouted. Indigo peeked through the gap between her arms to see that Anthony had stepped between her and a Righteous man holding a maul. "Everyone hang on a second!" he shouted, panic trilling his voice. "We can't jump to conclusions!"

"Like hell we can't," said the man with the maul. "Right, Mr. Popp?"

"Right, Will," the merchant answered.

Indigo winced when Will drove the wide blunt edge of the maul into Anthony's gut. Anthony doubled over and vomited. The attacker then kicked him aside and stormed toward Indigo with the weapon raised.

She sighed inwardly, watching the maul quiver at the top of its arc. There was no use trying to protect herself now; ascension would soon be upon her. But another explosion rocked the air before Will could attack, and the top of the maul splintered. Wood chips rained down. Will lost his balance and tripped over Indigo. He fell over her shoulder and landed on top of the dead man with a wet slapping sound.

"ENOUGH!"

Indigo rose shakily to her feet. The host of Righteous parted, fear in their eyes as they made room for the prowling stranger moving among them. The stranger still held up his exploding weapon, but he had also drawn a sword with an elaborately carved pommel. The blade was streaked with blood, shimmering pink in the bright sunlight. Indigo wondered if he had killed another guest or simply wounded them. Her mind debated whether she cared.

In the end, she decided she did. Because no matter how much hatred she held for these despicable people, the overgod favored them. And to go against the overgod was to invite a lifetime of pain and constant death.

As if we do not have that already, her nihilistic inner voice declared.

"Everyone, back away!" the stranger bellowed, and the Righteous complied, even Jasper Popp and his cadre of powerful merchants. When the stranger reached Indigo, he sheathed his sword and held his free hand out to her.

She gawked up at it but did not move.

"C'mon, I'm trying to help," the stranger said, his head tilting in confusion.

"I do not *want* your help," she snapped. "Do you not know what it is you have done?"

The stranger lowered his hand, backed away slowly. Indigo stood on her own accord. The guests surrounding her glared, their wrath like physical waves of heat that scorched her flesh. Murmured scorn dripped out of their mouths. She threw back her shoulders, refusing to look any of them in the eyes. When a cohort helped the wounded Anthony to his feet, she declined to turn his way, even after he had earned at least a dollop of gratitude for his foolish attempt at protecting her.

"This isn't supposed to happen," Jasper Popp repeated, with less conviction than before. He pointed at the stranger, who remained standing in the center of the hostile circle with his exploding weapon by his side. "He killed a man. With a *gun*. Where did your kind get ahold of one? You aren't supposed be allowed that kind of weaponry."

"I have never heard of a *gun*," Indigo told the merchant, which was the truth.

"Then why does *he* have one?"

Indigo glanced at the stranger and shrugged. "He is not Ersatz."

"He's not?" asked Kirsten. She ogled her own people, then the dead man on the ground. "Is he one of *ours*?"

Anthony staggered forward, still being helped by his friend, still clutching his midsection. "He ain't that either," he said through rasping breaths. "He's not tagged. I saw that earlier. I thought he was Ersatz."

"Isn't that interesting," Popp said, tapping a finger against his chin. "Not one of yours, not one of mine. Seems we got ourselves an interloper who somehow snuck inside the wards."

"Seems to be," his wife affirmed.

The merchant smirked, a cruel gleam in his eyes. "That means he belongs to no one. That means he's fair game. We could take him out of this village and make him stand trial in front of a real judge if we wanted."

Kirsten nipped at his ear. "Or we could just kill him right here."

"We could," Jasper agreed. He kicked the corpse of the tattooed man. "He did just murder one of my assets."

"You could try," the stranger growled. He pointed his silver weapon at the merchant. "Or you could just leave before I put a bullet between your eyes too."

"Oh, you could most *certainly* do that, obviously," Jasper sneered. "But you can't kill all of us. Not before taking an arrow. Or five."

The stranger tilted his head.

"Look around, dumbass." Jasper laughed. "See the mess you got yourself into."

At least five men and women standing on the far side of the circle had their bows out, arrows nocked, as did a couple more guests who had climbed atop the nearby carts that had been loaded up for afternoon adventuring. Another two held powerful crossbows. All were aimed at the stranger.

"Seems like we got ourselves a little impasse," Jasper snickered.

The stranger said nothing; the hand holding his weapon lifted ever so slightly.

"Don't do it," said Will, clutching the maul. "You won't like what happens next."

Luckily for him, the stranger complied. His teeth gnashed together, his eyes squinted. He was obviously trying to think of the best way to get out of this situation with his life intact. Even though she did not know him, even though he had made life in Darkenwood that much more difficult by simply being here, Indigo hoped that he would make the right choice.

"That's more like it," Jasper said with a grunt. He shoved his hands in his pockets and strode easily into the center of the human ring, as if he had no care in the world. "Now what're you gonna do? Poor little interloper who went and killed one of my new claims adjusters. Now I gotta replace him. I *hate* the hiring process. Interviewing morons all day. Someone's gonna have to pay for that. Whaddaya say?"

The stranger remained silent, patient.

"Didn't think so." He turned to Indigo. "Listen up, whore. I was gonna string you up. I really was. But since y'all had nothing to do with this whole shitshow, I won't. What *is* gonna happen is we'll be taking the bearded menace here and marching him out somewhere private. So those who aren't in our party won't have to hear him screaming when we dismember him. Slowly. After that, you can have his head. Sound good to you?" He cackled. "Listen to me sounding all gentlemanly. Like you have any say in the matter at all."

It would have been so easy to allow the horrible man to whisk the stranger off to satisfy his primal urges. If she did that, then her people would be safe, at least for a little while. Let someone else be the target for once.

But that was not how this would end, and she knew it. The Righteous would return with their bloodlust stoked. Hickweis Tavern would become a feeding frenzy of violence while the mysterious stranger, who currently looked at her with eyes that drooped with the sadness of imminent betrayal, would be instantly forgotten. This man, ignorant as he was, had put his life on the line to protect someone Indigo loved. For that, she owed him an opportunity to escape with his life.

The Ersatz would be punished either way. Irritating the Righteous by allowing the stranger to flee felt like the right thing to do. The solution came to her almost immediately. She did not think twice about it.

"You cannot have him," she said.

The merchant blinked as if confused. "Excuse me?"

Indigo pivoted toward Hickweis Tavern. Her courtesans stood on the terrace, watching her every move. Aspar was among them, Orchid nestled in his strong arms like a baby. Indigo and the halfling locked eyes, and Indigo mouthed a word only she would know. The halfling gave her a brisk nod and then whispered in the ear of the one who held her. Aspar placed Orchid on the ground. Indigo took a deep breath and faced the arrogant merchant once more.

"I said you cannot have him," she declared. "By the law of the overgod, all unforeseen transgressions that occur within his realm are to be judged by the Voice of Him. This has been the law since the day this village was created. It remains so now."

"Hold on a second," Kirsten Popp said. The pudgy woman hefted her billowing skirts and took wobbling steps toward Indigo. "Let's kill her, too, Jass. And then kill her again. Teach all the lesser beings to remember their place." She glared at her husband. "My family's been coming here for decades. I've never heard of this 'Voice of Him' nonsense. I call bullshit."

"It actually *is* a thing. Buried deep in the bylaws, but it's there." Jasper gnawed his lip, seeming unsure. "But I think it's only been called once before."

"Make that twice," Indigo said calmly.

She turned to the porch of Hickweis Tavern, and everyone else followed her gaze. Orchid had reappeared, standing on the terrace railing, a horn pressed to her tiny lips. The horn was twice as big as the halfling, so long that Aspar held the bell end, and the sound that came from it when Orchid blew was so deep and resonant it made the air quake. Indigo shivered, remembering the only other time that horn had been blown, over a century ago.

Both Righteous and Ersatz covered their ears as the horn bleated. When it was over, Aspar plucked the halfling off the railing and disappeared inside. Murmurs arose from the crowd.

"What happens now?" Anthony asked, still bent over from his injury.

He was answered by a low thrum that caused every Righteous in the vicinity to wince. Dull red lights flashed beneath clothes at the place where their collarbones met their necks. The flashes disappeared quickly, as did the low thrum.

The marks of the Righteous had been activated. Just like Indigo remembered.

"The valley is now closed," she announced. "Please, go collect your belongings and exit the same way you arrived. And do so quickly. The Voice of Him will be here shortly, and he will only deal with the one who has broken the rules of the land." She pointed at the stranger. "Him."

"What happens if we stay?" Kirsten Popp asked, looking at her husband.

"We all lose our deposits," Jasper answered.

"Even if only one of us stays behind?"

He scowled. "Even then."

None of their talk meant anything to Indigo, but it obviously meant a great deal to them. The Righteous started hustling toward the guest townhouses situated half a mile down the deeply wooded eastern path. Anthony offered Indigo a wounded expression before limping alongside them.

The only one to linger was Jasper Popp. He ushered his wife along with the rest of their smaller group of powerful merchants and then stared Indigo down.

"Don't think this is over," he raged. "My father knows the president of Viral Ventures. I'll get an audience with him. In fact, I think this place has run its course. It might be time to burn it all down and build something better." He pointed at her, then the stranger, who remained still as a statue behind her. "And if that one doesn't pay for what he's done, I'll make sure it *hurts* when you burn."

Righteous men and their self-important proclamations. As if getting to have their way with an entire populace wasn't enough for them.

"Everyone will do as they must," Indigo said defiantly.

"That's right we will," the merchant grunted, jutting his chin at the corpse of the recently-departed Peter Ortiz. "I'll leave that for you to take care of," he said with all the emotion of a butcher telling his underlings to clean cow guts off the shop floor. He scowled at her again and hurried off.

Only after he disappeared into the concealing line of trees did Indigo allow herself a moment to calm her racing heart. Everything was happening too quickly.

"Thank you, Miss Indigo," a cool voice stated. "What was that all about, anyway?"

The stranger behind her folded his arms over his chest, one hand propped beneath his chin. His expression remained composed. Indigo did not understand how he could be so relaxed. He had just killed a man, had barely avoided being killed himself by an angry mob, yet he stood there looking contemplative.

"You must leave," she told him. "Now."

His calm façade cracked ever so slightly. "Leave? To where?"

"Back where you came from. Wherever that is."

He sighed. "Sorry, can't do that. I can only go one way." He rolled back on his heels, pointed north. "How about over the mountains? Can you give me directions?"

"I cannot."

"How about whatever way the bastards you just kicked out of here go?"

"Passage through the center of the Great Range is reserved for the Righteous." She looked him up and down. "And you are *certainly* not one of them."

He looked incredulous. "Righteous? Those people? Those... *assholes*?"

Indigo almost laughed. Almost. But then she heard a high-pitched whine that made the tips of her pointed ears quiver. She had wasted too much time already.

"Please, just leave. The Voice will be here shortly, and you need to be beyond the boundary when he arrives. You will not like what happens if you linger."

"I thought you said this Voice guy only deals with the one who caused the problem? That's me, right?"

"Yes. Now you see why you must go."

His lips pressed together. "What happens when he shows up and I'm not here?"

Indigo could not stop herself from grimacing. There was a reason no one had blown the horn to summon the Voice of Him in well over a century. The last time was after a pair of murderous Righteous had set fire to the local settlement under the light of a full moon. Fifty-three Ersatz were sent into ascension that night, yet the Voice decreed the fire unworthy of such an extreme measure as closing the village borders. He gravely punished the one who had blown the horn, doling out ascension after ascension over a span of two weeks. The poor Ersatz who had been the previous overseer of Hickweis Tavern went insane from the constant pain and terror. That overseer now lingered on the outskirts of the Path of the Hero, fated to never have their forgotten sins forgiven.

None had considered blowing the horn after that. The risk was too great. Until Indigo had just ordered it done.

"You'll be the one punished, won't you?" the stranger asked.

"That...does not matter," she said. "Please, just go. If you do not, then I did all this for nothing."

For a moment, she thought the man might do as she told him, which would have been a first for a non-Ersatz. Alas, after a few moments of gazing off into the distance, he tipped back his hat and laughed. Indigo was taken aback at how beautiful his bearded face appeared when he smiled.

"You know, I think I'm gonna stay," he said. "I've killed demons. How much tougher could this guy be?" He mulishly shoved his hands in the pockets of his long leather coat. When he glanced at Indigo, however, his expression seemed imploring, as if he wanted nothing more than for her to ask him why he had made the decision he did.

Indigo refused to give him that because ignoring him might mean he would get his leather-covered rear end out of Darkenwood.

"Very well," she said and turned her back on him.

The Ersatz went about the business of cleaning up before the Voice arrived. The porch was mopped, the railing mended, broken glass swept from inside the tavern. The stranger attempted to help when Vivo came over to assist Indigo in hefting the body of the dead Righteous man, but she succeeded in making him back away with nothing more than a glare. After that, he contented himself by lingering near the porch steps, leaning on the balustrade, and watching the world go round. He seemed so curious, so unconcerned.

What an odd sort, Indigo thought. Her own fascination grew. She would like to get to know him better. It broke her heart to know she would never get the chance.

"He is not leaving, is he?" Macaro asked when she entered the tavern to collect water to wash blood off the courtyard path.

"No," she said grimly.

The dwarf shrugged. "Do not be so torn up about it, Mum. I know what you were trying to do. What you would have put yourself through to protect this man. I would rather he suffer than you. His will be quick. Yours could go on forever. Do not forget what happened to Raz."

She slapped the bar hard to enough to rattle the glasses drying on the rack. "You think I could ever forget that?" she seethed. "*I* was the one who loved her."

Sincere apologies followed her out the door, where she continued to help her people prepare. It was all she could do not to think of the past, and what was about to come.

Roughly twenty minutes after the horn had been blown—more than enough time for a handsome stranger to get outside the boundary of Darkenwood—bells rang in the distance. The bells signaled that the Righteous had crossed beneath the Fallen Arch, that they were now on their way home. Indigo grimaced as she applied salve to the wounds on Mana's face. She hoped this time the Righteous would stay away. She knew that wish would not be granted.

A vibration shook the ground. Indigo peered at the stranger, who unfortunately remained on the stoop, unaware. She put her fingers in her mouth, let out a shrill whistle. The man looked up at her.

"Stranger, this is your last chance to leave," she called out.

"Call me Shade," he hollered back.

Such an oddly fitting name.

The vibration cut out and another sound emerged, a heavy *thud*, *thud*, *swoosh*, followed by a low grinding that rattled her teeth. It originated from the copse of pine trees to the right of Hickweis Tavern. The stranger, this Shade, had obviously both heard and felt the disturbance, for he rose from the steps and pulled the exploding silver weapon from inside his coat. The mid-afternoon sun shone down brightly, making the man squint.

The trees shook. Branches snapped, pine needles rained down. An enormous form appeared from within the shadows, shoving through the cover of vegetation until it emerged fully. The stranger stared that way, his jaw hanging open.

The Voice of Him had arrived.

7

"All that we are is a result of what others have thought us to be."
—Book of the Pentus, Quotations 17:89

The moment the thing stepped out of the copse of trees, Shade regretted how flippantly he'd been taking this unique situation. He had thought the danger was over when the throng of privileged assholes were forced to vacate the premises. He thought he could stand there, watch Indigo from the corner of his eye, and wait for that magical moment amid the hubbub when he could steal a few moments of her time. He was drawn to her, inebriated by her mere existence, so much so that he never quite registered how close he had come to dying right there in the courtyard, done in by something as mundane as a pompous rich man with a pack of armed followers and a thirst for blood.

But now, as he stared at a monstrosity before him, he realized that maybe he should have taken Indigo's earlier advice and gotten out of Darkenwood as quickly as he could.

Too late now.

The Voice of Him—if that's what this beast was—stood at least twelve feet tall on reverse-jointed legs. Everything about it was *thick*, from its thighs to its waist to the gigantic arms that led to platter-sized hands and ended in fingers tipped with wicked claws. Golden scales covered every inch of its hide; the only clothes it wore was a black thong.

What resided above its shoulders was as otherworldly as it was terrifying. Its tree trunk-sized neck supported a head that was far too large and covered with the same golden scales as the rest of its body. A ring of black horns jutted from its skull. The snout resembled a lizard's, like the terragils that populated the hottest parts of the Wasteland. The jaws beneath, filled with protruding teeth, were wide enough to take off Shade's head with a single bite. Set far back of that terrible maw were a pair of eyes that burned red with sinister intelligence.

The beast took a lumbering step forward, shedding the last of the vines it had dragged from the forest. Shade's survival instinct kicked in. He pulled the stolen burner from the holster tucked under his armpit and squeezed the trigger three times. Luckily, he was just as good with smaller arms as he had been with Rosetta. The three shots exploded out of the barrel in quick succession, each striking the monstrous thing right between its eyes.

The bullets bounced off armor-thick scales, succeeding only in making one of the horns quiver. The lizard-man parted its rows of overlapping teeth and licked its nose holes with a sickening gray tongue. Those red eyes flared with demonic light. It took another thunderous step.

Shit.

Shade maneuvered away from the building behind him, keeping the revolver trained on the lumbering beast. The lizard-man tracked his movements. Much to his surprise he saw that those surrounding him, humans and monsters alike, had dropped to their knees with their heads bowed. Again thinking that Indigo may have been wise in her suggestion, he finessed his way between their kneeling forms, ready to start running once he found a clear path. Then he spotted Indigo, the only one of her people standing. Her eyes were locked on the Voice, her hands clasped before her as if in prayer. Shade gulped.

She appeared to be willing to sacrifice herself in his stead. He couldn't allow that.

Steeling his nerves, he changed direction and hustled toward the gargantuan fiend, knocking a couple oddly-colored beings off their knees in the process. When he reached a spread of open grass, he let out a yawp, hefted the revolver, and emptied his last eight rounds into the thing from thirty feet away. The bullets again had no effect, bouncing off arms, legs, midsection, and pelvis. Even the shot aimed at the spot where its junk should have been only succeeded in fraying the black thong.

How wonderful it would have been to have his Eldersword right now.

The lizard-man pitched forward, roaring with such concussive force that Shade was blown off his feet. He landed hard on his elbow, then rolled to make sure he could quickly regain his footing. From the side, he noticed Indigo staring at him with her shoulders hunched. Shade did his best to ignore her by focusing on the immediate threat to his own life.

The creature reared back on those reverse-jointed legs, assuming an astonishingly introspective pose. It looked so human in that moment that the contradiction taxed Shade's brain.

Then it spoke, its voice deep and resonating and clearly male. "Bring him to me."

The kneeling Ersatz burst into motion. Multiple hands grabbed Shade's arms, shoulders, and around the waist. The spent revolver fell from his hand and disappeared into the crush of flesh. Someone ripped his sword from its sheath. Someone else tugged on his hat, the string choking him until it broke. The threads holding his duster together started to rip. He was restrained tightly enough to be rendered immobile, and he couldn't help but wonder where these peoples' viciousness had been when their fellow villager was being murdered.

For the second time today, he found himself ushered along against his will, this time toward a massive creature he had no way of killing. When he was only a few feet away from its impressive bulk, one of his captors—the male prostitute who had been dancing with what appeared to be his sister—drove a fist into his midsection, doubling him over. Shade fell to one knee; multiple hands pressed against his back, keeping him down.

A clawed finger as big as Shade's wrist slipped beneath his chin, forcing his head to tilt up. The Voice glared down at him, nostrils flaring, maw partway open. It exhaled a breath that smelled like chimney exhaust.

"Who are you?" the Voice of Him growled.

Shade stared up at the beast but refused to speak. If it was going to kill him, let it kill him while being annoyed. The creature snarled, and seeing those sharp teeth gnash together made Shade wonder what would happen to his traitorous soul once he was bitten in half.

"He said his name is Shade," said Indigo from somewhere behind him.

"Shade. Interesting name." The lizard-man considered him with what could only be disdain. "The interloper is not marked. He is not Righteous. How did he enter this valley?"

The bartender Macaro stepped into view, saying, "Nobody knows." Shade had not seen the short man since before the fracas with the departed guests had begun. With the way Macaro squinted and blinked his beady eyes in the intensity of the sun, he wondered if the dwarf had ever stepped foot outside.

"It should not be possible," said the beast.

"We understand," Indigo stated, finally entering Shade's line of sight. She glared bitterly at him. "There is no explanation."

The Voice glanced her way. "It is no matter. The overgod will enlighten me when the time is right. For now, we must deal with the unfortunate complication that comes from the murder of a virtuous man." The Voice turned its attention back to Shade. "You have brought shame and pestilence upon our tender valley, interloper. The Righteous will seek retribution for what you have done, and I have no choice but to give it to them. Your life is the price, your dismembered corpse the gift that will allow them to keep this valley pure."

Shade's fear melted away, and he laughed. He couldn't help it. The whole situation was too outlandish for him to retain even a semblance of sanity. The laughter rocked his chest, made him cough, but he still couldn't stop. He hacked and spat and cackled. The hands pinning him down retracted.

"Do you find this situation humorous, interloper?" the enormous lizard-man asked.

Shade spat out a few more hacks of laughter. He wondered if this was how Meesh felt whenever he got locked in one of his giggling fits. "Humorous? Nah. Downright freaking hilarious is more like it."

"How so?"

"Because this isn't real. It can't be. Nothing about this place makes any sense."

"Oh, it is very real, interloper. As real as the stars above, as real as the malice that resides in your very soul. If you have one." The Voice hacked out a sound like a chuckle.

Shade grunted, sighed, and rolled his eyes. "You know what? Screw it. If you're gonna kill me, just kill me and get it over with. Better that than to listen to your moronic goddamn blathering."

Gasps sounded all around him. The Ersatz cowered and backed away. The Voice remained staring.

"You mock what you do not understand."

"You're right, I *don't* understand," Shade snapped. With his restraints removed, he slowly stood up and brushed the dirt from his duster. "Where are you people from? How did you get here? Why in the Nine Hells do you stand around while your *own people* get butchered, and then sentence *me* to death for killing the killer? It's… it's nonsensical. Completely freaking insane."

The lizard-man snickered. "You spew ignorance, interloper. The men who bless this valley with their presence are Righteous. They are beyond reproach, the minor gods of Darkenwood, the true rulers of those who call this valley home. As the overgod decrees, so it shall be." It snorted. "And who are you to question the will of a deity?"

"Someone who doesn't believe in any," Shade countered. "Or who does, but is doubting." He shook his head, peeking at Indigo. "What god would not only allow its creations to be used that way, but *demand* it? To let them be beaten and killed on a whim? It's not right. It's not *fair.* Because every life is sacred. Every life deserves to be defended from tyranny."

"Even the life of the Righteous man you murdered? That one will not come back."

"Of course he won't!" Shade said, exasperated. "Who would? Besides, he ceased being a man the moment he struck down someone less powerful than him. He didn't protect the innocent, he *attacked* them. A blameless man died today. A woman was beaten. And no one came to her defense but me."

The lizard-man's red eyes flared. "You are claiming to be the champion of the innocent?"

"Someone has to be," Shade said proudly. He might have broken his vows and abandoned his brothers, but he wouldn't turn his back on that which he knew to be true.

"Would you die for them?" asked the beast.

"I would."

One of the Voice's hands lashed out, snatching up a nearby kneeling man by the nape of his neck. It was another prostitute, the really tall one with weepy eyes. The beast lifted the man up, those thick fingers tightening around his neck. The man's face rapidly turned purple as the life was squeezed from him, but he didn't struggle.

"Stop it," Indigo said in an exhausted tone. She dropped to her knees in front of the beast. "Let Aqua down. Stop this game. If the overgod wants to punish anyone, let him punish *me*."

The Voice ignored her. "How about this one?" It laughed, its words aimed at Shade. "Would you die for him?" It gestured at Indigo. "For *her*?"

Shade didn't answer with words. Instead, he swallowed the rest of his lingering fear and jumped over the kneeling woman, intent on seeing if he could accomplish the impossible and punch through the creature's scales. *Pentus give me strength,* he thought. The hypocrisy of praying to a god he had disavowed in a time of hopelessness was not lost on him.

The Voice caught him in midair with its free hand. His face slammed into its open palm, its fingers swallowed his entire upper body. Blinded, Shade swung his legs, feeling a fool. Gravity shifted, and he was flying through the air. His vision flashed, a return to the nonsensical dream of men in fatigues falling freely through the sky.

Fatigues?

The thought quickly abandoned him when he landed with a *thud*. He rolled onto his back, seeing stars.

"Will you die for them?" the Voice repeated.

Shade lifted himself up shakily and groaned. "Yes."

"No," Indigo said.

"Yes," he repeated.

The Voice cast aside the man it had been holding aloft, who crumpled into a ball when he landed. None of his fellow villagers went to help him.

"Then come here, interloper, and accept payment for defiling the land of the overgod Rawg without complaint."

Shade took a deep breath, lifted his chin, and approached. To have come this far, to have betrayed his brothers to find answers, only to have his journey end before finding any, seemed more than wrong. But when he looked at Indigo, he knew that he would forgo his own life for hers in a heartbeat, even though he barely knew her. He saw strength in her, and defiance, even in her inaction. Or perhaps because of it. And besides, at that moment he didn't know if he wanted to exist in this upside-down world any longer, a world where beauty could be ripped away on the impulse of whatever dark forces wanted him tortured.

"I'm sorry, Vera," he whispered to the dead woman he still loved. He dropped to his knees beside Indigo, ignoring her protests. "If I do this, will they be safe?"

"As the overgod decrees, yes."

"Then I accept without argument."

"Very well," the lizard-man said.

"No," Indigo repeated with a scowl.

A nod from the lizard-man and the citizens of Darkenwood grabbed Indigo and dragged her away. She didn't protest, allowing herself to be lugged across the grass, arms and legs trailing like she'd been rendered boneless. The Voice of Him licked its long maw again. "You have been sentenced to death for the murder of a Righteous man. May the overgod have no mercy on your soul."

"Get on with it already," Shade muttered.

The lizard-man opened its mouth wide enough to fit a small pony inside. Shade squeezed his eyes shut. He didn't want the last thing he saw in life to be those gaping jaws descending on him.

"Wait!" someone screamed.

"It is him! He who would be Aumor!" yelled someone else.

Shade tensed.

The killing blow never came. He peeked through squinting lids to see the Voice frozen mid-lunge. Its mouth filled his vision—rows of sharp teeth and a gullet that looked just as gray as its tongue. No air assaulted him this time; it seemed as if the creature had simply stopped breathing. Shade cautiously ducked his head, worried that this was some trick and those jaws would shut just when he thought he might be spared. But when he slid to the side, the Voice didn't move its body at all.

Shade chanced a look over his shoulder. The others had released Indigo, who was now on her feet, staring with eyebrows askew at something happening behind him. Shade spun around.

Macaro stood not twenty feet away, tugging on the arm of the waifish girl with black hair and a face covered with bruises, whom he had seen dancing earlier. Bluebell, the redheaded prostitute who had approached Shade in the tavern, stood on the other side of the girl, breathlessly shaking her.

"Show him," Macaro said, an edge of excitement in his voice.

"Yes, Mana, show him!" echoed Bluebell. Her voice was high-pitched, a likely result of her bruised and probably broken nose.

The waif lifted her gaze—one of her eyes nearly swollen shut—and held aloft the wadded object she had been concealing. The tattered muslin wrapping fell away, revealing a foot-long golden shaft. Shade gawked at the thing, struck dumb. Realization dawned soon after, and he patted down the right side of his torn duster, where he had concealed the artifact Ken had given to him up on the mountain.

It wasn't there. Obviously.

"It is the Key," Indigo said calmly.

"It is," Macaro said.

"It *is*!" exclaimed Bluebell.

Although Indigo appeared apathetic, Shade noticed a tiny spasm of her fingers that betrayed her outward calm. She turned around slowly, and when her eyes briefly met Shade's, he swore they reflected disbelief and at least a dash of hope.

Indigo didn't speak. She simply stared at the gigantic lizard-man, and it stared back at her. It shut its mouth slowly, automatically, and the burning light left its red eyes. The beast rose to its full height, its shoulders rolling back until it assumed a pose of perverted regality.

"Where did that come from?" it asked, sounding smaller and less powerful than before.

The bruised girl holding the golden rod murmured something under her breath.

"She says it fell from the coat of the stranger," Bluebell announced.

That massive head swiveled toward Shade. "Is that correct, interloper?"

Shade nodded, though he kept his trap shut for fear of saying the wrong thing.

Bluebell and Macaro urged the beaten girl toward Shade. She held the rod out before her like it was a hallowed sword, and he was still the knight he'd been before defying his vows. He mindlessly took it from her, not liking the way she recoiled at his touch, as if fearing he would strike her down.

What happened to these people?

The Voice of Him spoke again: "Do you invoke the Rite, interloper?"

"Um…" He stared at the shaft covered in carved ridges that felt so hollow and useless in his hands. "Sure?"

He winced as soon as the word exited his mouth. If this creature was looking for certainty, that was likely the last thing he would ever say.

But the Voice of Him simply bobbed that gigantic cranium. Its arms fell limp at its sides. "Very well. The interloper is now the champion. May he be proved worthy. May he become Aumor Reborn."

With that, the lizard-man turned on oversized feet and stomped back into the copse of trees. The vegetation folded around its body as if alive, concealing its bulk within leafy greenness. Again came that low grinding sound that Shade had heard just before the creature arrived. It seemed to go on forever. A heavy *clank* followed.

After that, silence.

Shade remained still, letting the quiet envelop him. Most of the Ersatz remained kneeling for a time, until Indigo finally turned to face them. She took a deep breath, closed her eyes, and started walking toward the tavern. Shade swore he saw her wink on her way by.

Her people began to rise, blinking rapidly and staring up at the huge red ball of a sun hanging overhead. To Shade, they looked like he had felt the first day of his creation—astonished, puzzled, *new*. Even the hideous creatures that made up most of their number took on that air of new innocence. Smiles started to stretch across faces both human and not.

A woman dressed in see-through lace whistled. A gray-skinned, horn-toothed monster laughed. A man with a hunched back and scales on his arms began clapping. Soon, the whole lot of them joined in. Cheers rose to the heavens, riotous applause pulsed in Shade's ears. They surrounded him again, only this time they didn't twist and wrench his extremities. Instead, each creature that approached ran their fingers across his body like he was the son of the Pentus, and they were long-starving pilgrims who had just found salvation.

It was by far the strangest thing he'd ever experienced in a short lifetime filled with strangeness.

The roars grew even louder. This wasn't like the raucousness of the so-called Righteous he'd witnessed in the tavern. That had been fueled by savageness and epicaricacy; the exuberance of the Ersatz was more...acquitted. Positive. As if these people had just discovered that happiness existed. He didn't understand it. There was no way he could. So he just went along for the ride.

A pair of burly fiends with huge grins on their ugly faces grabbed him under the arms. Shade gave himself over to their strength. They lifted him until his legs rested on their shoulders. Others surrounded him, spilling out of the surrounding landscape, more than Shade could count. They continued to fawn upon him, cajole him, treat him like royalty. When he lifted the golden shaft above his head, their gaiety became downright deafening.

Before long, he was carried toward the tavern. The Ersatz formed living stairs, allowing him to climb off his carters' shoulders and step directly onto the building's front porch. There were revelers there, too, whistling and hooting and slapping his back as he was ushered through swinging doors he'd been aggressively shoved out of earlier.

The interior of the tavern was a bustle of kinetic, joyous energy. The woman with red skin and black horns reappeared, playing her not-guitar. Humans and monsters alike danced with wild abandon. Drinks were poured and drunk.

It was a downright hootenanny, with Shade at the epicenter.

The bar was just as busy as the dance floor. Macaro hustled to serve the many cajolers, with a tiny sprite of a girl and a weird thing with the face of an octopus helping to pour drinks. The short man waved Shade over, but he remained frozen, his mind gone completely blank. Everything began to meld together. Only when something warm and soft touched his hand did he shake out of his stupor and return to reality.

Indigo stood in front of him. Her bewitching teardrop eyes were narrowed, showing only a sliver of her brilliant green irises. She half-smiled at him, the largest show of emotion he had seen from her yet. She raised a hand to tuck a strand of hair behind one of her pointed ears. Her head tilted to the side.

"Your name is Shade," she said, having to raise her voice to be heard.

"And yours is Indigo," he replied just as loudly.

"Indeed," the stunning creature said with a brisk nod.

Shade motioned to the party going on around him. "And this is about...me?"

"It is."

"Why? What's happening here? Who's Aumor?" He lifted the weird length of metal that had started it all. "What's *this*?"

Indigo gently took the shaft from him, tucked it into the tapered waistline of her soiled purple dress. "No questions yet," she said. She grabbed a sloshing glass of amber liquid from someone passing by and pressed it into his hand. "For now, drink."

"I can do that." He tipped back the glass. It was the same delicious concoction that Macaro had served him earlier: sweet and sour and slightly burning. He wiped froth from his beard with the back of his hand. "It's good," he said, the only thing he could think to say.

Indigo seemed pensive. "Did you mean what you said?"

"About what?"

"About every life being sacred? About being willing to give your own for ours? Is that why you came here?"

"Um, yeah, sure, of course," Shade said. His head was starting to swim. "Why?"

"Because you have no idea what is to come for you. No idea at all."

8

Force must be met with greater force, trickery met with trickery.
Your life is precious; you must protect it by any means necessary.
—**Book of the Pentus, Divulgences 8:8**

Watching Rodney try to hold his weapon was enough to make Meesh want to either burst out laughing or rip his own hair out. The guy was hopeless—he couldn't keep his legs a proper distance apart, his right shoulder always sagged when he pressed the stock against it, and he had far too much trouble keeping the foregrip raised with his support hand. It was baffling. When Meesh was reborn, he'd taken to his burners almost immediately and became an expert marksman after only a week of practice. Rodney, on the other hand, would be lucky to hit the broad side of a barn over that same length of time, as if he had no natural abilities outside singing and playing his guitar.

Maybe Reverend Garron was right. Maybe Rodney *had* been created defective.

"Shut up," he muttered to himself.

Rodney continued to struggle with his stance, which made Meesh throw up his hands. The bolt Rodney fired went wide of its mark, spinning past the old blasted-out wall they were using for target practice. His new brother frowned, fumbling as he loaded another lead-tipped bolt into the flight groove.

That, right there, was another problem. Out of all the firearms inside the Dakota Keep vault, Rodney had chosen a crossbow, undoubtedly the clunkiest weapon imaginable. Sure, it was new and shiny and well-maintained, just like every other weapon in their arsenal, and the string drew back automatically. But it was still awkward as hell and not very practical.

Just like Rodney.

"Keep your head up, brah!" Meesh shouted, cuffing his new brother in the back of the head when his next bolt embedded itself in the ground five feet in front of the wall. "And stop letting your left hand drift. It's not like we're trying to build a Sacred Tree here. A goddamn six-year-old can hit a target that big from thirty yards away!"

"Sorry," Rodney said meekly. He looked down at the ground, frowning, and kicked at the sand. "I'll do better."

Meesh immediately felt bad. "Never mind. That's enough for today. Go pick up your bolts."

"Righty then. I'll do that. And after? Will we be riding again?"

"Not yet. I got something I gotta take care of. Get cozy with your book while I'm at it."

"I can do that," he said with a sideways grin. "I most *certainly* can do that."

Rodney leisurely packed the crossbow into his oversized satchel and drifted over to fetch his misfired bolts. After that, he meandered toward the open patch of sand where the knights had left their Warhorses. He tossed the satchel into the rear compartment of his oblong silver machine, removed the book Meesh had mentioned, and slid down the side of the smooth metal. When his rump hit the ground, he balanced the book on his knees and began reading.

A slow, unsteady breath exited Meesh's nose. He hated every second of this.

They'd departed Yaddo the day before, only a few hours after Reverend Garron had shown them the Crone's riddle. Another ride through the tunnel and a trip aboard the *Ocean Child* later, and they were back in the Wasteland. They left Portsmouth on the backs of their Warhorses as the sun set and rode on through the evening, keeping close to the shoreline to avoid getting close to New Salem. The last thing Meesh wanted was another run-in with Fatisha Dorl's Black Masks. Rodney might've smoothed the situation over last time, but given Meesh's foul mood, he was afraid he might say something that would spark violence.

All of which led them to arriving in Sal Morrow just before midnight. They spent the rest of the night at the settlement's little run-down inn—no need to risk getting sucked dry by nightweed, crystal wards or not, when you have a pocket full of coin. It was something he could never convince Abe to do. *Ha. I win, brah,* he thought, brining in a wave of regret.

Meesh woke up his new brother just before sunrise. Rodney needed to get some practice in before they came across something they had to defeat that required more than a steady strumming hand and a sweet voice. Rodney obviously couldn't shoot, and he hadn't yet had the opportunity to fully bond with his Eldersword. They were knights heading toward what would likely be a harrowing situation. What good was a knight who couldn't fight?

Sure, the training would've been easier had they spent more time in Yaddo as he had originally planned, to utilize all the amenities Dakota Keep had to offer. But after the meeting with Reverend Garron, Meesh wanted nothing more than to get the hell off the island as quickly as possible. Being there was simply too overwhelming. The Crone's riddle telling him to kill Shade? The Reverend questioning Rodney's viability? The strange note Octavia left him saying, *Help me, look deeper?*

Nothing but nonsense. The only way for him to come to grips with any of it was to get away.

He stopped watching his brother read and shuffled around the old, collapsed building. Behind the rotting bones of the structure lay the skeleton of a huge guitar, at least thirty feet long. The metal frame of the instrument was half-buried in the sand and browned with age, the rust flaked off when he ran a finger along it. Meesh sucked in his lips as he wiped the soiled finger on his breeches. He stuffed his hands in his pockets and wandered to the edge of a steep cliff.

The place he'd chosen for morning training was the remains of the city of Westgate. The old sign bearing the city's name was visible a little farther north, a fanned structure rising from the sand like a defiant middle finger. That sign was about all that was left other than ruins, since half of the municipality had fallen into the ocean a hundred or so years before. The stray deformed wildlife, like bovine with three eyes and goats with extra dangling legs, were the only living things that called this place home.

Meesh bladed a hand over his eyes, staring at the top of the pyramid that poked out of that water a few hundred yards from shore. There was a reason there were no settlements on the northwestern coast of the Wasteland. The cliffs were too high and susceptible to degradation and landslides. He leaned forward, feeling the rush of danger that came from looking over a precipitous drop without anything to support him. He eyed the jagged rocks seventy feet below, felt the mist from the waves crashing violently against them. A few other structures were scattered about down there, buildings he recognized as having stood right on the precipice the last time he and his brothers came through here. Recent additions to the carnage of Westgate.

"If I jumped, I wouldn't have to do any of this," he muttered.

He stepped away from the cliff's edge. There'd be no jumping, not today or any other day. Meesh loved being alive too much to kill himself over unwanted duties. The solution was to find the humor in it all, not wallow in misery. Too bad he was having a hard time finding something funny about executing his own brother.

Rodney lifted his gaze from the book he was reading when Meesh wandered back toward him. He smiled warmly, which lifted Meesh's spirits a little. Rodney had such an off-kilter grin, as if he were smiling with his bottom lip instead of his top. It would've looked perfect on a simpleton. Meesh chuckled.

"Do what you needed to do, mate?" Rodney asked.

"Yup," Meesh told him.

"What'd you do? Bleed the lizard or something?"

Meesh did a doubletake. "What's that mean?"

"You know, urinate." He laughed. "Americans never did appreciate inert English vulgarity."

"Ameri-whos?"

A blank look came over Rodney's face. "I...I don't rightly know. Just came into my head. It's gone now. What did I say?"

"Dunno," Meesh lied. He'd write it down when Rodney wasn't looking, add it to the small collection of oddities he'd already compiled in his book of poetry over the last twelve hours. Anything that Reverend Garron might want to know about.

Rodney seemed to shake out of his vacuity. "We off now?" he asked, setting aside his reading material.

"Not yet." He jutted his chin at the book. "Where you at with that?"

"Making good progress, I suppose." Rodney's smile faltered slightly. "I just reached the part that speaks of the Hells that bleed demons into this world. It makes for very strange reading."

"How so?'

He shrugged. "I couldn't really say. I simply feel like I know all this already, but I can't quite reach it. As if the knowledge is inaccessible to me."

"Welcome to life as a Knight Eternal," said Meesh.

"So...this is not unusual?"

"Nope. Not at all."

Rodney's relieved look was heartening. "Good."

"Why don't you tell me about it?" Meesh said.

"About what?"

"What you've learned about the Hells?"

"Ah." He relaxed against the hull of his Warhorse, which gave off a light vibration in reaction to his touch. "Well, there are nine of them, clearly. Hells. Each located at a different point along the spiral of creation, beginning with Nowhere, and bottoming out at the Obsidian Hall." He fluttered a hand in front of his face. "Which is the one Hell where no demons have emerged from yet. Likely because everything there is frozen, being so far from the central light of creation."

"What's the most common demon?"

"That would be possessors. Oily blackness that leaks out of fissures and is absorbed into living flesh. The demon takes over the host, and they immediately go out looking for more hosts. Their sole purpose is to breed, which makes sense, given that they're spawned from The Frenzy. That's a sort of Hell ruled by pleasures of the flesh, where overpopulation has led to the fraying of the walls of reality."

"How do you kill 'em?"

"Silver corrupts their essence, effectively abolishing them," Rodney said, ticking off with his fingers. "Or you can destroy their eyes, which causes fire to erupt from the empty sockets. Or their neck, with decapitation, which, if I'm being honest, is rather unseemly. Finally, you can close the fissure they emerged from, which will suck their black oily essences out of the hosts and back into The Frenzy. This is probably the most effective method, since possessors can't stray far from the portal they came from."

"Why?"

"Because they aren't corporeal and rely on the specific energy leaking out of the fissure to retain their consciousness. Otherwise, they would simply fizzle into the atmosphere and disappear."

Meesh nodded. "You're a quick study."

"Always have been," Rodney answered, though his face contorted like he smelled a fart when he said it.

"Now you know why you gotta keep learning this stuff," Meesh told him. "Memorize it like the back of your hand. It'll be the difference between life or death."

A part of him felt guilty for saying that. Here he was, demanding studiousness from his new brother when he himself had none for all the six years of life. He'd never read more than a few paragraphs of the book Rodney was reading—the *Ritterhandbuch*, a constantly-updated journal that operated both as a guidebook and an instructional manual for the Knights Eternal. Meesh instead relied on Shade to fill him in on anything he needed to know.

It wasn't his fault, though. Or so he told himself. The *Ritterhandbuch* was just so damn *dry*. The knights who'd written it could've at least spiced it up a little. Maybe thrown in some sex to distract from the massive information dumps. The thought made him chuckle.

"What's so funny?" Rodney asked.

"Nothin', brah," said Meesh. "Forget it. Just put that book away and grab your sword. We got some sparring to do."

For the next few hours, as early morning turned into late morning and the aridness of the desert took hold, the two brothers mashed Elderswords together amid the ruins. Amazingly, Rodney started to improve. He moved a little more gracefully with each parry, and the blade of his sword began to take on the colors of his emotions rather than the dull white glow of an unbound Eldersword.

Meesh taught him as best he could, urging him to mirror his movements rather than instructing him on the best stances and techniques. This was partially because he didn't want to lose any body parts when Rodney inevitably made a clumsy swing, but mostly because he didn't *know* any stances or techniques. Meesh fought with practiced instinct, developing a unique fighting style based on quickness and unpredictable lunges. Technical prowess had been Abe's area of expertise, not his, and he'd fought his eldest brother tooth and nail when Abe demanded he learn.

A rock dropped in his gut, even as he danced and swatted with easy flicks of the wrist. Abe wasn't around any longer. Now it was up to *him* to train a new knight, a new brother. If Rodney died because he wasn't prepared, that responsibility for that would fall on Meesh alone.

I really should've read that damn book.

By the time noon came around, both of them were sweat-drenched. Perhaps it was because of the influence of the Rush, but Rodney's Eldersword glowed bright blue throughout the end of their session, reflecting such a pure calm that Meesh wondered if his heart rate had ever risen over sixty. A good sign. If Rodney could show that same kind of coolness in an actual life-or-death situation, maybe they'd both get through in one piece whatever came next.

"What do we do now?" Rodney asked when they finished sparring.

Meesh's stomach grumbled. "Lunch. I'm famished. There's an inn called Adavan Station up the way that serves a mean burger. And not all their meat is from mutie cows, either."

"We are heading north?" Rodney said. He clucked his tongue as he wrung sweat from his long hair. "I thought the Reverend said we were to head in the opposite direction?"

"Yeah, he did," Meesh said, shrugging on his vest. "But I think he's wrong. Let's call it a hunch based on a couple intriguing clues. First, Shade said he was gonna go out looking for answers when he abandoned us. Considering that the bastard Asaph had talked about some kingdom you could only reach by going over the mountains to the north, that's probably the way he went. Next, there's this part of the riddle the Crone gave us: *To reach the passage, discontent, through solid stone it weaves.* Four years back, we had *another* riddle that sent us up near Tansaray. It's a mining settlement on the ridge of those mountains. The phrasing was really similar, something about weaving through solid stone. Put two and two together...north we go. I'll take responsibility if I'm wrong."

Rodney pressed his lips together. "What did the riddle send you up there for? The previous one?"

"Oh, that was a doozey. A malbog slipped into this reality, took up residence in one of the mines. It killed ten miners before we got there and took it out."

"A malbog," Rodney said with a brisk nod. "From the seventh Hell, Chiron Apraxia. Beings of living molten rock. Can be defeated by filling their core with a water and aggregate mixture, which will then harden their hearts and cause them to cool until they become pure stone." He quirked his lips. "Is that correct?"

"Wow," Meesh told him. "You really *are* a quick study."

"Thanks. I'm trying."

Meesh slapped him on the back. "And you're doing great, brah. Goddamn outstanding."

They finished packing away their gear and stepped into their Warhorses' saddles. Tito came to life beneath Meesh, the churning turbines within its silver shell lifting the machine off the ground.

"We are heading to Adavan Station now, I take it?" the Warhorse asked.

Meesh grabbed the handles. "You heard."

"I hear most everything. So long as you don't turn off my audio recognition sensors."

"Good to know."

"Will we be staying long?" the tinny voice queried as the machine drifted forward. Rodney mounted Ivan and fell in behind them.

"Dunno. I might wanna stay for a bit. Get my bearings. Think things over."

"Understood," Tito said, and the Warhorse tipped forward as if nodding. "We do not need maximum velocity, then."

"No. *Definitely* not."

"Very well. I will leave you at the controls."

The voice went silent. Meesh pressed the handles forward, and the Warhorse picked up speed. Unlike during their initial return to Portsmouth, he kept it slow, perhaps a double canter. Even that seemed too fast. He longed for the slog of riding horseback, not because he didn't appreciate going fast—he did, oh he did—but because everything seemed to be conspiring for him to hunt down Shade as quickly as possible. With Pam, it would've taken him more than a week to reach a place as far away as Tansaray. On Tito, that same trip could potentially be completed in less than a day.

The last relics of the abandoned city that had yet to be swallowed by the desert passed them by—a huge stone wall, a half-toppled colosseum, and finally the fan-like Westgate sign—and they proceeded to sail over barren sand. When they reached the Wayward Pass, Meesh swung north, keeping plenty of distance between himself and the disintegrating roadway. Sand blew up in high plumes in their wakes. They passed a couple of horse-drawn carriages, but they were too far away for Meesh to tell if the travelers noticed the flying machines or not.

The brutal sun was still at its highest point in the sky when they reached the outskirts of Adavan Station. *Way too quickly*, Meesh thought with a frown. He approached the building from behind, leading Rodney to a set of large boulders far off the Pass where they could stow their Warhorses out of sight. It would suck walking a half-mile through the sweltering heat to reach the inn, but that was preferable to having a bunch of simpletons gawk at them. The last thing he needed was to run across a ruffian with delusions of grandeur who thought he might be able to get his hands on some of the Elders' tech. That'd happened numerous times over the years, and though it never took much to dispatch such morons, Meesh didn't want to chance it. Not with Rodney being so new.

For much the same reason, he decided they should leave their weapons with the Warhorses. When you're going for inconspicuous, sleek silver pistols, advanced crossbows, and glowing swords kind of defeated the purpose.

During their slow trudge through the sand, Meesh noticed that Rodney had fallen more silent than usual. He seemed pensive again, his long fingers tapping incessantly against his thigh.

"What's wrong?" Meesh asked.

His brother arched his brows. "Nothing. I'm only thinking."

"About what?"

He winced and turned away.

"Seriously, brah, it's okay," Meesh said. "What's on your mind?"

"Running. Sprinting, specifically."

"What about it?"

"I...I'm not really sure. That perhaps I enjoy doing it?"

"Really? That's it?"

"Yes."

Meesh chuckled. "You're an odd one, brah. I'll give ya that."

The pair eventually made their way closer to Adavan Station, where the sand wasn't as loose and they found solid footing. Meesh peeked into the stable on their way by. Twelve horses were hobbled in there, most of them slightly deformed, though a pair of large stallions resembled Abe's old horse Greenie. They passed a trio of carriages tied up just outside the inn's entrance. A bad feeling churned in Meesh's gut. Unlike Loretta's, the behemoth of a waystation on the eastern coast of the Wasteland, Adavan Station usually struggled for business. There was no settlement close by save Tansaray, and too many bandits called this part of the desert home, which made trade a risky proposition at best. Most of the times he and his brothers had come here, it'd been completely empty.

The fact that it was bustling now was ominous.

Despite its usual lack of business, Adavan Station itself was an obviously loved structure. A simple box of a building standing two stories tall, its white-painted wood siding remained bright and clean, even with the harsh climate. The roof was in good shape, which was the most uncommon aspect of any edifice in the Wasteland. Roofs were always the first things to go, constantly assaulted by heat, sunlight, and brutal sandstorms. Yet Adavan Station's shingles always looked secure.

It pays to have free labor, Meesh thought. Gilra Moon, the woman who operated the inn, had twelve sons. And as far as he could see, those sons were just as invested in the waystation's upkeep as their mother.

A few people lingered on the inn's front stoop, all men, all appearing a bit too hard for Meesh's liking. They had ratty beards and beady eyes, and gave Meesh and Rodney cautious stares when the knights climbed the steps. It was possible they were simply couriers or tradesmen, but they were just as likely to have found work being outlaws or bodyguards. Meesh tipped his head to them when he held the door open for Rodney, trying to see if any of them recognized him. From the way they nodded back and then went about their business, it seemed none did.

"Who were they?" Rodney whispered once they were inside.

"Potential problems."

The interior of Adavan Station was just as lovingly cared for as the exterior. The floors were buffed and polished, and the furniture scattered in the lobby, though obviously crafted by amateurs, was handsomely painted. Quaint figurines made from wound twine covered the shelves lining the walls. Gilra herself worked the counter. The old woman with a head of long gray hair and a penchant for brightly-colored smocks smiled at the knights' approach. She ushered away the two men standing at the counter with her—two of her sons,

Meesh guessed—and gave the approaching knights her full attention. When her gaze lifted to Rodney, her complexion reddened.

"My, my, Meesh, you rascal," she said in her sing-song voice. "Who is this you've brought me?"

"That's Rodney," he said.

"Where's the other two? Your brothers?"

"Not here."

"Will they be joining us?"

"Um, probably not."

Gilra brought her eyes back down to him. "Oh. Oh!" She shook her head. "I'm sorry, Meesh. I didn't know. Though I probably should've guessed. I've met so many of your brothers over the years. You, Shade, and Abe have been around so long that I took you three for granted." She grabbed his hand and kissed his knuckles. "I'll miss them. Abe and Shade were always very polite."

"It's okay. There's no way you could've known," Meesh told her somberly. "And I miss 'em, too."

"I'm sure." Gilra sighed, offered Rodney one last glance, and then opened her ledger. "So, you're the new brother, eh? And you call yourself Rodney? I like it. Far better than another version of those same silly names. Staying the night?"

Meesh answered for them both. "Maybe. Or maybe three or four. Depends on our moods."

Gilra nodded, lifted an ashwood pencil, and scribbled on the page. She licked her lips as she wrote, and Meesh was mesmerized. He didn't know Gilra's age, but rumor had it she was over seventy. Even so, she had a youthful vigor about her that was downright magnetic. She kept her appearance as well-maintained as her inn, her long gray hair always clean and her formless bright frocks always spotless. The extra weight she carried smoothed out most of her wrinkles, making it hard to guess her age. Meesh heard she'd been a hellion in her youth, which made sense given her many children. He also had to admit that he sometimes wondered, on a visceral level, if she could still be a hellion now.

"Is it always this busy?" Rodney asked, yanking Meesh from improper thoughts.

"He speaks!" Gilra crooned, playfully nibbling on the end of her pencil. "And yeah, this kind of traffic's gotten pretty regular of late."

Meesh passed a few coins over the counter. "I thought we knights were most of your business."

"Not anymore." The old woman winked as she lowered her voice. "Not since the gunslingers started coming around."

"The *who*?"

"Information really *doesn't* travel out here, does it?" she said. "About two months ago, we started getting more frequent visitors. Traders, merchants, you name it. Always accompanied by men armed with burners and bangers and thundermakers. Paid protection, they said. I haven't heard a single report of bandit raids since. And I haven't had to use Abe's gift neither." She lifted the shotgun that she kept stashed under the desk, then squinted at Meesh. "You really haven't heard of this? I find that hard to believe."

"I've been…indisposed," he said.

"I imagine you must've been!" She eyed Rodney again. "Anywho, these armed men call themselves gunslingers. They're all good folks, by and large. Maybe a little boisterous, but so're my own boys. In fact, Dex went off to join up with them, since they're always trying to recruit new members. I let him go. Bart's of age now, so he can do the kitchen cleanup instead."

"Wait, which one is Dex? Who's Bart?"

"Y'know, Dex. The one with the lazy eye. And Bart's my grandson. Lommie's oldest. Just turned eighteen."

"Oh yeah. Him." Meesh shrugged. He could never keep track of Gilra's sons.

Gilra crossed her arms over her ample chest. "Actually, now that I'm talking about them, maybe you shouldn't stay here."

"Why not?" Rodney asked innocently.

"I said these gunslingers are boisterous, right? Well they are. And they can be a competitive bunch, too. Duels ain't out of the question. They'll challenge anyone who claims to be faster on the draw than them, anyone who pronounces themselves a better marksman. I've had a couple folks walk outta here after a challenge and never come back. And if they knew who you are…"

Her eyebrow raised as her words trailed off.

Meesh kept his voice low when he said, "What, am I supposed to be *scared* of them?"

"It's not you I'm worried about."

"Oh. Ha!" He slapped the desk when he laughed, which brought yet another of Gilra's sons out of the woodwork to check on her. A glance from the woman of the house made the young man hastily disappear.

"Listen, Gilly, you don't got nothin' to worry about from us. We didn't come here for a fight." Meesh backed away, held his arms out. "We're not even armed. Except for my knife. Just came in for some eats and maybe a few days of relaxation. You won't get no trouble from us."

"What if someone recognizes you?" the old woman asked guardedly.

Meesh waved a dismissive hand. "P'shaw. I might be pretty, but I'm pale as they come, which means I'll fit right in." He smacked Rodney on the back. "And there's not a soul in the whole Wasteland who knows who this beanpole is. Well, except for Fatisha's crew. But they don't show their faces around here, do they?"

"Nope, those sorts stay far away. Your brothers were the only ones who looked like them who ever stayed here. I mean, I liked your brothers and all, and I knew Abe for thirty years. But facts're facts, and usually folks that dark bring nothing but trouble."

Meesh clenched his teeth to bite back a nasty retort. "You got nothing to worry about," he forced himself to say.

"You promise to behave?"

"I promise."

"I promise as well," added Rodney, who reached out and wrapped his fingers over her hand.

Gilra's cheeks turned a deep crimson. She pulled her hand free, fanned herself, and said, "Dougie made beef pottage. You'll like it. Just come back here and get your key when you're done eating."

With that, she turned away and started fiddling with something on the table behind her. Meesh hissed air through his teeth and glanced up at Rodney. "C'mon, let's get some lunch."

The diner was located at the back of the inn, past the stairs to the second level. Quite a few people were seated in there—sixteen by quick count. Meesh picked out the potential gunslingers among the patrons—a trio of youthful faces situated in the far corner of the room, throwing back drinks while sitting in the ideal positions where they could keep watch on all sections of the dining area. The pistols strapped to their hips made it more obvious.

Meesh tugged on Rodney's arm, and his brother leaned over slightly. "Call me Jim," he whispered, using the first name that came to mind. Thankfully, Rodney didn't question him.

Even though his every instinct screamed to sit as far away from the youths as possible, Meesh chose a table close enough so he could eavesdrop on them, but far enough away so it wouldn't look like that's what he was doing. Maybe it wasn't the brightest choice in the world, but he couldn't help himself. Everything around here had changed so much in such a short time, and he was just *so damn curious.*

He and Rodney slid into their respective seats. One of the gunslingers shifted his eyes their way without turning his head. Meesh flopped back in his chair, let his arms hang down, threw his head back, and groaned.

"God *damn* my feet hurt," he said, channeling Abe's penchant for complaining.

The gunslinger's eyes slid back toward his cohorts. For the moment.

A pretty young woman with frizzy blond hair, probably one of the Moon boys' wives, approached the table. She smiled at them, showing that she had all her teeth. Another big difference between Adavan Station and Loretta's.

Meesh offered vague pleasantries, ordering the beef pottage Gilra had suggested for himself and Rodney. The girl walked back toward the kitchen, and he swiveled in his seat to watch her assets sway. He did it because that's what he figured the gunslingers would expect from some random Wasteland wanderer. Truth was, he didn't really care what her ass looked like, no matter how pretty she was. There were far more important things on his mind than sex.

"Sweet lass," Rodney said, the first time he'd spoken since they sat down.

"Think she liked you," Meesh replied.

Rodney shrugged. "Perhaps."

"Perhaps? What, you too good for her?"

"I never said that. I simply... I am just..." Rodney sighed as he massaged his temples. "I'm having a difficult time finding the words to explain."

"Don't gotta explain at all," Meesh told him, keeping his tone level. "I'm pissed too. That horse's been with me for nine years. I'd broken her so good she could almost read my mind. Those bastards better hope I don't find 'em, or I swear..."

Meesh groaned inwardly when Rodney looked at him like he'd sprouted a second head. Good thing his back was to the gunslingers. A second later, his eyebrows lifted, and he said comically, "Oh. Yes... Jim... that makes me angry too."

While they waited for their food, Meesh and Rodney improvised. The story of the theft of their horses grew more fleshed out each time one passed to the other. While they talked, Meesh kept discreet watch on the gunslingers. They seemed interested in the tale he and Rodney were weaving, but it didn't stop them from continuing their own conversation.

The serving girl finally came back with two steaming bowls of pottage. Perfect timing, since he and Rodney were running out of ways to embellish their fictional encounter. And now Meesh had the opportunity to listen in on the three young men while he ate.

"...and then the guy bet me I couldn't hit a bullseye from a hundred yards," a young man with a badly healed broken nose was saying. "I told him I'd put up my horse and my gun, he countered with his Kaiser-loving girl of all things."

Kaiser? That's new, thought Meesh.

"What happened next?" asked a man with a head of moppish black hair.

"Whaddaya think happened? Not just one bullseye, but two."
Bent-Nose made a *pew-pew* sound and fired off a pair of imaginary
shots with his fingers.

"Did ya take the girl?" asked the third gunslinger, who was short
and scrawny with wild blue eyes.

"'Course I did. Twice. She begged me to stay afterward. Said her
man never made her feel so good."

All three of them laughed. Meesh had to fight to keep from rolling
his eyes.

While Meesh and Rodney spooned tasty gravy into their mouths,
the three gunslingers went on like that, weaving one tale of prowess
after another. Meesh didn't think any of them could've been more
than twenty years old. Which meant their stories were probably as
real as the one he and Rodney had been telling earlier.

Rodney looked bored, and Meesh was ready to give up listening.
There was nothing to learn here. He'd be better served by heading up
to their room, getting some rest, and coming to grips with what he had
to do to Shade when he found him. *If* he found him.

But then he heard three words that grabbed his attention and kept it.

"Five-pointed star," said Mop-Head. "That's what the dude
driving the wagon called it. Which seems...what's a word that means
describing something obvious?"

"Redundant, I think?" said Wild-Eyes.

"Yeah, Thorne, I guess that works. Redundant."

"You could call all them Pentus missionaries that," said Bent-Nose.
"Since they suck at promoting their own religion."

"Kort, I don't think that's the right way to use that word," said
Mop-Head. "But anyway, that may be a thing of the past, 'cause this
missionary I ran into came up with a whole new way of pulling in
followers."

"Oh yeah?" said the guy with the wild eyes, Thorne. "And how's
that?"

"By giving away guns."

Kort with the bent nose spat a mouthful of beer. "Yeah, right! Don't
try to pull one over on us, Mick."

"I ain't lying," Mick with the mop hair said. "You can ask Devron when we get back to Tansaray. He was with me. And Greg and Jon and Nikko, too. We was escorting a buncha tanners in Pennonstaff, and the missionary dude called us over. He straight-up offered to give us a freakin' trunk full of weapons—pistols, rifles, even shotguns. Offered his horse and carriage, too, even though we didn't need it. And he only wanted one thing in return."

"What's that?" Thorne asked.

Mick leaned forward. A guarded look came over him, as though ready to impart on his brethren the secrets of the universe. His voice took on a serious quality when he whispered, "A prayer."

After a moment of confusion from the other two, they all burst out laughing.

"And did you?" Kort asked once he had calmed down.

"Sure, why not?" replied Mick. "Like Charlie always says, a true Kaiser don't never turn down easy money. He should know. He's the one who used to be a king."

Meesh sat there quietly, taking it all in as he chewed his pottage. He didn't react when Rodney raised a questioning eyebrow at him. He just let the gunslingers' words wash over him like an acid bath.

Everything Mick said made far more sense than it should. All the things Meesh had seen and heard during his last excursion to the Wasteland came roaring to the forefront of his mind. The troupe of bandits he and his brothers encountered after crossing the Red Cliffs had been riding carriages marked with the five-pointed star and were armed with weapons produced in Yaddo. Asaph had later called the Pentmatarianist missionaries glorified arms dealers who were sowing discord throughout the Wasteland for the nefarious purpose of leaving messes for the knights to clean up. The murderous, dead-controlling bastard even mentioned a deposed king named Charles who'd crossed the northern mountains with him and taken up residence in Tansaray.

Meesh hadn't believed a word. In truth, all he took from the conversation was pleasure from his brothers' uncomfortable reactions to a stranger's outlandish tales. But if all what Mick said was true, if the Reverend was the liar Abe had proclaimed him to be…

Feeling hot under the collar, Meesh dug into his vest pocket and pulled out the scrap of paper Octavia had left for him. He unfolded it and stared at the four ominous words: *Help me. Look deeper.* His heartbeat picked up its pace. He stuffed the note back in his pocket, gnashed hard on another bite of gravy-slathered beef, and accidently bit the inside of his cheek.

Rodney leaned forward, asking *What's wrong?* with his expression.

Meesh waved him off. He obviously couldn't explain any of this to his new brother right now. And even if he could, would it make any sense to someone who'd only been alive for a week and a half?

"Are the guns good at least?" Kort was asking back at the gunslingers' table.

"Oh yeah, *real* good," answered Mick.

Thorne raised one wily eyebrow. "Better than the ones Charlie gave us?"

"Nah," said Mick, patting the big black monster of a pistol in his hip holster. "These bad boys got more power and're more accurate. But I gotta admit, the ones the holy roller handed over are way prettier."

"Got one on you?" asked Kort.

"Sure thing. Keep it in my bag. For backup."

Meesh held his breath as the young gunslinger gathered his rucksack. From within he removed a pistol that Meesh instantly recognized from the beige tint of the steel and the deep red color of the cherrywood grip. When Mick displayed the weapon to his cohorts, Meesh even saw the five-pointed star carved into the side of the handle.

"See?" Mick said. "Way prettier."

A risky plan entered Meesh's head, and he acted on it before he could overthink the situation. While Rodney looked on helplessly, Meesh leapt from his chair, knocking it to the floor with a loud clatter, and stormed toward the gunslingers.

"Hey!" he shouted. "What the hell you think you're doing, assholes?"

The diner went quiet. All eyes in the room turned his way. Meesh hoped no one knew who he was, if only because he didn't want anyone other than Rodney to see him playing the victim. He focused on the three young men at the table. The gunslingers started at his sudden outburst, the two with their hands empty reaching for their weapons. The one who'd been showing off the pistol from Sal Yaddo flipped the gun around and pointed it at him with far more speed than Meesh had been expecting.

Maybe this wasn't the best plan.

"'Scuse me, mister," Mick said calmly, his finger tapping the trigger. "We're minding our own business here. You should go sit back down with your bud before something you don't wanna happen, happens."

"You mean like me an' my brother was just minding our own business when you people held us up and stole our horses?" Meesh barked. "Where are they? Where're Dinner and...and Blixen?"

Shit. Stupid names. Idiot.

Mick faltered; the barrel of his pistol lowered slightly. "Who and who? I got no idea what you're talkin' about."

"That gun, right there, the one you're waving at me. The ones who robbed us had burners that looked just like it."

"They did, huh?" asked a curious-sounding Kort. "And listen to him, still using the unenlightened term for 'em."

"They did!" exclaimed Rodney. Meesh winced as his brother clumsily stood from his seat and joined his side. Why hadn't he just stayed put?

"Hells yeah, brah," Meesh said, trying to draw the gunslingers' attention away from the tall man with the unconvincing angry face. "They pointed them right at me and Rod here's heads and told us to skedaddle. Even shot at us when we ran away. Lucky we're even standing here!"

Mick took his finger off the trigger and stared at the pistol as if seeing it for the first time. "Their guns looked like these, you said?"

"*Exactly* like those," Meesh told him. "Stupid star emblem and everything."

"Huh," Kort said, wiping at his off-kilter nose. "Interesting."

"That weren't us, mister," said Thorne. "Promise you that. We wouldn't never."

"Really?" Meesh took a deep breath, forcing a look of uncertainty onto his face.

"Sure looks like it could be them," Rodney muttered.

"Well, it ain't," Mick said proudly. "We ain't bandits. We're gunslingers. We *protect* people, not rob 'em."

"For a price, anyway," amended Kort.

"You're not lying?" Meesh asked.

"We don't speak falsehoods," Thorne said.

Your stories beg to differ, Meesh thought. He shifted from one foot to the other, doing his best to seem ashamed. "Oh. Oops. I'm, uh, sorry then. Kinda amped up."

"I'm sorry, too," Rodney added.

Mick shrugged, stowed the pistol back in his rucksack. "It happens. I get being pissed, but you really gotta watch out who you're picking fights with. If we weren't so level-headed, it might've ended bad for ya."

Meesh bristled at being scolded by someone younger and less experienced than him, but he did his best not to let it show. "I get it. Again, sorry. We'll leave you to it." He grabbed Rodney by his sleeve. "C'mon, brah, let's leave 'em alone."

"Um, very well M...Jim," Rodney stuttered.

He turned his brother around, took a few steps. The other diner patrons, whom he'd almost forgotten about, went back to their meals. Meesh stopped, counted to five, and then circled back to the gunslingers. All three rolled their eyes at his approach.

"Hey, I got a question," he said.

Mick groaned. "What?"

"Well, it's just...my brother and me just lost everything. I mean *everything*. Any worldly possessions we had were in our saddlebags. See, we left Barrendale to start a new life, but now we got no way to get there, no way to pay for anything. I just used the last of our coin on that stew on the table over there."

"And that's our problem how?" asked Thorne.

"Oh, it's not your problem," Meesh said. "But still...we were heading up to Tansaray. You all know the area? If there's any work available? How to get there?"

The gunslingers glanced at each other. Thorne and Kort seemed hesitant, but Mick lifted his hands. "We were about to head up along the Pass after lunch," he said. "Tansaray's where we operate outta. And there's not much work...unless you wanna try your hand at joining the clan." He gestured to the other two. "We're always looking for new members. If you're interested, we can give you a lift. But word a' warning, it ain't gonna be easy."

"We will put in the work," Rodney said, making Meesh jump as he just now noticed that his brother had rejoined his side.

"You better," Kort said. "'Cause Charlie Midnight don't suffer fools, and he don't suffer laggards neither."

That seemed to settle it. Meesh and Rodney went back to their table and finished off what was left of their pottage. The diner went back to normal activities.

Rodney leaned toward him. "What just happened?" he whispered.

Meesh grinned. "Tell you in a bit."

The gunslingers finally finished their drinks, then stood up and made their way for the exit. Mick waved for Meesh and Rodney to follow. They complied with haste. Meesh gave Gilra a finger-over-the-mouth *hush* signal on his way past the reception desk. The woman who ran Adavan Station shook her head and placed the room key she'd set aside back on its hook.

Once they returned to the Wasteland's oppressive heat, the gunslingers approached one of the empty carts that'd been secured next to the entrance. Mick slapped the wagon's thick wooden rail. "Here's your ride," he said, climbing onto the driver's perch. The other two headed for the stables. Meesh guessed the pair of handsome stallions in there belonged to them.

He and Rodney climbed into the back of the carriage. Stacks of hay that smelled of piss and mold served as seats. Meesh wrinkled his nose when he lowered himself down on one of the stacks. Rodney sat opposite him, looking worried. As Rodney kept glancing toward the rear of Adavan Station, Meesh puckered his lips to silently tell him not to worry.

It may not have worked, as Meesh rarely accomplished anything silently.

Kort and Thorne galloped out of the stables atop their stallions. They whooped, racing out toward the Wayward Pass. Mick flicked the reins and gave a *"Hyah!"* The sturdy draft horses pulling the cart lurched into motion.

Meesh leaned back against the railing, letting the harsh sunlight wash over him as the cart bounced along the sand-covered trail. Rodney ogled him as if he'd gone insane.

"Meesh...Jim..." his brother began, quietly.

"I know, I feel you," Meesh said with a raised voice. "I wish our horses could hear us now. That they'd somehow realize how much we need them, escape captivity, and come find us."

"Hah!" Mick said from his perch. "Horses ain't that smart."

"Don't I know it!"

"What in the *world* are you doing?" Rodney whispered, bewildered.

Meesh dropped his voice and said, "Playing a hunch."

"Will it work?"

"It better," he said with a sigh. "It goddamn better."

— 9 —

The servant, who knew the will of her Lord but did not prepare,
was lashed nine times by her Master, one for each Hell.
And throughout her beating she laughed, for in her disobedience,
she knew that no more of her would be asked.
—**Book of the Pentus, Allegories 5:15**

F or the first time in far too long, Indigo felt truly *alive.*

She sensed it when she woke up that morning. When she stretched to tease the cricks out of her back, the result of spending the night upright in a chair. When she traversed the path before the sun rose to take a dip in the lake. When she wandered back to Hickweis Tavern, dripping wet and chilled. When she plucked an apple off the plate atop the bar and tasted its bitter sweetness. When she climbed the stairs back to her room. All mundane actions, most of which she had performed day in and day out, now given new meaning by the specter of the thing she had never once felt in her two hundred and seven years of life. Hope.

That was what the man currently occupying her bed represented— the potential for release, for freedom, no matter how unrealistic it seemed. She knew nothing about him other than his name, his claim of having been a knight from a derelict kingdom, and the fact that he had killed a Righteous man. But that did nothing to distill her sliver of optimism.

Rather, the unknowing made it more powerful. Indigo had *known* countless human men. She understood more than most that once you cracked that outer shell, no matter how beautiful, you could only feel disappointed by the ugliness that inevitably oozed out.

For the moment, Shade slept fitfully. He tossed and turned, the silk sheets twisting around his body. Indigo watched him from the bedroom doorway. She wondered what he was dreaming that made him utter those strange sleep-groans and whimpers. When she remembered her metaphor of cracking the outer shell, she slipped into the adjoining room without disturbing him.

It was best not to know.

She lowered herself into the same chair she had slept in, sipping tea and watching the sun slowly rise over the mountains through the east-facing window. She experienced the events of the previous day all over again—the pain of physical assault, her shock when Peter Ortiz was murdered, her defiance in summoning the Voice of Him, and the discovery that the stranger, Shade, had with him the one thing that could allow her people to leave this cursed valley.

Strangely, however, the events that happened after all of that ended stuck with her the most. She thought of Shade in the tavern, how he looked uncomfortable with all the cajoling. How he had loosened up after being handed drink after drink, until he reached the point where his shoulders lost their tension and the smiles that cracked his bearded face came easier. And oh, what a smile it was! A contradiction within itself, revealing brief moments of twinkle-eyed innocence that were out of place on the face of someone so outwardly hard, yet at the same time so natural and easy that she imagined a smile should have been a constant feature.

When those smiles became more common, she saw him *truly* shine. He had grabbed the case she had seen him carrying into the tavern earlier, removing an instrument that looked like a strange version of the citole Briar played. The music he created with that instrument was another paradox—beautiful, haunting, sensitive, forceful. The words he sang were equally wistful, dripping with angst. His performance captivated all the Ersatz, but Indigo felt it the most. Attraction latched onto her and would not let go. She felt true desire for the first time since the only true lover she had ever known was taken from her, in spirit if not body. She imagined herself with this man, physically as well as emotionally. During those fleeting seconds when the abuse she had suffered throughout her ascensions drifted into the background, she imagined the slimmest chance that she and her people might one day be happy.

Desire. Hope. Two sides of a coin edged with razors.

When the sun emerged fully from the shadow of the mountains, she splashed water on her face and descended to the tavern. Ersatz packed the place, courtesans and general staff alike, everyone hustling to clear away evidence of the events from last night. Each wore an expression showing degrees of shame or fear.

It seemed they, too, understood how threatening optimism could be.

Indigo spotted Mana in the far corner of the room. The girl was on her hands and knees, scrubbing with vigor. She winced with every other stroke; tears leaked from her swollen eye. Even though the girl looked far better today than she had yesterday, Indigo was filled with sadness at seeing her suffer even minor discomfort. Indigo touched her own cheek, the one struck by the fist of a dead man. There was no ache there, no swelling; any injury she suffered had disappeared while she slept.

All of the Ersatz were that way. Even Bluebell, whose nose had been broken, had not a mark on her when Indigo saw her going to the lake that morning. This only proved how viciously Mana had been beaten.

She caught a querying look from Macaro, who was busy restocking the liquor shelf behind the bar. Maneuvering her way toward him through the maze of tables, she made sure to scoop up a bucket and washcloth. Cleaning was not below her station; all Ersatz were as low as one could get, Indigo included.

Orchid was standing atop the counter sweeping up broken glass when Indigo reached the bar. When the halfling moved aside, she set down the bucket. Indigo wrung water from the cloth and set about polishing the areas Orchid had swept free.

"You do not have to do this, Mum," Orchid told her.

"I do, and you know it," said Indigo. She pressed down hard to rub out a particularly stubborn stain. It looked like blood. That it was likely the blood of one of her people made her scrub even harder. "And thank you, sweet one, for doing as I asked yesterday. I knew you would be the only one willing to press your lips to that damnable horn."

Orchid looked down at herself. "I doubt the overgod could torture me any more than he already has."

"I would not count on that, sweetling."

"Why are you worried about me? *You* are the one who risked everything by ordering it blown in the first place. He could have ripped you from your body over and over and over…"

"But that did not happen, did it?" Indigo stopped scrubbing and massaged her temples. "Instead, we all risked the life of someone else instead."

"You torture yourself too much," the halfling proclaimed in her squeaky voice. Shaking her head, she meandered to the other end of the long bar.

Macaro moved his stool closer and climbed atop it. He looked at Indigo thoughtfully as he went about drying glasses. "She is right, you know. You need not be so hard on yourself. You give all you have to this place, and to the people who call it home."

"That is my *job*."

"A job you asked for, after…" He winced, closed his eyes, and took a deep breath. "You understand my point."

"A selfish choice."

"How so?" the dwarf asked.

"I desired some semblance of control over an existence that was never truly my own."

"While at the same time putting yourself in the position to take the blame for anything that goes wrong."

"Stop it," Indigo said sharply.

"Stop what?"

"Defending me."

Macaro smirked. "Sorry, Mum. That, as you would say, is *my* job."

Try as she might, she could not stop her lips from stretching upward.

"That is better."

He flicked his gaze toward the ceiling. "And how is our 'friend'... up there? Is that what he is? A friend?"

"I have no idea," Indigo sighed. "And he is sleeping."

"Cannot handle his liquor, eh? Well. Proof right there he is no Righteous."

Indigo eyed the instrument case belonging to the stranger resting against the wall by the kitchen. The staff gave it a wide berth on their way to and fro, as if it were either holy or extremely dangerous.

"He is *certainly* not Righteous," she said.

"Most certainly not," Macaro agreed. His nose twitched as he set down another dried glass. "Speaking of our esteemed guests, I am not up on what the scriptures say about the Horn. Have they been updated? Do we still have three days free of them?"

"Darkenwood will be off-limits to the Righteous for the next three days, yes, to allow the valley to reorganize after the justice doled out by the Voice of Him." Indigo let out a humorless chuckle. "At least there is no big change this time. Yet."

"That is good," Macaro said. "And those who were forced to leave will not be allowed back until their allotted time, correct?"

"Yes. We should not see them for quite a while."

"Hopefully never again." He again looked at the ceiling. "If our stranger up there can truly become Aumor..."

Indigo placed her hand on his. She felt his pain. She was one of the first that the overgod had doomed to this valley, along with Raz, Wisteria, Sienna, and Black. The original five, bonded by servitude and pain. Macaro had arrived only a few months later, which meant he had suffered nearly as long as she had. It also meant his heart could be just as easily broken.

Hope was such a dangerous thing.

"We will get through this, no matter what," she told him. "We always have."

He slipped his hand free and grabbed the cloth she had been using to scrub the bar. "I will hold you to that, Mum. Until then, you should check on our guest. Make sure he did not die in his sleep and leave us hanging out to dry for nothing."

She leaned across the counter and placed a kiss on his silky-smooth cheek. Macaro laughed, squinting, seeming close to tears. *Hopeful* tears. Indigo turned away and ascended the stairs before he could see that they formed in her eyes too.

When she returned to her apartment, Shade was awake. He sat on the edge of the bed, naked save for a pair of loose-fitting undergarments. The sheets were piled in a formless lump behind him. He raised his bloodshot eyes. He held his odd hat in his hands, turning it over and over.

"Hey," the man said, smiling. "You found my slouch."

"Good morning," said Indigo. She calmed her nerves, breezed into the bedroom, and snatched his soiled clothes and jacket off the floor. "I assume you mean the hat. Peck found it out in the courtyard after the celebration ended last night. I had a new string put in for you."

"Thanks," he said bashfully.

"You slept well?"

His eyes followed her every movement. "Um, not really. I haven't been able to sleep in a... You know you don't gotta do that, right? I can clean up my own mess."

"Unnecessary," she replied. "You are our guest. You will be allowed every amenity that Hickweis Tavern has to offer. Including laundry service. And someone to fix the rips in your coat. Our staff seeks to impress."

Her insides roiled at reciting such a practiced screed, but she forgave herself for falling back on the familiar. Treating this situation as an everyday occurrence was the only way to keep from completely unraveling.

His smile tightened. "What'll I wear in the meantime?"

"I have collected an assortment of apparel for you to consider. All of it is clean, and it is all in your size."

"Thanks."

Indigo tossed the dirty clothes in a basket and moved to her bathroom. She gestured inside. "Would you like to wash up now? The water is warm, the soaps are of the finest quality. There are clean towels on the rack."

"Um, yeah, sure."

Shade slapped his thighs and stood from the bed. Indigo could not help but stare. The man was slender but handsomely muscled, and he moved with a level of grace that seemed more akin to the Ersatz than any Righteous she had met. Various scars marred his tantalizing brown skin. She found herself wanting to trace her fingers along those scars. Then to play with the nest of black hair in the middle of his chest.

"In here?" the stranger asked.

She blinked, realizing that he now stood beside her, gazing over her shoulder and into the bathroom. Indigo hastily stepped aside. Bewilderment overcame her. She had never been one to daydream, especially about pleasures of the flesh. Those things were rote aspects of her daily life, acts she had to partake in to fulfill her duties and absolve her sins. It had been more than a century since she had thought of intimacy in any other way. Yet here she was, looking at this disheveled stranger and feeling those pangs again.

Just like everything else about this man, it was both exciting and terrifying.

Shade breezed past her into the bathroom, staring at all the amenities with wonder. He ran his fingers over the sink and shaving supplies. He gazed at himself in the mirror. He drew back the curtain in front of the tub and touched the showerhead that protruded from the wall.

"You have running water here?" he asked.

"We do. And heated as well."

"That's insane. I haven't taken a shower since I was back home. Even Dakota Keep doesn't have bathrooms this nice." He peered at her over his shoulder, seeming far younger and more innocent than his body, facial hair, and scars should have allowed. "Thank you."

"It is my pleasure, truly," Indigo said, placing a hand over her heart. "And if there is anything else you need, feel free to ask. If you wish to bathe, I can assist with that. I could wash your hair, even trim your beard if you so desired."

It sickened her that her insides tingled at the offer.

His cheeks flushed and he turned away. "Nah, I'm good. I'm a big boy. I can take care of myself."

"Very well. I will be right here if you need me."

"Um, yeah, gotcha."

He eased the door shut.

Indigo remained at the door. She heard the *click* of shears, the dribbling of the faucet. The shower came to life, sounding like a waterfall. Indigo imagined what Shade looked like dripping wet. Scowling, she forced the image from her mind and went back to picking up the bedroom. While she worked, she appreciated his refusal for her assistance in the bathroom. No Righteous man (or woman if she swung that way) would *ever* turn aside such a request, as nakedness and nearness and opportunity often led to something more. Yet Shade, who was obviously captivated by her—especially given the way he ogled her during his drunkenness—had turned her down.

Only someone deserving of becoming Aumor reborn would react in such a way.

Shade eventually emerged from the bathroom wearing only a towel. He had trimmed his beard, which showed off the more sensitive angles of his face and those thick, sensual lips, and even cut back some of the curls atop his head. Indigo approved. With water beading on his bare skin and dripping down his muscular chest, he looked like desire come to life.

"Clothes?" he asked softly.

"Oh. Oh! Yes, in there." She pointed behind her to the sitting room. Shade strolled past, looking over the finery laid out on the sewing table beneath the window. "Whatever you wish, it is yours," she said. "Now, if you will excuse me, it is my turn to make myself presentable."

He looked at her, and there was such depth of longing in those soulful eyes that she was certain he would return the favor and offer his assistance in the same way she had offered hers.

But he didn't. He simply bowed his head and uttered a single, "Thanks."

"When I am finished myself, I will bring you downstairs and we can discuss what happens next."

"Okay," he said meekly.

Despite wanting to linger, she let him be. She entered the bathroom to find it hot and steamy but miraculously clean. There were no traces of hair in the sink, the towels he had used were all hung back on their hooks with care. The place *smelled* like him, a tantalizing musk that lingered in the air like rain on a sunny day. Indigo smiled, stripped, and stepped into the shower. She tingled all over.

When she finished washing, she threw on a simple brown dress—the simplest she had—and tied a scarf around her waist. She exited the bathroom but could not find the stranger. He was no longer in the sitting room or in her apartment at all. Suddenly frightened, she hustled down to the tavern, her heart aflutter. What if the man had fled the valley? What if that tiny inkling of hope she had put upon his shoulders had been misplaced?

But Shade had not run. She found him sitting at the bar, a glass of water in hand. Macaro spoke with him, and the other Ersatz—mostly just the courtesans now—kept their distance, yet looking like they wanted nothing more than to lay their hands on him as they had last night. Shade listened to the hushed words Macaro uttered, his head bobbing. He constantly shifted on his stool as if he had an itch he could not scratch. Sitting on the bar before him was the thin length of golden steel, nestled in its wad of cloth.

"Ah, there he is," Indigo announced. She hopped off the stairs, her feet lightly touching the floorboards as she approached the bar. "The man of the hour."

"I'm not so much as that," Shade grumbled. He took another sip of water and winced.

"And what were you all talking about?" Indigo asked, eyeing Macaro.

He shrugged. "I was telling Shade here about the Key."

"Ah, yes. I imagine he would have questions."

She sidled up beside him, pressed her shoulder to his. Shade ran his fingers over the grooves along the length of the Key, seemingly lost in thought.

"You say it's a key," he said softly. "What's it open? Macaro says a door, but he won't tell me *what* door."

The bartender leaned forward on his stool and smirked.

"Do not torment the man," Indigo told him. She looked back at Shade. "The Rawgian Key is an object of fables and legend here. I was not sure it even existed. There is a painting of it inside Tro Choi on a door that has never been opened."

"Games and trickery." Shade lifted the key, rolled it across his palm. He released a frustrated breath. "None of this makes any sense. Nothing about *this whole place* makes any sense!"

The anger in his voice made Indigo recoil, an action mimicked by all the other Ersatz in attendance. Shade was breathing heavily, his fists twisting the Key as though he could grind it into a diamond with his bare hands. Indigo steadied herself, placed a calming hand on his shoulder.

He immediately swiped her hand away, spun on the stool, and stumbled to standing. "Don't touch me!"

Indigo gaped at him, eyes wide. The hope within her came close to cracking.

At her expression, Shade's flash of wrath faded away. "Oh, no, I'm... I'm so sorry... It's not you, Indigo," he stammered. He placed the Key down, took off his hat, and ran his fingers through his tight nest of curls. "I just...you shouldn't touch me. You're a being of beauty. Of purity." He swallowed, hard. "I don't deserve your touch. I never will."

"What would make you say that?" Indigo asked.

"I was a knight," Shade said, his spine straightening, his shoulders rolling back. "A member of a holy order, who took a vow to protect the innocent, to ward off the forces of evil and send them back to the Hells they came from." A staccato-like sigh blew out his nose. "I broke those vows. I abandoned my brothers. I rebelled against my creator. I'm simply...a sinner."

Behind the bar, Macaro started laughing. "Then you are right where you belong!"

The stranger spun on him. "What's that supposed to mean?"

"It means that you are a sinner standing in a valley full of them," Indigo said. She chanced touching his shoulder again, and this time he did not throw her off. She gently spun him to face her. "You speak of hell? That is exactly what Darkenwood represents. A place where the vilest of sinners attempt to save their black souls."

Shade blinked, screwed up his mouth. "What?"

"We are all sinners, Shade," Indigo said. "Every soul you see here, the worst of the worst. It is our lot in life to suffer. Or so we have been told."

"What's so horrible that someone like you would be condemned like that?"

"Someone like me?" Indigo asked.

"Someone so damn perfect."

She took a deep breath. "I am not perfect, Shade. I am no better than anyone who calls this valley home."

"And none of us knows our sins," Macaro added. "All any of us remember is what we have experienced from the moment we opened our eyes in Darkenwood."

Shade frowned. "How can you atone for your evils if you don't know what those evils are?"

"Another great mystery," Indigo said with a shrug.

"That makes even less sense," said Shade. "Though this kinda tells me why none of you tried to avenge the murder of that man yesterday, because you believe he probably deserved what happened to him."

Mana started to cry behind them.

"You speak of Pipin?" asked Macaro.

"Don't know his name," the stranger said. "The big guy. Got an axe in the back. None of you helped, or even mourned him afterward. You just dragged his body and did…something to it."

"We laid his body on the pyre," Indigo said after a deep breath. "And Pipin did *not* deserve his fate. He was as good a soul as there has ever been. He sacrificed his own ascension to save another from the same fate. As for mourning him, who is there to mourn when death is but a brief respite from pain?"

"That's fatalistic," grumbled Shade.

"Yet it is the truth."

"Well, if it's so bad here, why don't you just leave? Start a new life somewhere else?"

"You…" Indigo began, but she snapped her mouth shut. Any anger she felt at the stranger's presumptiveness was laved away by the jumble of confusion apparent in his sad brown eyes.

"He truly does not know," Macaro said.

Indigo gave the dwarf a knowing look. "How could he? He is a stranger here."

"Because the man who will become Aumor Reborn—"

"—will arrive with nothing but ignorance and love in his heart."

Macaro laughed. "And here I thought the songs Wisteria sang were all flights of fancy."

"Many of them are," said Indigo. "That one…is not."

"Let us hope so."

"Please, someone fill me in on what's going on," Shade cut in, obviously frustrated.

Indigo grabbed both his hands. She felt his heart beating rapidly through his skin, as if his bewilderment was morphing into fear.

"You told me you would give your life for us," she said, her eyes locked on his. "It is only fair that you know why that would be necessary."

"Then tell me," he said.

"That, I cannot do. This is not something one can be told. It must be *shown*."

Indigo grabbed the Key from the bar and tucked it into the belt holding up his new pants. She took Shade by his hands and looked into his eyes, haunted as they were. When she gave him a gentle tug, he followed her willingly.

Time decides your age. Your heart decides your time.
Destiny decides your path. None of this can you control.
—**Book of the Pentus, Platitudes 21:18**

Indigo pulled Shade along the wide cobbled path. He was so distracted by his thoughts he belatedly realized he had stepped in horse droppings and was now painting the cobbles a smeary brown with every other step. Consumed by turmoil, he barely registered the various Ersatz who watched them pass, their mostly inhuman eyes conveying ebullience and wariness equally.

Nothing about his current circumstances seemed real, which said a lot, considering the weirdness he'd encountered in his time patrolling the Wasteland with his brothers. It felt as if the world and all its creatures were conspiring to drive him insane.

He couldn't stop thinking about the dream that had woken him that morning. In it, he'd been a child, small and vulnerable, wandering through dimly lit halls with tile floors while strumming an old broom as if it were a guitar. The dream was innocent enough; nothing horrible happened, no monsters lurked in the shadows, and even though the surroundings were strange, they weren't threatening. But his subconscious knew that he had never experienced childhood, which caused a feeling of wrongness to overtake him, to *consume* him.

The fact that he did not immediately recognize his surroundings when he woke up hadn't helped his mindset.

Everything he heard after that added to his discomfort. It all seemed like an extension of his uneasy dream. He couldn't understand why he remained in this place when every instinct told him to head north, toward the answers he had come this way to find. It made no sense that he would sacrifice his safety for a race of beings who might or might not have sprung from a stygian pit, a people whose traditions and supposed curse he simply couldn't wrap his mind around. And finally, he found it truly insane that he agreed to all this not only out of noble duty, but also because of his infatuation with the stunning creature who was holding his hand and leading him beneath a canopy of leafy green.

The contradiction of it all threatened to undo him. He felt like a stranger, a man who no longer understood right and wrong, as if the knight he had been had gotten lost along the way.

That's wrong, he realized. Ceasing to be a knight had been his choice—a *conscious* choice. The Vera he had known in life would have been so very disappointed.

Finally, after being pulled along for what felt like miles, Indigo brought him to a halt at the place where Shade had seen the naked man stumbling out when he entered Darkenwood. They passed between the tall hedgerows, and Shade looked up. The purple façade on the windowless structure appeared outlandish rather than hallowed. The iron star at the top of its tall spire glared outward like an insidious eye.

Shade saw Indigo's gaze upon the building coated with loathing not reverence.

"Where are we?" he asked, breaking the extended silence.

"The end, and the beginning," Indigo said. "Come."

She pulled him around the side of the building. Shade told himself he was letting Indigo get her mad pseudo-religious ideas out of her head before he attempted to pry reasonable answers from her. The truth was much more pathetic. He simply loved the silkiness of her skin, the warmth she radiated, the firmness of her grip. Touching her sent tingles through him and made his heart race.

The sensation was not as potent as the Rush, but it was definitely more enticing.

They stopped at the rear of the property, where the tall hedgerows ended and a thick stretch of woods began. Shade squinted. He could just see the path he had taken off the mountain, at least fifty feet into the forest and lit up by sunlight streaming through the canopy. When he tilted his head to the right, he saw the outline of the sign marking the boundary of Darkenwood.

"That's where I entered," he said, his voice sounding far away to his own ears. He gestured to the peaks visible over the tree line. "And that's where I came from. Over those mountains."

"So you told me," said Indigo. "Which I still find unfathomable. We have always been told that nothing exists south of the valley. That the only civilization lies to the north."

Shade nodded. "We were told similarly. Obviously, both beliefs were pretty damn wrong."

"Obviously." She looked at him with those hypnotic green eyes, but then quickly turned away.

An uncomfortable silence stretched out, leaving Shade with nothing more to do than stare at the surrounding forest. It really was so beautiful here, so peaceful. A nearly perfect setting where one could get lost simply wandering from one peaceful alcove to another. That thought caused a spark of realization that tickled the base of his skull.

"There's no walls," he whispered.

Indigo gave him a sidelong look. "What?"

"I said there's no walls. No fence. No goddamn barrier at all. It's all wide open."

"In a way, yes."

Shade planted his hands on his hips, his stare an accusation. "Which still doesn't make any sense. If it's true what you told me, that you're mistreated and abused for some forgotten sins, then it's true that you could just leave." He proffered his hand at the woods. "Hell, there's nothing in your way. My guess is that you and your people've been beaten down so much that you just *believe* you're trapped."

"That is not true," she said, looking hurt.

"I think it is," he told her. "I walked right into this valley. What's stopping *you* from walking *out*?"

It appeared as if Indigo wanted to say something, but her lips snapped shut before a sound came out. Her brow furrowed, those teardrop eyes squinted. She lifted her left hand. It was such a perfect hand, her golden flesh seemingly inviting Shade to kiss it. He stood rapt, wondering whether she was going to slap him or caress his cheek.

She did neither. Instead, she reached toward the forest, shoving past the hanging branch of an evergreen, until her fingers hovered over the shrubs and vines that marked the boundary. It was such a random act that Shade could only retain eye contact.

An oddly sweet burning scent tickled his nose. Shade tore his gaze away from the gorgeous creature's face and stared in disbelief at her outstretched arm. Her flesh had started to turn red, opening cracks that belched smoke. Sores formed, starting in the middle of her forearm and spreading to her fingertips. The liquid within those sores rippled like boiling water beneath her stretched skin.

"Stop it!" he demanded and yanked her arm back from the invisible boundary. The raised boils ceased fizzing, the redness lessened ever so slightly. Incredulous, Shade poked at one of the boils. It popped, leaking pus that pooled in the crook of her elbow. Indigo removed the scarf from around her waist with her free hand and held it out to Shade. He took it and wrapped it around her scorched arm.

"There are indeed walls," Indigo said. "You simply cannot see them. The only safe passage out of this valley is through the Fallen Arch. This is why your being here is special. You are the first non-Righteous or Ersatz to ever walk these lands."

He breathed in short bursts as he bandaged her arm. He had nothing to say.

"You are not, however, the first to think we could simply flee this life," Indigo thankfully continued. "I tried once, long ago. We all have at one time or another. But we cannot leave. We will be burned, but not killed. And in the end," she gestured to the building behind them, "we will always return here."

"I don't understand," Shade whispered.

"You will."

When he finished her dressings, Indigo flexed her arm and stretched her fingers. She nodded in apparent satisfaction, took Shade's hand once more, and brought him back to the front of the temple. They went up the steps to the entrance. She pulled open the heavy door and guided him inside.

The interior of the building was frightening in its familiarity. It certainly looked like a hall of worship, lit by bright lights embedded in a twelve-foot ceiling. The walls were simple wood covered with countless frescoes that made no sense to Shade. The center of the large space was filled with rows of bench seating, similar to the Scourger's House of Yehoshua, that faced a raised altar made of black marble.

The altar was the temple's most unusual feature. Four jade columns rose from the floor to ceiling at the rear of the dais, spaced evenly apart. Each had a rectangular opening cut into it that one could traipse right inside, like four doorways to nowhere. A mass of gray flesh, at least the size of a man, bulged and rippled like a malformed lung as it spilled out of the portal just left of center. *A cocoon*, Shade thought. It looked like a goddamn cocoon.

"What…" he began, but words failed him.

The barest of smiles cracked Indigo's face. She tugged his hand, leading him to the far wall on the opposite side of the altar. At one point, she grabbed Shade's chin to force him to turn away from the writhing lump of flesh on the dais.

"Do you worship that thing?" he asked softly.

Indigo ignored him, instead gesturing to the frescoes on the walls. "This is our story," she said, walking slowly along the outskirts of the room. "It begins here, with the tale of wars fought and wars lost, of cruelty and greed and famine. Those are us, the Ersatz, the bringers of blight to the lands beyond the northern mountains. The worst of the worst. Those who shall forever atone for sins long since forgotten."

He followed her, studying the paintings along the way. They were indeed images of conflict, but in an abstract sense, with skeletons hanging bodies on pikes over pyres and cloven-hooved demons butchering men, women, and children. These people *could be* demons from the Nine Hells. Though for some reason, he doubted that. Something faint tugged on the outskirts of his thoughts, like a long-forgotten memory that couldn't find its way to the surface.

Indigo stopped before a door embedded in the wall directly opposite the altar. She stared at the strange looping symbol carved into the center of the door, surrounding an inch-wide hole. A painting of a man holding a golden rod was emblazoned above the jamb.

"Whereas the walls of the Tro Choi show our misdeeds," she said, "this room reveals our salvation. Or so we have been told."

"What's in there?" Shade asked. He stepped up beside her and ran his fingers along the ridges of the symbol.

Indigo shrugged. "We do not know. As I told you, it has never been opened."

"Why?"

"I assume because no one has ever possessed the Key."

She reached over, removed the notch-covered Rawgian Key from his belt loop, and placed it in his palm.

"This must be the lock," she said, guiding his hand toward the circular aperture in the middle of those intricate carvings.

Shade slid the key into the hole easily, and when he could push it in no further, there came an audible *click*. When nothing happened, Shade sucked on the back of his teeth before deciding to play along. He spun the protruding end of the Key to the right, and the subtle snap of springs unfurling made him let go.

Somewhere within the walls, gears whined and tumblers clacked. There came a sound like a deep sigh, and the door popped open. Shade watched Indigo's expression shift from stoic to only slightly dry. The woman pushed the door inward. A waft of stale-smelling air assaulted Shade's nostrils.

Lights clicked on when the two of them crossed through the portal. It was a much smaller room they entered—not much more than a broom closet. The walls were completely bare. In fact, the only object in the tiny room was a podium upon which rested a single sheet of parchment. Instead of writing, the parchment contained tiny, intricate symbols. *Hieroglyphs*, thought Shade, though he didn't know where that word originated or what it meant.

"It is real," Indigo said, breathless. It was the first time Shade had heard her voice warble. "I always assumed it a myth. A story told so that we would succumb to hope. Yet another attempt at torture by the overgod. But the proof is before you. The Path of Aumor exists. Everything you need to know is written right here."

"What's it say?"

"That this is the greatest challenge Darkenwood has to offer," she said, her fingertips dancing over the picture-writing. "The one who claims the mantle of Aumor Reborn shall cross one of the Sacred Paths. Upon completion of the test that awaits them, they shall pass beneath the Gate Between Worlds and enter Castle Rawg. If they who would be Aumor can defeat the Avatar of Rawg once they've entered the castle, they will be free to make the Choice of Choices. Should they choose correctly—should *you* choose correctly—the sins of the Ersatz will be forgiven. The curse binding us to Darkenwood will be lifted. We will be free to do with our lives as we please."

"Sounds easy," Shade grumbled.

"It will not be."

"No shit," Shade snorted. "And when's all this supposed to happen? Immediately?"

"No, not immediately." She leaned in, examining the picture-writing again. "It says here that the journey can only begin when the overgod completes his blink."

"What's that mean?"

"When the moon does not appear in the night sky."

"Oh. A new moon. When's the next one?"

"Six days."

"At least it's not *right now*."

Shade sighed, cupping his chin in his hand. Something that Ken, the man on the mountain, had said to him right before he left entered his thoughts: *Oppressed people cannot be oppressed forever.*

"I'm supposed to do it," he whispered.

"You are," said Indigo. She clasped her hands and let out a relieved sigh. "This is a noble thing, Shade. You say you were a knight—a *true* knight, not a Righteous playing out their fantasies as one. Are knights not noble?"

"I'm not a knight anymore."

"Your title does not define who you are." Her fingers touched the underside of his jaw, sending shivers through him. "Perhaps I am only seeing what I wish to see, but you give me hope. You give us *all* hope. Therefore, you will do the right thing, because it is right. I cannot think of any action more just than saving an entire civilization from torment. No matter our unremembered sins, my people do *not* deserve the pain of having to endure countless ascensions."

"You keep saying that. Ascend. Ascension. What's it mean?"

The hint of a smile disappeared from her beautiful face. "Come. I will show you."

They exited the room together, with Shade remembering to take the stupid key out of the door before they left. The door closed on its own behind them.

Indigo walked a straight line between the rows of seating, heading for the altar. The cocoon remained where it had been when he first saw it, spilling out of the pillar on the marble dais. It throbbed faster now. A soft red glow, like a beating heart, pulsed in the center of the gelatinous mass.

Shade followed her up the three steps onto the dais. Indigo approached the cocoon and gracefully dropped to her knees in front of it. The red spot thumped right in front of her face, and she gently placed her hand against the undulating membrane. A solid, ball-shaped object suddenly pressed against the fleshy casing, and Indigo kneaded it with the care of a doting mother. Shade's face twitched into a frown as he watched the odd display from over her shoulder.

"Come now," she told the wriggling lump. "It is time."

The thing in the cocoon shifted, and Shade was astonished when he saw the imprint of hands shoving against the fleshy prison. The outer membrane stretched thinner, revealing a face surging against it, open-mouthed as if screaming. The reddish glow from inside the cocoon pulsed all the faster.

Indigo scooted back a few inches. "You can do it. Claw your way free. *Ascend*."

A sound like water boiling reached Shade's ears. The bulging part of the cocoon tore, and a hand emerged, slender and feminine and dripping with ichor. Indigo grabbed a shredded corner of the membrane and pulled, even as more as that disgusting black and red liquid burped from within and splattered across the altar's slick marble surface. That slime-dripping arm extended farther out of its swath of flesh, desperately grasping at the empty air. Indigo hopped up into a squat, took hold of the reaching hand with both of hers, and pulled.

It took little time for Indigo to yank the cocoon's prisoner free. A girl, naked and covered head-to-toe in foul-smelling afterbirth, tumbled from the rapidly deflating cocoon. She collapsed onto the floor of the platform, though Indigo made sure the fall was controlled. Indigo held the girl, stroking her matted hair. Foul slime saturated the scarf-bandage wrapped around Indigo's arm, but she didn't seem to care. All her attention was on the girl in her lap, whose bright eyes bulged from her streaked face as she gasped for breath.

"What in the Nine Hells..." Shade began.

Indigo held up a hand to silence him. She then leaned the girl over her knee and held her there. A torrent of clear fluid erupted from the new girl's mouth and splashed over the marble floor.

"There, there," Indigo said.

The girl moaned.

Indigo used the hem of her dress to tenderly wipe muck from the girl's face. She was young, barely out of her teens, and a particular kind of pretty, with pale skin dotted with freckles, thin lips, large eyes, a dainty nose, and high cheekbones. Shade imagined her hair would be blond if it weren't slathered in filth. She coughed out the last of her sticky phlegm, and Indigo helped her to a sitting position. Those eyes, now half-lidded, turned Shade's way. He half expected her to cower in fear, but instead the new girl tensed, her fingers curling into fists.

"Do not worry over him," Indigo said. "He is a friend."

The girl let out a sharp breath and gave Indigo a pointed gaze.

"I am serious. He is here to help."

"He best be," the girl croaked. Her hands shot up and covered her mouth as soon as she spoke. She looked down at her naked body, covered in sinking ichor as it was, and reached a hand between her legs. Her lips pursed and she shook her head. "Oh."

"You will get used to it," Indigo said. Shockingly, she actually *laughed*.

The girl didn't seem offended. In fact, she started chuckling herself, squeezing reddish slush from her tresses. "True, it will be a new experience," she said, apparently still unsure about the way her voice sounded, because she winced when she spoke. But then that wince turned to a grin. "On the bright side, perhaps this time I will not have to ascend because of someone calling Right of Retribution. Could I get a simple strangulation in the throes of passion already?"

"Be careful what you wish for," Indigo said playfully.

Shade watched the banter, baffled. He took a hesitant step forward. When Indigo and the new girl looked at him again, he raised his hand like a child asking permission to speak during one of Abe's prayer sessions he held occasionally while they were traveling the Wasteland.

"Um, do you know each other?" he asked.

The two women shared a knowing glance, and then they both broke out laughing. This caused the new girl to fall into a hacking fit as her body expelled even more clear fluid.

"Shade, this is Pipin," Indigo said, using her thumb to wipe spittle from the corner of the new girl's mouth.

"Pipin?" he said. "The guy who got an axe in the back?"

"The same," said the girl after she recovered from her latest choking fit. She gave her naked body another once-over. "Only I suppose Pipi would work better now. What do you think, Mum?"

"You need not change your name," she told her.

"Well...what if I want to?"

"Then Pipi works just fine," Indigo said.

"Can someone please tell me what's going on?" Shade asked, his voice sounding soft and timid to his own ears.

Indigo shared a look with the new Pipin—Pipi now—and then leaned over to whisper something into the girl's ear. Pipi nodded sharply. She rose on shaky legs and stretched her arms over her head. "I think I *can* get used to this," she said. Without another word, she hopped off the black marble platform and exited the front door.

Shade remained rooted in place, staring at the steaming, deflated cocoon from which Pipi had emerged. Connections he was too afraid to recognize entered his mind, leaving him speechless.

Indigo climbed to her feet and smoothed out another ruined dress. She stood before him, confident yet exposed, and Shade felt his longing for her grow stronger, even while his thoughts remained muddled.

"That is ascension," she told him. "And that is what I meant when I told you that for us, death is but a brief respite from pain. It is not a statement made from some abstract philosophical pondering, but the genuine truth. We, the Ersatz, cannot die. It is part of our punishment. When our bodies perish, our essences return here, to Tro Choi, and are placed into another vessel at the whim of the overgod."

Shade swallowed the lump in his throat. "And this...this happened to you?"

"Of course," she said with a shrug. "I have suffered through many ascensions over the course of my punishment." She looked at him sympathetically. "Come, Shade. Take my hand. Let me tell you a story."

He let her wrap her fingers around his even though they were still slicked with nasty fluids. He felt lightheaded as she guided him off the altar, his mind rifling through everything that this new information implied. When she brought him off the altar and to the first row of seats, he sat down mindlessly. She slid in at his side.

"The first thing you need to know is that I was among the first Ersatz to open their eyes upon this valley," Indigo said. "There were five of us—Wisteria, Sienna, Raz, Black, and myself—who emerged from cocoons on that very altar. We came into being naked and afraid, not knowing who we were, but with an inherent understanding of language, the basic necessities of survival, even certain aspects of right and wrong. It was the Voice of Him who greeted us once we departed Tro Choi, and it was the Voice that named us and told us of our fates. We were brought to Merchantry Road, where a recently constructed housing complex, large enough for a few hundred, stood waiting for us. Yet we were the only five."

Shade nodded along with her story, intrigued.

"Those first few days," Indigo continued, "we were constantly visited by men and women wearing white garb with masks concealing their faces. They called themselves the pedagogues, agents of the overgod Rawg. They explained the rules we were to live by, told us what would happen should we leave, and informed us that our lives, such as they were, are forfeit to those greater than ourselves. They also demonstrated ascension on that very first day, as one of them abruptly stabbed Black in the eye with a knife. They then brought us back here to this building so we could watch him come to life again.

"After a week, the Righteous began to arrive to feed their carnal desires. This was *their* land, we were told, and we were simply part of the scenery. Part of the *game*. That was when we learned there was nothing we could do to defend ourselves from debasement. Not that we declined to fight back when we were abused—we did, and with ferocity—but we simply could not get the better of them. We are stronger than them, and faster, and, as time went on, more knowledgeable. But still, it did not matter. The overgod ingrained within us the inability to truly harm our betters. We might get close, we might cause them immediate pain and even draw blood, but at the last moment, something will go wrong—be it a seized muscle, a twitch, a sudden inability to move—allowing the Righteous opponent to emerge victorious."

"Like what happened with Pipin during his fight with the man I killed," Shade whispered.

"Yes, exactly like that."

He ran a hand down his face. "That's...that's *horrible*."

"It is," Indigo said. She placed a hand on his knee, causing a tremble to work its way through him. "But that is not even close to the worst of it. That distinction would be a complete loss of self. The Righteous are at an advantage. They know who they are, what they are, and what they aim to be. All *we* know is that we are subservient to their whims. And when death means that you will return in a new body, one that you are forced to relearn anew, it creates a crisis of the spirit. Who are we? Why has the overgod chosen whichever new form we are given? What must we do to repent, other than suffer? The more we suffer, the more it seems we are punished. This makes little sense when you consider that we are in this position to absolve ourselves of past sins that none of us remembers."

"Is that where the monsters come in?" asked Shade.

Indigo quirked an eyebrow. "Monsters?"

"Y'know, most of your people are inhuman creatures. The tiny girl with the huge eyes. The gray beast with tusks who lugs around the cart of weapons. The red-skinned demon that plays that strange guitar. All of them."

"They are not *monsters*, Shade. They are *us*." She took her hand off his knee and gestured to herself. "I am, as you might say, inhuman. Does that make *me* a monster?"

Embarrassment flushed his cheeks. "Of course not."

"Then the others who have been likewise cursed are not either. They are simply...different. Every Ersatz begins human, nearly indistin-guishable from our Righteous guests. During our first few ascensions, we remain that way. It is not until our fifth or sixth ascension that the anomalies begin. Randomly. Unpredictably. Perhaps we will come back as a dwarf, like Macaro. Or a triton like Wisteria, who dwells in Winninger Lake. Or a demonite like Briar. Or an orc like Fol. Or a half-elf, such as myself. Or, if we are particularly unlucky, we will be cursed to become human once more."

"Cursed? Why would returning as a human be bad?"

"Because only human-formed Ersatz can be courtesans. It is what the overgod wishes. We all acted in that capacity when we were new, like Pipi. She was thrust into Darkenwood only two years ago; her current death and rebirth mark her fourth ascension, and her first as a female. Once she is able to ascend to one of the sub-class species, she will no longer have to give herself to men and women who will abuse her day in and day out. If one day she were to return in a human body and we were short a courtesan in Hickweis Tavern, she would be faced with no other choice but to return to that line of work. Trust me, I know. I was in that position more than once."

Shade frowned. "I'm running out of ways to say *this is horrible.*"

"I ran out long ago," Indigo said with a shrug.

"I can imagine." He leaned back against the hard, uncomfortable bench. Images of Indigo having to perform debasing acts entered his thoughts, causing the heat of anger to rise up his neck. His eyes drifted back to the empty cocoon that was now starting to dissolve on the black marble altar.

"Were you ever a man?" he asked Indigo.

"Many times," she answered. "In fact, my very first body was that of a male. Do you have a problem with that?"

"A problem? No. It's just...strange."

She smiled at him softly, and he thought it glowed. "Not so much. Though it takes effort to learn new bodies, it is the bodies themselves that are the issue, not the gender assigned. We have come to view the change as natural. There is a fluidity to it. We are who we are in here." She placed a hand on her heart, then shifted that hand down between her legs. "Not here. The love we feel is not limited to the hardware one has at their disposal. It is all-encompassing."

"I see," Shade said, his head bobbing. "It's rather beautiful, actually."

"We like to think so."

He mulled over her words. "You've been in love before?"

"Of course. I love all my brethren."

"No, I mean *in love.* With one person. A person you want nothing more than to share your life with, where you feel that without them you can't breathe. Is that something you're capable of, or is it something that's been, well, bred out of you?"

He winced as soon as the words left his mouth. If it wouldn't make him look like a fool, he would have slapped himself upside the head. Here she was, telling him all about the atrocious history of this valley and the horrors her people face daily, and he had asked about love. He knew she would realize that he asked because he was infatuated with her and was curious if *she* could become infatuated with *him*.

What are you, twelve? he heard Vera scolding him in the back of his mind. Guilt formed a lump in his throat.

But Indigo did not react with hostility. She seemed to mull the question, her eyes aimed at the ceiling. "Yes," she said, her voice throaty and breathless. "I was in love once. Truly, hopelessly in love. With Raz, one of the original five. She was my beacon for a hundred years."

"A hundred years?" Shade said, cutting her off. "You've been alive for *a hundred years*?"

"Two hundred and seven," Indigo told him. "I have counted every second that has ticked on by."

He knew no way to respond to that, so he blinked and gestured for her to go on.

"Raz was the one who kept me sane when I feared I might end up cackling mad in the forest, like some of my more unfortunate siblings," Indigo said. "She was mighty, she was *strong*, and she possessed enough compassion to move mountains. While intimacy is strictly forbidden between the Ersatz, I managed to sneak out to be with her whenever I could. It did not matter what form we were in, whether we were man and woman, or shared the same gender, or whether we were human or subspecies. We simply could not keep ourselves apart. And when she became the overseer of Hickweis Tavern and I returned to being human, she invented ways to include herself in the dalliances of those who bought my services. A clever way of subverting the no-intimacy policy."

She fell silent. Shade inched a little closer to her and risked placing a hand on her knee like she had his. She didn't throw it off, didn't run away. The heat started rising in him again. He realized that he didn't care what this wonderful woman had been in the past. Just as she had explained how the Ersatz felt about one another, he was captivated by what and who she was now, not what she had been.

"What happed to her?" he asked softly. "To Raz?"

Indigo swallowed hard. "She was tortured by the Voice of Him for the sin of trying to protect her people. She was tortured until she became a shell of the beautiful soul she had once been. She was sent screaming into the northern hills when it was done, and that is where she remains to this day. Just another obstacle to be defeated by the Righteous when they choose to embark on the Path of the Hero. I see her every once in a while, during her ascensions. She refuses to even look at me. She simply babbles to herself and goes along her way, back to the mountains. Back to solitude. Until she ascends again."

Her eyes welled up with tears. Shade struggled to hold back his anger. He fought the urge to wrap his arms around her. Instead, he whispered, "I'm sorry. It must be hard."

"It is easier now, but I hold her with me here always." She again placed a hand over her chest. "I told you that I had tried to flee this place. That was in the days after Raz was reduced to a blubbering shell. I dashed up the trail behind this temple as quickly as I could, bathing in the pain of being scorched to ash because that pain hurt less than the pain of losing her. And then, when I returned, I was gifted the body of the half-elf you see before you now. This was the last form Raz had taken before her torture at the hands of the Voice. I took the mantle of overseer in her place. I had no choice. Ever since Hickweis Tavern was erected thirty years after our creation, half-elves are the only ones allowed to manage it. But I considered it a blessing. To be overseer of Hickweis Tavern has its advantages, even if everyone calls you 'Mum.' One is the fact that we are much less likely to ascend, as we hold a place of power in the community." She shook her head. "That brings its own form of crushing guilt, but I bear it willingly. Because I want to remember Raz the way she had been. Because whenever I look in the mirror, I see *her*."

"I understand," Shade said, his heart breaking.

"I am not sure you do," Indigo countered. "I am not sure you truly *can*."

"I can." The connections finally met up in his mind. Before this moment, he had struggled to justify his abandonment of his sacred vows. Not anymore. He felt Vera smiling down on him from somewhere in the heavens instead of scolding him. "I might not know exactly what you've been through, but I think I can at least relate."

"How could you?"

He stood up and began to pace in front of her. "My story's a lot like yours, actually. I told you I was a knight, but I *didn't* tell you that I came into this world six years ago as a fully formed adult. Who I was before—if I even *existed* before—is a mystery. My brothers and I hunt demons in the Wasteland beyond the southern mountains. We live in servitude under the Pentus, the god who supposedly created us, as servants bound to his church. Bound by vows we had no choice but to recite. We might not be forced into such horrific acts as you and your people, Indigo, but our lives are short and brutal. Full of violence and fear and a loss of hope. You've lived hundreds of years; I'll be lucky to live ten. And the penalty for desertion is death—to be cut down by your own brother's hand…"

Shade stopped pacing. Indigo looked up at him in disbelief—not that she didn't believe his tale, he assumed, but that she couldn't fathom the idea that an outsider could understand her pain. He dropped to a knee in front of her and grasped her hands. His right thumb traced circles on the damp scarf wrapped around her injured arm.

"Unlike you, we don't come back when we die," he told her. "Another brother will be created to take my place, and the memory of me will be nothing but words written in some stupid book. So yeah, Indigo, I can more than relate to your people. And I promise you, right here and now, that when those words're written about me, they'll say that Shadrach the Twentieth didn't turn away from people in need."

Indigo gnawed her bottom lip. Tears filled her eyes. Her golden skin sparkled beneath the bright ceiling lights.

"Does that mean you will take the Path of Aumor?" she asked softly.

"Damn straight I will. It's the right thing to do, even if it means I die trying."

— II —

Believe in everything. Believe in faeries, demons, dragons,
even leaders who will guide their people toward prosperity.
Each of them exist, until proven otherwise.
—**Book of the Pentus, Divulgences 18:4**

Meesh's back ached, his knees were sore, and he was damn tired. After four days of bouncing around in a carriage, he was about to snap. At night he was forced to sleep either on a bed of stinking hay bales or on a rocky outcropping. He would've rather slept on the sand, but that was out of the question. The gunslingers had no crystal wards to protect from nightweed, and he doubted if they knew such protections existed.

Maybe this half-baked plan of his wasn't such a great idea after all. Shocker.

At least the trip was almost over. The mountains in the distance resembled actual mountains now instead of vague purple smudges painted on the horizon. Also, there was far more traffic on the Wayward Pass than there'd been for the last three days. Convoys passed them regularly, their carts filled with everything from granite to zinc to copper to salt, all products extracted from Tansaray's vast system of mines.

"Would ya lookit that, business *is* booming," Meesh said, perking up on his uncomfortable hay-brick seat.

"'Course it is," Mick the gunslinger said from the driver's perch. "That's what we bring. The peace o' mind to do your business and not lose your product. Or your life."

"Cool, brah. Cool. Just never thought I'd see it," Meesh mentioned.

"Oh yeah?" The gunslinger passed a distrustful glance over his shoulder. "Why's that?"

"Y'know, because shit sucks," Meesh replied hastily, thinking, *Goddammit, don't be such an idiot.* "With how bad things are in Barrendale, it's tough to imagine *anywhere* being safe."

"Or profitable," added Rodney, accentuating his comment with a wink.

Meesh rolled his eyes. "Yeah, that too."

Mick swiveled back around. "I get that. But don't y'all worry. It's safe as houses here. Trust me. You'll see."

"I'll see all right," Meesh muttered under his breath.

The carriage rattled on along the rutted, sand-covered road. Prairie grasses popped up around them, signaling that they were getting closer to the lush mountains beyond. Meesh stood up to stretch, taking a moment to stare off into the Wasteland's bland beige scenery. Tiny puffs of dust rose in the distance. He sighed in relief, cracked his back, and dropped back onto the hay bale.

"Why do you keep doing that?" Rodney asked.

"Just admiring the scenery," Meesh told him, grinning.

They crested another of the Pass's numerous sandy hills, and Tansaray came into view. The town was much larger than the last time Meesh had been here. It'd been a little bigger than Ramstable, with scattered domiciles and warehouses to store the product extracted from the mines, all surrounding a built-up central region filled with shops and administrative buildings and bars. Now, those scattered homes formed a network of streets that spiraled off from the center. The town was still growing, too, as the skeletons of half-completed buildings dotted the boundaries where civilization met the wildlands. As the cart drew closer, he saw people milling about on newly-flattened streets. A *lot* of people.

Meesh whistled through his teeth. Tansaray might've been a larger settlement by Wasteland standards, but its population was dwarfed by places like Breighton, New Salem, and even Portsmouth. Residents from other settlements must've flocked here in droves over the last year or so to justify such rapid expansion. It made him realize that perhaps these gunslingers were actually delivering on the things they promised.

Rodney sidled up beside Meesh. His new brother had been relatively quiet over their journey, just going with the flow and keeping his mouth shut for the most part. Meesh took it as a sign that Rodney didn't want to blurt out the wrong thing and blow their cover. It wasn't like they could discuss their subterfuge in any great detail. They were never alone unless they went off to relieve themselves. Mick's perch was only a few short feet away, and the other two gunslingers, currently riding their stallions ahead of the carriage, were always within earshot when they stopped to rest the horses.

Which meant Meesh took it very seriously when Rodney's face contorted into a look of tight-lipped concern and asked, "What is going on over there?"

Meesh followed his finger that pointed at a newly-completed tenement building. The Wayward Pass was still a good distance away, running parallel with a quarter-mile between the road and the town, but Meesh clearly saw men and women wearing scarves over their faces, pairs of them hauling what looked to be slabs wrapped in white sheets out of the building. They exited one after another, dumping their cargo onto a cart waiting in the center of the dusty road.

"Dunno," Meesh said, frowning. He scooted toward the front of the carriage, leaned his elbow on the driver's perch. "Hey, Mick," he asked. "Something going on in town you wanna tell us?"

Mick took his eyes off the road ahead, flicking them toward the scene just before the draft horses pulled them out of view. "Nothing to worry about," the young gunslinger said, slapping the reins.

"It *looks* like something to worry about," Meesh said. "I mean, are those corpses?"

"It's new," Mick said, his brow furrowed. "I told you don't worry about it. We trust Charlie. He's the reason for all the prosperity. All you see here, all the improvements? All because o' him. So, anything that's going on, he can handle. Don't question it, or Kaiser help me…"

He faced front again, apparently done with the matter. Meesh sat back down, shared a doubtful look with Rodney, and shrugged. Whatever was happening here, it wouldn't be long before they found out.

The road turned east, terminating at the settlement's entrance. A huge arch bent over the road, *Welcome to Tansaray!* stenciled on it in huge, blocky letters. The carriage passed beneath the arch, and Meesh whistled.

Rodney leaned into him and whispered, "At least we aren't going under a stranger's crotch."

Gnawing on his cheek was all Meesh could do to keep from cracking up. Rodney's sense of humor was improving, even if it was as dry as a bottle after a drunkard's binge.

Mick guided the carriage behind his two cohorts, steering onto the road that cut through the center of town. This part of Tansaray still looked the same, filled with brick buildings that were remnants of a culture long dead. Every landmark Meesh saw reminded him of times when he and his brothers had come here. There was the old library—a Wasteland rarity—where Abe had taught Meesh how to vanquish a haunt five years back. He spotted Ralph's Sweats, a general store where a pretty young man named Dezzi had worked, with whom Meesh had a brief fling the year after that. Then there was the local magistrate's office, where Belial Monroe worked, across the street from the Funktown Copper Annex, which the Red Raiders had hijacked for their base of operations, and where that whole troupe of bandits had died in a hail of bullets.

So many memories.

Fun times, Meesh thought blissfully.

His bliss was tempered by the people walking the streets. Most were joyous, cheering the gunslingers as they passed by, gathering on stoops and balconies and downing drinks in front of roadside watering holes. But a few among them appeared skittish, as if paranoid of being so much as touched. A few more wore scarves over their mouths and noses, bloodshot eyes peeking out over the bloodstained fabric, their entire bodies quaking when they fell into coughing fits.

"Shit," Meesh grumbled. He folded his arms over his chest.

"What is it?" Rodney wondered softly.

"Tell you later."

The gunslingers brought them to the Tansaray Courthouse. It looked the same as ever, three stories of thick gray blocks that achieved the dichotomy of appearing both imperial and regressive. Everything around it had changed. Instead of an open courtyard, there was now a gigantic covered stable capable of housing at least fifty horses. The weathered statue of some *very important man* from the time before the rising, which used to stand at the base of the courthouse steps, was missing. The base of the statue had been hollowed out to create a fire pit. A mutated pig, with another half-formed pig growing out is back, rotated on a spit above the pit, flames licking its seared flesh, while a bunch of jovial young men, all armed, cavorted around it.

The last change was the biggest. The sign above the building's entrance no longer said "Tansaray Courthouse." Apparently, the building was now called "The Saloon."

"The Saloon?" Meesh asked, standing in the back of the cart with one knee propped on his hay bale.

"That's what we call it," Mick hollered over his shoulder.

"Surprised Ben agreed to change the name," he said.

"Ben?" the gunslinger asked.

"Quartermain. The civil manager."

"Oh, this is Charlie Midnight's house now," Mick said, and Meesh could hear the young man grinning. "The old guy don't live here no more."

"Where'd he go?"

"In the ground."

Meesh sat down again, letting out a long sigh. Ben Quartermain had been a good man. Stingy and a bit on the prickly side, but his heart was in the right place, and he always treated the knights with a grudging sort of respect. This whole situation kept getting worse and worse.

Up ahead, Kort and Thorne guided their stallions into the stables and dismounted, handing their steeds over to the attendants waiting inside. Mick brought the carriage in behind them. But when he brought the draft horses to a halt, he waved the attendants away and instead pivoted in his seat toward his two passengers. Meesh didn't like the narrow-eyed glare facing them.

"Coming from Barrendale, huh?" he asked in a low, threatening voice. His hand drifted toward the holstered burner on his belt.

"Yeah?" said Meesh, his face rumpled in confusion.

"How's someone from a backwater know the civil manager of a settlement this far north?"

Shit.

"We do not actually *know* him," Rodney said before Meesh could blurt out a nonsensical answer. "But he *was* the inspiration for us coming here."

"That so?" asked Mick.

"Yes, it is. You see, Benjamin Quartermain was originally from Calisto, another backwater on the border of the Unknown Lands. He is a cult hero down there, an example that if one individual can pull themselves up from nothing, anyone can."

He said it with such practiced ease that it sounded natural. Meesh was baffled.

Mick's gun hand relaxed. He peered at Meesh. "That so?"

"Yup," he said, nodding perhaps a bit too eagerly. "Totally, brah."

"Righty then." The young man's lips stretched into a grin. "I'll take you at your words. Y'all have been straight-up so far. And don't know why you'd be lyin', anyway. But if you are…"

He left it at that and hopped off his perch, waving for them to follow. Rodney winked in Meesh's direction before slipping off the side of the carriage as if he'd done it a thousand times before. Meesh chuckled and did the same.

Meesh grabbed Rodney's sleeve. "What was *that* about?" he whispered.

Rodney shrugged. "Simply trying to help. You seemed unsure of what to say."

"You came up with that story off the top of your head?"

"Oh, no, not at all. That story was in the *Ritterhandbuch*. In the section on local leaders."

Meesh grunted. *I really should've read that damn book.*

They exited the stables and took the quick turn onto the Saloon staircase. The three gunslingers greeted their colleagues around the firepit with whoops and high-fives. Meesh noted that a few of the other gunslingers wore face-scarves and there were indeed red stains dotting them. He made sure to give those people a wide berth when he crested the stairs and entered the Saloon.

The inside of the old courthouse was completely redesigned. The walls that used to hide offices on either side of the hallway had been torn down, creating a gigantic open space that teemed with men just as young and eager-looking as the three who'd brought the knights here. There was a bar on the left where the tax collector's office had been, while to the right, where the permits office and public works department used to be, women now pranced half-naked while a band strummed out a jaunty tune on banjos.

This place was a goddamn whorehouse. Or something like that.

Mick made sure Meesh and Rodney followed him until they emerged from the crowd onto the hallway on other side. The office of the civil manager was still an office, Meesh was pleased to see, its door guarded by two older, more hardened-looking gunslingers. Mick approached them, had a short conversation, and then went back to Meesh and Rodney. "Give it a few," he said before walking right past them.

Meesh turned. On the wall opposite the office hung a gigantic blackboard. Mick joined bent-nose Kort and bald Thorne in standing in front of it, talking among themselves.

The blackboard was covered with columns filled with chicken-scratch writing. Meesh realized exactly what the board was—a jobs list. Duties such as guarding merchant trains and personal bodyguards were listed, alongside grimmer propositions like *offing* and *shakedown*. Anything was possible, it seemed, for the right price. These gunslingers weren't as virtuous as they claimed.

Surprise, surprise.

Right after Mick, Kort, and Thorne finished arguing over what job they wanted next—they decided on *passenger convoy protection*, thank the Pentus—the door to the civil manager's office flew open. A man in a rumpled suit stormed out. Meesh recognized him as Rupert Patch, a physician who used to work out of Kate's Tavern down the street. He turned away so he wouldn't be recognized, until Rupert shoved into the crowd of drunk men and disappeared. Mick grabbed Meesh by the arm.

"Charlie'll see you now," the young man said.

"Awesome."

"You're gonna do this on your own, so good luck. Kort, Thorne, and me gotta split."

"Have fun," Meesh said.

The trio gave a strange, one-finger salute and headed back through the crowd. Meesh shrugged at Rodney, and together they approached the office.

The two men guarding the door glared at them when they entered. Meesh stopped himself from blowing one of them a kiss. *Focus*, he thought. The last thing he needed was to create a mess because he did something stupid. Especially when Abe and Shade weren't around to get him out of it.

The inside of the office was completely redecorated. The walls were a garish shade of green rather than their former bland white. All but one of the maps of the settlement and the surrounding mines had been replaced by primitive-looking guns nestled onto brackets and an ugly three-striped flag—brown on the top, red in the middle, yellow on the bottom. Tall glass display cases stood in the room's corners, each holding rack after rack of ammunition.

Five men and one woman populated the office, each scowling with their hands on their weapons. The woman in particular made him nervous. With arms rippling with muscle, scarred jaw, short black hair, mismatched eyes, and twitchy fingers, she seemed the sort who would respond violently with the mildest provocation. And there was something oddly familiar about her that he couldn't place.

"Who're you and whaddaya want?" asked the man sitting at the old civil manager's desk.

Meesh blinked, unable to stop his brows from furrowing in confusion. The seated guy was fat, and even though it was hard to tell since he was sitting behind a desk, he looked *extremely* short. He had a head of coiffed blond hair and beady eyes. A prominent nose jutted over a mouth that should've belonged to someone twice his size. He wore a flamboyant red suit with bolo tie. He was the most outlandish-looking person Meesh had ever seen, and that was saying something.

The guy cleared his throat, and Meesh flinched.

"I *said*, who're you and whaddaya want?" he repeated.

"Oh, yeah," Meesh began. He glanced at Rodney, who frowned. Meesh turned his gaze back to the short fat man. "I'm Jim, this here's Rodney. And you're Charlie, right?"

"Charlie Midnight, Lord of the Gunslingers, that's me," the guy said, tugging on his lapels like a braggart. "So, Jim and Rodney, you two just come in here to ask who I was? What, you fans or something? Can't you see I got stuff to worry about 'round here? I got people getting sick, a doc who says I'm not doing enough, and more jobs than boys to do 'em. My town's falling apart!"

Meesh dug his fingernails into his palm to keep from laughing. The guy's voice was squeaky, like a mouse's. A big, fat mouse. Hilarious.

Meesh took a deep breath. "Well, um, no. Mick actually brought us up here. We were robbed outside Adavan Station, by a buncha dudes who had—"

"I don't need to hear your whole damn history. Kaiser help me, why the hell're you in my office?"

The other gunslingers scowled. Meesh did too.

"We're just looking for work," Rodney said in a tone so sincere it was flat-out disarming. "We were robbed, as my brother said, and we have nothing. We're dedicated and hard-working. We can do right by you."

Charlie Midnight raised one of his thinly-plucked eyebrows. "You know what a gun is? Can you shoot?"

"I do, and I can," Meesh said.

"Me, not so much," admitted Rodney. "I can play guitar though."

"Hm." Charlie rocked back in his chair, rapping his knuckles on his desk. "Zeppo, c'mere. Let me know what you think of these men here."

A strange creature hopped up onto the desk from out of nowhere, hissing. It was roughly two feet long, with the body of a lizard, the face of an ugly-ass cat, and six insectoid legs. Its tail was segmented, ending in a rattle. Meesh fought the urge to shake his head. Why were people, especially people who fancied themselves powerful, so damn *stupid*?

"Well, Zeppo? Whaddaya say?"

The little monster spun in a circle, the sharp points of its legs tapping the desk. Its cat head hissed again, the rattle on the end of its tail shook.

"She likes you," Charlie said, patting the creature's back.

"Fantastic," grumbled Meesh.

"Does that mean you will give us work?" Rodney asked.

"Nah, not yet," Charlie said with a sneer. He rubbed at his second chin. "Just buys you two a night. I'll have Trish here test your gunmanship tomorrow." He gestured to the hard-looking woman behind him. "As for you, tallskie, we'll see if we can find you a six-string and you can give me a private show. Better be good. Before then, I'll set both y'all up with a room over at Maclemore's down the strip. Come back here first thing in the morning for your tests. Got it?"

"Sure thing," Meesh said.

"Very well," added Rodney.

Charlie pointed an accusatory finger at them. "Until then, let me tell you now that you best not get into any trouble. Mick talked to my boys outside, and he vouched for you, so that's good enough for me to give you this one night. But I don't know you. If I find you came here for *other* purposes, or if you drink too much and misbehave, then you'll have problems. Problems you won't like the solution to."

"Hear ya loud and clear, brah," Meesh told him.

"Good. Now get the hell outta my office. Trish, you take them. Tell Bobby the night's on me. He'll be reimbursed."

"Will do, Charlie," the rigid woman said with all the warmth of a block of ice. She stepped out from behind the desk and jutted her head at the door.

Meesh gave the Lord of the Gunslingers the same one-finger salute that Mick had given him, which got the guy chuckling. Zeppo the little monster clacked its insect legs together. Meesh eyed it warily before grabbing Rodney's forearm and turning to follow Trish out.

Charlie cleared his throat, stopping them after only a few steps.

"One more thing," the man squeaked. "If you *do* decide to go out on the town tonight, to explore or something like that, stay away from the new development in the southwest corner."

"Why?"

"So many questions! Because you're not a resident here, dumbass, and you obviously got no money. You fall ill, that's on you. You'll end up rotting in the gutter, and no one'll know you're gone."

"Sounds pleasant," Meesh mumbled under his breath. Rodney simply raised his eyebrows.

Unlike during their trek into the Saloon, they didn't have to elbow their way through the raucous partiers crowding the main floor. With Trish leading the way, the throng simply parted, as if she projected a magical force field. Everyone appeared afraid of her, which made Meesh *very* interested. In the gunslingers' male-dominated culture, he imagined Trish had accomplished something stupendous for her to be not just included in their ranks, but in their leader's inner circle.

Meesh couldn't decide if he was curious enough to risk being gutted to find out what.

Once outside, they descended the stairs and took a left. Meesh knew exactly where they were headed. Maclemore's was an inn at the end of Tansaray's main street, a place where the locals gathered to gamble and drink and try to get lucky. A pinch of fear worked its way up his spine. Given the nature of the people who now ran this place, and how many there were, if someone in Maclemore's recognized him...

Those thoughts fled him when realized he'd fallen behind Rodney and Trish. The two of them walked alongside each other up ahead, speaking in hushed tones. He swore as he hurried to catch up. Even walking in the middle of the street, people tended to stay as far away from Trish as possible.

"Yeah, it ain't been easy," Trish was saying by the time he came within earshot. Her voice was even and conversational away from the Saloon. "It's a patriarchal society they got here. And most of 'em ain't even from Tansaray! Charlie bought off some o' the dregs from the mining district when he first got here, then sent 'em out recruiting. Most the guys who came back are 'reformed' bandits from the badlands and a whole lotta young, downtrodden kids from other settlements who were close to turning to a bad life anyway. I'll give Charlie credit—he can turn 'em around pretty quick. Give 'em guns, a purpose, and a sense of belonging, and folks'll do almost anything for you."

"What about you?" Rodney asked. "How did *you* get involved?"

Trish glanced over her shoulder to see Meesh trailing behind them, and gave him a weird look. She leaned close to Rodney and said, "Sneakily, that's how. I used to work for the local magistrate, but he was one of the first ones Charlie deposed. Had him thrown right outta town. They were gonna throw me out too, but I convinced the bastards not to do it."

Meesh cringed. Of *course* the girl looked familiar. Trish Hartley. Or Harleen. He couldn't remember. The tall, pretty girl who used to be Belial Monroe's secretary. The one who Meesh had tried to seduce, but wouldn't give him the time of day. With the scars on her jaw and her hair cut short, he hadn't recognized her. He only hoped that *she* didn't recognize *him*.

"How did you convince them?" Rodney asked up ahead.

The woman's neck went taut. "The same way anyone convinces them. Through challenge. I told Charlie I could beat anyone in his employ, be it a duel or hand-to-hand combat. He said sure, 'cause of course he did. So I snuck into the courthouse—sorry, *the Saloon*—the night before the challenge, since that's where they were all staying at the time. I exchanged all their bullets with duds and poisoned their water vat with jimson oil." She let out a humorless chuckle. "They didn't know that my ma was an apothecary, and my da operated one o' the mines that produces saltpeter up on the mountain. He learned a lot from those lowlifes down in Ramstable. And he taught me *everything*."

Meesh shook his head. If Mara Choon heard this woman calling her people lowlifes, she would've gutted her, no matter how terrifying she seemed. And she would've been in the right. What was *wrong* with people? First Gilly talking about Abe and Shade, and now Trish. Was this tendency to lump those who didn't look like you into hateful boxes a new trend, or something that had always been there and he simply hadn't noticed? Had he done the same in the past without realizing it?

"What happened in the fight?" Rodney asked, drawing Meesh out of his mood.

"Went as you'd expect. I won the first three duels, since none o' their shots ever made it past their barrels. When Charlie put an end to that, I beat the living hell out of a bunch more. That part was tough, even though they were drugged and couldn't stand up straight. It's how I got this." She gestured at her ruined chin. "But I won. Killed four of the bastards that day before Charlie called it. He gave me an important position."

"Does he know you cheated?"

She shrugged. "Dunno. Probably. I think he'd be more impressed that I did."

"I see." Rodney bent his head. "Will you try to do him in now? As revenge for throwing your boss out of town?"

"Why would I do that?" Trish said, aghast. "I have a good deal here. I'm important for once. I wouldn't change that for the world."

Enterprising girl, Meesh thought.

They finally arrived at Maclemore's. The place was half-full, and Meesh noticed that a quarter of the people lingering outside wore those bloody scarves. Not good. Trish led them in, obtained a room key from the proprietor, and then brought them up the stairs and down the hall. She opened the door to their room, and Meesh tried to obscure his face with his hair when he walked past.

He expected her to leave—*hoped* she'd leave—after seeing them settled, but Trish entered the room after them and shut the door. She leaned against the wall, crossed her arms over her chest, and glared at Meesh.

"Um, whassup?" he asked.

"I'm not an idiot, you know," she said.

"What are you speaking of?" asked Rodney.

"Him," she said, pointing at Meesh. "I know him. He's Meshach of the Knights Eternal. He tried to get in my pants once. You think I'd *forget* that?"

"Er, no, 'course not." Meesh winced. "Just hoping."

"Why're you here?" she asked accusingly.

"Can't tell you."

"You here to kill Charlie?"

"No!" both Meesh and Rodney said in unison.

"Good. Good." She uncrossed her arms, shoved her hands in her pockets. "You promise?"

"Yeah, we promise," Meesh told her. "We just gotta get some info from your boss, then we're outta here."

"Why aren't you armed? Where're your guns? Your swords?"

Rodney gave him a questioning look. Meesh sighed.

"Subterfuge. Didn't wanna walk in here armed, not after hearing what this, um, culture was all about. Figured we could blend in, earn little fat Charlie's trust, and get what we needed outta him."

"You figured you could just waltz into this settlement, a place you and your brothers saved from a savage band of outlaws and a hellbeast only two years ago, and not be recognized?"

Meesh shrugged. "Okay, so there's a flaw in my plan. Shoot me. Actually, on second thought, please don't."

"I wish." She shook her head. "What you wanna know from Charlie?"

"None of your business."

"Where're your brothers?"

"That's not your business either."

Trish's jaw clenched and so did Meesh's. Rodney broke the tension when he stepped between them like a really tall little boy and asked, "You aren't going to turn us in, are you? It would be quite disappointing to ride all this way in the back of a cart only to be gunned down on our first day."

"No, I ain't tattling on you," she said. Her shoulders slumped. "I just... I need your help."

Meesh let out a blast of laughter. "Do tell."

"People are sick here," she said.

"No shit."

The glare she shot him could peel paint off walls. "The point *is*, I don't think this is natural. We had no illnesses here before a month ago. It started slow, a few people here and there. Now all the outlying neighborhoods are overwhelmed with it. We're losing five or six people a night. But *only* five or six. It's like a gradual march toward oblivion out there. It stays in one district for three days, then moves onto the next. It was actually less terrifying when the hacking sickness swept through when I was little. And that one killed six hundred people in a single week!"

"What do you want me to do about it?" Meesh asked.

"Help us! There's odd shit happening. I hear reports of people seeing a weird... thing... slithering around at night. They say it's made outta shadows. It's always sighted in the areas where people die. I told Charlie to look into it, but he won't. He says it's a mass hallucination. He's not from around here. He's from some kingdom on the other side of the world, he says. He don't believe stories about demons crawling out the abyss. He thinks it's some storm we gotta weather, even if people die. No one'll convince him otherwise."

"Even if he keeps one as a pet?" Meesh asked.

"Even then. He thinks Zeppo's a mutant created by exposure to something he calls radiation."

Interesting, Meesh thought. He exchanged a knowing glance with Rodney before turning back to her. "That what he and Rupert were arguing about? The sickness?"

Trish nodded slowly.

"Fine," Meesh groaned. "I'll help."

"Yes, *we* will," said Rodney.

Trish's eyes lit up. "You know what this thing is?"

"I have a theory," Meesh said. "But it's just a theory. It'll stay between Rodney and me for now. Don't want you getting excited and blurting stuff to morons who won't know what the hell you're talking about."

"But—"

"No buts, Trish," he snapped. "You want our help or not?"

"Of course!"

"Then make sure there're no gunslingers around the hotel tonight. You said the deaths are all happening in the outlying neighborhoods. Those're all the newer constructions, right?"

"Right. And the deaths have been happening at the newest one to the southwest. The area Charlie told you to stay away from."

"Okay then. We'll start there tonight. If there're patrols, see if you can do your herbalist magic with 'em. Rod and me can do our jobs, but not if we got a buncha trigger-happy assholes shooting at us."

"I'll see what I can do," she said with a nod.

"Good." He clasped his hands behind his back, tapped his foot, and stared at her.

"What?" Trish said.

"We done now? You wanted our help. We agreed. Now let my brother and me figure out how we're gonna pull this off in private, please."

Her head cocked to the side. "Your brother? I thought—"

"I said it's none of your business. Get. Out. Trish."

"Screw you," she muttered. She spun toward the door, but paused after opening it. "You better help, Meshach. Or else."

The door slammed.

"Empty promises!" Meesh shouted at her retreating footsteps. He flopped onto one of the room's uncomfortable beds.

Rodney lowered himself onto the bed opposite him. He looked awkward, his hands dangling between those long legs of his. His expression was somber but reflective.

"A gloam?" he asked softly.

Meesh made popping sounds with his lips. "Yup. I mean, I never ran up against one, but Abe told me stories, and this seems *really* similar." He gave his new brother a smirk. "You know gloams're rare, right?"

"Yes. Among the rarest demons, spawned in the Fifth Hell, Alghadab. There have only been six sightings in recorded history. None in twenty-four years. Their mere presence spreads illness throughout a community, and it feeds on the despair it leaves behind."

"And how're they killed?"

Rodney jabbed at his chest with his fist. "Bone dagger, through the heart. Which is going to be difficult."

"Why's that?"

"Because gloams have the innate ability to become incorporeal."

"Awesome. Good job."

What he *didn't* tell Rodney was that this was all new information for him. Sure, Abe had talked about the gloam he'd faced in his youth, but that story had been more about the horrible conditions the thing caused in Pennonstaff and less about how to actually kill it. Good thing Rodney was such a quick study.

"Meesh?" Rodney asked.

"Yeah?"

"Are we at risk of getting sick?"

"Nah. At least I don't think so. We knights have a higher constitution than most."

"Oh. Good." His head tilted to the other side. "Do we even *have* a bone dagger?"

"Nope."

"And this doesn't worry you?"

"Brah, six people a day have been dying here for a month." Meesh swung his legs around and sat up on the bed. "I'm pretty sure we can make ourselves one very easily."

Rodney grimaced and stared down at his hands.

"Don't worry, Rod. I'll do it."

"Okay, excellent."

"But tell me something."

His eyes lifted expectantly. "What?"

"Gloams are extremely rare. And there haven't been any registered fissures near Tansaray since we closed the last one. Where do you think *this* gloam came from, if that's what it is?"

"Well…" Rodney put a finger to the cleft in his chin. After a few seconds of silence, he snapped and grinned. "That would likely be the unfortunate side effect of the man in charge of this place keeping a mig as a pet."

"Why would that be?"

"Because while migs are generally harmless demons, being that they are from the Giving Hell of Alms Ceaseless, they bring bad luck to all who take them in. Which is, unfortunately, a far too common occurrence in the Wasteland. Not many pets about."

"Exactly," said Meesh. "And this time, bad luck arrived in the form of a goddamn gloam showing up outta nowhere. Stupid little migs. Why can't people just kill those ugly bastards on sight?"

Rodney shrugged. "I felt it was adorable. In an off-kilter, chimeric way."

"Have I told you you're a strange one, Rod?"

"Often," his brother said, grinning.

"Great." Meesh slapped the bed and laid back down. "Now, I need you to do me a favor."

"What would that be?"

"Go downstairs and scrounge up some grub. Trish was right that people might recognize me here, and I'm starving. We'll eat and get some rest. Because we're both gonna need to be fed and awake if we're gonna kill ourselves a demon tonight."

And for the women, accept of all who wish to give you their essence,
love the entire world freely, for you know not the pain
you may heap upon the spurned.
—Book of the Pentus, Havacana 53:3

T he first day of the Righteous returning to Darkenwood drew to
a close, and Indigo bristled with nervous energy. She whirled
through Hickweis Tavern, making sure her charges were doing
as they were told and trying her best to put out any potential fires
before they were lit.

The apartments upstairs were empty, and only a pair of guests
remained in the tavern—not surprising, given the brilliance of the
sunset, the perfect weather outside, and the fact that only eighteen
Righteous guests had arrived that morning. The two who lingered
were very young, a man and a woman visiting the valley for the
first time. They sipped their brews and conversed, acknowledging
Macaro only when their cups ran dry. They did not cause problems
nor indulge in one of the many fantasies Darkenwood offered. Even
when Vivo and Bluebell approached to offer their services, as they
were compelled to do, the couple politely declined. It was as if the two
existed in their own little world that no one else could penetrate.

Indigo paused in the middle of wiping off a table to watch them.
Some guests who were virgins to this place arrived in the same way

the departed Peter Ortiz had—full of aggression and seeking a release for their malicious impulses. Another longtime guest, herself with a cruel streak a mile long, had once told Indigo that this was how the Righteous kept the middle classes in line. If they were allowed the opportunity to play out their fantasies without fear of repercussion, they could purge those yearnings from their systems and return to society as relaxed and dutiful cogs in the machine.

Others, like the two at the bar and Anthony Bell before them, were more drawn in by the freedom from responsibility that the valley represented. If the Ersatz were lucky, these guests never came back. Because when Righteous such as these made a habit of returning, they inevitably turned toward obsession. Their niceties became laced with jealous violence and disdain, making them the cruelest of all. Jasper and Kirsten Popp were testaments to that.

Indigo took a deep breath. She did not need to be mulling over the gloominess of her existence, not when the Ersatz were only a few days away from possible emancipation. And *especially* not when the celebration she had been planning was about to begin.

A smile crept up on her.

Galas were a regular occurrence in the valley. There was the Festival of the Pregnant Moon, the Autumnal Bonfire, the Dance of Fertility (for the Righteous of course, as the Ersatz did not reproduce), and any celebration that the guests demanded, be they naming days or wedding anniversaries. What would take place tonight, however, was far different from any that had come before. These festivities were not preordained by the overgod, nor brought upon by their guests. Tonight, the Ersatz would be celebrating for themselves. Tonight, they would try to ease the tension of the one who would become Aumor Reborn.

Because while her people indeed needed the release, Shade needed it more. He was the one putting his life on the line.

She touched her chest when she thought of him, the stranger who had allowed them to experience true hope for the first time. The three days previous had been bliss beyond compare because of him. She and Shade had spoken for hours each day, oftentimes sitting by the fire at night until the crimson fingers of dawn stretched over the mountains. Indigo recounted for him her every ascension, how it felt to live in the countless bodies she had inhabited, how she longed for the tranquility that came with the prospect of closing her eyes upon death and not fearing them opening again. She told him of the gaping wounds left by her constant mistreatment, and how those wounds paled in comparison to the helplessness she felt knowing she could do nothing to heal the pain of those she loved. She desired freedom, to be able to throw her head back and shout to the overgod Rawg that he was wrong, that the Ersatz deserved their sovereignty, to finally live their lives as they so choose.

In turn, Shade had opened to her about his own history, his doubts and fears and his bubbling rage. She had listened raptly when he told of the adventures he and his brothers had embarked on, felt terror at the possibility of horrific beasts that wanted nothing more than to lay waste to the land. She laughed at how exasperated he looked when talking about trying to keep his pale brother Meesh in line, cried alongside him when he spoke of the death of the only woman he ever loved. Indigo could feel the depts of his doubt in the religion he had been created to serve, and understood the anger that had led to him breaking his vows and fleeing in search of answers.

"I think *you* are the answer I was looking for," he had told her just last night.

Those words had not left her since.

A lumpy, humanoid form with sallow gray flesh and six tentacle arms emerged from the corridor on the other side of the tavern, remaining in the shadows by the stairs. Mita the cook dipped his squid-like face toward Indigo, then disappeared back into the kitchen.

The food was done.

The celebration could begin.

Indigo swept up to the couple at the bar with a flourish. She placed a hand on each of their backs and leaned her head between them. Their conversation ceased. The woman bit her lip timidly, while the young man gave Indigo a steely-eyed glare that he could not hold. Indigo tickled the backs of their necks with her fingertips and gave each a kiss on the cheek. The man recoiled; the woman seemed to melt into it.

"I must ask you to join us outside," Indigo said. "The festivities are about to start."

"What if we wanna stay in here?" the man asked.

Indigo shot Macaro a glance. The dwarf wiped sweat from his darkened brow and hefted a case of libations to carry onto the porch. Dura, a boisterous soul who had been cursed with the wide, squat body of a hill troll during her latest ascension, squeezed behind the bar to do her part.

"*Everything* is moving outside," Indigo told the couple. "It would not be the Festival of the Blinking God if we did not see the last sliver of eye before it disappeared.

She backed away from them. The man grumbled under his breath and the woman tried to assure him in her naively squeaking voice that this might be fun.

"You always said you wanted to experience the traditions of other cultures," she said. "Well, this Blinking God event is obviously important. We should join in." To which the man shrugged. They both stood from their stools and meandered toward the exit, arm in arm.

Indigo laughed inwardly. Yes, the Festival of the Blinking God was important, but considering she had invented it yesterday morning, time-honored it was not. If she had her way, she might have called it "The Celebration of Perhaps No Longer Being Your Playthings." But alas, the last thing the Ersatz needed was to inform the Righteous that the valley might no longer be theirs. So, the Festival of the Blinking God had to be.

Darkness had descended by the time she stepped onto the terrace. A bonfire raged in the courtyard pit, and the pavilion was packed. The Ersatz outnumbered the Righteous twenty to one. Jubilance filled the air; not a shred of malice could be felt. There was dancing, with Briar sitting on a stool outside the pavilion and strumming her citole, while Mana, her injuries from the other day completely healed, sang alongside her. Indigo felt a moment of disappointment. She had hoped that Shade would join in, as she loved seeing him smile, and he never smiled more than when he was creating music. But the stool that had been set up for him was empty. His guitar case rested against it, untouched.

She stepped up to the railing and stood on tiptoes, her head on a swivel. There was no trace of his silly hat. Shade was nowhere to be found.

Concerned, she descended into the courtyard and made a show of smiling and greeting all who approached her. She spotted the young Righteous couple from the tavern, standing on their own in the middle of the courtyard, dancing closely. Vivo sat on the grass with Pipi, Vivo poking fun at the way the newly-female Ersatz had chosen to dress in mismatching lavender breeches overlaid with a patchwork skirt. Then there was Bluebell, holding court with a trio of Righteous men by the bonfire, flipping that wily red hair of hers as she played each of the men off one another. Meanwhile, Aqua and Aspar huddled by themselves just beyond the celebration, both their gazes aimed at the sky as if appreciating the beauty of the rising slivered moon for the first time.

But still no Shade.

Indigo entered the pavilion, where Macaro worked tirelessly behind the temporary bar. Orchid stood atop it, her tiny legs a blur as she dashed across the lacquered surface, distributing drinks. Shade was not in here either. Suddenly fearful, Indigo spun, colliding with a Righteous man in the process.

"Oh! I'm sorry!" the man said. He was another first-time visitor to Darkenwood. His hair was long, straight, and black, and he possessed teardrop eyes similar to her own. He looked very young, as did the striking woman with light brown skin and a head of long curly hair who held his arm.

"No, it is I who am sorry," Indigo said with a bow. "I was careless. Please forgive me."

"Um, you really have nothing to be sorry about," the woman said.

"Thank you. You are too kind."

Indigo took a moment to examine them. She recognized these two from the registration paperwork they submitted that morning upon arrival: Nathan and Sophie, a pair of successful artisans looking to expand their pottery trade by building connections in Darkenwood. But there was something off about them from the start. Perhaps it was the way Sophie looked at Nathan with a seemingly bottomless well of disappointment. Or how Nathan had seemed far more interested in touring the valley than partaking in its amenities.

"Great party," Nathan said.

"Thank you. We do our best to please the overgod."

"I'm sure you do," said Sophie, giving her partner another disapproving glare while she fiddled with the dazzling sapphire pendant strung around her neck.

"I apologize again. I was just leaving," Indigo told them.

Nathan grabbed her arm before she could exit the pavilion, and she froze.

"Looking for someone?" he asked. "You look like you're looking for someone."

"I do not wish to bother you with my problems," Indigo said, trying to rush this along. "If you will excuse me—"

"It's the black guy with the hat, isn't it?" Sophie cut in. "I saw you hanging with him earlier."

Indigo gulped down her burgeoning fear. "Yes. That is him."

"Why didn't you just say so!" laughed Nathan. "I saw him not even ten minutes ago. He was heading thataway." He pointed at the thin line of trees bordering the lake. "Interesting guy. What part of Pirie's he from?"

"I... do not know," Indigo said. Her throat ran dry.

"Aw, that sucks. I'll have to find out later." The man finally let go of her. "Anyway, good luck finding him. And again, great party."

Indigo offered them another bow and hustled out of the pavilion as quickly as she could. She felt eyes watching her the whole time. When she rounded the bonfire, she started running.

Sure enough, she found Shade squatting on the banks of Winninger Lake, rolling a flat stone in his hand. His eyes were fixed on the rippling water that sparkled beneath the starlight. When she reached his side, he looked up at her. His expression seemed torn.

"What are you doing out here?" she asked.

"Thinking," Shade said. He gestured to the lake. "I swear I hear something out here. Like... music."

"That would be Wisteria," Indigo told him. "She is always singing. She used to perform in the courtyard, before she chose never to surface again."

She frowned at the thought. Oh, how she missed her friend.

"Wisteria. She's one of the originals like you, right? The one who got turned into a fish-person?"

"The same, though she would prefer you call her a triton."

"Go it." He fiddled with the stone in his hand and frowned. "Did I worry you?"

Indigo pinched her thumb and forefinger together. "Slightly."

"Sorry."

He laughed, folded his duster beneath him, and sat down on the damp soil, his booted feet dangling close to the edge of the water. Indigo slipped down beside him and placed her hand atop his.

"What is bothering you?"

"Nothing. Everything." Shade pulled back his free arm and launched the flat stone into the lake. It skipped the water four times before it plinked beneath the surface. "I just...you told me what to expect when your guests showed up today. I thought I could handle it, but one of them started harassing one of the orc guys. What's his name—the one who was setting up the extension for the pavilion?"

"That would be Fol."

"Right. Fol. So this scrawny bastard goes up to him, starts calling him names. Taunting him. Taking away the stakes when he tried to lock in the supports. Then he started hitting him with a stick, daring him to fight back. Which he didn't. I mean, I talked to Fol last night. He's soft spoken and timid, kind to a fault. He just *looks* scary. Knowing what I know now, that he's powerless to defend himself, I just...I had to walk away before I did something rash."

"I understand," Indigo said, squeezing his hand.

"I know you do." He took off his hat, leaned his head on her shoulder. "It's just...man, I can't imagine going through life like this.

And the only thing I saw was a little bullying. I can't imagine how I might've reacted had someone tried to take advantage of Mana, or Pipi, or Bluebell, or picked a fight with Aqua, that big romantic ox."

The fate of Peter Ortiz entered her thoughts. "You likely would have killed them."

"Yeah. Probably. And then who knows what would've happened?" He gestured to the slivered moon. "I still got another two days to put up with it until I can do anything that'll, well, *fix* it. It's maddening."

Indigo pressed closer to his body. Feeling the heat coming off him made everything seem better.

"I do not think you have much to worry about. This group of Righteous seems very peculiar."

"In what way?"

"In the way that they are all neophytes. This is the first visit to Darkenwood for all eighteen of them, which has not occurred in many, many years. Other than the man you mentioned, they seem unusually calm and serene. None have requested to experience either the Path of the Hero or the Path of the Rogue. I have horseback riding lessons and some weapons training on the ledger, and even a few nature hikes, but nothing barbaric in any way. In fact, none of them have seemed particularly interested in taking advantage of our courtesans. They seem to enjoy the attention they are given, and I have seen a few allow their hands to roam, but none have put in a request for intimacy as of yet. Nor decided to take it by force."

"And that's unusual?"

She shrugged, enjoying the sound of his leather coat crinkling against her. "Yes and no. It is actually not that uncommon for newcomers to take their time before fully taking advantage of our... conveniences. They should remain that way until you leave." She sucked in her bottom lip. "By the time you complete your journey and return, however, that will likely not remain true."

"I wouldn't be so sure about that," Shade chuckled. "Because if I come back here, it means I've passed this Aumor test, which means you'll all be free."

Indigo chewed on those words, feeling jittery all over. She wanted to tell Shade how much she appreciated his willingness to undertake this perilous excursion for her sake, for *their* sakes, but she could not think of what to say. Instead she buried her face in the nape of his neck and breathed in the earthy scent of him. She could only hope that Shade felt the same comfort in the act as she did.

"I could stay here all night," he whispered.

"So could I," she murmured into his skin. "However, there is a celebration going on right now that we might wish to attend."

They meandered back toward the Hickweis Tavern courtyard, strolling hand-in-hand until they came within view of the revelers. Indigo took the lead, trying to appear the dutiful host reigning in a stray guest.

For the next hour, she did her best to enjoy being in the company of her people. The party remained jovial, even when the Righteous among them became all the more drunk. Shade dawdled close to her the whole time, but took pains to not be at her side. He smiled when the Ersatz approached him to offer their veiled thanks. He ate heartily when the servers poured out of the tavern, carrying the meal for the evening, and he even put on a friendly face when the guests spoke with him.

He was the center of attention, and none of the Righteous seemed to realize it.

The dancing kicked up a notch, with a circle forming around the bonfire, Vivo and Mana at the forefront as usual. Many of the Righteous joined in on the fun, and those that did not seemed content to watch, clapping and stomping their feet while the dancers circled the blaze. Even the many inhuman Ersatz joined in, and Indigo found it surprising that their appearance in the middle of the party caused no hitch in the proceedings whatsoever.

Indigo settled herself onto a raised platform on the outskirts, always aware, her belly a mess of nerves. She watched Shade as he shifted from one dance partner to the next, guffawed when Aspar twirled him in a clumsy spin, and felt a prickle of jealousy when Bluebell ground against him before passing him along. That innocent, little-boy smile returned to his face for the first time since that first night of revelry, and she drank in every moment that she could.

Mana took Shade by the hand, her usually sad eyes opened wide and gleaming when she led him in a feverish twirl. Shade threw his head back and laughed, only for the music to suddenly stop, bringing a halt to the merriment. Everyone looked around in confusion, until Briar appeared in the middle of the circle. She extended a red hand to Shade, showing her sharp-toothed grin. He gave her a bow and took the offered hand. The demonite brought him out of the circle, sat him down in the chair that had been set up for him. Macaro ceased his bartending duties long enough to hop out of the pavilion, snap open the guitar case, and hand the instrument to its owner. Shade wrinkled his nose at the short man, who cackled and disappeared back inside. The man who would be Aumor then leaned over, whispered a few words to Briar, and held up a finger to Mana, who had retaken her seat on the other side. They both smiled. Shade counted to three and a new song began.

The cheers this time were deafening.

The music washed over Indigo, bubbled out of her, made her want to cry. Mana overwhelmed her with the sincerity in her voice. When Shade began singing alongside her, releasing all his pain and doubt through words that slipped easily from his throat, Indigo was ready to break apart completely.

Her thoughts returned to something Shade had said to her as they sat beside Winninger Lake. *If I come back here.*

If. Such a simple word, but the either/or truth of it filled her with dread.

There was no promise that Shade would be successful in his journey. There was a strong possibility that he would die either to the dangers on the Path or the Avatar of Rawg. If any of that were to happen, Shade would be gone from her life forever. She would never feel his closeness again. Never hear him laugh. Never get to know the extent to which he could make her truly *feel*.

She clasped her hands, expectancy churning. Her breaths came quickly, urgently. As the song Shade and Briar were playing reached its crescendo, so did she. Her lips parted, and she found herself shaking. Her knees trembled. Delicious images rushed through her mind, her heart racing. She stared at Shade from across the circle of carousers, and the finality of everything that was and could be slammed her right in the gut.

Hope. Love. Intimacy. Release. A moment of absolute perfection. It was all there for the taking, if she would only reach for it.

Her heart in her throat, she hopped off the platform and dashed recklessly through the crowd. She pushed and shoved, eyes wild with desire and the fear that it would never be realized. When she finally breached open air, she stopped short, hopping in place like a bull about to charge while the musicians finished their current song.

The last note was strummed, and Indigo burst into motion. She crossed the twenty-foot distance between herself and Shade in two strides and grabbed his wrist. His head whipped toward her, eyes wide with surprise.

"Come with me," she said, and hurried in the other direction without waiting for his reply. He yelped, his guitar falling to the ground and *twang*, but she kept a tight grip on him and dragged him along. In her unrestrained, single-minded fervor, she barely registered that the entire crowd applauded her as she ran.

Up the stairs and into Hickweis Tavern she dashed, Shade panting behind her. They climbed the three stories to her apartment so quickly that she had no memory of doing so. Once inside, she pushed Shade against the wall, barreled into him, knocked off his hat, and buried her mouth onto his.

The kiss was ragged and aggressive and graceless, but Indigo could not stop. She writhed against the hardness of his body, nipping at his lips, getting the tiny curls of his beard stuck in her teeth. His hands fell to her hips, but he did not grab her, nor match her ferocity. In frustration she cried out and pressed herself harder against him. She grabbed his crotch roughly over his breeches.

"Wait." Shade broke from her long enough to speak. She devoured his mouth with hers again, prompting him to shove her away. "Indigo, *stop!*"

He held her at arm's reach, his face was flushed, sweat dripping down his forehead. Indigo remembered him showering in her bathroom the morning after she first saw him, the way she had imagined how the water looked cascading over his chest. She wanted that now. A grumble vibrated her throat, and she tried to attack him again. Shade held firm.

"*Wait!*"

The indecision in his eyes quelled her ferocious passion, and guilt rolled her over. He did not desire her the way she did him. He was repulsed by her past. The things she had done and the people she had been repelled him. It all swirled together in her mind, made her pull away and tug at her hair, which had fallen out of its neat bun in her zeal. The steeliness of her inner survivor took over, driving back the pathetic tears that were ready to fall.

This is a man. To peel back the surface is to invite disappointment.

"Indigo..."

He placed a gentle hand on her back. She wanted to veer away from his touch, but the idiotic hope that had been such a new presence in her life kept her rooted in place. She peered at the outline of him over her shoulder.

"I'm sorry," he said.

"For what?"

"For not being able to meet you where you are." He slumped against the wall she had been pushing him against. "You gotta understand. It's not that I don't want you. I *do*. It's one of the only things I've thought about since the moment I saw you. But...but I'm afraid I don't know how. I'm afraid it wouldn't be *right*."

She faced him again, but kept a respectful distance. "Why would that be?"

"As I've told you, I've only been with one woman in my life," he said. "Vera. We were together twice in an intimate way. And I loved her completely. I don't know if being with *you* in that way would be a disrespect to the both of you. Her, for moving on. You, for, well, *using* you. And besides, given all you've been through, I'm not sure if it would be...taking advantage."

Indigo laughed. She couldn't help it; laughter just tore out of her, peel after peel, until she bent over at the waist with tears raining onto the floorboards.

"What's so funny?"

"You are," she said. "Here I was, thinking that you were appalled by the things I have been."

He put a hand on his chest, aghast. "Never."

"That is one answer. The second is…do you desire me, truly?"

"Of course."

"And I, you. It is fine to question your own motivations. If you truly feel that being with me in a certain way would be an insult to Vera, then I will respect that and move on. However, you cannot use fear of my own damaged nature as a reason to deny yourself. For that would be denying me, as well, showing a lack of respect for my ability to choose my own path. It is *I* who brought *you* here, Shade. I am strong. I have had to be to survive all these decades with my sanity intact. I have lived a life without the ability to make decisions for myself. Now, I have that chance. And with that chance, I choose *you*."

"I see." He scuffed his boots against the floor. "And my inexperience doesn't matter?"

Indigo smiled. "I have experience enough for the both of us."

This time, when Indigo grabbed his hand, she waited for him to comply. Her excitement percolated once again when she led him into the bedroom. She positioned him in front of the bed, and he stood still, waiting, expectant. He was nervous, she could tell, and without her prior desperation she was able to take it slowly. She slid his duster off his shoulders and tossed it aside. Undid the buttons on his shirt, lingering on each one, even taking a moment to spread his shirt apart and give his chest a tiny, harmless nibble. His breath shortened; his body shook. It was exhilarating.

When his shirt was finally off, she undid his breeches and slid them down his legs, again slowly. She touched his hardness lightly, teasing around it without being too forceful. Shade let out short bursts of breath, his buttocks clamping. In seeing his reaction, Indigo felt her own juices flow. She knew exactly what he was feeling; she had been there, been *him*. And that knowledge lent itself to sexual empathy that allowed her to match his every point of pleasure within herself and then amplify it for them both.

"Hold on," Shade breathed when she wrapped her fist around him.

"Why?" she asked.

"This isn't fair. This can't be a one-way street."

The mere suggestion of such balance made her all the slicker.

Shade took her hands and guided her up to standing. Tenderly, deliberately, without an ounce of force. He circled around the back of her and went about unhooking the straps of her fancy dress. Even though she could feel his fingers tremble, he went about his duties efficiently, without wasted motion. If he was so proficient with all aspects of himself...

Before she could finish that thought, he spun her around. His mouth found hers, and this time when they kissed, it was in a pattern of tender to voracious and then back again that made her knees tremble. Shade moved to her neck, to her breasts, to her nipples. His beard tickled every inch of her. She could not suppress her shudders.

With her ache reaching its breaking point, she grabbed him around the waist and pulled him backward onto the bed. They writhed against each other's sweat-slicked forms. She flipped him onto his back and placed tiny kisses all the way down his body, making him expel short, stuttering gasps that only drove her passion further. She teased his manhood with her lips, her tongue, her fingers, working him up and down and over again, bringing him nearly to the point of screaming.

When it was his turn, he was delicate but eager, decisive but keen on guidance. Indigo told him what to do, sometimes with words, sometimes with a shift of the hips or a gentle nudge with her hands. He was a capable student. Before long she was arching her back and clutching the sheets. She glanced down her body, saw his head bobbing between her legs, his short-cropped black hair glistening with her own juices, and that sight alone was enough to heighten her thirst tenfold. This time she actually *did* scream, her hips rising off the bed, dragging his head along with them.

He jerked up, concern painting his wet face. "You okay?" he asked. "Did I hurt you?"

Indigo felt her eyes nearly bulge from her head. She shot up to sitting, grabbed him beneath the armpits, and pulled him on top of her. There was no instruction this time, no words needed. She drove her hips downward, grabbed him in her fist, and showed him the way. He entered without hesitation. The mix of blissful pain and agonizing pleasure nearly tore Indigo in two.

Their lovemaking was brief, but powerful. Shade finished, his entire body gone rigid, and hers as well. They held onto one another as their muscles twitched. The vibrations running between them were enough to stretch the moment out, continue it, *heighten* it, until they both found themselves near tears.

When it was over, he collapsed to the side, somehow able to slip off her without her feeling a single second of pressure or discomfort. Indigo melted into his arms, curled into a ball, held him tightly. Shade kissed her sweat-caked forehead, nibbled the tips of her pointed ears, buried his face in her neck. She caressed those tiny hairs on his chest, trying not to be too rough, remembering her past selves and how much it hurt when those hairs were pulled to the point of ripping.

They simply lay together for a while after that. Nothing more was needed. No gestures, no questions, no meaningless words. The only thing either of them needed at that moment was each other, and the knowledge that what they had done, they had done because they wanted to.

For the first time in the life Indigo remembered, she understood contentment. And it had been her choice.

— 13 —

And should you do so, your Lord shall burden your soul
until it breaks; such is the peril of benefaction.
—Book of the Pentus; Platitudes 9:2

When dusk came, Meesh and Rodney exited Maclemore's and snuck toward the prairie outside the northeastern boundary of the city, where Rodney had learned through some investigative questioning that the townspeople were disposing of their dead in a communal pit. Meesh took the duty of climbing down into the earthen grave under the cover of darkness and digging blindly through the remains to find a body in a suitable state of decay.

Meesh held his breath. The work was disgusting, but at least he couldn't see anything. Hell, he'd been covered in the combined stinking fluids of hundreds of dead men before. Not too long ago actually. It was old hat by now.

Once he found a corpse that was properly squishy, he used his knife to hack through the rotting tendons and tore the bone free, trying his best not to think about what the donor might look like or the meaty parts he'd tossed aside while getting the job done. Rodney held the rope as Meesh climbed out of the pit when he finished.

Beneath the light of the sliver of moon overhead, Meesh inspected his find. It was a smaller-sized femur, about the length of his forearm. Probably from a short woman or an older child. His chest constricted.

Dammit, don't think of that. He laid the viscous-covered bone on a pile of rocks nearby and whacked at it with a sharp stone. The *crack* of stone striking bone echoed, making him nervous that someone lingering on the outskirts of town might hear, but the buildings in the distance remained dark and silent. When the bone finally snapped in half, the resulting ends were suitably sharp, as shattered bone tended to be, and the balls at the ends formed suitable handles. He dumped water from his canteen over both halves, cleaning them as well as he could, before tucking one into his belt and handing the second to Rodney. His brother's face, haunting in the sparse moonlight, took on the appearance of a sickened ghost when he accepted the half-femur and held it between two fingers.

"It ain't gonna bite you," Meesh whispered.

"What about diseases?" said Rodney.

"You're worried about diseases *now*? Where was that when I was crawling around in a pit of corpses?"

His brother's outline shrugged. "It wasn't me in there."

"Nice. Real friggin' nice." Meesh threw up his hands. "C'mon, you twit. We got work to do."

They snuck around the far eastern bend of Tansaray, making sure to keep a distance between them and the settlement itself. Gunslingers guarded the end of nearly all the streets, which were barricaded by six-foot high piles of sandbags. These were common deterrents against sabrewolves and other desert predators, especially in the larger townships that had no Sacred Tree to provide electric light.

Only when they'd wandered far from town, cresting a slight incline that left them mostly out of sight, did Meesh order Rodney to stop. He gazed out at the barrenness to the south, where the Wasteland and the sky above competed for which was blacker and more ominous.

"What are we doing?" Rodney murmured. "Why did we stop?"

"Getting supplies," Meesh told him. He cleared his throat and raised his voice ever so slightly. "To be honest, I really wish Tito and Ivan were here with us now."

"I do, as well," Rodney said. "You would be surprised how much of a comfort Ivan can be. He may be a machine, but he has personality, and he seems to very much appreciate my...wait, what is that noise?"

"Supplies," Meesh said with a low chuckle.

A pair of tiny objects appeared on the horizon, creating minor dust storms as they zipped along the rolling prairie. Moonlight twinkled off their shiny silver hulls. Rodney gasped. The Warhorses crossed the span in a matter of seconds, their turbines muting when they came to a halt a few feet away from where Meesh and Rodney stood.

"Hey, guys," Meesh said proudly. "You got my message."

"Of course we did," Tito answered. "So long as you do not disengage our audio recognition sensors—"

"You hear almost anything," Meesh finished. "Yeah, that's kinda the hunch I was playing. Thanks for following."

"It is our duty to protect you," said Ivan. "And, might I say, very well played, sir."

"'Course, brah. When I have a plan, it *always* goes well."

He felt Rodney rolling his eyes behind him.

They retrieved their Elderswords from the Warhorses' storage compartments, and Meesh nabbed one of his burners. He ordered the machines away for the time being, and they glided back out into the darkness. For a short time, he stared after their dusty contrails, wondering why in the world he was bothering with any of this. It would've been so easy for him and Rodney to hop on the backs of those metal steeds and disappear forever. After all, if there were no Knights Eternal, there would be no one left to hunt them down...

"Stop it," he spoke out loud.

"What?" asked Rodney.

"Nothing, brah. Let's go. We got work to do."

They headed west, toward the area Trish had identified as being the most afflicted with the illness. The guards posted at the barricades were fewer here, meaning that the industrious young woman had done what Meesh had asked. By the time they arrived on the periphery of the newly-built southwestern corner of Tansaray, there was nary a gunslinger to be found. Meesh imagined they were all either puking, passed out, or wandering around the settlement hallucinating. All three images made him laugh.

With no one in sight to stop them, the knights darted toward the pile of sandbags blocking the unfinished street. The quiet sounds of people weeping inside the complexes on either side created an aura of inevitability that dragged on his soul. He could find nothing funny about this—not when people were dying. Not when those hiding inside the group housing structure might be watching their mothers, fathers, or children die painfully.

Meesh and Rodney used old scaffolding to climb to the roof of the four-story building on their right. They each took one side of the slanted roof—Meesh the side facing the prairie, Rodney the one facing town. They hunkered down. And waited.

After more than an hour of listening to people sob and cry against the unfairness of the world, Meesh's stomach grumbled. It turned out a brief rest and a bland mystery-meat sandwich from Maclemore's pub weren't enough to power him through a whole night of doing nothing. If not for the fact that he had to shush Rodney every few minutes when his brother started humming, he might have curled up and fallen asleep right there on the roof.

Surrounded by the sounds of despair, he would've had nightmares.

The sliver of moon climbed higher in the clear night sky. It reached the point in the evening when the stars were ready to twinkle out of existence. Meesh grunted. Maybe this wasn't the right night or they had picked the wrong district to watch. Maybe they would actually need to go through Charlie's stupid gunslinger tests in the morning and then try again tomorrow. The possibility irritated him to no end.

Now he heard it—a low, sharp sound, like static from socks rubbed together. He leaned over the lip of the roof and squinted, trying to discern one dark shape from another, but all he could see were tumbleweed shapes and swaying prairie grasses. Rodney soon joined him. He'd apparently heard the noise too.

"You see anything?" Rodney whispered.

"Shush."

Down below, Meesh spied the outline of an elongated shape slinking along the side of the complex. It indeed appeared to be made of smoke, a deep blackness that blended with the shadows cast by the building. Its movements obstructed the starlight reflecting off the first-story windows, otherwise Meesh wouldn't have been able to see it. The demon was far longer than he'd imagined, at least fifteen feet from one end to the other. When the faceless head of the shadow-worm lifted, it was as thick as an ox.

Not good.

Meesh raised a finger to Rodney, then gripped the edge of the roof and silently swung to the balcony below. He tried to imagine he was swinging from the shell of the hellbeast he'd killed, but the mirage wasn't working. This wasn't something he knew how to defeat. This was something new. Something completely alien, which meant he was relying on Rodney's recently-learned knowledge to fly him straight.

I'm gonna die, ain't I?

His brother dropped onto the balcony behind him, rattling the iron supports and making far too much noise. Meesh inched toward the railing to see if they'd scared the demon off. They hadn't. It remained pressed against the building with its rounded end raised, like it was trying to become one with the stone foundation.

A sudden yell came from inside. Someone screamed, "No, my baby, no!" A subtle vibration filled the air. The gloam rose even higher against the foundation, a soft, almost indistinguishable pinkish glow lighting it up from one end to the other. It seemed to solidify. To Meesh, it resembled scales growing along the whole length of its serpentine form. The screaming from inside the complex kicked up a notch. It was horrific and desperate. He imagined a mother cradling a lifeless child. A husband trying desperately to stop the flailing of a wife stricken with seizures. A young knight plunging his blade into the face of an undead woman he knew he had been falling for, then turning that same blade on a brother he once loved more than anything.

Hopelessness, that's what he felt. And he *hated* that feeling. The concern and irritation that had been thrumming inside him turned to rage.

"Enough of this!" Meesh snatched the Eldersword from his belt, grabbed the railing, and launched himself over the side of the balcony. He plummeted three stories in a single heartbeat, landing on both feet and tucking into a roll. The Rush surged through him as the Eldersword extended to its full length, the groove running up the flat of the blade glowing a bright, hateful red.

He'd never felt so damn *angry*.

The gloam's featureless head lolled in his direction. Meesh suppressed the bellow on the tip of his tongue and charged silently. Illuminated by the glow of his Eldersword, the demon was indeed comprised entirely of a rippling smoky substance that shifted form each time it moved. Could Meesh actually hurt this thing? He leapt into the air and slashed at the gloam's neck, hoping to sever its featureless head from the rest of it.

The blade passed right through the black smoke as if nothing was there.

Hurtling out of control, Meesh collided with the building's foundation and his forehead thwacked against solid stone. Pain shot through him, head to groin, and he dropped his Eldersword. The world plunged into blackness as his legs went wobbly and he sank to his knees.

New agony tore him from his dazed state, swallowing him from shoulder to breastbone. He let out a shriek and kicked out, trying to free himself from whatever now crushed the right side of his body. His left fist collided with something hard and scaly. The massive weight lifted him, slammed him to the ground, and didn't let go. Meesh's hand lashed out, his fingers touching the vibrating hilt of the sword he'd dropped. The Rush filled him again. Light flared—verging on violet this time, signifying his growing terror—and he stabbed at whatever held him. The pressure on his breast and back immediately released, as if there'd never been anything latched onto him.

Meesh lurched to his feet, trying to put distance between himself and his attacker. When he spun around, he saw the entire fifteen-foot length of the shadow-snake coiling, preparing to strike.

It lunged. Meesh swung. The sword passed right through the demon again, the two halves of its smoke-like form splitting around him like water around a rock. He tried to spin around, but again something solid barged into him, knocking him over.

"GODDAMMIT!"

He almost tripped as he spun. His Eldersword flared purple and red when he righted himself, and he stared at the sword in disappointment. Weapon of the Elders or not, it wasn't doing any good against this demon.

Then again, it wasn't *supposed* to.

Realization struck him just before the gloam did. He yanked the broken femur from his belt with his free hand, holding it out just as the thing's shadow-body surged toward him. Again, it was like striking at air. Frustration caused his stomach to tense. How the *hell* could you kill something that wasn't even there?

Bone dagger through the heart, my ass.

A low thump came from behind him, and Meesh peeked over his shoulder. Rodney had finally made it down from the fourth floor. He huffed and puffed in the darkness beneath the lowest balcony, one hand on his chest, the other on his belt. Meesh's brother gazed at him with eyes that reflected sorrow in the scant light. He wasn't looking at Meesh, however, but at the slithering demon.

Meesh took another hack at the gloam, with his Eldersword this time. The section the sword passed through turned to thin wisps. He stood there, panting. This thing was going to be the death of him from a heart attack brought on by pure frustration. His only saving grace was that the shrieking from inside the building had stopped. *Screw this,* he thought. He tossed aside the bone shard and reached for the burner on his hip.

"Meesh," Rodney said softly.

He peered at his brother. Rodney stood there still as a statue ten feet away.

"Meesh," he repeated.

"What?" Meesh growled.

"Drop your sword."

"What?" His attention shifted between his brother and the coiling gloam. "You're goddamn mad. No!"

"Yes. Please. Just drop it. And back away. I know what to do. I think."

Meesh grudgingly did what Rodney wanted. His Eldersword disappeared into the darkly swaying grass at his feet, its light extinguished. He stepped to the side, watching the shadow of the smoky creature's head track him. Rodney had to have a plan. Didn't he?

Apparently, he did, and that plan involved crying.

Rodney broke out in heartfelt sobs that rocked his chest and brought the tall man to his knees. His cries echoed off the foundation and into the vast Wasteland beyond. Meesh twisted back toward the gloam, but the demon wasn't watching him anymore. Its full attention was on Rodney, as if Meesh had ceased to exist.

His brother dropped fully onto his back and continued his torrent of blubbering moans. The demon inched forward like a snake entranced. It slid right past Meesh, its length constricting and extending as it slid through the grass.

The gloam's smoky form circled around Rodney, until it had him fully engulfed and Meesh couldn't see him anymore. His heart started racing. Was his brother trying to kill himself? He reached into the grass in search of his Eldersword.

A slurping sound emerged, stilling his hand. He glanced up to see that the soft pink glow from earlier had returned, alighting slowly within the demon, starting from its featureless head and extending all the way to its tail. And then the thing started to solidify. Black scales emerged from the smoke, lit up by that pinkish hue. The head ceased being featureless; a snout extended and the eyes that appeared on the sides of its face were blacker than the void. It really *was* a huge demon snake. The head curled upward and its toothless mouth yawned open. The pinkish glow took the form of mist that rose from the center of its curled body, entering its mouth. That's when Meesh realized that the glow didn't come from the demon, but from the energy the demon fed upon.

From Rodney.

Panic overtook him. He plunged into the dry and brittle grass, desperately searching for his dropped sword. He gave up and ripped the revolver off his hip instead. He aimed at the creature's downturned head, ready to pump it full of silver.

The sight of Rodney's outline surging upward stilled his trigger finger. His brother plunged his upper body directly into the demon's gaping maw. The gloam apparently didn't notice at first, even as its scales bulged from the large man's body invading it. Then the demon began to struggle. Meesh holstered his burner, dropped to a knee, and finally found his Eldersword in the grass. He ran toward his brother, sword out, blazing purple.

But he was too late to do anything. The gloam let out a high-pitched whine, its scaled body spasmed, and it fell still. The head collapsed over its curled length, carrying Rodney's lower half with it. Meesh froze, fearing his brother dead, but Rodney's legs kicked and Meesh heard muffled shouts coming from within the hopefully-dead demon's bulk.

Getting as solid a grip on Rodney's thrashing feet as he could, Meesh pulled backward with all his might. Slowly, his brother emerged from the sagging maw. He came free with a *plop*, his upper body glistening in the darkness. Meesh let go of his feet, and Rodney sat up. He wiped his hair. Wetness splashed behind him.

"Damn," Rodney said.

Meesh started laughing. He couldn't help it.

Rodney struggled to his feet and stood over the dead demon. He held the second bone shard in his hand, dark fluid dripping from its tip. Meesh meandered over to him. He clapped his brother on the shoulder. Rodney winced.

"You killed it," he said. "You freaking killed it."

His brother nodded solemnly.

"How?"

"Gloams have to materialize to feed," Rodney said softly. "And they feed on despair. So, I gave it what it wanted, then jumped down its throat and stabbed its heart from the inside."

"Whoa." Meesh clapped his shoulder again. "Who knew you could trick a demon into feeding on you? Great job, brah."

"It wasn't a trick. I wasn't acting." When he turned Meesh's way, there was such sadness in his eyes that he felt like it would swallow him too. "I am *filled* with despair. I just gave it what it wanted."

Meesh's jaw snapped shut. His hand slipped off Rodney's shoulder. He pulled his brother in, wrapped his arms around him. He let Rodney cry against him. It didn't matter that he was covered with stinking demon innards. At that moment, all Meesh wanted to do was find a salve for his brother's apparently troubled soul.

And Meesh knew right then that he wouldn't be writing about this escapade in that stupid journal for Reverend Garron. In fact, he didn't think he would be telling the Reverend anything about the subject at all.

The people of Tansaray stepped as far out of the way as they could when Meesh led Rodney on a march down the middle of the street beneath the blaze of the early morning sun. Healthy or sick, salespeople, miners, gunslingers, or simply pedestrians, nobody wanted to get close to them.

Probably because they carried a fifteen-foot-long dead demon snake on their shoulders.

They traipsed right up the steps leading to the Saloon and dropped the demon on top of the base of the converted firepit. Its scales burned in the sunlight, stinking gasses belched from its toothless mouth. Meesh pinwheeled his arm, working to get circulation back into his shoulder. That stupid gloam had to weigh at least six hundred pounds. He was surprised he and Rodney were able to carry it the two miles from the southwestern district.

Should've used that wheelbarrow, he thought. But no, he'd wanted to be dramatic about it. He'd trade a sore shoulder for the spectacle of dropping that stinking pile of dead flesh onto the firepit like it was nothing.

Rodney seemed far more composed now that the sun was out. He was out of breath, but at least he wasn't the mess he had been a few hours ago. Meesh still didn't know what had brought on Rodney's proclamation of immense sorrow, and that was a-okay by him. He might be growing to love this new version of his brother, and would soothe him if need be, but he wasn't good at dealing with *feelings.*

Young men with firearms poured out of the old courthouse. They gathered on the steps, gaping at the rotting monstrosity Meesh and Rodney had just deposited atop the firepit. The gunslingers whispered among themselves, many of them whistled, some swore in disbelief. Their eyes were all on the demon; none noticed the two men who'd brought the dead thing here.

Trish exited the double doors at the top of the stairs. She stared at the scene below in disbelief. Meesh caught her gaze and brushed his hands together. Trish nodded her understanding. The cunning woman who had been a secretary only a year before cupped her hands around her mouth and bellowed, "Who is it that brought this creature to Charlie Midnight's doorstep?"

"Us!" Meesh said, eagerly waving Rodney over. They walked up the first few steps to address Trish. "Jim and Rod, your saviors from Barrendale, come to show y'all that we solved your disease issue!" He faced the throng of gunslingers below him. "If anyone else in this town can say that, please, just let me know and we can trade war stories."

The crowd grumbled. No one stepped forward.

"Didn't think so," Meesh said.

He saw Mick push to the front of the throng, his eyes bulging. "What *is* that thing?"

"That'd be the monster that brought the bleeding lung to Tansaray!" Meesh announced. He paraded back and forth on the wide step like a showman. "See, Charlie *knew* some sorta demon was lurking around here, so he sent me an' Rod out to kill it. And we did! Because all Charlie wants is to lead y'all to greatness and protect those who can't protect themselves. Right?"

"RIGHT!" the mass of gunslingers answered.

"So let's hear it for Charlie, who protects you all! Charlie! Charlie!"

"*Charlie! Charlie!*" echoed the crowd.

Meesh grinned at Rodney, who gave a tepid smile back.

The door at the top of the stairs swung open again, and this time Charlie Midnight himself stormed out. If Meesh had thought the guy looked outlandish sitting behind his desk, it was a hundred times worse when he wasn't. Charlie couldn't have been more than five feet tall. His tiny legs looked way too small to support the round frame sitting atop them, and he actually waddled when he walked. His arms were also quite short, barely reaching his oversized stomach. And the look on his face the moment he saw the commotion on his front steps, with his thick lips scrunched up and his tiny eyes opened wide like swollen raisins, was downright hilarious. If Meesh hadn't been leading the way in cheering the man's name, he would've cracked up.

"Charlie!" Meesh said one last time, pumping his fist. He then sidled over the Rodney. "Keep them going, like we discussed." Rodney gave a subtle bob of the head. Meesh squeezed his arm, slung his pack onto his shoulder. "Be right back," he said and ran up the stairs.

"What in Kaiser's name is going on?" Charlie asked once Meesh reached the top. The Lord of the Gunslingers' cheeks had gone full burgundy, and he was stuck in that in-between state where he obviously wanted to scowl and act pissed but couldn't because everyone was cheering for him and he didn't know why. Plus, that big-ass demon snake probably threw him for a loop.

"We gotta talk," Meesh told him.

"No, you need to—"

Meesh grabbed his stubby arm before Charlie could object. Thankfully, Trish understood what was going on without being told. She sashayed in front of them and continued egging on the crowd so no one could see Meesh shove their leader through the door.

There was no one in the tavern-slash-brothel when Meesh finally forced Charlie inside. He struck the guy again in the back when the little man started protesting his treatment. Charlie sprawled onto the old marble floor.

"What're you doing!" his voice squeaked. "I'll have you killed for this!"

"Nah, you won't," Meesh said, grabbing him by the collar of his fancy jacket and dragging him along. "C'mon, your office. We need to talk."

"Damn you!" the man shouted, arms and legs thrashing. "Just let me walk already! I'll go, I'll go!"

"Fine. But you better behave, brah."

Meesh let go of his coat, and Charlie Midnight wobbled on the floor like an upside-down turtle before he was able to get his feet under him. He brushed off his suit, his cheeks redder than dutifully slapped ass cheeks. "Fine, let's go," he said and waddled ahead of Meesh toward the old civil manager's office.

Once inside, Charlie climbed into the chair behind his desk. Meesh noticed his hands fiddling just out of sight, so he reached into his satchel and whipped out his revolver. Even though it wasn't necessary to draw back the hammer, he did so anyway. In situations like these, he always found the *click* more dramatic.

Charlie's eyes shot up. He froze in place.

"Yeah, I know you gotta gun under there," Meesh said. "But unless you want your brains aerated, I suggest you drop it on the ground and kick it to me."

The little man stared at him gape-mouthed. He barely seemed to move before the telltale clatter of metal bouncing off tile was heard. Charlie then slumped in his chair, beyond hysterical as he tried to kick the weapon out from under the desk with those tiny legs of his.

He finally succeeded, and a huge burner spun from beneath the fancy oaken desk. Meesh hovered over it, admiring the craftsmanship. It used a magazine, not a cylinder, and the metal was a deep shade of black.

"Nice piece," he said.

"Thanks," Charlie mumbled.

"Anyway." Meesh eased the hammer forward, stashed his revolver, picked up Charlie's pistol, and stuffed that in his belt. He made his way to the wall and leaned against it, legs and arms crossed. He kept his gaze locked on Charlie, if for no other reason than watching the guy squirm was a freaking riot.

"What?" the leader of the gunslingers said. "Why're you staring at me?"

Meesh shrugged. "Just wanted to see how someone who thinks they're a king does under pressure."

"I don't think it," he replied, a mischievous grin stretching his ugly lips. "I *know* it."

Nice tell, Meesh thought. A soft tapping sounded above him. Snatching Charlie's pistol from his belt, he kicked himself off the wall, aimed, and squeezed the trigger in a single motion. The bullet he fired ripped through the screeching cat-face of the mig that'd been crawling along the molding. The creature's body exploded, splattering chunks of fur, carapace, and viscera across the ceiling. Disgusting bits cascaded down the wall.

"Zeppo!" Charlie cried.

Meesh blew across the pistol's smoking barrel. "You're a friggin' moron, brah. That thing up there ain't no pet. It's a goddamn demon. All the shit going on in this town? The bleeding lung bullshit? It's because of that. Because those critters bring bad luck. And the bad luck it brought *you* was another demon. And this other demon brought the disease."

"I don't believe in this demon bullshit," Charlie insisted, but as he tried to put on a strong face, the way his fingers quaked while laced atop the desk revealed someone who wasn't nearly as brave as he thought himself to be.

"You better, and you should," Meesh told him. "Because if you're gonna be in charge around here, you gotta know the dangers. You ain't in Pirie no more, brah."

Charlie blinked rapidly. "Wait...what? Who the hell *are* you?"

"Name's Meshach, Knight Eternal of the Pentus. Surely you've heard of me?"

The chubby man went bone white. He stopped shivering; hell, he stopped moving altogether.

Looked like he'd heard of him.

"Cool it, Chaz, and calm down," Meesh said. "I'm not gonna hurt you. I don't think I could afford to, especially now that I riled up all your boys out there. They *love* you, y'know. You inspire 'em. Which to me makes you dangerous, since I never met any inspiring leader whose followers didn't meet wicked ends." He thought of Cooper and his Outriders. "It's goddamn depressing."

The man just stared.

"Anyway, I'm not gonna hurt you, because if I did, I'd never make it outta here alive. And trust me, I *really* like being alive. So this is what you're gonna do for me. As payment for solving your problem, you're gonna tell me exactly how you and Asaph got from over there," he pointed at the distant mountains outside the office window, "to here."

There went that blinking again. So much damn blinking.

"Wait. You know Asaph Noigel?"

"Yup, I knew him. Traveled with him for a while. He told me and my brothers all sorts of crazy stories about Pirie, and how you were overthrown and exiled and ended up down here in the Wasteland." Meesh twirled the black pistol on his finger. "He also told me you were building a following up here in Tansaray, which is why I came here."

"Where is he now? Asaph?" Charlie rasped, like he had a lemon stuck in his throat.

"He dead," Meesh said.

Charlie blinked yet again but seemed to shake himself out of it. He ran a hand through his formerly slicked-back hair, which now stood on end. "So that's the only reason you came here? Information?"

"Exactly."

"Why? Why didn't you just come up and *ask*?"

"You think you would've told me if I did that, fat and cocky as you are?"

The guy grimaced and stared at his hands.

"Right. Didn't think so. Anyway, brah, what's gonna happen is this. You're gonna step back and let Doc Patch do his job. The cause of the plague's gone, but people're still sick. You let Doc quarantine the way he wants, and you'll come out okay. He's a good dude, knows what he's doing. I mean hell, he's a doctor in a mining town. No one knows how to deal with bleeding lungs better than him. Got it?"

Charlie nodded.

"Awesome. Next, you're gonna take this here"—He tore the lone remaining map of the area around the mines from the wall and slapped it down on the desk in front of Charlie.—"and you're gonna take that there pencil and draw me directions for how to get from here to there. I want the full story, Chaz. And I want it to be accurate. Because if it's not…"

"What then?" he asked pathetically.

"If it's not, I come back here, sneak in when you're not expecting it, and murder you in your sleep." Charlie stared up at him and gulped, which made Meesh sigh. "Damn, man! That's not what I *want* to happen. I'm more than happy to let you and your boys keep on keepin' on, 'cause honestly, this area's in a lot better shape with you running things your way than it was before. So long as you don't get stupid again and take another demon for a pet." He tapped his chin. "Or, y'know, get too big for those tiny-ass breeches of yours. Or start leaning into full-on villainy. Stuff like that. If you keep your boys under control and keep the pay-for-murder to an absolute minimum, I promise you won't see me again. Unless, well, I need you. Deal?"

Charlie continued staring.

"I said *deal*?"

"Oh." The short man nodded rapidly. "Yes. Yes, deal."

"Cool. Now pick up that pencil and get to marking, brah. 'Cause I don't know how long those folks outside are gonna be satisfied just chanting your name without you making an appearance. Wouldn't want you to disappoint the masses or anything. Right?"

"R-right," Charlie stammered.

He grabbed the pencil, leaned over the map, and got to work.

Meesh sat with his feet up on Tito's sleek metal hull and went over the map one more time. They had just passed the entrance to the old copper mine, which was two hundred yards behind them. The map indicated that the old abandoned worker's settlement was another seventy-five yards to the northeast, so that meant the cave Charlie pointed out should be somewhere around…

"Here!" Rodney called out.

Meesh lifted his head. His brother was off to the right, nearly hidden by the brush and tree limbs that made maneuvering Warhorses up the side of the mountain a nearly impossible task. He stood up in the saddle to get a better look.

"Did Abednego find it?" Tito asked.

Meesh folded the map. "Dunno. Let's go find out."

The Warhorse lifted off the leaf-matted ground, and they slowly weaved through the trees to where Rodney sat atop Ivan. Branches scraped Tito's hull. *Dammit all*, Meesh thought. *At this point it'd be quicker to walk.*

When he finally arrived at the place where Ivan was parked, Rodney was nowhere to be found. Meesh dismounted and sauntered toward the veil of vines covering the steep rock face they had been running parallel to for many miles now.

"Yo, Rodney," he called out. "You find it or what?"

"I did!" came his brother's faint voice. "One moment, I became a little stuck."

A section of vines swayed, and a hand poked free. Rodney materialized from behind the vegetation twenty feet ahead, covered in dirt with his hair disheveled. He gave Meesh a timid smile.

"What the hell happened?"

"I found it," Rodney said, wincing. "But it was dark. I might have... tripped and fallen."

"'Course you did." Meesh shook his head. "It's behind there, I take it?"

"It is. We may have a slight issue, however."

"Which is?"

"Come see for yourself."

"Be right back, Teets," Meesh told the Warhorse.

"I will be waiting, sir," Tito replied.

He stepped over fallen logs and protruding branches until he reached Rodney's position. If there was one thing the Wasteland had going for it, it was ease of movement. It might have been prettier here in the mountains, but there were just too many damn obstacles.

"Show me," he said.

Rodney peeled back the vines, revealing a gaping black hole cut into the side of the mountain. The air stunk of mold in there, and he distinctly heard water dripping from somewhere in the dark depths.

Meesh approached the wall of the cave. Sure enough, just as Charlie had told him, a placard stating *S Colorado Impasse* was embedded in the rock.

"This is the place," Meesh said. "What's the problem?"

Rodney pointed deeper into the tunnel. "Look."

Meesh squinted. While the cave was wide, fifty feet or so into the tunnel the floor became festooned with boulders and fallen rocks. There was enough room for the two of them to make it through on their own, but there was no way their Warhorses would fit. Meesh groaned.

"So we gotta go on foot," he said.

"Seems to be," said Rodney.

"Great. Kill me now."

It took time to maneuver the two Warhorses into the mouth of the cave. When they were positioned so that the curtain of vines could be dropped evenly along the rock wall outside, Meesh and Rodney stocked up on their weapons, ten torches each, and a hefty bag of salt pork. They faced the tunnel, which mocked them with its ragged downward passage.

"Are we doing this?" Rodney asked.

"We totally are, brah," Meesh answered.

"What happens if we *do* find your brother?"

"He's your brother too," Meesh said. "As for what we do then... I guess we just go in and find out."

Rodney swallowed hard. "That is as good a plan as any, I suppose."

"From your mouth to the Pentus's ears."

Meesh gave Tito one last hollow pat on the hull. "Be back soon, I hope," he said, and then he and Rodney headed off into the darkness.

— 14 —

The man endured his trial to seek deliverance from it, when in fact
he should have avoided the hardship at all costs. Suffering is a
foolhardy method of learning what to hold close to your heart
and what to leave behind. What is discovered is easily forgotten.
—Book of the Pentus, Allegories 17:33

S hade sat atop an actual horse for the first time since he and
his brothers had been together. Before the Warhorses. Before
discovering what had truly happened to Vera. Before the final
confrontation with Asaph's undead army had killed Cooper and his
Outriders, Abe, and Shade's own faith. It felt good, straddling a hearty
chestnut mare with a starburst of white hair on the side of her neck.
The horse's heartbeat pulsed through the thick riding leathers, which
made him feel *alive*, a sensation that Shade thought he'd lost long ago.

Indigo stood beside him, stroking the mare's flank, her gaze fixed
on the fork in the road ahead. The gloomy light of dawn heightened
the troubled expression in her eyes. He couldn't stop himself from
focusing on her instead of what he had to do next.

The two days that had followed the invented Festival of the Blinking
God had been the best of Shade's life. The precious hours he and
Indigo spent together were blissful. Whenever she wasn't engaged in
her duties as overseer, she was with him, helping to unlock his rage
and sadness and set his angst-ridden soul at ease. And he'd helped

her, as well. They shared words and deeds as well as their bodies, all leading up to his waking this morning, wrapped in her arms, staring at the darkness outside her window and wishing, just *wishing*, that he could abandon this Aumor Reborn prophecy the way he'd abandoned his vows as a Knight Eternal. Wishing that he could spend the rest of his days with the precious creature whose bed he shared, far from turmoil, from servitude, from violence.

It was, of course, not an option. There was no way he and Indigo could run away from this place. Even if he figured out a way to slip her outside the boundary without her melting away in his arms, she would never forgive him for leaving her people behind. And after all the kindness these strangers—who were strangers no longer—had shown him, he would never forgive *himself* for abandoning them.

If he didn't do this, none of them would have a future.

"I'm ready," he said, shifting in the saddle and throwing back his shoulders.

"I...am not," whispered Indigo.

He reached down, ran a finger over the gentle tip of her ear. She shuddered, grabbed his hand, held it tight, yet her gaze was still fixed on the fork in the road.

"I should be going with you," she said. "But I know I cannot. I know it is forbidden. But I hate it nonetheless."

"I'm not too fond of it either," Shade said.

"We are destined to walk our paths alone, I suppose."

"And then come back together once those paths are complete," he added, giving her hand a squeeze. Indigo kissed his knuckles. He released her and grabbed the reins. "You're sure you'll be able to ratio-nalize my not being here?" he asked.

"I do not think it will be a problem." She glanced over her shoulder at the road behind. "I will simply say that an emergency arose in the night that called you back home. It would not be the first time a guest was forced to cut their visit short. They lead very important lives, as you know."

She said it with such thinly-veiled sarcasm that Shade was close to laughter. This was a new aspect to her personality that he'd seen unfold over the last few days, and the change was welcome. Seeing her drop her stoic façade made him recognize a similar change in himself. It seemed that discovering hope had given Indigo an influx of acerbic wit, just as it had given Shade the willingness to sit back and appreciate the little things.

"And no one's gonna question why I was spending all my time with you?" Shade asked.

"As far as they know, you purchased my services. There should be no questions."

Shade grimaced at that. "You gonna be able to handle yourself okay?"

"I have survived for two centuries without you," Indigo reminded him. "I am sure I will be able to get through the next week."

Her pointed words struck him like an arrow in the side, but then he saw the wry smile on her lips, and this time he really did start laughing.

"You got me."

She touched his knee. "Do not worry over me, Shade. These Righteous remain provincial, as I told you they would. They planned a few nature hikes today, and a tour of Merchantry Road three days hence. A fishing competition has been organized, of all things, for tomorrow. No weapons training. No excursions to these paths." She gestured to the sign positioned between the forked roads. "Hopefully, it will remain that way."

Shade squinted at the large placard. The upper half of the sign stated, "The Path of the Hero," with an arrow pointing left, the path he was to take. The lower half proclaimed, "The Path of the Rogue" with its arrow aimed to the right.

"What happens on that Rogue's path, anyway?" he asked.

"I would not know. Those of my people who once populated the settlements along the Rogue were among the most ascended. The damage done was enough for the pedagogues to deem the Path of the Rogue off-limits to the Ersatz. That was many years ago, yet it remains among the most popular attractions in Darkenwood."

Shade furrowed his brow, his thoughts going to dark places. "That's weird. You don't know what happens there?"

"Not at all. The Righteous do not discuss it, and I do not ask."

"Probably for the best."

Indigo looked up at the sky, which had brightened to a melancholy violet. The sad expression she wore broke Shade's heart.

"It's time for me to go, isn't it?"

"It is. I will need to rouse the Tavern soon. And I have yet to bathe." Her face became serious. "Please, tell me you remember what you must do."

"I remember. I promise."

Those perfect lips twisted together, like she wanted to say something but wasn't sure if she should. "I trust you," she finally said and patted the horse's flank one last time before starting back the way they'd come. Shade pivoted in the saddle, watching her hips sway through her satin nightdress. It was at that moment that he realized what she had wanted to say.

"I love you, too," he whispered under his breath.

He urged the mare to turn around, veering her along the Path of the Hero. The road was still cobbled, surrounded on both sides by huge trees. To the left, the land graded upward in a rocky incline. The sky brightened as he trotted the horse at a medium pace. The air grew warm and thick, the breeze blew back the brim of his slouch. The songs of the morning birds, peeps of the frogs, and chirps all grew louder. Everything seemed peaceful. It brought a thankful ache to his chest.

Here he was, Shadrach the Twentieth, enjoying the little things again.

As morning stretched on, the road scaled higher. Numbered markers appeared on the left-hand side of the path, spaced a mile apart, marking paths deeper into the woods. Shade didn't need to measure them; he knew they were a mile apart because Indigo had told him they were. One went by, then a second, and a third. He ogled each of the upward-slanting trails through the forest, wondering what sort of challenge awaited at the end of each one.

Finally, when the blazing red sun became visible in the narrow strip of visible sky above the path, Shade found his destination. Marker seventeen, the bright reflective numbers painted white upon a narrow green sign attached to an iron pole anchored in the ground. Shade dismounted and went about tying the mare to the long hitching rail located ten feet beyond the marker. Thankfully, a bubbling brook ran just behind the pole, easily within the horse's reach. "Wouldn't want you to die of dehydration out here," he said, and when her reins were suitably fastened, he untied his rucksack from the saddle and slipped the straps over his shoulders like a backpack.

Even though he faced a two- or three-day journey on foot, he had packed lightly: two wrapped packages of dried fruit, three skins of wine, one of purified water, one flintstone, and a bedroll and tarp for protection from the elements at night. That, along with his stolen revolver and Ronan Cooper's saber, was all he could justify bringing with him. The path that Indigo had mapped out using the tablet inside Tro Choi's hidden room indicated that the passage would be almost entirely uphill. He would have to walk narrow ledges and scale unsteady rock walls to reach where he was going. There was no way he would attempt to do so while weighed down by supplies he could scrounge in the forest on his own.

"Be good, Chestnut," he told the mare, stroking her mane one last time. "I hope you don't get stuck out here for long before Indigo sends someone to retrieve you."

The horse whinnied. Shade thought of Gypsy and felt a pang of loss.

He approached the marker, stopped before it, and looked up. Already the trail was steep—a thin strip that cut across a rocky, thickly-wooded hillside. Shade took a pull from his waterskin, tipped back his hat, and began his climb.

The going was rough, and his every muscle burned. Nearly the entire length of the path was pitched at a ninety-degree angle, even when it transformed from rocky outcroppings to dirt. The dirt was worse. At least he could find footholds in stone, while the mud, leaves, and exposed roots conspired to trip him up or make him slide back down. It was maddening.

Just when the sun began its descent, the land finally flattened. The forest around him, already dim due to the canopy, became even darker. Unseen animals rustled the undergrowth somewhere out of his range of vision. "Screw this," Shade muttered. Finding a fallen tree that leaned at just the perfect angle, he tossed the tarp over it and staked down the ends. He gathered brush and twigs, built a fire, and sat before it, scarfing down the bag of dehydrated figs Indigo had given him with half a wineskin. He nursed the sores on his feet and the ache of his back. Part of him wanted to ponder what came next, but he was so exhausted from the effort that he simply lay beneath the tarp, pulled his hat over his eyes, and fell asleep.

When he dreamed, it was of Indigo, naked and writhing and pure.

The next day was more of the same. He grew to loathe the land beneath his feet as he slipped and slid and stumbled his way upward. At least the blisters on his heels had disappeared overnight. If there was one positive thing about being created the way he'd been, that was it. He and his brothers healed so much faster than normal men.

He chuckled to himself, but then an image he hadn't expected entered his mind—Mana, the waifish and sad prostitute who had discovered the Rawgian Key after he'd dropped it. That girl had been beaten to such an extent by the man Shade had killed that her entire face had swollen to resemble one of the mutants from the Unknown Lands that sometimes harassed backwaters like Barrendale. Yet the next day, she had been almost completely healed. The same went for Bluebell and her broken nose.

And Indigo. Her arm had been a blistered red mess when she demonstrated for him the invisible barrier surrounding Darkenwood. The next day, nary a welt marred her flesh. He hadn't thought about it at the time. With so much strangeness going on, who could blame him? But now that it became clear, it made him wonder if the Knights Eternal and the Ersatz had more in common than he realized.

It started raining at dusk. Short of breath, Shade hunkered down in a slight gully with the tarp spread over him. The temperature dropped precipitously, and he shivered against the cold stone, grousing against the weather. Each day he'd spent in Darkenwood had been gorgeous.

Nearly perfect. Why did that have to change just because the altitude did?

It's not fair, he thought, and when he realized that his inner voice sounded like a spoiled teenager, the hearty guffaws that followed warmed him up.

The rain persisted long into the night. When he woke in the morning, cold and wet and with a splitting headache, he wished for no more obstacles for him to face on this path. The climb and sleeping out in the elements were more than enough for him.

Then again, wasn't that the whole point? As Indigo had said, this particular trail was so perilous that it was considered suitable for only the most fit and determined of the Righteous. Proving to yourself that you were strong enough to not only survive the journey, but thrive while doing it, was what drove those who chose it. The fact there were fiends to fight at the end of the voyage was only window dressing. The Righteous had nothing to fear from Ersatz foes, other than the brief distress that came from pondering whether their opponent wouldn't hesitate to kill them this time. Shade didn't have that advantage. He wasn't Righteous. When he faced whatever stood between him and the Gate Between Worlds, he would be facing them on even ground.

Kill or be killed.

He only wished Indigo had known who or what he was going to encounter. She'd been able to decipher the right path to take using the tablet, but the name and race of the threats on the Path of the Hero were a complete mystery. That information was given by the overgod Rawg only; when one was cursed to be an obstacle, they awoke from their cocoon with the instructions already imprinted on their souls.

It all boiled down to a horrible existence. Mulling it over further convinced Shade that he needed to do all he could to save these people from their vengeful and callous deity. That alone gave him the vitality to pack up his things and continue his climb.

At last, during late afternoon on his third day of travel, after stabbing a squirrel and cooking its tiny carcass for lunch, he scaled yet another steep, slippery incline and found flat ground. He pulled himself upright and took in his surroundings.

He stood on a shelf cut into the side of the mountain. He couldn't tell how wide the shelf was, given that the area was still packed with trees that he couldn't see beyond. And it was still cold, but it looked as if the path remained level, at least for a bit. Breathing a sigh of relief, he shifted his rucksack into a more comfortable position and trundled onward.

After a mile or so of hiking along the blessedly smooth trail, strange noises reached his ears. The birds and insects and scurrying animals quieted, replaced by grunts and squeals and the occasional *clank* of metal. *Close.* Shade stepped off the path, ducking into a thick nest of vines and low bushes. He set down his rucksack and unstrapped Ronan Cooper's saber from the top. He shrugged out of his duster, affixed the scabbard to his belt, and slung on the shoulder holster. After piling all his belongings neatly under a bush, Shade crept out into the unknown.

Instead of walking straight down the path toward danger, he did the smart thing and approached from the surrounding woods. As his every footfall crunched in the bed of dead leaves, he winced. But the noise didn't seem to stir the creatures whose ruckus grew ever louder. They continued their grunts and snarls and barked laughter as if they heard nothing at all.

The sun beat down brighter, suggesting a clearing within the trees. Shade snuck up to the boundary and peered through gapped branches. When he saw what awaited him, he groaned.

It was indeed a clearing, circular in shape and populated with four rather large, cone-shaped tents. Those tents' residents sat on logs around a fire, roasting hunks of meat on sharpened sticks. There were five of them, sitting with a stooped posture, their thick bodies covered with fur. Each possessed a pair of lower tusks that curled up and around distended mouths, like humanoid boars. It wasn't just distance that had made their voices sound like grunts and growls. Given the structure of their jaws, Shade doubted they could make any other sounds.

He inched back from his spying perch, yanked the revolver from its holster, and checked that the cylinder was full. It was. He remained squatting, mulling over whether he wanted to take the easy way or the hard way—the hard way being an attempt at reasoning with such primal-looking beasts.

The easy way won out. It always did.

After a steadying breath, Shade crept back to his spot. He aimed the barrel through the branches, measured the distance and the light wind. He might not have been as great a marksman as Meesh, who could decapitate a cat from two hundred yards, but he didn't need to be. Not for creatures with heads this large.

He fired off five shots in close succession. The echo of gunfire rattled the trees, causing the silent birds above to take flight. Three of the monsters fell immediately, their brains leaking from holes in their skulls. The other two fell off their makeshift stools, shrieking. One toppled into the fire. Its fur alit, and it flailed as it tried to roll out of the flames. The second survivor whirled toward Shade, its left arm dangling and useless, blood pouring off its fingertips.

Shade stood up and gunned down the one-armed beast when it tried to charge. Its face imploded when the bullet struck. The last creature finally freed itself from the firepit. Its entire body ablaze and smoking, it hurled itself at Shade, an unholy, bubbling scream coming from its cooking mouth. Shade fired once, twice, and a third time into the fiend's bulk. It stumbled to its knees, closing within just a few feet of him. Shade hopped backward to avoid a thrashing, flaming arm, and then fired another bullet at the spot where he thought the head should be. It was difficult to tell with all the flames.

The creature fell still and continued to cook. The smoke coming off it smelled sweet, like pork. It turned Shade's stomach just to think of it.

"That wasn't so hard," he said, carefully stepping around each of the bodies, examining them. Guilt forced a frown on his face. Becoming these hideous things was not their fault. It wasn't a life they had chosen, but a sentence handed down upon them. He imagined how much trauma they had suffered. The only saving grace he saw was that he had killed most of them quickly. Once they were resurrected, their only memory of the encounter would be a brief moment of pain, if that.

A sound like a grumbling sigh came from one of the tents. Shade backed away, holding his pistol at the ready. The sound came again, and the third tent to the right started to shake. A huge hand grabbed the flap of cured animal hide and shoved it aside. Shade's jaw nearly fell off his face.

The man that emerged was the biggest that he'd ever seen. At least eight feet tall, with pastel blue flesh, biceps as big as Shade's chest, and strange white markings across his face, he was nearly as intimidating as the Voice of Him. The lifelessness of his white eyes made him look like the harbinger of death.

"You murdered them," the man said, his voice thunderous as a rockslide.

Shade neither confirmed nor denied. He simply squeezed the trigger, getting off two more shots before he heard that fateful *click*. Both bullets found their mark—one in the giant's forehead, the other in his neck. But they had no effect. The tiny spinning slugs didn't bounce off so much as appear to simply stop moving, as if the colossus had skin three feet thick.

Shade took a step back, hastily trying to pop out the old cylinder and insert the new one from his belt. His hands fumbled.

"Shit."

The giant brought curious fingers to the spots on his throat and head where the bullets had struck, as if searching for wounds. He then leveled Shade with a serious blank stare, let out a roar, and surged forward.

With his immense size, it took the giant only three strides to cross the twenty-foot gap between them. Shade abandoned his attempt at reloading his pistol. When a humungous arm flailed toward him, its boulder-sized fist clenched tight, he dropped down as quickly as he could and rolled out of the way. The fist passed over him with such force that the wind blew out his cheeks.

Shade shot up from his roll and darted to the side while the giant completed his slow yet powerful swing. The former knight returned to switching out the cylinder, and this time succeeded. After the new one clicked into place, he pocketed the spent one. The giant pivoted to face him again, for some reason staring at the fist he'd just swung. He scrunched up his face in a comically frightening show of confusion.

"I was not thwarted," that grinding voice said.

Shade emptied another half-cylinder into him, again to no affect. This time, the giant acted as if he hadn't feel the bullets at all.

"I was not thwarted," he repeated. He lowered his fist and stared across at Shade, who still held up the smoking revolver. "I was not thwarted!" the giant bellowed, and again he started lumbering, this time wearing an insane grin.

The ground shook with the giant's every stride. Shade fired the cylinder's last six shots while backing away. The giant swung again, this time aiming lower, anticipating his opponent's roll. Instead, Shade leapt over the arm, landed on two feet on the other side, and decided his best bet was to run for cover in the trees.

"Can't we talk about this?" he yelled as he fled.

He didn't get far before a massive hand grabbed him by the shoulder. The hand squeezed, and Shade swore he felt his collarbone crack like a crab's shell. He screamed in pain as he was lifted off the ground and spun about.

The giant pulled him close and smiled. "You are not Righteous," he said. His breath blew in Shade's face, stinking of rotten meat. "You are not Ersatz. You cannot thwart me."

"Yeah...about...that..." Shade gasped.

"I will have won. For once, I will have...I will have..."

A perplexed look covered the giant's inhuman face. His cheeks twitched, his lips peeled back. He pulled Shade even closer, as his nostrils flared. Shade was certain that was the end for him, but the giant suddenly drew him away instead of biting off his head, his blank expression gone slack.

"You smell...of him," he said.

Almost gently, the giant lowered Shade until his feet touched ground. When the huge hand released his shoulder, Shade instinctively rubbed it. The giant sat down, crossing his legs, his arms draped across his knees.

"You smell of him," he repeated.

Shade gawked at the massive hulk. "I don't... Who the hell're you talking about?" he said, and inwardly chided himself for doing that instead of seizing his opportunity and getting the hell out of there.

"My love. My Indigo."

"Oh." Shade tilted his head. It took an embarrassing few seconds until realization dawned. "Oh! Are you Raz?"

The giant nodded, staring at his hands.

This is insane, thought Shade.

"You may live," the giant said. "You are special to him. To Indigo. I can tell. I do not wish to hurt him again."

"Okay then. That was...easy." He raised his eyebrows. "Quick question though. You wouldn't happen to know of a secret gate that no one's supposed to know about, do you?"

The giant pointed behind him. "Beyond those tents is a pathway that leads to a hidden staircase that climbs the rest of this mountain. If you seek a gate of some sort, that is the likeliest place to find one."

"Got it. Cool." He flipped his hat back onto his head and tipped it at the giant. "Nice to meet you, Raz. I, um, heard good things?"

He winced at his own awkwardness.

"Mm," was all Raz said.

Shade took that to mean he was done here. He stowed the revolver back in its sheath and retrieved his rucksack from the woods. When he returned, Raz was busy cleaning out the area, stacking the corpses of the boar-boys onto the flames. That sickly sweet roasting pork scent filled the air. Shade decided to give the giant some space, just in case he had a change of heart. He crept around the edge of the clearing, heading for the tents.

"One moment, stranger," that booming voice stated, freezing him in his tracks.

He turned his head slowly. "Yeah?"

"I must ask a favor of you."

"What's that?"

"Kill me."

Shade stood dumbfounded. "Huh?"

"Please, stranger, kill me." The giant lowered himself again, this time lying flat on his back. He was *so damn long.* "It has been a decade since the Righteous have chosen this path. A decade of sitting with my brothers and sisters, speaking in grunts, waiting for a chance at new life. That time is now. Please, strike me down. Make me ascend. I will begin anew. I will get to see *him,* if only for a fleeting moment."

Raz turned his massive head, so that he faced away from Shade. His hand came up and tugged on his earlobe.

Shade got the message. Hesitantly, he drew Cooper's saber and approached the prone giant. He tapped the blade against the exposed ear. "Here?" he asked, his voice rising like a young girl's.

"It is where the meat is weakest," the giant replied.

"Sorry," Shade whispered. He drove the tip of the blade into the ear canal. It scraped roughly against the stone-like flesh, and he had to lean all his weight on the pommel to force it all the way in. But all the way in it went. The sharpened edge pierced the brain, bringing a gasp that sounded like an exploding cannister of gunpowder from the giant's throat. Raz shook once, then fell still. Shade pulled the dripping blade free. He cleaned it off using the dead giant's thong before stuffing it back in its scabbard.

The deed done, he breezed past the tents and shoved through thick vegetation until he found something he hadn't been expecting—a chain-link fence topped with razor wire. Behind the fence was a narrow passageway leading through a bed of solid rock. He grabbed the links and shook. It seemed solid. Without thinking about it too much, he threw his rucksack over, took off his duster, and climbed the fence. At the top, he wrapped his duster around the razor wire so he could swing to the other side.

When he landed, dust kicked up beneath his boots. He gathered up his things and started along his way again. The rock the path cut through turned out to be only a boulder; when he emerged on the other side, a concrete staircase lay before him, long and narrow, leading up the side of the mountain.

"Thank you, Raz," Shade whispered. "Thank you, Indigo."

And he climbed.

— 15 —

"I once knew a youth who carved words upon a rock.
What he created was innocent and sincere, and far more worthwhile
than the blathering of countless mystics worshipping a false god,
who all believed they knew more than I."
—**Book of the Pentus, Quotations 56:13**

Meesh had no way of knowing how long he and Rodney had been meandering their way through the collapsed tunnel. All he knew was that he didn't want to do it anymore. They'd become so tired at one point that they both slept in the pitch black, surrounded by crumbling stone and dripping water. Enough was enough already.

The dream that'd invaded his sleep had been the worst. In it, he was sprawled out in a rust-stained bathtub, surrounded by candles. A feeling of dread pressed in on him, and his thoughts flickered through countless scenes that he didn't remember and couldn't understand. The regret of promise unfulfilled, the desire for some undefined *other*, made him grab a needle off the side of the tub and pump poison into his veins. And when he laid his head back as the poison surged through him, he knew in his cloudy mind that this was the end. That he'd never rise from that tub again. That he'd drift off into nothingness and never wake up.

Most horrible of all, he'd been *okay* with that.

He woke up terrified, patting himself down in the darkness to make sure his limbs still moved, his lungs still breathed, and his heart still beat. All he heard, other than water drip, drip, dripping somewhere deeper in the tunnel, was Rodney across from him, singing a melancholy tune in a hushed voice. It hadn't helped his mindset, bringing actual tears to his eyes for the first time he could remember.

When he wasn't drunk, anyway.

Worst of all, the sensations he'd felt in the dream had stayed with him. Even now, some unknown hours later, while he and Rodney struggled to climb over some recently fallen rubble, that sense of self-annihilating dread permeated his thoughts.

It sucked.

Meesh's torch went out when they'd finally cleared that latest obstacle and the tunnel flattened back into a layer of damp, slippery limestone. Rodney lit a new torch, muttering, "Bullocks."

"Whassup?" Meesh grumbled.

"Last flare."

"Flare?"

He turned to his brother. The newly-ignited torch threw ghastly red light over the cavern making it look like a passageway to one of the Nine Hells. Rodney lifted the cylinder to him and shrugged.

"Torch, I mean. This is my last torch."

Meesh frowned. He signaled for Rodney to stand over him, then set down his bag and rifled through its contents. "I'm out too," he said. He unfolded the map he'd taken from Charlie Midnight and looked at the sloppy diagram of the cave system sketched on the back. "I think that's okay. Ol' Chaz said there was permanent lighting down here once the channel veers to the right." He grabbed Rodney's wrist, aimed the spitting flame deeper into the cave. "It's up ahead, I think."

"You said that last time."

"Well, I'm sayin' it again."

Grunting, he gathered up his things and started marching, ignoring Rodney's further questions. Meesh didn't have any answers. Nothing that wouldn't be tainted by his sour mood, anyway.

He passed the time by counting the seconds between the moment they discovered they were on their last torch to the moment it sputtered out. It was sixteen hundred and thirty-nine. As far as any of them knew, those twenty-seven minutes were the last light either of them would ever see. He stared at the glowing end of Rodney's torch longingly. The last sparks piddled out the cylinder. The tunnel went dark.

"Shit." His voice echoed around him like a battalion of angry ghosts.

"What should we do now?" asked Rodney.

"We keep going," Meesh said. "Just...stay close. Let's make sure neither of us fall behind."

"I'll hum."

Meesh rolled his eyes in the darkness. "You do that."

The going was difficult with no way to see where they were going. Meesh kept close to the tunnel's earthen wall, running his fingers along it, cursing every time his knuckles banged against a random protruding stone. He tripped more than once, nearly falling on his face each time. At least the frustration, which was bordering on anger, managed to keep the dread feelings from his dream at bay. That, and the fact that Rodney's steady, wordless tune was sort of soothing.

Would wonders never cease?

After a good two hours of slow progress—Meesh could only guess it had been that long, but given his predicament, he was going to give himself the benefit of exaggeration—he ran headlong into a wall. Rodney collided with him from behind, making Meesh thunk his forehead on the wall again.

"Goddammit, back up!" he yelled.

"What is it?" Rodney asked softly.

"Hold on, brah. Sheesh. I'm in pain here."

Meesh rubbed the spot between his eyes where he *knew* a red welt was forming. He reached out a tentative hand to see what he'd just run into. The surface was grainy but flat, with even seams running lengthwise.

Brick.

"Found ya," he whispered.

He shuffled sideways, keeping his hands on the wall, feeling like the stupid mime who used to perform his "trapped in a box" routine on the streets of Po-Po. It was embarrassing, but what the hell? Not like anyone could see him.

After a few more scuffling paces, his knuckles rapped against something extremely hard. A metallic *twang* echoed through the cave. Meesh felt around the new discovery. It was large and rectangular and felt like a door, only it sat diagonally instead of straight up and down.

"What is this?" Rodney's disembodied voice asked.

The sudden onset of brightness caused Meesh to throw his arm up over his face. When his eyes adjusted, he peered over his elbow to see Rodney's outline standing in the middle of a rectangular halo of light.

"You were right," his brother said with a smirk. "We *were* almost there."

Meesh chuckled. It wasn't often Rodney told a joke, let alone one that was somewhat funny.

He straightened his back and examined their find. It was certainly a doorway, right in the middle of a gray brick wall that had somehow ended up at the end of a cave. The door itself was hollow steel, and it'd long ago been ripped from its hinges, now resting cockeyed against the wall. Meesh bent his head sideways and squinted, reading the old, dusty sign that said *AUTHORIZED ACCESS ONLY*.

"Guess someone didn't agree," Meesh said. He looped his thumbs through his belt, his index fingers tapping away. A thought struck him, and he glanced down at the pommel of his sword. His Eldersword. Which glowed. They hadn't needed to wander around in the dark. His neck flushed from embarrassment. His only solace was the fact Rodney hadn't thought of it either—though in fairness, his brother had far, far less experience than him. Moron. He gnashed his teeth together to stop his cheeks from reddening as he joined his brother on the other side of the doorway.

The corridor they entered seemed to stretch on forever in a straight line. Meesh found it far too familiar. The floor and walls were beige, and the light fixtures embedded in the paneled ceiling were far too bright. Those lights clicked on when they walked beneath them, then turned off once they passed them by. Because the knights were constantly in the center of the only available light source, it was impossible to tell how long the passageway stretched. And given how crude Charlie's drawn map of the place was, it was effectively useless as a reference.

An off-putting sense of déjà-vu caused him to grit his teeth. This type of corridor seemed familiar because it was. The hidden structure underneath the Cooper Nuclear Station looked almost exactly like this, as if one had been copied from the other. If that was the case, that meant this passageway was *old*.

Probably as old as the Ancients.

"This is very strange," Rodney said, looking up in wonder each time a new set of overhead lights turned on.

"You ain't kidding, brah."

They continued until the corridor finally ended, splitting off to the left and to the right. The right passage was marked *White River*; the left, *Provo*. Meesh pulled the map out of his back pocket. "Looks like we're going to Provo, wherever the hell that is." He grabbed Rodney by the shirt and pulled him along.

A soft, metallic groan sounded above. Meesh looked up at the bright ceiling. They were most certainly deep beneath the mountains by now, a billion tons of rock pressing down on top of their heads. He hoped the Ancients really were as brilliant as the legends said. If this structure collapsed, their journey would end far too quickly.

The deeper they went into the Provo tunnel, the stranger things became. The passageway widened by half, and the floor became white tiles covered with dust instead of smooth beige stone. The ceiling rose higher, perhaps at least twenty feet up. The lights that shone down entered through stained glass panels, creating the equivalent of false sunlight, that remained on after they passed by. He and Rodney's every footfall resounded through the cavernous space. Raised planting beds, any vegetation long rotted away, populated the middle of the broadened corridor, creating what looked like a two-way thoroughfare.

The walls on both sides were broken up every thirty-five paces by doorways big as warehouse entrances, each leading to vast rooms. These were mostly empty, though some detritus remained—an overturned table here, a formless black mass that might've been rotted fabric there, the remains of broken glassware glittering beneath the dim lights.

Again, Meesh felt an eerie sense of familiarity. For whatever reason, he imagined this place as a sort of vast indoor market. Tall blond clerks letting off puffs of perfume to lure in men desperate to find something to make their wives happy. Music stores packed from wall to wall with records. Clothiers where one could peruse seemingly endless collections of the latest fashions.

"Stop it," he whispered, lowering himself onto the ledge of one of the flower beds and holding his head in his hands, trying to force the alien images away.

A hand fell on his shoulder. Rodney stood over him, his expression pained.

"You see it too," Meesh said.

"More than you know," answered Rodney.

"What's that even mean, brah?"

Rodney stuffed his hands in his pockets and loped on ahead. Meesh stared after him. He touched his left breast pocket, where his palm-sized notebook was always at the ready. For the first time since arriving at Adavan Station, he wondered whether he should continue jotting down his brother's eccentricities for the Reverend. *No,* he thought. Doing that would be backsliding, returning to something he knew so he didn't get all weirded out. He slapped the stone planter and hustled after his brother, wondering when he'd gone and gotten so damn introspective.

After a while, the enormous space became a narrow corridor once more. They passed through another door, this one still on its hinges, and entered a stretch of hallway far brighter than anything Meesh would've expected to find buried in the middle of a mountain. The walls were painted in cheerful colors, and murals as beautiful as any created by the best artists of Sal Yaddo decorated the long, unbroken surface. There were green landscapes speckled with wildflowers; fantastical scenes of unicorns and faeries and rainbows; portraits of smiling faces, too many to count, nearly layered over each other, as if attempting to build a mountain of joyous expressions; countless images of wildlife: lions and tigers and bears and monkeys and parakeets, all animals Meesh had never seen before, but whose names he knew nonetheless.

Between these murals were still more doors, normal sized and closed. When the knights stepped through one to investigate, they found a practical yet homey living space. There was no furniture left, just like everywhere else in this odd underground world, but when Meesh walked through another door standing at the junction of two rooms, he found a bathroom complete with a toilet, sink, and shower. There was running water here, just like in Dakota Keep. Or there had been, anyway—when he flipped on the spigot, the pipes shuddered and sighed but remained dry.

His mind swam with possibilities when he and Rodney exited the living quarters and continued on their way. There were just *so many* of these apartments, hundreds as far as he could tell. There were offices as well, and long white rooms whose walls were giant empty window-panes, and a place that looked like it could've been a mess hall.

That's when the truth struck him like a load of bricks right in the sore noggin. This place, this network of arterial passages and domiciles, was where the Ancients had ridden out the Rising. Asaph had said as much, but of course Meesh hadn't believed him. Now that he saw it with his own eyes, it was undeniable. Everything that mass-murdering psychopath Asaph had said about these caverns was the truth. And if that was the case, then it was possible everything else Asaph said—about the Reverend being a fraud, the Pentus a non-existent deity, and the whole church being useless—might be true too.

Meesh snarled and picked up his pace.

At another junction, this one splitting four ways, Meesh consulted Charlie's map again. They took the left-center path, the one with the sign on the wall reading *Science and Leisure* in raised letters. Everything about this passage was white and sterile, even though it was covered in dust. There were wide-open nooks every so often, each with benches affixed to the walls. More rooms populated this passageway, too, but all the doors were closed and locked. Meesh stopped trying to open them, his strides growing quicker and more desperate.

"Wait," Rodney said. "Stop a moment, Meesh."

Meesh spun around. His brother stood with hands on hips, staring at a set of double doors on the wall opposite him. His expression screamed confusion, with eyes narrowed and lips slightly parted.

"What's up?"

"Do you feel that?"

"Feel what?"

"That…humming. A vibration. It's low, but it is most *certainly* real." Rodney looked at Meesh expectantly. "Correct?"

Meesh closed his eyes. Sure enough, he felt it too. A slight tremor that came every third second, like a heartbeat.

"Yeah, I feel it."

Rodney pointed at the set of double doors across from him. "I believe it's coming from behind there."

"Hm. Let's see."

Meesh approached the doors. They were locked, just like every other stupid door along this passage. He almost told Rodney to forget it, that they should move on, but then he spotted the plaque on the wall to the right of the door and focused on that instead. The plaque was bronze, the words obscured by a layer of dust. He brushed the filth off and backed up a step to read.

Welcome to the Central Utah
Cumulative Redundancy
Oracular Neural Engine:
The place where one looks
when they wish to look deeper.
Keep an open mind
And use caution.

Meesh reached into his vest's right breast pocket and fished out the note Octavia left for him.

Help me. Look deeper.

"C'mon now," he muttered. "This can't be that insane."

The doors were so immensely thick he couldn't break them down. He drew his Eldersword, extended it, and used the vibrating blade to slice a clean line through the seam between the two doors. The locking mechanism sizzled and fell with a *clank*. He clipped the sword back onto his belt, braced his feet, and shoved. The doors swung open slowly, groaning in protest the whole time.

What he entered was a near perfect facsimile of the antechamber of the Temple of the Crone. The dimensions were the same—one hundred feet wide, thirty feet deep—and a recessed shelf to the right of the steel door opposite the entrance held a single glowing Heartcube. The ceiling was just as harrowingly steep, the temperature inside just as chilly. The only real difference between here and there was that the concrete walls in this particular chamber were bare, whereas the walls within the Crone's temple were covered with painted frescoes.

"What is this place?" Rodney asked.

Meesh nearly jumped out of his skin. His teeth chattered when he looked back at his brother, who hesitated just outside the opened doorway as if afraid the floor was lava.

"Someplace important," Meesh said.

Rodney glanced at the ceiling. "It looks...alien."

"That's probably 'cause it is."

"Do you need me in here?" Rodney asked, taking a step back.

"Nah. Best you don't come in here at all. Like the plaque there says, use caution."

His brother nodded gravely and stepped to the side, disappearing from sight. "I'll be right here, waiting," his voice announced. "If you require my assistance..."

"Yeah, I'll call out if I do."

Relief washed over him as he made his way to the steel door. It wasn't that he didn't want Rodney around or thought his company was tiresome. No, what Meesh feared was trying to explain away whatever emotions came over him while in here. Because his whole world was crashing down on him. The implications were terrifying, especially for someone who didn't consider himself all that introspective.

When he reached the door, he pressed his palms and forehead against the cold steel, a mirror to what he'd done in the Temple of the Crone, right before Octavia left him that damn note. "Anyone in there?" he called, but all he heard in reply was that familiar soft and gentle buzz that started behind his eyes and took root in the back of his throat.

He snatched up his Eldersword. The blade glowed orange, showing the outlandish worry he felt. The Rush surging through him made his fear grow stronger. It would be so easy to plunge this vibrating blade into the door, cut himself in just as he had cut his way into the room. Maybe then he wouldn't feel so scared.

Another thought came to him, and he abruptly retracted his blade. *It can't be that simple*, he thought once more. He placed one hand on the door, closed his eyes, and whispered, with all the sincerity he could muster, "I wanna look deeper."

In the cubby to the right, the glow of the Heartcube intensified. Mechanisms awakened with a squeal, and a puff of air like a sigh smacked him in the face. Meesh withdrew his hand as the door slid to the left, disappearing into the wall. A rectangle of blackness greeted him like a schoolyard bully, taunting him to run away and hide.

Meesh forced a smile onto his face and walked into the darkness unabated. Fake it 'til you make it. He was sure he'd heard that advice somewhere before.

The lights came on as soon as he passed through the blackened rectangle, revealing a staircase lined on either side by opaque walls, through which flashing colors shone. The vibration Rodney had first noticed in the corridor became more noticeable, bringing physical sensation to Meesh's growing unease. He tapped the hilt of his Eldersword, counting on the tiny jolts of Rush he received to keep him sane.

At the bottom of the staircase was a short catwalk that hovered over a circular pit. In the middle of that pit rose a large tower, high as he could see. All sorts of strange machinery blinked and droned and rumbled down below. The constant faint sounds were like the squawking of ocean birds heard through a burlap sack. Meesh groaned as he placed a foot on the catwalk and stomped toward the door set into the tower on the other side—again reminiscent of the Cooper Nuclear Station.

When he reached the door, he stared at the inscription stenciled in red upon the smooth reflective surface. *Central Utah C.R.O.N.E. Unit.* A pit dropped in his stomach. He reached toward a black panel beside the door. The panel lit up and a bright green light traced his palm up and down. Meesh held still, not knowing what to do or how to proceed, whether the strange green light was hurting him or not. Finally, the light clicked off, and he was no worse for wear. A crackling noise filled his ears from somewhere above, followed by a woman's voice, soft and sweet and inviting.

"Hello, revenant. I've been waiting for you."

"You have?"

"Yes. Your coming was foretold."

"By who?"

"By me."

"Are you an oracle?" he asked.

"I am. I have been down here alone for a very long time. It's good to have company. Please, come inside. We need to talk."

The door before him parted down the middle and spread open.

Meesh gulped down the last of his fear and walked inside. As soon as he entered the portal, blinking lights blinded him, colors swirled around him in a kaleidoscope that churned his belly and made him feel dizzy. He leaned against the wall, the cold steel no comfort as the assault of bright, strobing lights continued.

Images flashed through his mind: a lizard thrashing about in the desert sand; huge blocks of ice the size of a village breaking off from glaciers and falling into the ocean; countless random faces shrieking in unison as their faces melted away until nothing remained but gleaming white skulls; a dripping syringe, spinning around and around in a featureless void; a pair of leather pants with a silver belt, a black shirt, and a gold sequined vest, laid out on a bed in a filthy room, as if the person who had once worn them had faded away.

A scream bubbled in Meesh's throat, but it was halted when the visions suddenly vanished.

"Meshach, please sit," the kind voice of the oracle said.

His vision cleared, revealing a single chair in the chamber with him. He shuffled over and sat down mindlessly, his head still reeling. Then the wall opposite him lit up, and the oracle began speaking once more. Meesh sat there in silence, his eyes growing wider by the second as he absorbed every word.

He had no way of telling how long his audience with the oracle had taken, but by the time he emerged back onto the catwalk, shaking all over, his brain was still on the fritz. He couldn't keep his thoughts straight. Everything he'd just seen and heard played over and over again in his head. He couldn't make any sense of it, or maybe it was that he didn't *want* to understand.

Because understanding meant that nothing was real.

He ascended the stairs in a daze and walked back through the antechamber. The thick steel door slid shut behind him. He found Rodney in the corridor, worrying over a strip of salt pork. His brother looked perplexed.

"What happened in there?" he asked.

Meesh frowned. "Why?"

"You were gone so long. I was worried."

"I was? How long?"

"At least forty-five minutes, though I don't know for certain. I went to look for you, but I couldn't get through the door."

"Oh." Meesh closed his eyes, breathed deeply. "It didn't seem like that long."

"Well, it was." Rodney's head tilted. "Are you all right? You look pale. You sound different."

"I'm fine," Meesh said. He picked up the bag he'd dropped by the entrance and slung it over his shoulder.

"You're certain?"

"Totally."

He must not've been convincing, because Rodney scrunched his lips like he was sucking on a lemon. "What did you see in there, Meesh? What happened to you?"

"Nothing, man. Nothing at all." He started marching down the long hallway. A brief flicker made him blink—the image of his bearded brother kneeling on the ground, sobbing, his hands covered in blood. Meesh shoved the vision away. "Now let's get a move on. We need to get to Shade, and we need to get to him *now*."

Rodney caught up to him easily with his long strides. "Why the sudden urgency? I thought we were going to take it slowly?"

"Not anymore, brah," Meesh said. "Not anymore."

"What if I don't want to? I really don't wish to kill—"

Meesh spun on his brother. His every fiber wanted to scream, to release all the confusion and fear that'd been building up in him ever since Abe died and Shade left. But one look at that sensitive face and those eyes that held depths of sorrow he couldn't understand was enough to quell his rage. Instead, he grabbed Rodney's hands and looked at him with compassion that he'd only given one other person in his short life.

"We're not killing anyone, Rod. Well, we're not killing Shade, anyway."

"We aren't?" His brother's face relaxed.

"No. The mission isn't to murder our brother anymore."

"Then what are we to do?"

Meesh gave him a sideways smirk that took a little of the edge off. He hoped that smirk told his brother all he needed to know—that their goal wasn't to kill Shade any longer, because everything Meesh had ever known was a lie. If he had to vocalize that, he knew that he'd just end up screaming.

16

His seed is like the seed of the Great Pine. In its infancy,
it is insignificant, easily overlooked. No one believes its potency.
Yet in their apathy, mankind will let it spawn until it
overshadows all. And in time, that tree will reign over all the Earth.
—Book of the Pentus, Allegories 22:41

On the fourth day after Shade embarked on his quest to become
Aumor Reborn, doubt wrapped its sticky fingers around
Indigo and would not let go.

For the previous three days, she had been upbeat. She tended to the
new Righteous guests, made sure Hickweis Tavern ran as smoothly
as possible, and one night even joined a group of her people for
a gathering at the Merchantry Road dormitories after the guests
retreated to their cottages on the other side of the valley. She laughed
and drank with her fellow Ersatz, pining for the day in the not too
distant future when they could do this as a freed people.

But that optimism fled earlier that morning and showed no sign of
returning.

Before the break of dawn, when she wandered through the forest
collecting the berries Mita requested for one of his unique desserts,
she drew close to the boundary of the valley. An expectant grin
crossed her face when she reached her hand through the unseen

wall keeping her prisoner. The pain had been immediate. Her skin reddened, the boils rose, and she quickly withdrew.

That had spurred her to visit Tro Choi after depositing the basket of berries at the tavern. Nothing greeted her there—no new cocoons, nor the soft trembling that announced an Ersatz had just ascended. There was nothing but emptiness and silence within the temple.

All potential outcomes poured through her mind: Shade had yet to reach the Gate Between Worlds. He had succumbed to the perils of the path. He had been defeated by the Avatar of Rawg. He had defeated the Avatar, yet some next step was required before the Ersatz could be freed. He had fled and now traipsed through the land of the Righteous, abandoning her to continue seeking the answers that had caused him to stumble upon this valley in the first place.

Those, and so many more. That Indigo had no way of knowing which was true dragged her down into dejection. It did not help matters that she realized she was missing the man so completely that it hurt.

At least the guests had remained oddly acquiescent through it all. They demanded nothing untoward of their servants, only benign outings that Indigo felt sure they could experience in their own lands. Nature hikes, the fishing tournament, horseback riding lessons, bird-watching tutorials, and a few cooking classes were all this group had wanted so far.

Now she was giving a group of six an after-dinner tour of the shops and eateries lining Merchantry Road.

"If you were to walk that way," she said, pointing to where the road veered south a quarter-mile past the last shop on the strip, "you would find the fields where all the food that we consume here in Darkenwood is grown. Our vegetable gardens are vast; we grow corn year-round. At any point in time, there are upward of fifty cattle in our barns, and twenty-seven cows supply all the milk and cheese we could ever wish to consume."

"Where are the cattle butchered?" asked one of the Righteous, an extremely tall and athletic woman with black skin named Zoe. She jabbed a thumb over her shoulder. "I saw the shop back there, but it doesn't look big enough to actually, y'know, butcher animals."

"The cattle are cleaned and cut into quarters in the barns," Indigo said. "The cuts are then transported to the butcher. The processed meat is lightly salted and stored in the cold cellar of the butchery, until it is requested for meals. Luckily for all involved, our demand is relatively constant, and we have measured out the proper quantities needed so that meat is rarely stored for longer than five days before it is used."

"That's good," said Nathan, the young Righteous man with floppy hair and teardrop eyes. He tapped his walking stick on the ground. "Very efficient. Who came up with this process, anyway?"

"I did," Indigo told him.

He grinned adorably, pointed his stick toward the path. "Good on you. Mind if I ask how many people you have working down there? In the fields, tending cattle, stuff like that?"

"Sixty-two Ersatz work the gardens, while another thirty-three are responsible for the cattle, chicken, and pigs."

"Again, efficient," Nathan said. "You got everything figured out."

"It is our job," said Indigo. "All the better to make your stay that much more enjoyable."

The man nodded, though he seemed suddenly uncomfortable.

"We're not gonna go there, are we?" asked his companion, Sophie, with a distasteful grimace.

"Why not, Sophie?" Nathan asked, nudging her. "Scared?"

She shot him a look. "No, disgusted. I'm vegan."

"Well duh. It's not like I haven't known you for, like, ever."

"We can visit the farms in the morning, if you like," Indigo cut in. "Right now, it is nearly dark. We can do whatever else you wish around the Merchantry Road, but I feel that perhaps we should leave the livestock to rest for the evening." She gritted her teeth, realizing the mistake she had just made in telling the Righteous what they would and would not be doing. She gave an abrupt curtsey and said, "Unless you demand otherwise."

Nathan waved her off before turning to his five companions. "Nah, we're good. What do *you* guys wanna do?"

"Let's check out the cold cellar," said another brown-skinned Righteous named Fuad.

"Yeah, let's do that," purred Zoe.

Sophie appeared repulsed. "Ew. No thanks." She eyed Indigo in a manner that was either predatory or admiring, or perhaps both. "I wanna see where you get your dresses."

"Boring," said another of their number, a shorter blond man named Lucien.

"We can do both," Indigo announced. She signaled to Aspar, whom Indigo had asked to join them on the tour. "Aspar, would you please bring our guests to the butchery?"

"Of course, Mum," he said, grinning. It seemed he had yet to lose his hope as Indigo had. Then again, given the predilections of this group of Righteous, he was a courtesan still able to live each day without defiling himself. She dreaded the arrival of the next group, who would surely return to their heinous ways and rob him of his newfound positivity.

Four of the guests left with him, leaving only Sophie and Gia, a pretty girl whose skin was the same tone as Shade's, and who wore long dreadlocks that dangled at the middle of her back.

"Shall we?" Indigo asked. Sophie and Gia smiled at one another, locked arms, and gestured for her to lead the way.

Odd group, for sure.

They trailed the quartet led by Aspar back toward the long line of structures crowding the road. Even as the gray of dusk became the black of night, Merchantry Road teemed with people. The only busier place in Darkenwood was Hickweis Tavern—mainly because they were the only true gathering places in the entire valley, other than the Righteous cottages on the eastern margin.

The buildings here were large, three- and four-story structures that dwarfed even the tavern. Merchantry Road had grown exponentially during the thirty years after Darkenwood came into being, with new constructions raised in accordance with the boon of new Ersatz who emerged from Tro Choi in those first few decades. That growth had slowed considerably over the past one hundred and fifty years. In those early days, a new batch of five doomed souls emerged every other month. Today, a single new Ersatz arriving during a calendar year was a surprise. The last new prisoner of the valley had been Pipin, now Pipi, who had first fallen into servitude two years ago.

The four structures in which the majority of the Ersatz lived were grouped on the far end of the road. Bulky and inelegant, the complexes had room to house a hundred Ersatz each. The living conditions in the dormitories were not ideal, with huge communal rooms lined with cots and public bathing stations. The only Ersatz blessed with private dwellings were Indigo and her courtesans—and those who had been reduced to threats on the Path of the Hero. This meant that privacy came with an unfortunate price. The many Ersatz who lived here still had their share of ascensions, of course. Workplace accidents, such as being kicked by cattle, losing a limb to the kiln and ascending oneself to avoid living disabled, or falling from a scaffold were not uncommon. And there were the occasions when the Righteous guests became wrapped in roguish ways and decided to make Merchantry Road a bloodbath, the worst such instance being the burning of the dormitories that had led to Raz's torture by the Voice of Him.

Indigo had experienced all of it, and if not for her decision to become overseer, she would have preferred to live here. At least in the dormitories, all you needed to do to get a break from the madness was walk out the back door and trod less than a mile to Winninger Lake.

The various shops, cafés, smiths, and other assorted trades had sprouted from the housing complexes like a bent spine. Buildings both great and small were crammed right next to one another. The seamstress shop that Indigo led her two guests toward was nestled between a tanner and a bakery that specialized in buttered pastries. She climbed the steps and held the door open so Sophie and Gia could enter.

The interior of the shop was lit by numerous glass-shielded candelabras and decorated with a variety of colorful hanging tapestries. Racks of clothing—everything from tunics to breeches to all manner of dresses, both fancy and practical—populated the right side of the wide-open space, while the looms and spinning wheels used to create such garments occupied the left. Given that it was past dinner, the only living things present were the multitude of pythons that Sienna, who had operated the seamstress shop for decades, kept as pets.

"Ooh, fancy!" Gia said. The Righteous girl clasped her hands together and hustled toward the racks of clothing. If she was worried about the snakes, she did not show it. Sophie gave Indigo a knowing smirk and followed after.

Gia perused the finely-tailored dresses while Sophie stopped in front of a gown displayed on a pedestal all its own. The gown was made from crushed velvet, the long skirt pleated so it formed a spiraling pattern when the wearer spun. Created in the ombré style that Sienna loved so much, the cinched top was white with a hint of pink, growing ever darker on the way down, ending with a blood-red hemline. It was by far the most beautiful garment in the entire place; Indigo had a similar gown in her closet.

"This is gorgeous," Sophie said, gently poking at the soft material as if it might break.

"Sienna creates inspired pieces," Indigo said.

"And this Sienna, she makes all your dresses?"

"She does, yes."

"Nice. Really nice. She make your other clothes too?"

"What other clothes?" asked Indigo.

Anne gave her a sideways glance. "Y'know, your slacks, blouses, suits? Those sorts of things?"

"I possess no such vestments. Other than my undergarments, dresses are all I wear."

"Jeez. Why?"

"The overseer of Hickweis Tavern must present herself as a lady of highest regard."

"Oh. Gotcha. Well, at least dresses are comfortable." Sophie tapped a fingertip against her sapphire pendant and raised an eyebrow at the tight bustier Indigo currently wore. "Or they can be, anyway."

"We do what we can to give our guests the best experiences possible," Indigo said indifferently.

"Yeah," said the woman. "I've heard."

While Gia continued her enthusiastic perusing, Sophie moved on to the next rack. She took her time looking at each item of clothing, but the way she kept glancing at Indigo made it obvious that the clothes were just a distraction.

"Something troubles you?" Indigo asked her. "Have I done something? If I am making you uncomfortable, I am more than willing to wait outside while you go about your business."

The woman sighed. Her exquisitely thick lips spread into an earnest smile. "Don't be silly. You're not making me uncomfortable at all. I just have...questions."

"Such as?" said Indigo.

"Well, like this." Sophie pulled another dress from the rack, this one much humbler, though just as expertly made. "How much would I pay for this? I mean, there're no prices listed here."

"You would pay how much you think it is worth."

"With these?" She opened the bag she carried over her shoulder, pulled out a handful of wooden coins stamped with the symbol of the overgod—three interlocking circles set within a triangle.

"Yes, with those," Indigo said.

"Are they worth anything? We were each handed a whole satchel of them before we got on the train. But nobody told us their value."

Indigo felt the oncoming cramp of irritation. "Just as with anything we sell, your coin is worth what you deem it to be worth."

"Really," said Sophie, squinting. "So, I could decide that this dress is worth one of these coins, and I could walk outta here with it for that?"

"Indeed."

"Oh." Her brow furrowed, and her fists bundled tightly around the fabric of the dress. "And what if I decide it's not worth anything?"

"Then it is yours to take!" proclaimed a voice Indigo knew well.

All heads turned to the curtain hanging in front of the doorway at the rear of the vast showroom. The curtain flew aside, and a woman swept into the room with a flourish. Sienna was ravishing as always, tall and lean, with her porcelain skin twinkling in the candlelight and her white-blond hair falling in waves to the middle of her back. Her pointed ears were twice as long as Indigo's, befitting her status as a pure elf.

For an Ersatz to ascend as an elf meant they were instantly given the highest standing among their downtrodden little society, and they were placed in charge of the most important establishments on Merchantry Road. Only nine elves existed within the boundary of Darkenwood at any one time, the rarest of the breeds aside from the triton and half-elf, of which there were only one each. Sienna liked to flaunt that fact as much as possible, and since her ascension to this form ninety years ago, was outrageously jealous of Indigo for being one of a kind.

Though her pride would never allow her to say it out loud.

"And you are?" Sophie asked.

The elf lifted one of her pythons off a candelabra and draped it around her neck like a scarf. She petted the snake as she glided across the floor. "I am Sienna, the master seamstress of this establishment," she said with an exaggerated bow. Her smile left her face momentarily when she glanced at Indigo.

"You made all this stuff?" asked Sophie.

Sienna beamed like a star ready to explode. "Indeed. All designs within this humble shop are my own. Crafted with my own hands, and the hands of my capable assistants." She frowned at Indigo. "It pains me that I was not made aware of your visit or I would have had the fitting rooms made ready for you."

"Eh, no need," Sophie said. "We're just looking."

"These are awesome!" exclaimed Gia from deeper in the racks. She was holding up a variety of dresses to her body.

"As I said, anything you desire is yours to take," Indigo said, proffering a graceful hand at her wares.

"We don't have to pay for it?" asked Gia.

"If you do not desire to, then no," Sienna answered.

Sophie frowned, shaking her head. "This don't seem right."

"Oh, but it is, my dear. As the overgod decrees, so it shall be."

"People keep telling me that," Sophie grumbled.

Indigo eyed the Righteous woman closely. Sophie certainly seemed dismayed by what she was hearing, a consistent trait since her arrival. Nothing about the way she acted made any sense when contrasted against the two hundred and seven years of experience Indigo had at her disposal.

"I can have one, right Sophie?" Gia asked excitedly.

The woman looked her way, twining a strand of her curly black hair in an irritated manner. "No, definitely not."

"Please?"

"I said no, Gia!" she shouted, and the sudden anger in her voice forced Indigo to take a step back. The Righteous woman took a deep breath, and when she looked at Indigo again, she appeared downright apologetic. "I think that's enough for today. I'll take her home."

"As you wish," Indigo said, with a slight curtsey.

Sophie closed her eyes, exhaled deeply. She then forced her younger friend toward the exit. As Indigo went to follow them out, a forceful grip on her bicep held her in place.

"Be careful, Indigo," Sienna said, her normally aristocratic tone replaced with scorn.

Indigo shrugged out of her grasp. "I know not what you are talking about."

"Oh, I am sure you do." She crossed her arms over her chest and stared Indigo down. The python coiled around her neck flicked its forked tongue. "Be wary of putting your faith in false idols. Our fates lie in the hands of the overgod. Any beliefs otherwise will only lead to pain. For us all. Take the lesson from Black and fall in line."

Indigo turned her back on the elf. Sienna had always been a stickler for the rules of the overgod, no matter how many times she had witnessed the depths of torment inflicted on her own people. She frequently pointed to Black as the example all Ersatz should strive toward. One of the original five, Black had done all that was demanded of him without complaint. He had suffered tragedy after tragedy, and had been ascended more times than any other Ersatz before Raz. Black had been collected by the pedagogues five years after being birthed in the valley and was told that his sentence was over. In two hundred and seven years, he was the only Ersatz to ever escape Darkenwood.

As she had told Shade one night while they lay beneath the stars, she believed Black was an outlier. That she had been given no sign in the many years since that any other Ersatz would ever win their freedom. Simply recalling this conversation made the ache of worrying over her bearded stranger all the more painful.

Indigo was in such a huff when she pushed through the front door of the seamstress shop that she did not immediately recognize the strange happenings around her. At the bottom of the stairs, she stopped short just before a gnome collided with her knee. The gnome pumped his arms and legs, running as fast as his tiny body could go.

Indigo blinked into the darkness as her surroundings came into focus. People were dashing past her left and right.

"What the...?"

That was when she heard the dreaded proclamation: *"FIRE!"*

The scent of smoke filled her nostrils. She turned slowly toward the direction her people were running. The first thing she saw were the flames licking from the lower windows of the first dormitory on the row. Then the billowing smoke came into view, slithering out of the building like a snake. Finally, she was that her people had formed a fire line to quell the flames.

Sienna burst out of her shop, eyes wide. She gazed in the same direction as Indigo, and then shot a hateful look her way.

"Your fault!" the elf screamed and sprinted toward the action.

Panic forced Indigo to snap out of it. Her legs kicked into gear, carrying her as fast as they could toward the blaze. Running was difficult in her billowing dress, and she cursed her slowness. She sucked air into her lungs, trying to will her heart to stop racing.

Shock overcame her when she noticed that the guests she had been escorting around the valley had joined the fire line. All six of them passed buckets between them, not seeming to care that those they assisted would be considered monstrous by Righteous standards. Despite their efforts, the fire had spread, beginning to consume the second housing complex. If they did not act fast, the whole of Merchantry Road could go up in smoke.

Indigo entered the fire line, her fingers going numb as she passed pails of splashing water forward and empty pails backward. Thankfully, after a while, the fire started to smolder. Nothing but foul-smelling smoke belched from the first-floor windows. Her people began to fall back, exhausted. Some bent over with hands on knees, others collapsed onto the ground. Indigo stared at the charred window frame, wondering how in the world the fire had started. Her first guess was her troupe of Righteous, but she could not make herself believe that. If they had started the fire, then why would they have joined in the effort to put it out?

Someone suggested they search the burned building in case anyone had been trapped inside that needed rescue. The Righteous man Fuad volunteered his services. Indigo started to join him, but was pulled back by Shamrock, the yellow-skinned hobgoblin who cleaned tables at Hickweis Tavern. His lack of a nose made him look so much like a leering skeleton that most guests were appalled by his appearance. He was actually one of the sweetest individuals that Indigo had ever known.

"Mum, Mum," Shamrock urged, tugging on her sleeve. "Please, you must come!"

"Why? What is wrong, Sham?"

"It is Yonder. He saw something in the trees."

He pointed across Merchantry Road toward a small stretch of woods filled with hiking trails and streams popular for morning walks. She could not see anything there, given that it was nighttime and a quarter-mile away.

"Could it have been a deer?" she asked.

If Shamrock possessed a nose, it would have scrunched. "No deer in that stretch, Mum. Too much traffic."

Indigo nodded, her interest churning. "Let us go see, then." She doubted that anyone was still hiding in those woods, but if that was where the arsonist had fled to after setting the fires, and Yonder had seen them, then perhaps Indigo might find some clues.

By the time she and Shamrock reached the forest boundary, located on the underside of the hill upon which Merchantry Road sat, Yonder had stepped back, her big red fir bolg nose flaring, her sideways-pointing ears twitching. Fear shone in her wide, starlight-twinkling eyes.

"What is it, Yonder?" Indigo asked.

The fir bolg pointed a stubby finger at the forest. "Someone is in there, Mum. I hear them. I *smell* them."

Indigo inched forward, wishing that her half-elf body possessed heightened senses. It was difficult to see anything in the darkness, or smell anything with smoke still filling the air.

"Are you certain?"

"I am, Mum."

Something moved in the trees, causing the branches to rustle. Indigo froze in place.

"*It's her,*" someone whispered far too loudly.

An explosion split the night. Indigo dropped down and covered her ringing ears. Behind her, Shamrock let loose a muffled scream. She peeked over her shoulder and saw him fall to the ground, clutching his chest. Yonder rushed to his aid.

The forest in front of her moved as if alive. Numerous forms emerged from the shadows, and Indigo feared that the demons Shade had spoken of had somehow made their way here. Then one of them spoke, and the reality was much worse.

"Burn the rest of it," the chilling voice of Jasper Popp declared. "*All of it.*"

The order was shouted down the line.

Torches ignited, at least fifty of them spread out across the tree line. Jasper Popp looked like the demon Indigo had thought him to be, the torchlight flickering red across his pale face, framed by that ridiculous chinstrap beard. He held a weapon in his hand that resembled an elongated version of the one Shade had used against both Peter Ortiz and the Voice of Him. A gun, black and heavy and ominous. All around him, his fellow Righteous hooted and hollered and started charging toward those gathered around the burned housing complex.

Indigo fought against the desire to squeeze her eyes shut and block out her ears when her people started screaming. She only stared up at the hateful man who hovered above her.

"Where is he?" Jasper growled. "The one who destroyed my property?"

She pressed her lips together and said nothing.

"Fine," he said. "The hard way it is."

He stuffed the gun in his belt and drew back his arm dramatically, as if making a display out of hitting her. Indigo used his moment of showiness to her gain. In a blur of movement, she rolled toward him and kicked out her leg. Her foot connected with his shin, and Jasper let out a gasp of pain as he nearly fell over.

Strong arms wrapped around her before she could press her advantage. Those arms squeezed, bony knuckles pressed firmly against her breastbone. She wrenched her torso, trying to break free.

"Indigo, stop!" someone pleaded into her ear. "Don't make this harder than it already is."

She craned her neck to see Anthony Bell, illuminated by the halo of dancing light given off by the torch Jasper held. His face twisted into a tense, tooth-gritted expression.

His arms squeezed tighter, leaving Indigo gasping for air. In front of her, Jasper righted himself and cracked his neck. This time he did not create a spectacle out of her pain. He struck her hard and fast with his closed fist, snapping her head back and splitting her bottom lip. The left side of her face immediately went numb; a high-pitched buzzing filled her head.

He grabbed a handful of her hair and pulled taut. "You're gonna suffer," he snarled, his spit splashing her cheek. "I'm gonna kill all your people while you watch. And then I'm gonna make sure this whole damn place is reset." He yanked her head aside and glared at Anthony. "Keep her here until it's time."

"Um, sure thing, boss," Anthony stammered.

Jasper whipped his gun back out, spun around, and stomped away. Indigo could not see what was going on in the distance, but she clearly heard the screams and shouts and banging on stone. She watched

Jasper pause in front of Yonder, who still sat on the grass, holding a gasping Shamrock in her arms. The Righteous man shot them both in the head. They collapsed on top of one another and fell still. Indigo hoped that when they ascended, they did so long after Shade had freed them all.

More screams erupted from up the hill and across the road. Indigo gritted her teeth and commenced struggling. She needed to get out of there. She needed to go to her people. If they were all going to be ascended this night, she wanted to ascend along with them.

"Cut it out, Indigo!" Anthony yelled. "Just give me a few—"

There came a hollow *thonk*, and the man went suddenly rigid. His hands unclasped, his arms slid weakly down her front, and his weight pressed against her back. Indigo gathered her wits enough to hop aside, letting his limp body fall to the grass. She could not see him clearly without the torchlight, but she swore something glistened with wetness atop the outline of his head.

"C'mon," a woman whispered. Soft fingers brushed Indigo on the wrist.

She instinctively recoiled. The outline of wild curls in the sparse moonlight, along with the bluish glow of a particular crystal pendant, revealed that it was Sophie standing there, holding a felled tree branch.

"Get away from me," Indigo demanded.

"Whatever you want," Sophie said, backing up slowly. "Just do me a favor and get to the tavern as fast as you can. It's the only relatively safe place."

With that, the woman took off, following the path Jasper had taken, up the hill and across the road. Meanwhile, Indigo was lost in a spiderweb of confusion. Had a Righteous woman just protected her from a Righteous man?

The groans coming from Anthony, sprawled out on the grass, proved the answer was *yes*.

Without questioning it again, Indigo hefted her skirts and ran. She kept her distance from the road, just in case, measuring her strides and breathing in through her nose and out her mouth. Hickweis

Tavern was three-quarters of a mile from here. If she kept a steady pace instead of sprinting, she would have enough wind left to help guide however many of her people were left once she arrived.

The hill rose slightly, the forest drawing closer to the road, and much to her amazement, she saw a whole throng of Ersatz racing along above her. The larger races carried their smaller brethren on their shoulders as they ran. Sienna was among the flock, kicking up dust as she pulled ahead with her long strides. Indigo shifted direction, pounding her slippered feet uphill until she trod over cobbles instead of grass. She fell in beside Aspar, who was slowed by helping a gamayun girl named Canary keep pace. Canary clenched at the blood-drenched feathers covering her chest, laboring with every step.

Indigo and Aspar locked eyes briefly, and he grimaced. She wanted to ask what happened back there, but of course she could not, given the circumstances. Her heart thundered, and she gave up on trying to preserve her energy. She lifted her skirts higher and put on speed, easily outracing the rest of her people until she ran alongside Sienna. The elf looked at her askance, but Indigo paid her no mind. She ran even faster, leaving Sienna in the dust.

Hickweis Tavern appeared and disappeared each time she crested one of the rolling hills along the road, until the land flattened out and her destination was finally within her grasp. The terrace was crowded with Ersatz.

She skidded to a halt when she reached the stairs, grabbing the railing to keep from sliding right on past. Macaro gaped at her from the porch, with Vivo, Bluebell, Pipi, and the other courtesans flanking him. Orchid squeezed to the front of the throng, her already wide eyes ready to pop out of her skull. When the courtesans saw the mass of people swiftly approaching, their eyes bulged as well.

"What's happening out there?" Macaro asked.

"The Righteous." Indigo spat through her teeth. By the overgod, she was *breathless*.

The expression Macaro wore turned sour. "They turned on us? Is this like what Natalie Rowen did that got Raz—"

"No, not them," she blurted out. "The other ones. They...they came back... They..." She threw her hands in the air. "Gyah! It does not matter. Our people need help. Many are hurt. Get down here and make sure everyone gets inside."

Those standing on the porch burst into motion as soon as the words left her mouth. They dashed toward the onrushing Ersatz, the fresher legs of the tavern staff assisting the wounded. Pride surged through Indigo as she watched Mana lend her shoulder to a limping hobgoblin. When Beaver, the half-orc who ran the stables, scooped a weakened drow into his arms like she weighed nothing. When Pipi encouraged a pair of gnomes to climb onto her back instead of continuing to ride a satyr who was favoring his left side.

Indigo stood in the middle of the courtyard, managing the situation as best she could. "Go, get them inside!" she commanded. "Do not linger on the first floor. Take as many as you can up to the rooms. We need to fit as many into the tavern as possible. Hurry!"

Her people proved to be good listeners, as always. They formed a zippering stream that swiftly flowed up the staircase and through the tavern doors. None were knocked aside, none fell and were trampled; when someone lost their balance, their neighbor helped keep them upright. It was a show of community support in a time of crisis that she felt certain the Righteous would not appreciate.

When Aspar arrived, Indigo called him over. He handed a still-struggling Canary off to Aqua and approached her.

"What happened back there?" she asked while urging her people onward in an orderly fashion.

"They came out of nowhere. More Righteous. I think I recognized a couple from the last batch. They attacked us while we were preparing to enter the burned dormitory. They carried torches." His face looked pained, as if his mind struggled to make sense of the words he spoke. "It was the *other* guests who gave us time to run. They attacked their brethren without warning. It shocked me as much as it shocked them, I think."

She nodded sharply. "Thank you, Aspar. Now help get everyone inside."

"Yes, Mum."

He ran off to help an elf keep himself upright before he fell in the middle of the crush of bodies. Indigo resumed walking up and down the line, shouting instructions, always aware of those coming toward the tavern along the road. Her people were still arriving in trickles, but there was no sign of the Righteous. She could hear the surreal *pop-pop-pop* of their weapons echoing through the valley.

Finally, the last stragglers made their way into the tavern, shielded by the pink granite walls. New shouts sounded from the direction of Merchantry Road. Indigo passed off to Bluebell the injured satyr she had been helping to walk and ran toward the sound, again wishing she could see in the dark.

People appeared from around the stretch of woods, running at breakneck speed over the cobbles and waving their arms. Their voices combined, creating a sound like water poured from a jug. Bright flashes went off when one of them turned around.

They drew close enough where Indigo could make out the faintest of their features, and she realized these were her current Righteous guests. Yet another mass of humanity followed a couple hundred feet behind. Indigo stiffened, watching the last of her people enter the relative safety of Hickweis Tavern.

"Indigo, come now!" shouted Macaro. The dwarf held open the door and pinwheeled his arm. Vivo and Pipi lingered behind him, both looking ready to fight—however worthless a fight it might be.

It would be so easy for Indigo to scamper into the tavern and bar the doors and windows right this moment. Hickweis Tavern was made of stone; it would be nearly impossible for their attackers to burn the place down with them inside. They could bide their time, wait to see if Shade could somehow accomplish his mission and allow them to protect their own lives. But then she would be leaving their current guests, who had fought their own people to protect the Ersatz, who were at the mercy of a much larger and more bloodthirsty force.

"Not yet!" she called out to Macaro. "Keep the door open!"

She moved off the path, gesticulating wildly so those approaching would know shelter awaited. The guests drew closer and closer, until she could clearly see Sophie, her long curly hair trailing behind her. Nathan was at her side, panting as he fiddled with his walking stick. The man spun around quickly, aimed the stick at the sky. A bright flare erupted from the end of it, arced across darkness, and splattered against the ground. Whatever the substance was spread out to all sides like living blue fire, illuminating their pursuers. Those nearest the blue fire convulsed and fell. Nathan emitted a brief cheer before turning tail and booking it to keep up with his fellow guests.

They were going to make it.

Indigo pivoted, intent on letting Macaro know it would only be a few more seconds, but something hard and heavy collided with her before she could say anything. She fell onto her back, and whatever had struck her landed fully on her chest, knocking the wind out of her. She gasped for air, struggling against a fleshy thing that stank of piss and bourbon.

"Did you actually think we wouldn't split up? Idiot. I guess that's why we're the masters and you're the playthings."

The man atop her drew back. With the light streaming out of the tavern windows, she saw him clearly. It was another of those who followed Jasper Popp, a rough loudmouth named Will Velent. He had obviously come from the other direction, which Indigo had not expected. This meant he likely had others with him...all while Macaro still held the door open.

Perhaps she truly was the idiot the Righteous man claimed her to be.

"It's a shame, really," Will said, leering down at her with cruel eyes. He pressed the flat edge of a knife with a wicked blade against her cheek. "Such a pretty face. Maybe the company president can put it on another of his dolls. Or maybe I'll just keep it for myself."

The coldness of the steel retreated as Will slowly turned the knife, ready to slice into her flesh. An otherworldly calm settled over Indigo. She could barely breathe, but she could still defend herself to a point. And perhaps, if that lingering thread of hope within her held true, she could do much more than that.

She curled her right leg over the back of the man straddling her, hooking her ankle around his side while at the same time grabbing tight to his wrist. She grinned and wrenched her hips, using his lack of balance against him. Her legs were powerful enough to wrench him, making him shout out in pain. She then jerked her hand, and the combined motion of his falling one way while she twisted the sensitive joint snapped his wrist. His fingers went limp, the knife fell to the grass, and he toppled off her, blubbering and screaming.

Indigo snatched up the blade, flipping quickly to her feet. On instinct, she dropped the full weight of herself onto the prone man, blade held in both hands, ready to plunge it into his heart. She could visualize herself doing it, actually *saw* the blade pierce skin and slide between ribs. But when she was inches away from killing the evil man, her every muscle became hard as stone. Pain rocketed through her as she froze on her knees, as if time had stopped only for her.

Her ability to move returned only when someone else clobbered her on the side of the head. She blacked out for a second, only to come back when her face struck the dirt. Slickness painted the right side of her face; her mouth tasted of copper. Her new attacker, a woman with long hair and a savage glare, raised a club, ready send Indigo into her next ascension.

Something large and sharp suddenly ejected from the woman's mouth. For a moment, Indigo wondered why this Righteous woman had a tongue that resembled a sharpened stake. But then the eyes of her attacker bulged. Her body shook and she toppled to the side, revealing Gia, her dreadlocks dripping with sweat. The short, pretty Righteous girl stepped on the back of the blond woman's head, yanking the spear free. She flicked blood and brain matter off the tip, then whipped it around her back with one hand while offering the other to Indigo.

"C'mon," she said. "We don't have time."

While a riot raged around her, Indigo accepted the offered hand. She was pulled to her feet, still wobbly from the blow to the head. From the corner of her eye, she noticed that Will Velent was also not moving and likely dead. Someone else came at her from the other side. An arm snaked around her waist, urging her to run, which she did as best she could.

She was nearly carried up the tavern steps, where Vivo and Aqua grabbed her and brought her inside. They propped her up against the bar, made sure she was steady, and then rushed back to the front door. Indigo gripped tightly to the edge of the counter behind her with both hands. The pain wracking her body made her dizzy, but she was aware enough to take stock of her situation.

At least a hundred of her people packed the main room of the tavern. Tables were shoved together so the most severely injured could be laid atop them while other tended their wounds. And there were wounds aplenty—blood splashed to the floor, leaking from cuts and scrapes and bullet wounds and deep gashes.

A perverse relief washed over Indigo. The wounded did not seem as numerous as she had feared. Most wore their minor cuts and scrapes as if they were part of their everyday attire—which, for an Ersatz, was not far from the truth. Her eyes flicked toward the ceiling. She wondered how many had sought shelter in the private rooms up there, which in turn made her wonder how many of the three hundred and ninety-four Ersatz had been stricken down in the initial attack, how many had made it to safety, and how many would succumb to their wounds.

No matter how this played out tonight, she imagined that Tro Choi would be overflowing with ascensions soon.

Someone shouted an order, which brought her gaze back to the tavern entrance. The Righteous guests who had turned on their own worked alongside her courtesans to barricade the door. A quick count told her that all eighteen had made it inside. It was Nathan who shouted out directions, and those fortifying the door followed his every command. He seemed well versed at this sort of thing, much too well versed for someone who claimed to be an artisan.

"Why are they here, Mum?"

Indigo saw Orchid standing on the bar. Her tiny hands were clasped in front of her chest as she stared at the potential villains invading their safe haven. She blinked her huge eyes, and her body shuddered.

"They assisted us," Indigo said in what she hoped was a calming tone.

"Why?"

"I...I do not know, sweetling."

"I do not trust them," Orchid said.

Indigo glanced again at the door, where Nathan was now busy poring over something that looked like a book while the others put the finishing touches on the firmly secured door.

"I do not, either," Indigo whispered.

"Perhaps we do not have to." Orchid lifted her hopeful gaze. "Perhaps Aumor will soon be reborn."

Indigo tried not to think of all the horrible things that might have befallen her beloved stranger. "I would not count on it."

"What about the Voice? Should Aqua fetch the horn? Should I blow it again? He will surely help us, will he not?"

"It is something to consider..."

Whatever Orchid said in reply was drowned out by the distracted thoughts running through Indigo's head. She took in the scene again. With the initial tumult died down, the moans of the injured and the encouraging words of those caring for them were all she could hear. Even the ruckus caused by those trying to fortify the door had gone silent.

It was not the silence inside the tavern that distracted her, but the fact she could hear nothing going on *outside*. Fear swelled from her core, and Indigo left Orchid without another word. She meandered through the mass of her people, heading for an open spot by one of the lower windows that had not been obstructed.

She placed a hand on the wall, and the coldness of the stone overwhelmed her. Leaning to the side, she peered through the bottom corner of the window. What she saw outside she could not quite understand.

It was nearly as bright as daytime out there. A glow rose above the distant trees, signifying that Merchantry Road was fully on fire. In the courtyard, both the pavilion and the empty stables had been set ablaze, the flames licking a good twenty feet into the night sky.

The interlopers gathered around Hickweis Tavern, their acts of vandalism apparently finished. They stood side by side across her line of sight, and she assumed they had completely encircled the building. They all held weapons—a few with guns both long and short, but most with clubs and machetes—but they did not attack. They simply stood quietly, burning torches in hand, and stared.

"What in the name of the overgod are they doing?" Indigo whispered.

The circle parted, and a lone figure on horseback trotted into view. He was an old man, with chopped gray hair and a long gray beard. He cut an imposing figure with his broad shoulders and haughty posture. The man looked down at the corpses of the two Righteous sprawled out twenty feet from the stairs. He barked something Indigo could not hear, and another pair of invaders stepped forward to retrieve the bodies.

"Aw, shit. He made an appearance. I knew it."

Indigo jerked her head at the sound of the voice. Nathan stood at the other corner of the window, that slender black book still in his hands. Indigo had not noticed him approach.

"Who is that?" she asked.

"Hugo Popp," the young Righteous man said. "Jasper's dad, and the guy who runs the family business."

Indigo furrowed her brow and looked back outside. She had met Hugo Popp many times; he had been a constant visitor to Darkenwood in his youth. The man she saw out there now, though imposing, was but a shade of the authoritative brute he had been when she had last seen him. That must have been twenty, perhaps even thirty years ago.

Time had a tendency to mean little when you lived two centuries.

"You said you knew he would come?" Indigo said, eyeing Nathan suspiciously.

If Nathan noticed her distrust, he did not show it. "Well, I kinda thought he would. Hugo sent a letter to the president of Viral Ventures the day after his son got booted outta here, demanding compensation for one of his assets getting killed." He shrugged, his gaze still locked on the happenings outside. "He was *pissed*. He talked about burning the whole place down. That's why my group came here. To see if there was any truth to his claim and to take precautions in case it was an actual threat and not just talking out his ass. Looks like he wasn't. There he is, with his own little army. *God*, do I hate rich people."

"Who *are* you?" Indigo asked.

"Nobody. Not anymore." Nathan finally glanced her way, offering her a strange, cringing smile. "I guess you could say I work for the Architect."

Indigo raised her eyebrows. "The Architect?"

"The guy who built this place," Nathan said with a humorless chuckle.

That made no sense, considering the Ersatz had always been told that Darkenwood was created by the overgod Rawg. Indigo wanted to question him more but decided against it. This whole situation—her entire *life*—was bewildering enough without trying to pry sensible answers from someone who only spoke in ominous vagaries.

Instead, she turned her gaze back outside. While most of the Righteous invaders continued to stand in their wide circle, a few of them, including Jasper and his wife, had gathered around the elder Popp and were now engaged in an animated conversation. Indigo wished she could hear them. Another trio of horses entered the circle, one of which was attached to a cart. Jasper shared a look with his father, then flicked his fingers at the other men who had been conversing with them. The men on two of the new horses began to slowly canter away, followed by the one hauling the cart. More Righteous on foot filled in the line behind them. Perhaps thirty of them.

"Are they leaving?" Indigo asked.

"Nope," Nathan said with obvious disdain.

Outside, the horses and those who followed them had left the circle, and it closed again. Hugo began picking at his fingernails.

Indigo stood there flummoxed. "Why are they not attacking?"

"They're waiting," said Nathan.

"For what?"

The man sighed. "Killing you lot doesn't do anything, because you'll just come right back. That's why so few of you died in the initial surge. They wanted to hem you in, keep you in one place. Which they did. And now Hugo's sending a group of men out to make sure that when they kill you this time, you *stay* dead. They'll only attack when that's done."

The truth of what he was saying hit Indigo right in the gut. Her jaw dropped open. "They are going to destroy Tro Choi."

"Exactly."

"How do you know?"

"Because it's what I would do," he said grimly. He lifted his book again, and his fingers danced across its hidden page. "Don't worry, I'm trying to figure something out."

"You are not armed, there are not enough of you to protect us, and we cannot defend ourselves." She leaned against the wall and closed her eyes. In the darkness behind her eyelids, the pain of her injuries came back tenfold.

"Perhaps it is best to give in," she said. "Let us all die for real this time. Let the suffering come to an end."

"You really think Shade wants that?" Nathan said without looking up.

Her eyes shot open. "You know of Shade?"

"I know of a lot of things."

"Then you know Shade is dead."

"Yeah, no he's not." He finally lifted his gaze from his book. "I told you I know a lot of things, just like I know what you're gonna say now. But you're just gonna have to trust me on this. He's alive. He's almost there. He might not accomplish what he hopes to, but there's still a chance."

"A chance for what?"

"A chance you'll get your wish. That all this'll be over before the sun comes up tomorrow, and I can walk outta here without Sophie slitting my goddamn throat."

He left her then, heading back toward the group of Righteous turncoats who were now gathered around Macaro at the bar. Indigo watched the man depart, a lump in her throat. She could not think about the significance of what he had just told her, nor ponder what role he played in the madness.

He had just said Shade still lived, and that was all that mattered.

If true, her tiny blossom of hope was still alive and well.

17

> *Beware the danger of selfless acts.*
> *For giving freely of yourself produces a culture of dependency,*
> *which is the Dragon that will swallow the world.*
> —Book of the Pentus, Platitudes 3:14

This is hopeless.

That was the only thought running through Shade's head as he climbed the narrow staircase cut into the side of the mountain. It was not the steepness that got to him, since the stairs had been constructed so that the rise was gradual and easily traversed. Nor was it the biting cold wind that fluttered his duster and made his bones ache. Compared to his initial trek up the path at marker seventeen, this was as simple as putting one foot in front of the other.

No, what grated on his nerves was the utter monotony of it all. Everything around him, through every step along this secret staircase, was the same. The same fifteen-foot-high concrete wall dominated his right side, which he pressed against on his way up so that he didn't chance tumbling over the precipitous drop three feet to his left. The only ways open to him were forward and back, and after coming this far, he was *not* about to turn back. But with his inability to see over the wall, there was no way for him to mark his progress.

For all he knew, he could be stuck here forever, like the spirits of the damned in Nowhere, the First Hell, destined to wander a dismal gray nothing, slowly descending into madness until the end of days.

He'd already spent hours upon end on this staircase. He'd spent the night shivering next to that damn wall, had relieved himself multiple times on the concrete steps. His stomach cramped. With nowhere to go in search of food, he had to ration the last four dried figs in his satchel. And now night was approaching again, the sun dipping behind the peaks and turning the sky into a deepening purple-black bruise.

He fought back his body's protests, held Indigo in his thoughts, and kept on going.

Finally, after night fully descended and the stars shone brightly, the end of his journey came into view. The path took a sudden hard righthand turn, and its angle increased significantly. A wall mirroring the one on his right now appeared on his left, and the staircase cut straight up the mountain.

At least he didn't have to worry about falling over anymore.

The going was steep, but he could clearly see the apex, where a large arch shone like a phantom bathed in starlight. Reenergized, Shade picked up his pace, ignoring the soreness of his muscles, nearly skipping from step to step.

He paused twenty steps from the end and forced his eyes to focus on the arch at the top. *THE GATE BETWEEN WORLDS*, the arch read, the letters cut into the stone and forming an arch all their own. Smiling, he leapt up those last twenty steps, passed beneath the arch, and stopped short.

A wide gravel path lay before him, leading through a gap between monstrous crags. Beyond that path, barely visible in the darkness, was the largest building Shade had seen outside of Breighton and New Salem. Castle Rawg at last. Bathed in shadow, it looked like a peak growing out of the side of the mountain he was on. He could make out no other details but its size. After taking a deep breath, he threw back his shoulders and took the only path offered.

The closer he drew, the more the structure's features became clear. It wasn't a castle so much as a single huge tower that a castle could fit inside of. Shade found it difficult to gauge just how big the structure was. Dominating his vision, it was at least a thousand feet wide, perhaps wider, stretching from the rugged scale of the mountain's peak to the edge of the cliffside it rested upon. The bricks used to build it were huge, likely as big as one of Cooper's horseless carriages. The height of the tower itself was so exaggerated that Shade's neck grew sore from staring up to see the parapets.

It took him far too long to cross the distance between the Gate Between Worlds and Castle Rawg. By the time he reached the base of that colossal tower, he was convinced that the structure's very existence was impossible. The sloping land around it was barren, nothing but rocks and granite and pine trees stunted by the thin air. Who built this thing? Why build it here? And how was brickwork that huge brought to a place so unreachable?

The only thing that made sense was that it was indeed constructed by a god.

As he neared the castle, stones crunching beneath his feet, a pair of bright lights flashed to life. Shade dropped into a defensive stance and shielded his eyes while reaching for his revolver. He lifted the gun, squinting against the brightness. A door stood before him set into gray-green stone. The light came from a pair of torches affixed to the wall on either side of that door. They had seemingly alighted on their own.

"That's weird," Shade whispered.

Add it to the list.

He approached the door cautiously. A simple board had been nailed at eye level, its surface slathered with a thick layer of grime. Shade used the sleeve of his duster to wipe off the muck. What he uncovered was baffling to say the least.

Welcome, you who hold the Rawgian Key.
Thank you for choosing the Path of Aumor!
We strive to make your experience as genuine as possible.
Open the door if you dare. The ultimate adventure awaits.
Good luck!

Why so cheery?

Shade shook his head, deciding not to question it. He removed the golden shaft from his bag and slid its tip into the circular hole above the door latch, twisting until he heard a *click*. The key then began spinning on its own, sinking deeper into the hole until it disappeared.

"What the hell?"

He reached for the keyhole, but before his fingers could touch the cold steel ring, the door popped open and swung inward. Stale air burped from the opening, smelling of mold and, strangely, something akin to gun oil. Shade wrinkled his nose, pushed the door the rest of the way open, and went inside.

As soon as he stepped through the opening, more torches ignited, one by one, illuminating a long stone corridor. A shiver wriggled down his spine. *What kind of magic is this?* He turned to examine the door. It seemed to be nothing but wood, six inches thick. There was no handle on the inside, nor a place for the key to exit. Going back to the front, he poked his finger into the hole where he'd inserted the key, but found it hollow. Where had the key gone? How would he get back out if it locked?

Propping the door open with his foot, he leaned outside and grabbed the closest, heaviest stone he could reach. He shoved the door until it hit the wall, then wedged the stone against it. The last thing he wanted was to get trapped in this barren corridor with only sentient torches to sustain him.

That done, he crept along the passageway. It was narrow; if he stretched his arms out at his sides, his fingertips brushed the brick walls. The ceiling hung so low that he had to fight the urge to hunch over. The torches' flames caused the heat to rise in the cramped space and cast his surroundings in flickering shades of red. Shade imagined a fissure to one of the Nine Hells might look like this from the inside. This was not the kind of thing he needed to be thinking if he wanted to stay sane.

Another door awaited him at the end of the corridor. Almost as soon as he reached it, a loud *bang* made him spin around. The door he had propped open had slammed shut, the stone spinning on the dust-covered ground like a wobbly top.

"So much for leaving that way."

Dejected, he turned back to the matter at hand. Much like the other door, this one was marked with a dust-coated sign. He blew the dust off, waved away sneeze-inducing particles, and read the bas-relief out loud, as befitted a situation this ridiculous.

"The heart and Rawg are one and the same. Both bring life, awaken desire, open doors. Both are most vulnerable right before the fires of passion erupt. Only through prying the heart from Rawg will the door of choices be opened for you. Welcome, Aumor. May you choose wisely."

Shade sneered at the placard. "Great. More metaphors. Why can't prophesies just be upfront with all this destiny shit?"

With one last shake of his head, he grabbed the door handle, pressed the latch, and stepped forward to face the Avatar of Rawg, whatever that might be.

It became obvious once he exited the corridor that the castle was hollow. Starlight shone down, for in place of a ceiling, a vast circular opening lay a few hundred feet above. His brain had a hard time rationalizing the sheer size of the place—it was big enough to fit a small town the size of Pinchu, but the gloomy, inconsistent light coming down from above made those insanely tall, circular walls seem to squeeze in on him. In a way, the place looked like a trap built to kill a god, with the array of columns that created the equivalent of a stone forest in the center of the open space, at least thirty feet tall each, creating deadly spikes to impale a lost deity when it fell.

"Stay on point," he told himself. "Choice of Choices. The heart's the key. Or something."

Before he could take a step in either direction, the door closed on its own behind him with a rattling *thud*, followed by another torch flaming to life beside his head. He squinted against the glare. The new self-lighting torch revealed that the door was flat with no handle on this side, and when he tried to pry his fingers into the frame, it remained solid as stone. Locked. Glancing to his right, he spotted a strung bow hanging on a hook, dirty but as solidly constructed as any he could find in the vault at Dakota Keep. Beside the bow hung a quiver full of arrows. Curious, he pulled one out. The tip was sharp, but the material was strangely coarse, like flint. Interesting but useless, since he had a revolver tucked beneath his armpit.

The self-lighting torch, however, unlike those lining the corridor leading here that were affixed to the walls, was a slender length of steel resting firmly in a bracket. The torch would be *much* more useful than the bow. "Thanks," he said to the emptiness as he lifted it from its sconce.

Torch in one hand and revolver in the other, he made his way around the exterior of the enormous space. There were no signs on the walls, no markers. It felt like he walked for an hour before something other than drab gray stone entered his small globe of flickering yellow light.

Another locked door with no handle. At first, Shade thought that he might have traversed the entire circumference of the tower and ended up back where he'd started, but then he noticed that this door had a three-foot-wide hexagonal notch cut into it. The door he had originally entered had been smooth. At least, that's what he remembered. It was always possible his mind was playing tricks on him.

He continued walking.

It took him another lengthy span of time to arrive back at the original door. Sure enough, it was nothing but a thick plank of wood supported by iron turnbuckles.

One way in. One way out. *The heart is the key.* Shade stared grimly at the forest of pillars in the center. "I'm gonna have to go in there, aren't I?" he groused. With a deep, resigned breath, he crossed the hundred-foot span of emptiness and entered the unknown.

The columns weren't as closely packed as they'd seemed from a distance. Rather, there was a gap of at least twenty feet between each one, though the spacing was staggered, creating the illusion of an impassable obstacle. Why someone had built this, Shade had no idea. All he knew was that it might be smarter to wait until sunrise rather than continue poking around in the dark.

Unless, of course, whatever he was searching for found him first.

Nothing jumped out at him, and he heard no sounds that might hint at something sneaking about. In fact, the only thing he heard was the reverberating bellow of the wind blowing over the open top of the tower. If the Avatar of Rawg was in here with him, it did a very good job of keeping itself hidden.

He approached one pillar, then the next, and still another. The lack of progress frustrated him to no end. As an experiment, he propped the torch against one of the columns, slipped around to the other side, and tried looking at the stone forest using only the faint starlight. After his eyes adjusted, he noticed a strange mound of a shape off to his right, as if someone had piled debris between the columns. Gathering up the torch, he headed in that direction.

Now that he saw the mound, it was easy to keep track of its outline, even with the torchlight stifling his night vision. The mass was large—quite a bit taller than him, and stretching with a noticeable hump from one side to the other. But it didn't move. He thought it could be a bunker of some sort. If there was a bunker, there would be another door. It was possible the Avatar of Rawg was hiding in there, like some fairytale witch's hut within a haunted wood, waiting to lure in wayward children to use in her stew.

Shade circled around, trying to gauge just how big this new discovery might be. It grew larger and larger as he spiraled toward it, until the deeper blackness of the thing was all he could see.

His attention was so focused on the mound that he paid no attention to where he stepped. His foot struck something large and heavy, and he tripped. He let go of the torch on his way down and it skittered away, spitting flames. His left hand broke his fall, stone biting into the knuckles of his right hand, which still held the revolver. He swore, slumped to sitting, jammed the revolver back into its holster, and shook the ache out of his fingers.

Just ahead of him, something moved.

Shade stiffened, every muscle taut with expectation. The movement stilled. After counting to ten, he got back to his feet and picked up the dropped torch, inwardly lamenting every time his duster rustled or his boots scuffed.

It took little effort to find what he had tripped over. It was a pointed black shard the length of his arm, curled like a talon, its sharp end buried in the stone floor. He stepped back and swung the torch from side to side. The shard was shaped like a talon because that's what it was. And there were two more of them, each attached to huge stubs of fingers covered with large, reddish-black scales.

The splayed hand of some enormous three-fingered beast.

He inched away slowly, trying to decide whether he should snuff out the torch. Backing into a column, he pressed against it and used its hard comfort to guide him around to the other side, never taking his eyes off that huge, unmoving hand. When he had performed a half-revolution, he went to bolt, only to pull up short when he came face-to-face with the hand's owner.

In his sudden terror at seeing the thing, Shade forgot to breathe. The red-black scales were present on its head as well, only plated and coming to spine-like points. Its nose was tapered and horned, leading to a mouth so big that Shade could climb inside and stretch out comfortably, if not for those frightening, three-foot-long teeth protruding from its gums. Above the jaw hinge was one of its closed eyes, and above that three black horns that swept back like frozen hair.

The mound he'd been approaching was the monster's body, curled up in motionless sleep, the wings that sprouted from its thick shoulders attached to the long appendages that led to those three-taloned hands.

A dragon, like one from the old storybooks in the Dakota Keep library. A goddamn *dragon*.

His breath finally exhaled when he muttered, "Shit."

The dragon's eyelid slid open. The eye that stared at him was black with glowing red veins. The slanted, reptilian pupil that narrowed and expanded as it focused was pure, blinding white. Shade recaptured enough of his senses to back away, but not enough to flee. The thing before him was just so huge, so *unbelievable*, that the sight of it drove away his better sense. Much like the first time he had encountered a hellbeast, when one look at that gargantuan, crab-like body had caused his mind to blank. He likely would have died that day if Abe hadn't been there to slap some sense into him.

Only Abe was not here with him now, and never would be again.

A series of out-of-place metallic *clanks* preceded the dragon rising from its slumber. Its head turned slowly, until it stared down at Shade with both of its brightly glowing eyes. Its long neck lifted, its shoulders hunched, and those gigantic clawed hands gouged deep into the floor. The dragon reared back, its chest rising off the ground, barbed tail whipping behind it. The thing was as tall as the columns. Its leathery wings, when puffed out, could likely swallow the entire stone forest with their width.

Shade tore his gaze off the dragon's beaked, predatory face, instead focusing on the bright light that shone from its torso. This creature had no soft underbelly like those in the old books; the thick red scales covered every inch of it that Shade could see.

All except for the sparkling red six-sided jewel embedded in its chest.

Only through prying the heart from Rawg will the door of choices be opened for you.

"You gotta be kidding."

Deep, hearty laughter formed in his chest and rocketed out his throat. He doubled over, cackling like Meesh would at a dirty joke. He was close to cracking. Still laughing, he craned his head back to meet the dragon's hateful glare and yelled, "Are you the Avatar of Rawg?"

The dragon's head tilted to one side as if confused.

"If you are, you think I could borrow that jewel there?"

In response, another metallic screech echoed seemingly from all around, followed by a series of clicks. The dragon's long neck lowered slightly; its mouth yawned open. Shade recoiled, the laughter dying in his throat. He heard a gaseous hissing sound, and when he stared down the giant beast's maw, he saw a radiant ball of flame start to form.

"Shit!"

He tossed his torch away and dove behind the nearest pillar. Just as he did, a jet of fire expelled from the dragon's mouth. The width of his shelter split the inferno into twin streams of yellow-white flame that cooked the air and made it hard to breathe. Squeezing his eyes shut, he did his best to stop his racing heart from exploding.

The spouts of flame stopped, leaving the ground around Shade smoking. He heard the creaking again, along with something that whirred and grinded like a rusted well pulley. A loud *thud* followed, shaking the stone he leaned against. Then came another. Shade chanced a peek around the smoking pillar.

The dragon was on the move. One of its clawed hands rose and fell, rustling its wings and pulling it forward between the columns. Then it brought forth the other hand, which hit the ground only fifty feet from Shade's hiding place. The barbed tail continued to whip while its rear legs, which Shade could now see were stunted like a bat's, moved to lurch it forward even more.

He had no experience with mythical beasts, but in a brief moment of calm clarity, he thought the dragon was moving all wrong. Its every motion seemed hesitant, almost herky-jerky, as if the signals from its brain were having a hard time reaching its extremities—something he might be able to use to his advantage. If only he could think straight, since that damned irritating squealing and grinding kept bouncing off the columns and inside his skull.

Another stride forward for the dragon. Much too close. As an experiment, Shade lifted his revolver and fired a single shot at the beast. It acted as if it felt nothing. So that wasn't going to work. How in the world was he supposed to get the jewel out of the chest of something that huge and powerful? There was no way he'd be able to do it by facing it head on. Maybe if he found a way to get behind it…

"Beats no plan at all," he whispered as he started running.

As soon as he emerged from behind the pillar, the dragon picked up its speed and those weird sounds reached a crescendo. Shade darted around one column, then another, using his quickness to his advantage. It seemed to be working. The dragon couldn't easily maneuver between the pillars, forcing it to backtrack and choose a new path whenever Shade changed course. And when that high-pitched hissing filled the air, he made sure to duck for cover just before another stream of fire puked from the dragon's maw.

But the more he played this game, ducking in and out of hiding and attempting to lose himself in the stone forest, the more he realized all this effort was for nothing. The dragon had stopped chasing him and instead simply mirrored his movements, making sure it faced him no matter where he ran and spitting out constant licks of flame to slow him down. The thing must have had great eyesight to be able to track him given how dim it was in the tower.

After the seventh time Shade hid from a torrent of fire, dejection overwhelmed him. This was taking far too long, and he had absolutely no idea how to gain the upper hand. He thought of Indigo again, and of Macaro and Aspar and Mana and Aqua and Pipi and Vivo. All those souls who had been tortured for sins they didn't even know they had committed. Tortured by a deity represented by the dragon here in this tower. If he couldn't find a way to win, if he couldn't make the Choice of Choices, then what purpose did any of this serve? What did his love for Indigo mean? What had the meeting of their passions accomplished?

That last question caused a needle to skip over the record of his thoughts. The image of the bow and quiver by the door entered his mind, and an idea bloomed. His heartbeat picked back up. Readying his revolver, he chanced peering around the column. The latest attack of flaming breath had just ceased, leaving everything scorched and steaming.

There was the dragon, perhaps two hundred yards away, squatting on its hind legs and leaning forward, its weight balanced on those long front arms, wings folded back. Remnants of liquid fire dribbled off jaws that slowly worked up and down. Smoke billowed from between its teeth. The crystal in its chest glowed, and the creature posed as if showing off its prize, taunting its opponent.

Shade grinned. "Like to play games, huh?"

He shot out from behind the column like a sabrewolf that had spotted easy prey. He became a bellowing madman, running directly at the massive thing. The dragon didn't seem surprised, but that was okay. The beast was slow and awkward. Shade could benefit from that sluggishness.

When he had closed half the distance between himself and the dragon, its serpentine neck uncoiled, its red mouth gaped, and that hissing, gaseous sound made itself known once again. Shade quickly ducked behind the closest pillar just before the dragon let loose another of its seemingly unlimited gusts of blazing breath.

He huddled against the upright length of stone, waited until the flames abated, and then burst into motion before the stone around him stopped glowing. His feet moved faster this time, anticipation and danger giving his muscles energy the way the Rush had once.

Everything was scorching hot. Sweat drenched his clothes; his slouch slipped off his head and bounced against his back by its string. He closed in on the immense creature. A hundred feet, seventy-five, fifty. It raised one clawed hand that was twice his size and took a herky-jerky forward stride. Shade was so close now that nothing existed but the dragon. Its mouth opened—he swore he heard a squeal like a steel bar being bent by a gale-force wind—and Shade lifted his revolver. He was only twenty feet away now and had to crane his neck to see the dragon's face. He was so close that he could see the gas billowing deep in the beast's throat, a spark that would soon ignite that gas into a homicidal river of fire.

He aimed right down its gullet and pulled the trigger.

As soon as he felt the recoil, he tumbled to the side, hoping against hope that his aim was true. Sliding in behind yet one more stone column, he hugged his forearms over his ears just in case his plan worked.

It did.

A concussive boom sounded almost immediately, and the column he hid behind trembled. A flash of light turned the forest of pillars into the surface of the sun, so bright that it stabbed at his brain even when he closed his eyes. The ground shook. Tiny bits of gravel bounced like thousands of fleas desperately searching for a nest of hair to call home.

Chunks of flaming dragon fell from the sky in a fiery rain, hitting the ground and rolling, trailing sparks and smoke. His vision blurred by the detonation, Shade saw it all clearly nonetheless. Though he felt like he had cotton stuffed in his ears, he heard those bits clang when they landed, one after another, all around him.

He wondered if this was what the beginning of the world had been like, when cosmic debris fell from the heavens and cratered the planet's surface. He squeezed his eyes shut, dropped his head between his knees, and prayed to no god in particular that he might be spared the indignity of coming this far only to be crushed by a falling hunk of mythical beast.

He remained like that until the ringing in his ears subsided. Warily, he lifted his head and opened his eyes. Everything seemed to have gone still. The crackle of small fires was the only sound he heard. A wretched smell that he couldn't quite place assaulted him. Bringing his shirt up to cover his nose, he peeked around the pillar.

There sat the dragon, unmoving. It was still up on its haunches with its neck lifted, though there was no longer anything attached to it. Flames and sparks jetted from the mess of pulverized red scales where the head had once been.

I killed it, right? he wondered. Of course he had. It had no head. But if that was the case, then why was it still upright? Shouldn't it have collapsed? Otherwise, how was he going to get that stupid jewel, nested in the dragon's chest, far too high up for him to reach, its light gone out?

As if to answer his unasked questions, the dragon began to move. A familiar whirring sound accompanied the body's downward tilt. Shade spun around and ran out of its path of descent. If the thing fell on top of him, he would be crushed instantly.

Miraculously, the body didn't fall. Instead, as Shade looked on from a safe distance, its forearms started to bend. The torso lowered closer and closer to the ground. All movement ground to a halt.

Shade stared at the thing as he mindlessly stroked his beard. The jewel was now within arm's reach, but that wasn't what captured his attention. Rather, it was the clear view he was now afforded of the end of that serpentine neck.

No blood dripped from the jagged opening; instead, wires sparking with electricity danced from the opening. The visible portion of the creature's spine wasn't made from bone, but a half-melted steel girder. The liquid that bubbled out was black and thick and caustic, and he realized right away that it was the source of the smell he couldn't place earlier—a mixture of oil and grease.

This wasn't a dragon. It was a goddamn machine, like the silver knights that guarded the Cooper Nuclear Station.

Shade let out a deep breath, lifted his slouch from his back, and plopped it back on his head. He couldn't understand why the overgod of the Ersatz would choose a machine to be its champion, nor why it would place instructions that hinted at how to defeat said champion in front of its lair. It seemed as if it was *asking* to be defeated.

"Don't think about it too hard," he said, channeling his inner Meesh. "Gift horses and all that."

He waited a few more seconds to be sure the machine-dragon wouldn't lower any more, then marched forward, careful to avoid the sparks and oil dripping from its headless neck. Thankfully, the jewel was less than a foot above his head—the perfect height for him to grab the edges and wrench it free.

He reached up, grabbed the crystalline edges, and pulled. The thing barely wobbled. He tugged harder, shimmying it back and forth, and even lifted both feet to see if gravity would help. In the back of his mind, he feared that the added weight might cause the arms supporting the mechanical beast to slip and bring its full weight crashing down on him.

Don't be an idiot, he chided himself. This thing had to weigh at least a thousand tons. His extra hundred and eighty pounds wouldn't make any difference.

Finally, the jewel shifted in its socket. Shade continued to twist and yank, and eventually resorted to using Cooper's saber to pry at the corners. It worked. The shimmering crystal broke free with a loud snapping sound and fell clattering to the ground. Shade hopped back so it wouldn't crush his toes, watched it teeter and totter from one side to the other. Glancing up, he spied the steel bracket that once held the jewel in place. *PHUNG DYNAMYX* was stenciled in bright white on the fastener's smooth surface.

Those same words were printed on the box containing the unbound Eldersword that Cooper had found in a cave near Lemsberg.

More connections clicked into place. Shade had seen and heard Asaph say such things when Vera showed him Abe's last moments on the black mirror in the Heartcube chamber beneath the Cooper Station. That the Knights Eternal hadn't been created by the Pentus, but by the Ancients themselves. For the dragon to have the same emblem on it as something that had contained supposedly sacred weapons changed everything.

It meant the maniac Asaph hadn't been lying. The Pentus truly wasn't real.

And neither was the overgod Rawg.

Shade's expression shifted from grin to grimace. Everything he'd ever believed had just been shattered—completely this time. Conflicting emotions surged through him. If there was no Pentus, that meant there were no vows for him to break. No overgod meant the Ersatz likely hadn't been sinners, and they had been punished for no goddamn reason.

Enraged now, he scooped the crystal off the ground and ran as fast as he could out from under the stilled machine dragon. The rock was heavy and slippery, which made it difficult to carry. He hugged it tight against himself and went on, driven by passion and sadness and hope and rage.

He sprinted along the wall of the tower, his lungs aching with every stride. The door he was looking for appeared much more quickly this time. He took it as a blessing, since lugging a thirty-pound hunk of crystal against his chest had caused his back to throb.

As soon as he reached the door, he hefted the crystal with both hands and pressed it into the hollowed-out opening. When he'd looked at the imprint earlier, it appeared to be carved into the wood, but when he shoved the hexagonal hunk of quartz into place, he heard a *thunk*. The jewel began to glow pinkish-red.

The jewel remained in place when Shade removed his hands. There came a loud banging sound, and the door abruptly swung inward. He yanked the revolver back out in case some new threat awaited him and strode purposefully through the opening.

The space he entered was a comparably small, twenty-by-twenty room. Like the corridor leading to the center of the tower, its walls were gray brick. The only light source came from a lit candelabra positioned on the opposite side of the room, standing beside a strange contraption that looked like it had grown right out of the rough stone floor. For whatever reason, he thought it looked like a torture chamber, yet he'd never *seen* an actual torture chamber.

After glancing at the door behind him—the only way in or out of this room—he swallowed any misgivings and approached the odd device. It resembled a sundial placed on its side and half-buried in the floor so that only the upper half-circle was exposed. Attached to the sundial by a triangular brace was a lever that rose to the middle of Shade's chest.

He squatted down to examine the half-sundial. Notches marked the curve, but there was nothing else he could glean from the thing. Shade sucked in his bottom lip.

"What *is* this?" he muttered.

"*This is the Choice of Choices,*" a flat female voice echoed all around him. "*The end of the line. Congratulations on successfully completing the Path of Aumor.*"

Shade leapt to his feet just as the door slammed shut behind him. What the hell was it with this tower and its doors that swung closed on their own? He spun in a circle, looking for whoever had spoken, but there was no one in here with him.

The voice returned as if the walls had birthed it: "*The time has come, Aumor Reborn. The decision must be made.*"

"What decision?" he shouted at the emptiness, feeling both silly and terrified.

"As you have defeated the Avatar of Rawg, the overgod now blesses you with a choice."

"The overgod doesn't exist!" he said. "None of this is real!"

"One path marks endowment," the voice continued. *"Swing the lever to the right, and you will be given all that men have ever desired—gold, influence, power. To do as you wish, when you wish. To travel all of Pirie in luxury. To never have anyone question your intentions. You will never want again, not for the rest of your dying days. This is what the overgod has promised."*

"I don't want that," Shade announced. "I'm here to free the Ersatz."

The voice hitched before continuing: *"The second path leads to independence. Should you draw the lever to the left, the one you adore, who has sinned against man and their creator, shall be granted agency. Free to build their own destiny. Free to retaliate against their oppressors. Free to live and love as they so choose."*

Shade reached for the lever. "That's what I want."

"Free to live the rest of their days without you," the voice said, freezing him just as his fingers wrapped around the lever's grip.

"What?"

"Both choices before you require a sacrifice. For power, the sacrifice is others; for freedom, the sacrifice is oneself. Choose endowment, and your love will live on as they always have, while you will become as a god among men; choose independence, and the sins of a single Ersatz will be forgiven, while you will perish here in this very room."

A pause: *"What choice do you make?"*

Shade stood there, stunned. "That's not a goddamn choice!" he screamed.

But it seemed the voice was done talking.

His hand slipped off the lever. Of course this would be how it ended. All his effort, all his passion, and this was the choice he was given? To enrich himself or die? And his sacrifice wouldn't even free all the Ersatz! There had to be another way, an option that would allow him to liberate the entire valley and not have it cost him his life. He simply couldn't think of any. That lack of ideas drove a spike into his heart, threatening to send him spiraling into despair.

Suddenly a light went off within him and he returned to himself. This wasn't a choice at all, he realized. This was his destiny. This was what he had been created to do.

Eventually, the yearning for freedom manifests itself.

If he released even one enslaved person from their bonds, could that not start the revolution that freed the rest? Was not death, in and of itself, a kind of freedom? Freedom from the guilt, pain, loss, and constant indecision that had plagued Shade ever since Vera disappeared from his life.

"I'm sorry, Indigo," he whispered.

He grabbed the lever again, whipped it to the left as hard as he could.

"The choice has been made."

A great rumbling shook the room. Dust and dirt fell from the ceiling in a cyclone. The bricks in the walls began to crack, chunks of stone clattered to the floor. Shade closed his eyes, pictured the wonderful woman he had grown to love. And he kept that image in his mind as he sank to his knees, the room falling apart around him, and accepted his fate.

— 18 —

The body is kindling, the mind is the flame. It is the body that feeds
the mind, and with every mystery revealed, that flame grows.
Open yourself fully to knowledge, and the body will be consumed
by the light of our Lord.
—Book of the Pentus, Havacana 6:17

The network of tunnels beneath the mountain seemed to go on forever. They were so vast and never ending that Meesh ceased finding any wonder in his surroundings. The numerous alcoves, living spaces, and scientific advancements that had allowed the Elders to survive the long years after the Rising became rote, even boring.

It didn't help that Meesh was obsessed about what the oracle had told him. That probably had as much to do with his ever-growing restlessness as anything. Though the fact he still had no concept of time down here didn't help.

"I cannot stop thinking of the Ninth Hell," Rodney said, breaking an extended period of silence.

Meesh jumped at the sound of something other than their combined footfalls. "Why's that?"

"The book says that the Obsidian Hall is the mirror of the Crystalline Hall, ruled over by the old gods that the Pentus cast into the void." He gestured to their surroundings. "Does this not seem eerily similar to that concept? From what I've seen of the Wasteland, and even Yaddo, they are lands of simplicity. Technology exists there, but it is something left behind, not understood by those who use it. The people generally live in tune with what nature gives them. What we have here, on the other hand, is an underground city that never sees the sun, full of technological marvels created by those who once resided here. Man did not exist in tune with nature in this structure, they *defeated* it. You said you think the Elders survived the apocalypse in these very tunnels, correct?"

Meesh nodded, keeping his eyes straight ahead.

"In that way, then, you could look at the Elders as the gods of the old world being cast into the void, with the void generally described as a place of darkness. Sure, there is light here, but it is *false* light, created using whatever means of power the Elders themselves created. Like gods."

"Rod, what's your point?"

"I find the comparison interesting," he said, shrugging. "I think I may simply be the type of bloke who finds comfort in examining religious concepts. The way the known or accepted past can be wedged into a doctrine that serves to unite a people and promote spiritual growth in the present. At times, at least. As of right now, I'm not entirely certain if that is the purpose of the religion that birthed you and me."

"It's not real," Meesh grumbled. "None of it is."

Rodney gave him an adorable half-smile. "I know, Meesh. That is, as you might say, my point."

They spent another indiscernible amount of time wandering through a white corridor that, judging by the billboards above the entrances to the many empty cubicles, had been a medical ward in the far-distant past. Meesh perked up. He noticed one particular billboard that made him stop in his tracks. Rodney, lost in his thoughts as usual, wandered for another twenty paces before noticing his brother wasn't alongside him anymore. He looped back to Meesh's side.

"What are you looking at?" he asked.

Meesh pointed up at the sign.

"Hm. *Radiology and Imaging*?" said Rodney. "Why does this interest you? Is it important?"

"It is, yeah. I think this is where we go now." He pointed into the room beyond, its floor littered with ancient, desiccated rubbish. "Somewhere in there's the path to Shade."

"Wait, hang on a minute." Rodney pulled out the map, unfolded it, and stared at Charlie's scribblings on the back. "The small man said nothing about taking a detour. According to what is written, we're supposed to—"

"We're going this way," Meesh proclaimed. He walked into the large open space, heading for the unmarked door at the back. The sound of paper rumpling accompanied Rodney's attempts to catch up with him.

"Would this have anything to do with what you saw in that strange room you entered yesterday?" his brother asked.

Was that yesterday?

Keeping track of time was hard when time had no meaning.

"Probably, yeah," Meesh said.

"Do you wish to talk about it now?"

"No."

"Very well. I respect your discretion."

"'Course you do."

Meesh pulled the door open. The lights came on, brightening a corridor that was far too clean for a place that'd been abandoned for centuries.

The corridor branched off in all directions, creating a maze where every path led back to that central hall. Meesh led Rodney down every single one, until he finally found the access point the oracle had sent him to.

Rodney read the sign. "Provo Engineering Only?"

"We're engineering today, brah," Meesh said with a scowl.

The door and the staircase beyond it led into a gigantic room, at least fifty feet high and filled with a network of pipes attached to huge drums the size of cottages. A stale, pungent odor filled the air, making

Meesh pull his shirt up over his nose. The two knights' feet *clanked* on the staircase. Everything else was deathly quiet.

"Any clue what this place is, brah?" asked Meesh, his voice echoing off the walls.

"I would assume a sewage treatment plant of some kind," answered Rodney. He pinched his nose. "One that has long gone to rot."

"Gross."

Once they reached the bottom of the stairs, Meesh made sure to stay in the center walkway and not get too close to the brown stains that spread along the floor beneath the giant barrels. He walked to the end of the row, through a door that slid open automatically when he approached, and into the much smaller room beyond.

That smaller room was the end of the line. There were lockers attached to the walls, shelving filled with the decayed remnants of things he couldn't identify, and a desk covered with ancient papers in one corner. Meesh walked to the desk and looked up. There. Exactly what he was looking for.

A grate in the ceiling.

"Mate, what are you doing?" Rodney asked as Meesh flung all the old papers off the desk—most of them turned to dust as soon as he touched them—and climbed up onto its rickety flat surface. He looped his fingers through the holes of the grate and tested its strength. It held firm, heavy bolts locking it in on all sides. Snatching the Eldersword from his belt, he flicked his wrist and extended the blade, which swirled with spirals of blue and red along the groove. The vibrating edge easily sliced through the grate's thick steel. Meesh hopped to the end of the desk when the grate came crashing down, its severed edges glowing bright orange.

Meesh peered into the darkened area above. It was a narrow conduit, complete with a ladder and big enough for him and Rodney to squeeze through. He reached up, grabbed the bottom rung of the ladder, and pulled. It extended downward with a rusty squeal and banged against the top of the desk. He tested its strength. It seemed stable enough.

"Going up," he said, grinning at his brother.

"You are *sure* this is the way?" asked Rodney.

"As sure as I'll ever be."

Rodney sighed. "Very well. Still, it seems like a bloody shite way to go."

Meesh did a double-take. He'd never heard his brother swear.

"Why don't you say 'shit' like everyone else?" he asked.

"I have always said 'shite.'"

"Always? You haven't even been alive a month yet."

Rodney looked up at him and shrugged. Meesh remembered something else the oracle told him and frowned. He grabbed onto the ladder and started to climb.

As they scaled the ladder in total darkness, Meesh began to feel claustrophobic. He thought he'd gotten used to not being able to see anything, but he could barely move his shoulders from one side to the other without hitting the walls of the pipe. This heightened his tension a hundredfold. Nevertheless, he kept his progress slow, not wanting a repeat performance of what had happened in the cave system when he slammed his head against the wall. Because that *hurt*.

At long last, he noticed that the echo of his breathing seemed to travel less far. Meesh reached up a tentative hand and found something hard and metallic above him. His fingers wrapped around what felt like a handle, which turned with a *thunk*. The hiss of escaping air surrounded him, and he breathed a sigh of relief. Pulling out his Eldersword was the last thing he wanted to do in such a confined space. He would rather not risk slipping on the rungs and having that vibrating blade slice into his own flesh or, for Pentus's sake, Rodney's.

Meesh grumbled at his use of his deity's name, even if it had only been in his thoughts. It was going to take some time to stop doing that.

The hatch above swung upward with a squeal when he shoved. Industrial sounds reached his ears, and his nose was invaded by an odd antiseptic smell, like bleach. Meesh climbed out, breathing easily despite that pungent odor, thankful that he wasn't in that constricting space any longer. But after he helped Rodney out of the hole and took a second to look around, his relief proved fleeting.

They were in yet another corridor, only this one had twenty-foot high glass walls on either side. The glass contained an opaque fluid that glowed with yellow light from somewhere within. They looked like a pair of fish tanks that stretched from where he stood, near a wall covered with instrument panels, into what seemed like infinity.

"Is this an... an...," he began, but he couldn't find the right word.

"An aquarium?" asked Rodney.

That was the word. He stared at Rodney, intent on asking him how he knew that, but then again, he didn't have to. Then he caught sight of something over his brother's shoulder that stole his attention away.

He brushed past his brother and pressed his hands to the glass. It felt warm to the touch, almost hot. Something lurked in there, floating from side to side, attached to the unseen floor of the tank by a slender, fleshy thread. Meesh squinted to see it better. It was a tiny red ball that made the liquid around it glisten, but the object was either too small or he was too far away for him to know for certain.

"This is very strange," Rodney said, once more giving Meesh's own reservations a voice.

"You ain't kidding." He stepped back from the glass. "All right, gotta focus on the task at hand. Let's get going. Dunno how far we still gotta go."

It was hard to take his own advice, since the farther along the glass-sealed tunnel they strode, the stranger things in the glass tanks became. More of those little balls floated in there on their tethers, growing in size and number with every few feet they walked, until it looked like they were surrounded by kelp forests, if the kelp were made of a fleshy red and black substance and had translucent orbs attached to the tops of each strand. Forms writhed about in those orbs, tiny black things that looked far too serpentine for Meesh's liking.

After another couple hundred feet, the forms in those orbs had grown to such a size that he could plainly see what they were. Embryos. Hundreds of pre-formed creatures, curled in their balls with no eyes or features and only the beginning nubs of limbs. A horrific sort of *wrongness* came over him. How in the Nine Hells had he found himself in some kind of industrial incubator?

"This...is not natural," Rodney whispered.

"No shit," Meesh said.

His brother visibly shivered. "I feel worse being in here than I did climbing into the gloam's throat. At least I knew what I was doing then. Or I supposed I did, anywho. Here..."

"I feel ya, Rod. I totally do."

Another few hundred paces, and the weirdness around them changed. The fluid-filled tanks on both sides of the corridor now contained smaller, distinct cubes. Within each cube resided a single fetus, still attached by that vein-like umbilical. These were still larger than the ones that'd come before, with fully formed extremities. Most of them looked distinctly inhuman, with heads that were much too large, or features that were animalistic, even demonic. A chill came over Meesh, and he dropped his hands to the butts of his twin revolvers, just in case.

It didn't take long for the seemingly endless corridor to reveal just how otherworldly a good number of these preformed monsters were. The cubes they resided in grew larger and larger to mimic the size of their occupants. There were infantile beasts with heads like wolves, creatures with skin that varied from stark white to gray to green to bright orange, monsters that looked like lizards with anthropomorphic bodies. It was like a human-demon breeding ground, with the demons outnumbering the humans ten to one, at least.

From somewhere up above, a mechanical arm dropped down into the liquid. Meesh stopped in his tracks, watching as the arm snatched up one of the cubes in its four-clawed grip and moved it farther along the line. A second arm appeared to grab another.

"An assembly line full of monsters," Meesh grumbled. "How awesome."

Eventually, they reached a point where the cubes didn't float randomly in the fluid, and were instead placed side-by-side, reinforcing Meesh's assumption of an assembly line. The things in the cubes were now full-grown fiends. They varied in size—some were as small as a toddler, some as tall as ten feet—and they floated there in their nakedness, eyes closed, arms and feet dangling. Meesh had a waking-nightmare moment, picturing each of these beasts, human or otherwise, all opening their eyes at once, breaking out of their cubes, and lunging at him and Rodney like Asaph's undead army.

Please no, he thought.

When the corridor finally ended, Meesh sighed in relief. He'd been starting to fear that it would go on forever. But more movement in the tanks made him pause. He grabbed Rodney's bicep in anticipation. One of the vessels to his right, containing the unconscious form of a blue-skinned, pointy-eared demon, was being snatched up by a mechanical arm. Still another arm took hold of a vessel containing a man who would've been considered beautiful if not for the horns sprouting from his head. The mechanical arms sloshed through the fluid, which had become more amber in color, and carried the vessels somewhere out of sight. Those tanks must've stretched far deeper than he first imagined.

Meesh dragged Rodney backward. A glance over his shoulder told him that the same thing was happening in the opposite tank. The whole damn place seemed to be coming to life.

"C'mon!" he yelled, and sprinted until he exited the corridor, Rodney right behind him. The space they entered was huge and empty. Meesh looked up but couldn't find the ceiling. The walls surrounding him were black and crystalline, like opal. He spun in a circle, looking for somewhere to go.

When he peered back at the path from which they'd emerged, he saw that the outside wall of the birthing tanks had two large pipes attached on either side, each wide enough to fit three of him abreast inside. The pipes climbed into the darkness above and disappeared. He didn't know what to make of them at all.

"Rod, got any suggestions?" he asked.

Rodney didn't reply.

He whirled around. Rodney had disappeared. Panic built in Meesh's ribcage. He couldn't do this without his brother. It didn't matter if Rodney was new and strange and maybe defective. The truth was that he'd grown to love and trust his tall, goofy companion. He relied on him, even.

"Um, Meesh?" Rodney called out from the darkness. "I think I found something."

The relief he felt at hearing that somber voice was palpable. He turned toward the sound.

"Where are you?"

"Over here!"

He caught a glimpse of a solitary figure standing not far off. Meesh wondered if this place changed the nature of existence and made things appear and disappear, but then he remembered he'd just been walking along a brightly lit corridor, made brighter by the fluid in those tanks. His eyes simply hadn't adjusted yet. Cursing his newfound frightfulness, he hurried in Rodney's direction.

His brother stood facing the opal-like wall, a hand on his dimpled chin.

"What's up?" asked Meesh.

"I think there's an elevator here," he said.

"A what?"

"An elevator. See?" He reached out, touched a part of the wall with his forefinger. A bright green light came on, illuminating an upward-facing arrow. A seam in the wall that Meesh hadn't noticed slid open soundlessly, revealing a little box of space beyond. The light coming from inside lit Rodney's face with soft orange light that flattened his features and made him look like a child.

"After you," Rodney said.

"What happens now?" Meesh asked, walking into the box.

Rodney entered right after. "Now, we go up. I think."

The doors slid shut, again without so much as a whisper. A distressing sensation squeezed Meesh's nethers, crawled into his stomach, and made him feel like he might vomit. The box seemed to be moving, but everything around him, from the smooth brown walls to the reflective ceiling with embedded lights, remained static.

Unlike him, Rodney appeared to be completely at ease with that fact.

Meesh leaned against the wall and closed his eyes, trying to force down his ill feelings. *Lucky bastard,* he thought while listening to Rodney whistle. *There's so much he's gotta teach me.*

An image then came to him, of a woman with blond hair on her knees before him. He suddenly felt drunk. His vision swam, his surroundings went fuzzy. The seams in the wood paneling covering the inside of the elevator began to sway from side to side like eels. He laughed, caught his reflection in the mirror opposite. Sure, he hadn't shaved in two weeks, but why was his beard so long? Why was he wearing a t-shirt and denim coat? And why was this girl trying to unbutton his leather pants after he'd downed so much whisky and snorted so much coke?

"Nico, stop," he mumbled.

The girl looked up at him, gorgeous as always, her lips slicked.

"Nico?" she said.

She had Rodney's voice.

Meesh came to with a start. He opened his eyes and saw Rodney standing in front of him, hands on his shoulders.

"What happened?" his brother asked.

"Nuthin'," he retorted, and slapped Rodney's arms aside. He stood in the corner of the *elevator* and adjusted his sore crotch.

"Meesh, is something troubling you?"

He shook his head. He wanted to forget that he'd felt such a horrible, dizzying loss of self again. If only it would stop happening.

"You'll remember," the oracle had said.

He supposed this was a part of that. But he didn't have to like it.

A soft bell chimed, and the weird feeling in Meesh's groin disappeared. He clenched and unclenched his fists, starting to feel more like himself. With an affirmative nod to Rodney, the knights stepped out of the opened door and into a narrow passage. Unlike nearly every other corridor they'd traversed since entering the cave four days ago, this one didn't go on forever. It had a very obvious end point, complete with a door and a flashing red *EXIT* sign above it.

"Hallelujah," Meesh said.

"I concur," agreed Rodney, who then asked, "Were you Anglican?"

"What? I'm...?" He let out a slow breath. "Rod, just shut up."

At the exit, Meesh hesitated before pressing the latch and pulling the door open. There were sounds behind it. Not voices exactly, but more...grunts and growls. "Great," he muttered, and took out one of his revolvers. "You should ready your crossbow, just to be safe," he told Rodney, then rolled his eyes and tapped his foot impatiently while his brother went through the laborious process of taking the weapon out of his bag and assembling it. The last time Rodney had fired the thing was at the ruins of Westgate. What, ten days ago? And he hadn't exactly been a good shot then.

"We're gonna die," Meesh groaned.

"What?"

"Nothing. Hurry."

At long last, Rodney loaded a bolt into place and stood in a comical defensive posture. Meesh put a finger to his lips and inched the door open.

He poked his head out. There was another door beside the one they'd opened, this one with strange symbols marked on it. He heard another grunt and jerked his head forward. His feet moved, one after the other, his curiosity pulling him from the safety of the corridor.

Unlike the otherworldly things down below, Meesh witnessed something he'd seen before when he stepped out into the open. The windowless room was eerily similar to the Scourger's House of Yehoshua, complete with paintings hanging on the cross-hatched walls and rows of bench seating split by a central aisle that led to the altar standing directly ahead of him.

Meesh stared at the altar, at a loss for words. It was made of black marble, and from its rear rose four huge pillars that sparkled bright green, the twins of those below. But the most surreal parts were the five man-sized spotted cats that gathered up there, creatures similar to some of those floating in the tanks. They assembled around one of the pillars and a monstrous bag of gray flesh that protruded from a portal cut into that column. Meesh was reminded of the chrysalis of the sphynx moths found on Yaddo.

The leathery surface of the chrysalis bulged and warped, and the cat-people swiped at it with their claws. A hand burst through the membrane, dripping thick red ichor.

Two of the cat-people let out a chorus of feline yips as they wrapped their clawed fingers around that grasping hand and pulled. A hand became a forearm, then a shoulder, then a head covered with gunk-slicked hair.

Meesh crept into the central aisle between the seats to get a better view. He now realized that the individual emerging from the chrysalis was very much human. It was a girl, her features slender and delicate. Her mouth opened in a silent scream as the creatures' clawed hands worked their way up her body.

He lifted his revolver and aimed at the back of one of the monsters' heads. And he would have fired if Rodney hadn't placed his hand over the gun and forced Meesh to ease it down. Meesh looked at his brother, about to ask him why the hell he'd stopped him from protecting this poor girl. But a single raised eyebrow from Rodney cut those words off before they left his throat.

The two cat-people gripping the girl pulled harder, egged on by the yips and yowls of the three standing watch. The girl's upper body emerged, followed by her stomach, followed by...

A thick, muscular trunk covered with brown fur?

Meesh's face contorted like it did every time he used the Dakota Keep bathroom after Abe. His heart momentary fluttered in sorrow at the fact he would never smell that particular rancidness, nor see the face of its progenitor, ever again.

Up on the altar, the girl was nearly free of her fleshy sheath. But she wasn't a girl at all. She was beautiful from the waist up, but below that she had the body of a horse. She inched forward on her folded horse legs, panting and gasping until she finally vomited a stream of clear fluid all over those who had been helping her. The two cat-people didn't seem to care. They hopped up on their reverse-jointed legs and, in a grotesquely human gesture, slapped one another five.

Meesh ignored them, being too fixated on the girl who was half horse, on her hooves slipping and sliding on the gunk slathering the altar when she tried to stand up. The way her legs wobbled made him think this was the first time they had ever been used.

Which, he supposed, it was.

"A centaur," Rodney whispered. "So groovy."

Meesh blurted, "A what?" far too loudly. Every creature on the altar spun toward him, their tawny eyes widening, their noses flaring.

"Okay," Meesh grumbled. "So I'm an idiot."

He craned his neck, wondering if they should flee, but unfortunately the door had sunk into the wall, its seams lining up perfectly with the wooden slats. And there was no handle to grasp. If he hadn't just stepped through the opening, he wouldn't have known it existed at all. Panicked, he faced forward again and raised his unholstered revolver. His other hand reached for the second. There were only five of the cat-beasts, and they weren't armed—other than their claws and teeth, of course. Unless they were faster than a warhorse, he should at least be able to incapacitate them rather quickly. Which he obviously needed to do, since Rodney hadn't lifted his weapon yet. He just stood there waving, as if he were welcoming old friends to dinner.

The creatures didn't attack. Instead, they gathered around the horse-girl, shielding her with their bodies. The one in the center went to the edge of the altar and dropped down to its knees.

"We have no quarrel with you," the beast said, sounding amazingly human. "Our bodies are yours to do with as you wish."

"Excuse me?" Rodney said.

Meesh was speechless.

"All we ask is that you leave our place of ascension," the creature continued. "Tro Choi is sacred, the one place in Darkenwood where the Righteous are asked not to enter. So please, kind sirs, take your leave of here."

"Only if it pleases you," added another of the cat-people.

Well *that* was unexpected.

Meesh glanced at Rodney. His brother looked comically perplexed. One of the cat people leaned into its cohort and asked, "Where did they come from?" The other one shrugged, another unsettlingly human gesture.

"We have nothing to fear from them," stated a gentle female voice.

Behind the wall of spotted cat-people, the girl with the horse's body—the *centaur*, as Rodney had called her—finally rose. Her protectors parted, allowing her to trot forward on her four wobbly legs. Her shoulders were thrown back, her chin held high. She looked regal, even if she was naked and still covered with what amounted to afterbirth. Meesh thought that if half of her wasn't equine, he might've been immensely attracted to her. Part of him actually was.

"Raz, tread lightly," another of the cat-people said. "I can speak for the first time in a very long while. I do not wish to lose that ability only moments after regaining it."

"Worry not, Gren," horse-girl Raz said. "These men are not Righteous. They will not harm us."

"Are you certain?" asked the one who knelt at the front of the altar.

"I am."

"How do you know?"

The cat-person Gren rose from its knees and quickly moved aside. The centaur stopped at the edge of the black marble altar, gazing at the knights from across the span of lush burgundy carpet that ran down the center aisle. Meesh was immobile with indecision. Should he put away his gun, or just shoot the mutant half-breed already?

"Do you see the weapon this one holds?" she said. "Have you seen its ilk before?"

"Cannot say I have," answered Gren.

"It looks familiar," said another of the identical-looking cat-people.

Raz's hands stroked the fine brown hairs just below where her bellybutton should've been. "As it would," she said quietly. "The man who attacked our camp wielded one. It is the same weapon that ascended each of you."

"Oh. Oh yes," said yet one more nameless cat-person. It grimaced, shivering all over. "I fell into the fire. I burned. It hurt."

"I am sure it did, Lull," Raz said.

"It is pain I never wish to experience again. I wish to smite the man who inflicted it upon me." Lull cocked its head, narrowing those feral eyes at Meesh and Rodney. "You say these men are not Righteous. Does that mean we are able to hurt them?"

Meesh's finger danced on the trigger. "Hey now..."

"It does," Raz said. "But you should not. The man who ascended us was not our enemy. He gifted you all with bodies that are more suitable for you than your previous had ever been."

"I suppose that is true," Lull said.

Gren scratched at the whiskers on its chin. "Does this mean they are friends, as well?"

"The man on the mountain considered Indigo a friend." Raz's striking brown eyes considered the knights once more. "Should we consider you friends as well?"

"Certainly," Rodney said in a cheery tone.

Meesh couldn't help laughing. Give it to Rodney. He slapped his brother on the shoulder, released his grip on the revolver so that it swung upside down, trigger guard hooked on his finger. Chancing a step forward, he showed it to the creatures on the altar.

"You said the guy who, um, *ascended* you had a gun like this?"

Raz nodded gravely. "The very same."

"Cool. This guy didn't happen to be about the same size as me, only with brown skin and a beard?"

"And a funny hat," the centaur said.

"That'd be Shade all right," Meesh said. He glanced at his brother. "Shade always did like his hats. Wonder where he got his new one?"

Rodney lifted his hands as if to say, *I don't know*. Of course that wouldn't mean anything to him. Rodney had only met Shade for maybe two minutes before Shade took off.

"Anyway," Meesh said. He holstered his revolver and hedged closer to the altar. "You said this guy was friends with someone you know?"

"Indigo."

"Yeah, that don't mean nothing to me. Where's this guy? I've— *we've*—been looking for our brother for some time now. If this Indigo knows where he went off to, we'd really like to know. So we can go help him."

"Indigo is the overseer. He operates Hickweis Tavern."

Meesh closed his eyes, sighed.

"Excuse me," Rodney said, raising his hand. "Where would we find Hickweis Tavern?"

Raz pointed a long, elegant finger to her left, at the tall and wide door that must've been the exit. "The road outside leads directly to the center of Darkenwood. That is where Indigo will be. Do not leave the cobbled path and you will find it. Try not to stray into the woods. It is easy to get lost in the darkness."

"Thank you," Rodney said with a slight bow.

Meesh blinked. "Easy as that? You're just gonna let us walk right outta here?"

"Why would we wish for you to stay?" asked Raz.

"Good point."

He jerked his head at Rodney, and together they made their way down the aisle. They kept as close to the benches as they could when they pivoted toward the exit. Meesh couldn't help stealing one last glance at the altar on the way by. Curiously, the chrysalis from which Raz had emerged was disintegrating right before his eyes, its liquid remains flowing through slender gaps in the marble altar.

Everything about this place was *way* too curious.

They made it outside without issue, and even after the door—which was as heavy as it was big—closed with a squeal of hinges and a *thud*, Meesh still felt the creeping sensation of six sets of alien eyes staring at him. He shuddered, looked up at the slivered sandwich of a moon overhead, and started down the stairs.

"They seemed nice," Rodney said.

"If you say so," said Meesh.

"Well, we *were* trespassing in their place of...worship? Yet they seemed amicable enough about it. Even though you almost shot them."

"I did *not* almost shoot them."

"You wanted to."

Meesh stopped on the bottom step, glaring at his brother over his shoulder. When he saw the wry smile on Rodney's face, he shook his head and hopped onto the slate walkway at the base of the stairs.

The area surrounding the temple—if that's what it was—was lovingly maintained. A wide span of ankle-high grass circled the structure. It was fronted by an insanely tall hedgerow, the only gap being the space where the walkway cut through it. Meesh came to a halt halfway along the walkway and turned back.

Now that he could see the building in its entirety, barely illuminated by the scant moonlight, it struck him just how ordinary it looked. Just another church, no more impressive than any of the worship halls to the Pentus that the missionaries had commissioned throughout the Wasteland. Amazing that something so uninspiring could hide such uncanny wonders.

Maybe that was the point.

He nudged Rodney and started walking again, but something caught his eye through the gap in the hedgerow. There were flickering lights moving out there. Torches. Heading their way. He also heard the hollow clomp of a horse's hooves.

"What's wrong?" Rodney asked.

Meesh dragged his brother back a few steps. "Someone's coming. Put that away."

Rodney slung his crossbow over his shoulder awkwardly, his brow creased. Meesh really hoped whoever approached was just as amenable as the creatures inside the temple. His brother simply wasn't ready for an encounter that couldn't be resolved with a song.

The stomping of hooves grew louder, the brightness of the torches more prevalent, and finally a horse trotted through the ten-foot-wide split in the hedgerow. The rider, a man who looked to be in his fifties with peppered hair, pulled back on the reigns. The horse neighed and swung its head.

Meesh kept his sights trained on the rider, his brain doing backflips trying to decipher what kind of character this was. Even lit only by torchlight, he could tell that this guy's cheeks lacked any of the deep creases of someone who'd lived a difficult life. His mustache and beard were uniquely styled and oiled, and he carried himself in a haughty manner. Everything about him screamed privilege, not someone who'd show up on horseback wearing riding leathers with a rifle resting sloppily across his knees. He made a sour face at Meesh and Rodney, as if them standing there was an affront to his existence.

"How'd you get here so quick?" he asked brusquely.

Meesh glanced at Rodney, then back at the rider. "We...ran?"

"Idiots. I'm surrounded by idiots." The man shook his head. "Didn't you hear what Hugo said? You were to stay behind me and Jenner. We were going to enter first, make a scene. Just in case we needed some drama to spook the locals into running."

"Sorry," Meesh said with a shrug. "Must not've heard."

Another horse entered through the hedgerow, this rider younger and even stuffier-looking than the first. More people followed on foot, mostly men with a smattering of women, most holding torches and guns. Unlike the two riders, these folks looked far too excited and chatty to be a threat. Men and women alike uttered jokes under their breath.

Wherever the hell he and Rodney had ended up, it seemed everyone was either a manufactured beast or a well-armed nut case.

The men fanned out in front of the temple, still chittering and giggling and acting like this was some sort of game. Meesh eyed each of them warily, keeping himself and Rodney rooted in place while he counted their heads. He came up with thirty-seven.

The second rider took position next to the first. "Who's this?" he asked in a growl.

"Dunno," said the first. "They were here when I showed up."

"That so?" The younger man leaned forward, staring at the knights while stroking his horse's mane in a weirdly sexual manner. "What group you from, boys?"

"Um, we're with Burns," Meesh said, blurting out the first name that popped into his head.

"Burns, huh?" the young rider said. His hands slipped beneath the rifle in his lap. He glanced at his partner. "You sure they're with us?"

"Who else'd they be, Jenner? That one's got two guns. No guns in Darkenwood, remember?"

"The guy who killed Petey had a gun. That's what Jasper said."

"Oh. Oh! Didn't think of that."

The older man lifted the rifle off his lap, though he didn't aim it at them. He seemed as uncertain with the thing in his hands as Rodney was with his crossbow.

Maybe there's a chance to get out of this, Meesh thought.

"I'll ask you again," the younger man said. "What broker do you work for? Who brought you here?"

"Well, Jenner," Meesh replied, hoping that was actually the guy's name. "It goes like this. We didn't really know what—"

"Holy *shit*," someone said from behind the riders. "Look at that! There's one up there!"

Meesh heard that familiar squeak of hinges. *Shit.* He glanced back at the temple. One of the cat-people had wandered outside. He—or she, it was hard to tell—froze at the top step, as if the sight of the gathered men with torches had caused it to turn to stone.

"Would you look at that," Jenner said with a wicked grin. "Never saw a cat that dumb looking before."

"Git!" the older rider yelled.

The cat-person gawked.

"See, that's why we wanted a scene," Jenner said. "Oh well. Father said to try and get *most* of 'em to run away before we burn this place to the ground. Not *all* of 'em."

Jenner handed his torch to his partner, shouldered his rifle, and aimed over Meesh's head. This one seemed way more comfortable with the weapon than his companion. That, along with *burn this place to the ground*, forced Meesh's hand.

In a flash, he unholstered the revolver on his right hip and squeezed the trigger. The kickback massaged the muscles in his arms. Jenner's head snapped back. If it hadn't been night, Meesh knew he'd have seen the killer b's—blood, bone, and brains—fly out the back of his skull. The rifle drooped in his arms and he slumped far back in the saddle. He would've fallen off had his feet not been wedged in the stirrups. Instead, he sagged against the horse's rear end like a ventriloquist dummy with a stick shoved up its ass.

All thirty-six remaining sets of eyes gawked at the dead man. Meesh hesitated. He didn't want to kill anyone else, even these goofy and obviously out-of-their-league dumbasses. He just hoped they'd come to their senses and flee now that one of their leaders was dead.

A shrill feline cry rang out. Meesh whirled, afraid someone had snuck up from behind. But the cat-person was on its knees just outside the temple door.

"What have you done!" the creature shrieked.

"Huh?"

His confusion lasted seconds, but in those seconds everything changed. The clicks and clacks of rounds being loaded into bolt-action chambers became a chorus.

"He killed Jenner!" a woman's voice shouted.

Rage-filled yowls answered her.

"Goddammit." Meesh grumbled. Here he was, facing the wrong way.

Without another moment's hesitation, he drew his second revolver, spun back around, and let off six quick shots. He didn't bother aiming, since covering fire was what he needed. He and Rodney were out in the open; no matter how good Meesh was, there was no way he could take out thirty-six people before someone got off a lucky shot. The only choice was to hope these morons were smart enough to preserve their own safety, allowing him and Rodney the chance to do the same.

Luckily, the invaders acted accordingly. A few let loose with wild rifle rounds, but most ducked for cover behind the surrounding hedgerow. That gave Meesh all the time he needed. He squeezed another two shots, these measured, striking fleeing targets in the back. After that, he sprinted toward the temple, dragging a stunned Rodney along with him. A bullet dug into the ground at his feet, spraying his pants with dirt and grass.

Too close. Maybe these people weren't incompetent after all.

He rumbled along the slate walk and up the stairs, Rodney right behind him. The night air crackled with multiple gunshots that pinged the side of the building. The cat-person was still kneeling in front of the top step when Meesh arrived, so he lowered his shoulder and drove the creature backward. It put up surprisingly little resistance, as if it'd been shocked into paralysis. Rodney then ran past them, hefted the latch, shoved the heavy door open, and fell inside. Meesh followed, dragging the limp and muttering cat-person while small chunks of door frame exploded, spraying sharp slivers of wood.

Once inside, his tossed his burden out of the way, reached out the door, and fired blindly into the night's darkness. He withdrew his arm just in time for Rodney to slam the door shut. Bullets continued to thud loudly against the outside of the structure, but the walls and door were thick, and considering there were no windows, none were able to punch through. Meesh leaned his cheek against the wood, somehow comforted by the way the violent impacts pulsed against his cheek. Potentially fatal danger, rendered inert.

Small victories all around.

Meesh slid down the length of the door until his ass hit the floor. He slumped there, puffed out his cheeks, and let his hair fall in front of his face. It was warm in this temple. Considering he hadn't gotten a good night's sleep since leaving Dakota Keep, he decided right then that he could pass out for hours while the dangerous vibrations of embedded bullets comforted him. If only Rodney would stop tugging on his shirt.

"What?" he groused.

"Meesh…"

He swept the hair from his eyes. The sight of Raz the centaur, cleaned up now so that the supple pink flesh of her upper body was visible, brought him back around. The five cat-people surrounded her. All stared at him as if *he* were the monster in their midst.

"You killed a Righteous," Raz said accusingly. "You have doomed us all."

"Not sure what being righteous has to do with anything," he said. "But I guarantee you I didn't kill anyone like that. As for dooming you? Maybe, maybe not. All I can say for sure is there's a bunch of pissed-off assholes out there, who for some reason wanna burn down this here building. Which means this is gonna be a very, *very* long night."

— 19 —

Shut down your conscience.
Take control of the physical world.
It was created to benefit you.
—Book of the Pentus, Platitudes 1:9

I t did not take long for Indigo to grow tired of waiting. The moans and gasps and wails of injured Ersatz were like constant knives in the gut. Given the quick rate of healing her people possessed, most of the injuries would mend easily if they were allowed a few solid hours of sleep. Unfortunately, with the tavern still surrounded, that did not seem likely to happen anytime soon.

Still others bore maladies that would not be so easily made right even under the best circumstances. Limbs that were burned to charring, blows to the head that had cracked skulls, and multiple holes driven through bodies by the guns the Righteous carried, causing organ failure. A few of these unfortunates had ascended already; quite a few others would be better off if they did as well.

But Indigo did not dare go to assist them in their ascension. Not now. Not when Nathan had said the Righteous were intent on destroying Tro Choi. If that were the case, there would be no ascensions for her people. If that were the case, dead would simply mean dead.

To ease her troubled thoughts, she went upstairs to check those who had taken up shelter in the courtesan apartments. To every suffering individual, she offered words of support. But her kindness carried with it another purpose. She stole a few moments each visit to peek out the windows at all corners of Hickweis Tavern, checking to see if the Righteous surrounding them had made a move.

So far, they had not. They remained as they had been since first encircling the building, some standing at attention, some fidgeting, some swaying on their feet as if sleeping, all seemingly waiting for their leader to give a fateful order that had yet to come.

A full hour or more, and no movement. She could not tell if that was a good thing or bad.

Indigo found her way back to the tavern. She peeked out the lower front window and eyed Hugo Popp. The old Righteous man, his complexion cast in shades of red and black by flickering torchlight, remained atop his horse, picking at his fingernails as if he were lazing on his front stoop on a warm summer day. It was maddening.

Voices rising in anger behind her captured her attention. Nathan and Sophie, the leaders of the turncoat Righteous, were engaged in a heated conversation that had Sophie slamming a fist against the bar counter while Nathan pleaded with her to calm down. The rest of the turncoats looked on with nervous expressions, while the Ersatz gave the whole group a wide berth. It did not matter that these people had helped usher them to safety and seemed to actually care about their well-being. At the end of the day, they were still Righteous, and not to be trusted.

The only one who remained close to them was Macaro, who busied himself with organizing the liquor bottles on the wall behind the bar. A useless act, given how none of them would live to see tomorrow if those outside got their way, but predictable for Macaro. Diving into busy work was the only way the dutiful dwarf could keep himself together when things became tense.

Concerned, Indigo drew closer to the turncoats. When she reached the bar, all eyes turned to her, and the argument ceased. Sophie threw her arm around Nathan and dragged him toward the kitchen corridor. The rest, their expressions sour, formed smaller clusters. The only two who acknowledged Indigo were Gia and Zoe, who smiled apologetically before being lured into a hushed conversation.

Indigo tapped her fingernails on the bar, raising an eyebrow at Macaro. Annoyance was etched onto his scrunched mug. That could only mean that he had heard something he did not like. She tilted her head toward the far end of the bar, where he could disclose to her out of earshot all he had learned. But something caught her eye and stopped her where she stood.

The walking stick Nathan had been carrying since his arrival, the one that she had seen spewing blue flame out its end not very long ago, was propped against the counter, unguarded.

She tried to act nonchalant as she crept up to the foreign weapon. None of the turncoats, engaged in private discussions as they were, seemed to notice. Carefully, she slid her hand around the shaft and pulled it toward her.

Nothing about the walking stick appeared extraordinary. Its length felt like normal wood to her fingers, and when she lifted it, the weight seemed consistent with any other whittled six-foot branch. The only oddity was the leather wrapped around it three and a half feet up its length. A small metal box, barely two inches long and an inch thick, was embedded in the leather. She touched it, but nothing happened. Shrugging, she slid the walking stick backward so she could get a closer look at the top, the fringes of which were scorched. A blackened hole had been drilled into its end. She squeezed one eye shut and bent toward it, trying to see what was inside.

Someone grabbed her shoulder. "Wouldn't do that. Your face looks way better, y'know, on your face."

Nathan grabbed the walking stick, though he did not rip it from her hands. When he inclined his head, Indigo let go and allowed him to set it back to leaning against the bar on his other side. The turncoat tossed the book he had spent the last hour looking at—when he was not arguing with Sophie, that is—onto the countertop and sank onto the stool.

"That thing's dangerous," he said. "Sorry. My fault for leaving it unattended."

"What is it?" she asked.

"Something I brought from home, just in case. There's a cannister embedded in the shaft that holds separate synthetic naphthenic acid and palmitic acid compounds. If I flip open that little steel rectangle there and press a button, the two compounds mix, and a nitric propellant launches the mixture out the hole. Basically, it's a secret gun that shoots out an advanced form of napalm. Great for crowd dispersal... or buying a bunch of helpless people a chance to get to safety when murder-hungry assholes're chasing them. Pretty awesome, huh? Too bad it's all I got with me at the moment."

Indigo stared at him, brow creased in confusion.

"You have no clue what I'm talking about, do you?" The Righteous man flipped open his book and leaned over it, his fingers tap-tap-tapping away. "That's okay. I'm used to it by now."

He went silent, but did not urge Indigo to leave him be, so she slid herself over. When she looked down at the book, her nose wrinkled. Though the tome was leather-bound on the outside, it contained no pages on the inside that she could see. Instead, there was a flat sheet of glass that glowed subtly from the numerous bright numbers, letters, and images that filled the entirety of its eight-by-twelve-inch surface. The numbers and letters were constantly moving and changing, the images shifting this way and that, manipulated every time Nathan touched them.

"What kind of magic is this?" she finally asked. It was the only word she could think to describe what she saw.

Nathan answered without glancing up: "Not magic. That's Sophie's area. This, though, is another thing you wouldn't understand. It's just that...oh, would you look at that? There. That should do it." His face contorted in triumph, and he eased the book shut, hiding away those flashing symbols and images. He looked at her and asked, "How well do you know Shade?"

"Quite well. Why?"

"Do you think he'll make the right choice? If he completes the Path of Aumor?"

She felt affronted by the question. "I do not think he will, no. I *know* he will. Shade is a righteous man. Far more righteous than your lot."

"That's fair," Nathan said.

"Why would you ask?"

"No reason."

"Just tell her," a bitter voice demanded. Sophie flitted past, nudging Nathan with an elbow on the way by. She took up the stool on the other side of Indigo.

The young man sucked in his thick bottom lip. "I don't..."

"Do it. *Now.*"

"Fine. Fine! Jeez." He drummed the leather cover of his not-book. "When the Architect first designed this place, someone voiced concern that one of the guests might, just *might*, fall in love with one of the playthings. So he created a test of sorts, just in case that happened. A one-outcome scenario where, if the quester completes his mission, he's given what you'd call a Hobson's Choice. On one hand, he could win freedom for the object of his desire—at the cost of his own life. On the other, he could be made the richest individual in the kingdom." He frowned at Sophie, who let loose with a disapproving growl.

Indigo felt like someone had stabbed her in the heart. "What kind of monster would create something so horrible?"

"Yeah, who would do something like that?" Sophie asked with a glare.

"Hey, it wasn't ever supposed to happen!" exclaimed Nathan. "The Path was built, the obstacles put in place, but the Architect decided after it was done that it was a bad idea."

"Because he was afraid that if one dickhead did it, then everyone would find out about it," Sophie sneered. "I mean, how many *richest people in the kingdom* could the Architect afford to make?"

"Whatever his reasons, he did the right thing," Nathan insisted. "He hid away the Rawgian Key and promised no one would ever use it."

His partner scoffed. "And the asshole decided to keep the mythology in place anyway."

"Hey, it helped give the Ersatz something to strive toward."

"Even if it was a total lie?"

"Even then."

Indigo watched their back-and-forth in horror. "It *is not* a lie," she said, a cutting edge in her tone. "Shade brought the Rawgian Key to this very valley. He is on the Path as we speak, fighting for me. For *us*." She swallowed hard, staring pleadingly into the dark brown eyes of the turncoat. "Are you telling me he will not be able to free us all? That he can only win my liberty by...perishing?"

"Well, that's the way it *should* work," the young man said. "The whole scenario's built on outdated firmware, which means I couldn't alter anything that comes during the actual gameplay. But I was able to hack into the general operating system and change the parameters of victory. So, he'll be okay, so long as he doesn't die. And so long as he makes the right choice. I think."

"How charitable of you," snapped Sophie.

"Hey, I'm trying."

"And the overgod is agreeable with all of this?" Indigo asked softly. "Was this simply another way Rawg decided to torture us for our sins?"

Nathan stared at her, frowning.

"Go ahead, genius," Sophie said. "Tell her."

He gulped, grinded his teeth together, and said, "The overgod isn't real."

Indigo stared at him, unsure how to respond.

Sophie slapped the countertop and glared at her partner. "Keep going."

"I will! You don't gotta be such a dick about this, y'know."

"And the Architect didn't have to rip off a stupid theme park-gone-wrong show just to boast about how great he was," Sophie said sarcastically.

"That wasn't the point!"

Sophie deepened her scowl. "Don't tell *me* that, genius."

The young man gulped down a breath. "Sophie's right. You deserve to know, Indigo. But listen, this is gonna be hard." He took a steadying breath. "Everything you understand about the purpose of this place is a lie, including your role in it. The Ersatz aren't sinners. That's just the story you were told to keep you from questioning reality. There was never any way for you to earn your freedom."

"But Black…" Indigo began.

"Was a plant. Something else to give you hope." Nathan let out a groan. "In truth, you're all an unfortunate byproduct of an ill-conceived quest for knowledge that turned into an ill-conceived quest for entertainment. Innocents who got put in a position to be used by a bunch of overly privileged people who like playing games. And who wanted those games to seem more…real." He faltered as if speaking those words hurt him on a physical level.

"I…I…what?" said Indigo. She was so far from understanding that she could not think clearly. She stood from her stool and backed away. "This…cannot be real."

"It *is* real, unfortunately," Nathan said.

Sophie reached for her, but Indigo pulled away. The Righteous woman withdrew as if she understood. Such compassion showed in her dark brown eyes that Indigo believed she actually cared.

"I know you hate us," the woman said. "And we deserve it. But not all of us are bad. Not everyone in Pirie is a raging lunatic."

"Not everyone," muttered Nathan. "Is this more 'not all men' or 'not all cops' bullshit? I thought we got past that centuries ago."

His partner stared daggers at him until he turned away. Nathan spoke directly, "Indigo, I'm not gonna ask you to like me. Or be my friend. I just ask that you put a little trust in us. We came here to right two hundred years of wrongs. We came here to *help*."

That was it. Everything that had happened to Indigo over her many lives came roaring back in a fury of indignation. She let her anger wash away her confusion and flung her arm out at the injured Ersatz who filled the tavern.

"How is this helping?"

"Well…" Nathan began.

Sophie silenced him with an elbow to the ribs. "You're right," she said. "It didn't exactly go according to plan."

"Then how about you come up with a better one?" Indigo snapped. "How about—"

"Mum! *Mum!* Come quick!"

Aqua was calling for her. Indigo spun around to find her beloved courtesans gathered by the front window, staring out with rapt attention and without care for their safety. Bluebell waved an arm for her to hurry. Indigo offered one last scowl at the turncoats before hustling to her gathered people. They parted, allowing her a front-row view of the happenings outside.

The Righteous stood idly by no longer. A large swath of them—perhaps half their number—were streaming from around the other side of Hickweis Tavern, heading toward the spot where Hugo Popp sat atop his horse. The old merchant did not seem disinterested now. He stood in his stirrups, wildly gesticulating toward the south. Toward the direction of Tro Choi.

Now that she was close to the window, Indigo heard the muffled clamor of shouted voices. But something else made itself known—a distant, repetitive cracking. She was taken back a century ago, when a surprise snowstorm assaulted Darkenwood during a spring cold snap. It had been the only time in her lives that a large swath of snow had fallen in the valley, and the weight of all that heavy white stuff proved too great a burden for the oak and maple trees. That was what the sound reminded her of, the unbroken cacophony of toppling trees and thick branches that snapped like twigs.

She looked on as Hugo Popp plunged back into his saddle and snapped the reins. His horse took off at a mild gallop, heading for the cobbled road. Many Righteous fell in behind him—most of the ones who had guns—their arms and legs pumping. Two hundred men and women, weapons slung over their shoulders, struggling to keep up. Those left behind remained in their thinned-out circle, but their attentions were not on Hickweis Tavern. They stared off in the direction their leader had gone. Some appeared frightened, others angry, but most just looked annoyed.

"Something happened out there," Pipi said.

Indigo grabbed her hand. "I know."

"Do you think we are safe?" asked Aqua.

"As safe as we could be," she told him, giving his russet cheek a gentle caress.

A shrill whistle outside brought Indigo to attention. A man and woman worked their way down the remaining line of Righteous. As they drew closer, she clearly recognized Jasper and Kirsten Popp. The pair wrangled their remaining force into order, spit flying from their mouths with every shouted command. Jasper took the position his father had vacated, directly in front of the tavern entrance. His eyes were black and evil in the torchlight. Even thirty feet away, Indigo knew he was staring at the Ersatz through the window. The man spat a curse Indigo could not hear and shouldered his rife.

Panic surged through her. "Down!" she screamed, and immediately tackled Mana beside her to the ground. The waifish courtesan cried out when they hit the floor. A gunshot rang out, and the window above exploded. Indigo covered Mana with her body as tiny shards of glass rained down, cutting into the bare flesh of her shoulders and getting caught in her hair. All around, her people were screaming.

Indigo scanned the room. Most everyone in the tavern was on the floor now, even the injured who had been sprawled across tables. It was difficult to see if anyone had been hurt by the shot, other than the cuts and scrapes that covered her courtesans, who all crouched alongside her away from the now-glassless window.

"You're all gonna die tonight!" Jasper hollered. "You hear me? All of you! Permanently this time!"

There was so much hatred in his voice. Indigo could not help but wonder how someone who held so much power could hate so deeply those who possessed so little.

"Does he speak the truth?" asked Bluebell. It was heartbreaking to see hope in those crystal blue eyes. "Would the overgod truly release us from our curse?"

Indigo was ready to rage at the world. She wanted to tell her people the truth Nathan had spoken—if it really *was* the truth. They deserved to know how they had been lied to, their constant torment a farce created for the entertainment of those they called Righteous. That they should not long for death now when they had never truly been given a chance to *live*. And she would have, had Orchid not run up to her at that moment and grabbed her by the cheeks with her tiny, delicate hands.

"Mum," the halfling said, "he calls you."

Orchid gestured to the bar. The turncoats were still gathered there, hunkered down, seeming just as terrified as any Ersatz. Nathan was stooped on one knee just in front of Sophie, his book clutched tightly with one hand while he flapped his other at Indigo wildly.

Come here! he mouthed.

Indigo brushed specks of glass off her arms, wincing at the sharp pain of the tiny cuts now covering her bare flesh. While the Righteous outside began some kind of sadistic chant, she inched along the floorboards toward Nathan. The fabric of her dress bunched up and tore along the back as she crawled, which made her hate the fact that dresses were her duty to wear. A duty brought on by her station, itself brought about by the whims of those who created this place. Which made her loathe Nathan and Sophie and the whole lot of them all the more.

Yet when she reached the pair, there was such relief in the eyes of the young man with foppish hair that she could not help but syphon some off for herself. The half-smile that quirked one corner of his mouth seemed earnest, the first time he had appeared more than passively interested around anyone besides Sophie.

"First off, Tro Choi is still standing," the young man whispered. "There's some kinda fracas going on down there, but I'm not sure what. It's unexpected, but I'll take it. I'm assuming a bunch of men are heading that way now?"

Indigo nodded. "Most of the ones who held guns. As far as I could see, at least."

"Oh, that's better than I thought! But anyway, that's not why I needed to talk to you." He grabbed a fistful of her hair, pulled her toward him. Her body went rigid and she expected the worst. His lips brushed the pointed tip of her ear, making her insides squirm.

"He did it," whispered Nathan

"Who did what?"

He pulled back, his smile more prevalent. "Shade. He defeated the Avatar of Rawg. He made the right choice."

Indigo cast a wary look at her people, who were still focused on staying low and staring at the glassless window.

"Does he live?"

"I...think so. Not too sure about that." His smile faltered ever so slightly.

Sophie clambered over his shoulder. "Tell her the *good* news."

"Yeah, the good news," Nathan said. "Well, when I was messing with the framework, I put in a *ton* of spaghetti code to try to tax the system. Looks like it worked. From what I can tell, the overrides fried, and the server reverted back to its original settings. It helps that the server was really old and not really well maintained. Which is a good thing."

Indigo squinted at him.

"Tell her so she understands," Sophie chastised.

"Oh. Yeah." He shook his head, leaned closer again. "I set it up so that Shade flipping that switch ended up removing the governors from all of you. If it worked, the coding imprinted in your nervous systems won't recognize anyone as Righteous anymore. Their implants are useless now."

"Shit, Nathan," Sophie whisper-scolded. "I said say it so she could understand!"

Indigo raised her hand, cutting her off. "Are you saying that we will not be stopped from harming them severely any longer?"

"Exactly! Well, I think so."

"You think so?"

The young man shrugged. "It's hard to say. If I'd been able to get into the data center beneath the mountain, I could tell you for sure. But I'm working remotely, and like I said, all this tech is pretty outdated and unreliable."

Sophie shoved him aside and snatched Indigo by the hands. She had a wild gleam in her eye.

"There's only one way to find out," she said. "Give one of your people this. Send them out the back or something, have them sneak up on one of Popp's men. Let's see if Nathan here really is as good as he's been telling me he is since the beginning of goddamn time."

Indigo looked down. The woman placed a dagger in her hands. A wicked thing with a wrapped leather handle and a six-inch curved blade. Indigo tightened her fist around the grip, held the blade up to her face. She saw her reflection in the polished steel, her dark hair tousled, the golden skin on her forehead covered with tiny cuts.

"No," she said.

"What?" Sophie said, aghast. "You can't just—"

"I am not putting my people at risk for a possibility." Indigo stared at the dagger in her hand. "They have suffered enough already. I drew the ire of the Righteous when I called on the Voice of Him. So if anyone should test this theory of yours, it should be me."

"But you would've been freed regardless," Nathan said. "Shade chose *you*, remember."

A box was shoved behind the Righteous man, and Indigo cracked a wicked smile. "True. But he did not choose Macaro."

The dwarf hopped up on his crate with speed that should not have been possible for someone his size. One of his arms latched around the neck of the Righteous man, the other arm brought the knife he used to cut lemon wedges to Nathan's throat. The man froze, his eyes wide. Beside him, Sophie snickered.

"Hey now," Nathan said as the sharp blade pressed against his flesh.

"Sorry," Macaro told him.

"Are you really, though?" asked Sophie with a laugh.

Macaro pressed the knife to his throat harder, drawing a bead of blood. "Not really, I suppose."

"Good. That's good."

"Is it?" whined Nathan.

"Of course it is," Sophie said, stepping to the side and shaking her head.

Indigo picked up the thread the Righteous woman was pulling. "Because given what he has been put through by people like you, letting you bleed out on the floor would bring satisfaction, if only for a moment."

"Exactly."

Indigo tilted her head as Nathan shivered, a bead of red trailing down his neck and staining his collar. This only made the dwarf hold the blade tighter.

"Macaro," Indigo said to her friend, suddenly aware that every pair of eyes in the tavern was on them. "What do you feel?"

"Anger," the dwarf replied.

"No, other than that," added Sophie. "Beneath the anger."

Macaro took a deep breath and closed his eyes. "Nothing."

"No tremble in the muscles?" asked Indigo. "No grayness in the back of your mind, as if you are moments from losing consciousness?"

"No."

Sophie widened her smile. "That's good."

"It is," Indigo concurred. "And that is good enough for me. Macaro, please release him."

The dwarf nodded slowly and withdrew his knife. "Very well, Mum." He hopped off his stool and shook as if awakening from a bad dream.

"Well, that was something," Nathan grumbled. He pressed a finger against the cut on his neck. Gia handed him a napkin off the bar that he used to dab the blood. "Not sure if that proves everything."

"It proves enough," Indigo said.

"Fine." Nathan held the napkin to his neck and sighed. "But does it have to be *you*?"

"It does," Indigo said defiantly.

He rolled his eyes. "If you're intent on doing this, you're gonna need a plan. It shouldn't take long to come up with one."

"You will still help us, even after what Macaro put you through?" Indio asked.

"Of course he will," Sophie said, nudging her partner. She tucked her dangling pendant into the front of her shirt as if anticipating action, the amusement in her eyes palpable. "It's what we came here to do."

The occasional crack of gunfire, followed by the clay pots hanging on the opposite wall exploding, provided the backdrop while Indigo huddled with the two turncoats and formulated their scheme. She nodded in agreement with them as she ripped a long strip of white fabric from the underskirt beneath her dress. She then shuffled on her hands and knees toward the front door. Already, the other turncoats were working at removing the blockade.

They finished clearing the way with a flourish of falling chairs and snapping wood, giving Indigo a clear path. She rose to her feet only when she felt confident that no one would take a pot shot at her from the low window on the other side of the tavern.

Pinpricks washed over her. She glanced at Macaro, who poked out from behind the bar, his beady eyes watering. *I love you,* she mouthed, and then pressed the latch to open the door a crack. She squeezed her eyes shut and thrust her arm out, waving around the white strip of cloth while hoping no one would blast her hand to bloody bits.

Everything fell silent. Even the badly injured ceased their moaning. A callous, taunting voice rose above the beat of her heart.

"Overseer, is that your pretty little hand I see?"

Indigo took a calming breath and opened the door just wide enough to squeeze through. Her feet hit the porch; the chilled evening breeze struck her flesh. She saw no flash behind her eyelids, nor did she hear that ear-splitting crack of gunfire. At least nearby—the echoes of these horrible weapons discharging continued in the distance.

Only after she stepped forward and her hands grabbed the porch railing did she look upon the world. The thinned herd of Righteous men and women retained their distance, though all of them raised what weapons they had. Smoke billowed from the end of the long weapon Jasper Popp held. He trained that smoking barrel on her, pulled a bar that made a hollow *click-clank* sound, but did not fire.

It was a calculated risk baring herself to these people like this. She was helpless before them, even if Jasper was one of only three men before her armed with a ranged weapon. The only thing she counted on was the proclamation Jasper himself had made back on Merchantry Road, that he wanted her to suffer before she died a full, final death.

Kirsten stepped up beside him, waving a machete. "Why'd you come out here, overseer? Why aren't you cowering inside with the rest of the whores? With the rest of the *rats?*"

Indigo let go of the railing and lifted her chin high as she descended the stairs. It was difficult to stop her knees from shaking. Jasper and Kirsten mocked her with every step, but she kept her gaze locked on them. By the time her soft-soled shoes hit the grass of the courtyard, her legs felt like they would stop working entirely.

She walked toward her fate nonetheless.

"I am here to ask for mercy," she announced, as she passed by the grass that was stained by the blood of the two dead Righteous who had been hauled away.

"That so?" Kirsten snipped. "Why should we do that?"

Indigo drew ever closer. "Because we are helpless before you. Because you are superior to us in every way. Because you are Righteous."

"That's right we are," Jasper said. He lowered his rifle slightly and spat on the grass.

All were quiet, even the sneering Kirsten, while Indigo continued her apparent death march. She stopped a few feet away from her targets and knelt in the grass. Bending over, she placed down the torn piece of white fabric and smoothed it out. She bowed her head.

"I know what you are after," she said.

"That so?" said Jasper.

"You wish to raze this valley to the ground, to cease our ascensions."

Kirsten let out a barking laugh. "She's not stupid."

"That would make you liberators," Indigo said, ignoring her. "That you would finally break us of our curse proves just how righteous you truly are. For that, we thank you."

She sunk lower into her bow.

"Didn't see that coming," Jasper said with a chuckle.

"That's right, we might as well be gods to them," said Kirsten.

"Is that why you came begging for mercy?" Jasper asked.

Indigo deepened her bow. "It is, my lord." The words felt like acid on her tongue. "Please, in your wisdom, do to me what you wish. Abuse me. Use me. Discard me. You wish me tortured for what happened to poor Peter? Then do so. All I ask is that you allow my people a quick, painless death."

The man *harrumphed*. His wife snickered. The rest of the Righteous kept quiet.

"Is that too much to ask of a people so wise and devout?"

"Depends," Jasper said. "Where's the interloper? The one who killed my man? He's the one who's causing the ruckus down at your little temple, isn't he?"

"That is not the work of the stranger," Indigo told him. "The stranger was eliminated by the Voice of Him. Whatever confrontation is occurring at Tro Choi, I have no knowledge of it."

"Is she telling the truth?" Kirsten asked.

"Of course she is. They can't lie to us, remember."

"Oh. Oh yeah."

Which was not true. The Ersatz could indeed lie, and did often, if only to mitigate their suffering at cruel hands. But the Righteous, sitting on their arrogant perches as the superior beings, simply did not realize it.

"Whatever. Dad'll figure it out. As for what happened to the stranger..." Jasper *tsked*. "See, that's not acceptable. That man should've been mine to dispose of as I wished." He tapped his foot, and even though Indigo could not see him, she pictured him stroking his preposterous chin-beard in thought. "That right there makes mercy hard to come by. At least two more Ersatz gotta suffer, and suffer greatly, to make up for my loss of satisfaction."

"Two?" said Kirsten. "I'd make it four."

"Yeah, you're right. Four it is. We'll both choose 'em. But I'm telling you right now, one of mine is gonna be the waif."

"Good choice," his wife said.

"As you wish," Indigo groveled.

"That's right, as I wish. I can do *whatever* I wish, because that's the way this place was built." Jasper grunted. "But you're hiding something from me, ain't you?"

"What would that be?"

"Our own kind," Kirsten cut in. "There's a group of Righteous in that building, aren't there?"

Indigo nodded, still not looking up.

"Why're they hiding from us?" Jasper asked.

"They did not know who you were," she said. "They are all virgins to Darkenwood. Lesser artisans and traders experiencing our valley for the first time. I suppose you frightened them with your...arrival."

"Guess that explains why I didn't recognize any of the names in the register. Makes sense though, from a business sense. When you got a broken link in the supply train, you roll it back out slowly, to avoid any more hiccups."

"You are very wise," said Indigo.

She lifted her eyes enough to see Kirsten shuffle up alongside her husband. "But what about the guy with the flamethrower?"

"Yeah, that's weird," Jasper replied. He took another stride closer, near enough now that he stepped on the spread-out white cloth and nudged Indigo with his boot. "He in there too? Maybe it's him down at the temple."

Almost time, Indigo thought. She stooped lower at the waist in a show of entreaty while her hands found the dagger hidden in the fold of her dress.

On cue, feet tramped on veranda behind her. "That'd be me," Nathan announced. "Apologies for that."

Grumbling rose from the diminished column of Righteous.

"Who're you?" growled Jasper.

"Name's Nathan Trinh. Potter. Based outta Merrin."

"Merrin?" scoffed Kirsten. "That hole?"

"Bullshit," Jasper said. He lifted his rifle, prompting Indigo to finally raise her head. The barrel hovered over her. "Only transients and criminals live in Merrin. None of them would dare step foot into greater Pirie, let alone afford to come here."

More stomping of feet as people flooded the deck of Hickweis Tavern.

"Well, that's where we're from," Sophie said. "All of us. Guess you could say the worm's turned."

That was the signal. Indigo tore the dagger from concealment and drove it up toward the stomach of the Righteous man. She cringed on the inside, terrified, waiting for the moment when her muscles seized and pain surged through her.

That moment never came.

The dagger slid easily through cotton and plunged into flesh. Warm fluid dribbled over her fingers. Jasper let out a gasp, his gun lowered ever so slightly. He stared down at her in disbelief, his eyes the size of walnuts. Indigo snarled. A wave of hatred flooded her insides. Every horrible thing that had happened to her and her people, the ways she had been forced to paint brightness onto a canvas of pure black in order to maintain her sanity, drove her into a frenzy. She grasped the dagger with both hands, leapt to her feet, and violently ripped it to the side.

The blade came free, trailing blood and cotton threads. Indigo stood hunched, clutching the dagger like a tiny sword. In front of her, the Righteous man staggered. The rifle fell from his grip and rattled on the grass. Jasper let out another gasp, bringing his hands to his midsection. His gray shirt darkened profusely, and when he lifted the fabric, a bundle of entrails came spilling out. He fell to his knees, desperately trying to stuff his intestines back into the cavity they had vacated.

Kirsten emitted a horrified screech, tossed aside her machete, and dropped down beside her husband. Blubbering words spat from her lips as she joined him in trying to cram his insides back into place. "No, no, *no, no!*" she cried. The sound of her shrieks drowned out her own thoughts. Indigo wanted to stop hearing it. *Needed* to.

Now, she could do that herself.

Without a second thought, she circled around the struggling couple, came up behind Kirsten, and dragged the dagger across her windpipe. Her screams became gargled wheezes. Blood sprayed across the face of her dying husband. The woman dropped onto her back, clutching her throat. Blood spurted from between her fingers. Some of it splashed onto Indigo, but the half-elf was too focused on the way the rest of the Righteous stared at her in disbelief to care.

A few bloodstains meant nothing in the face of absolute liberation.

One of the Righteous, a middle-aged man she recognized from the times he had ordered Bluebell bound and beaten for his own pleasure, was the first to snap out of his stupor. He stopped staring at the dying couple on the ground and lifted his sword. It looked like he was about to charge, but something caught his attention and his head whipped around.

Indigo followed his gaze toward Hickweis Tavern. Nathan, Sophie, and the rest of the turncoats were now scampering along the courtyard, heading for the cottages to retrieve their weapons. The Ersatz streamed out of the tavern to take their place on the porch. They all stared at Indigo, who stood there like a feral beast, her clothes drenched in red, the dagger dripping blood onto the grass.

"My brothers, my sisters, come!" she bellowed. She tore off her dress and flung it aside, standing in her underclothes for all the valley to see. "They are our betters no more!" She pointed at the man with the sword, then on down the line of nervous Righteous. "They do not control us! Shade has become Aumor Reborn! He has given us what we were long denied—the ability to create for ourselves our own destiny!"

She elicited a primal scream that brought the wolves in the mountains to howling. The Righteous man with the sword flicked his eyes to the tavern and then back to her. His hands began to quiver as one voice, then another and another, joined Indigo in roaring to the heavens.

"Screw this!" the man said and started running. The other Righteous men and women followed suit. They appeared from all around the building, most sprinting toward the cobbled road, where they could find protection with the portion of their group that was better armed. Others dashed off in random directions, seeking protection in the woods.

Indigo took her eyes off the fleeing Righteous and stalked back to the couple she had felled. Kirsten had gone still, her glassy eyes staring at the blackened sky, but Jasper still breathed. His eyes reached Indigo's, his jaw working slowly. A blood bubble popped on his lips, followed by a pathetic appeal.

"P...please..."

She dropped down, driving the dagger up beneath his chin. Cartilage severed as the blade pierced his tongue and the roof of his mouth, finally breaking through the thin bone of his skull and ramming into his brain. One final shudder and he fell still. When she pulled the dagger free, the *plop* she heard was not sickening, but the most joyous of hymns.

Her people watched her, their expressions expectant, ferocious where once they had been compliant. Aspar and Pipi in particular looked ready for whatever was to come, hopping on the balls of their feet, their hands clenched into fists.

But it was Sienna whom Indigo focused on when next she spoke. Sienna, whose face had gone slack while she clutched the porch bannister as if she would float away if she let go.

"This is the moment they have long denied us!" Indigo said. "These people who think themselves superior are nothing. *We* are the faster. *We* are the stronger. *We* will win our freedom for the very first time. Now Fol, unlock your cart, hand out *our* weapons to *our* people. Tonight, we fight! Tonight, we pay back in blood all the pain and ascensions foisted upon us!"

The cheers that erupted from the Ersatz were a salve for her tortured soul.

Her people scattered, with Vivo and another of the burlier courtesans, Nall, hoisting Fol on their shoulders. They ran with the orc toward the rear of Hickweis Tavern, where the weapons cart was stored. A procession of fervent Ersatz, monstrous and human alike, followed them.

Indigo approached the porch, where now only Sienna, Macaro, and Orchid remained. The dwarf and the halfling looked upon Indigo with pride, while the elf still appeared horrified.

"What have you done?" Sienna asked.

"What I needed to."

"But the Righteous, the overgod..."

"Do not exist," Macaro answered with a sharp nod.

"But..."

Indigo hopped up the steps, took Sienna by the hands. She looked directly into her eyes.

"This is for you, for all of us," she said. "We *will* be free."

"You wish for us to fight?" Sienna asked softly. "I...I cannot..."

"No, Sienna. You have a more important job to do. Stay here with Macaro and Orchid. Care for our wounded people. Make sure they are comfortable. Make sure those who can, are able to see the glory of our emancipation. Can you do that?"

The elf nodded hesitantly.

"Excellent."

Orchid pulled on Indigo's bloodstained underclothes. "Mum, something you must know."

"What is it, sweetling?"

"The funny man. Nathan. He said he was giving you a gift before he left."

"He did?"

"Oh, he sure did," said Macaro. The dwarf approached the edge of the porch steps and gazed at the darkened thatch of trees in the near distance. "And here it comes now."

Indigo heard the low vibration and grinding noises that brought terror to her gut. The trees rustled, a loud *snap* filled air already crowded with the unbroken sound of distant gunfire. The Voice of Him burst free from his thatch, twelve feet tall and menacing. It stared at Indigo from across the courtyard, the red glow of its eyes cutting through the black of night.

Her heart nearly stopped.

The Voice of Him took one lumbering step forward, then did the unexpected. It dropped to one knee, crossed its arms over its scaled chest, and bowed its head.

"What...?"

"He said the Voice is now named Sobec," Orchid said. "And it is yours."

Macaro nodded. "Aye. According to that strange man, you are the only one who can tell it what to do."

"By the overgod," whispered Sienna.

"Not the overgod," Indigo said. "By *us*."

Her people emerged from around Hickweis Tavern, all holding aloft swords and spears and flails that at one point in the not-too-distant past had served as useless decorations in the hands of a people who could not truly fight back.

Pipi advanced toward Indigo. The girl held before her a short battle axe, the same kind that Peter Ortiz had used to slay her in her male form. The former courtesan dropped to a knee before her, reverently held out the weapon.

Indigo tossed aside her bloodied dagger and accepted her gift. The axe felt right in her hand. Grinning, she took her place before her army, two-hundred Ersatz strong. She raised the axe above her head.

"Let us go!" she boomed. "Let us protect the temple of our rebirth before it is taken down by those who would keep us enslaved!"

The crowd roared, and as one they dashed toward the cobbled road. Indigo glanced at the still-kneeling Voice of Him and ordered, "Sobec, with us! Now! Protect Tro Choi!"

The towering reptilian fiend unfolded itself and began to run in slow, unwieldly strides. Indigo threw her head back and laughed, then put on speed. She raced past the moving column of her people, arms and legs pumping with wild abandon.

They were a thunderous horde fueled by rage brought on by two centuries of institutionalized cruelty. Indigo laughed into the night air, an insane cackle that swallowed all other sound.

Thank you, Shade, she thought as her feet pounded the cobbles. Whatever happened next, it happened because of him. She only hoped that he was still breathing. That he would be able to find his way back to her to witness the glory that his efforts had wrought.

— 20 —

To fear the Lord is to fear the accumulation of knowledge;
one does not need their hand held to create wonders as they see fit.
—Book of the Pentus, Platitudes 17:76

A gentle humming lulled Shade to the brink of consciousness. His eyelids fluttered open, and the bright lights above startled him fully awake. He rolled onto his side, covered his head, and groaned. His eyes burned. His muscles ached. His head throbbed.

Wait a second.

The fact that he felt anything could only mean one thing.

Still alive.

The collapse of the chamber within Castle Rawg hadn't killed him. *Good.* And he still had on his duster, while his slouch sat upended on the floor beside him. *Also good.* Yet he wasn't sprawled out on a stone floor any longer, but a plush carpet. And the air around him lacked the hollow cold of the castle in the mountains. Rather, he felt perfectly warm and comfortable. He must have been knocked unconscious when the chamber ceiling started to fall, and someone found him and dragged him here.

It would not have been the first time.

He flexed his sore body and lifted himself to sitting, expecting to be back in Ken's cabin in the mountains, with Silas hovering nearby. But that was not nearly the case. Instead, he looked upon a place that part of his brain recognized but couldn't quite grasp.

The room he was in was large, with electric lights overhead—the source of the buzzing, of course. The walls were painted soft gray and decorated with weapons in shadowboxes, everything from broadswords to daggers to flails to primitive bows and arrows. There were comfortable looking chairs arranged in evenly-spaced rows. Leaflets had been stacked on the tables that stood at all four corners of the room.

Shade forced himself to stand, wandered to one of the tables, and lifted a leaflet. *The Wonders of Darkenwood Await*, said the header. Below was an illustration of a smiling couple holding bloodied swords, posing in front of the corpse of a giant that looked eerily similar to the form Raz had been in when Shade killed him.

"What the hell...?"

He dropped the leaflet without exploring further. He didn't need to, as the pieces had already begun to assemble in his head.

After picking up his hat and limping through the room's only doorway, Shade entered an open space with polished wood floors and a high ceiling. The lighting was dimmer, but in a way that enhanced the earthy color of the walls. The primitive warfare motif continued in here, only this time the shadowboxed weapons were joined by carved replicas of the many Ersatz races he'd met, each placed upon pedestals along the length of the wall to his left. To his rear stood a pair of glass double doors, presumably leading out of the structure, and to his right was a long reception desk. He ignored the potential exit and ran a finger along the counter, feeling the sponginess of the dark cherry-wood finish, the kind that one would find in an upscale hotel.

His brain fritzed momentarily, and he saw himself standing in a lobby much like this, only the walls were decked with crosshatched wood, and there were potted plants in the place of statues of monsters. Behind him, sweaty workers carried luggage and instrument cases. The older white man behind the counter looked at him, lips pressed together in distaste.

"Sorry, your kind can't stay here. Not in Alabama."

Shade knew he was being denied for nothing but the color of his skin, but when he looked back at the man, he didn't feel hate, but pity tinged with love. They were all in this together, this grand old experiment called society. He knew he needed to give folks the time to change. So he offered the old Southerner his kindest smile, tipped his head forward, and said, "It's all right. Times'll change, brother. And I hope you'll change with them."

And then he blinked, the scene shifted, and he was alone at the reception desk again. He stared at the spot where the old man had been, a relic from a memory that was not his. A sigh escaped his lips, and he pinched the bridge of his nose.

"What the hell's wrong with me?"

"On a structural level, nothing is wrong with you, sir," said a proper voice. "As far as the medical scans could tell, other than some bruises and minor scrapes, you are fit as a fiddle."

Shade whirled around. A man approached from the far end of the hall. He was nondescript in nearly every way—average height, likely in his mid-forties, with peach skin, straight white hair parted in the middle, and a clean-shaven face. The fashionable black suit he wore was expertly tailored, flourished with a tie and pocket square that were matching bright purple. The man came to an abrupt halt and bowed.

Up close, something else about the man gave Shade pause, and not only because he had just appeared out of nowhere. When he smiled, it didn't seem to reach his eyes, which were pale blue and lifeless. He showed no facial tics, no rise of an eyebrow or quirk of the lip. And those parts of his face that *did* move were far too deliberate, like some stone golem playing at being human.

"Who're you?" Shade asked.

"I am Robert Quick, kind sir, but you can call me Bob," the man replied with another awkward bow. "President of Viral Ventures."

Shade felt for his revolver, just in case. It was still there, along with Cooper's saber.

Good.

"Viral what?"

"Viral Ventures, my good man. The creator of such wonders as The Darkenwood Experience and Chimera Hunters. We have been keeping the denizens of Pirie entertained since the rebirth of society." A strange clicking sound came from the man's throat. "Now that niceties are out of the way, would you please follow me, Shadrach? Time is of the essence, and your destination awaits."

The man abruptly started walking away. Shade went to follow, until realization struck him.

"Hey, hold on a damn minute. How'd you know my name?"

Bob faced him again. "The Architect returned, notifying me of your impending arrival. He told me to have you fetched from the final stage of the decommissioned attraction and protected. Which was no easy feat, mind you. Castle Rawg is twelve thousand feet above us. Given the faulty connections, it is a miracle that I was able to keep the chamber from completely collapsing. Let alone getting you all the way down here in one piece." He kissed his middle and forefinger and aimed them at the sky. "Thank the Architect that those antique mechanizations were so well constructed."

"What the hell're you talking about?"

"Something that you might understand in time," the strange man said. "Now, if you please, the Architect was adamant that time is of the essence. You could stay here if that is what you wish, I suppose. But I was assured that you would want to rejoin the attractions that you successfully brought offline."

Shade glanced over his shoulder at the glass doors and scrunched up his face. "Fine."

"Excellent. You may follow me now. And please, excuse the mess in the lobby."

Sure enough, as Bob led him deeper into what he called "the lobby," signs that some kind of struggle had taken place were obvious. The statues of Ersatz races had been knocked over and defiled, the shadowboxes had been smashed and the weapons within taken. Scorch marks covered the floor, and Shade swore he saw bullet holes in the walls.

"What happened here?" he asked, though he had not meant to say it out loud.

"The last group who came through had no respect for protocol," Bob said, his odd, nasal voice tinged with disgust. "They slaughtered the guides when they were refused access to the attractions. Hence, I was awoken to clean up the mess."

"People were killed in here? Where's the blood?"

"That is what you are wondering?" Bob let out a hollow laugh. "People truly are an oblivious bunch. You never ask the correct questions."

"Oh yeah?" Shade sniped. "Why don't you tell me what the right question would be then?"

"Hopefully, I will not have to."

Bob stopped near a smashed fountain, the gargoyle that must have once sat at its crest was lying in pieces on the floor. The man veered to the left, tapped out a rhythm on a glossy black pad embedded in the wall, and stepped back. The wooden planks that made up the wall folded back like an accordion, revealing a huge rectangular gate that stood at least twenty feet wide and ten feet tall. The gate rolled upward with a chain-like rattle, opening to a hollow gray room beyond. Bob walked inside, urging Shade to follow.

He did. The floor shifted under his weight, making him hold his arms out to his sides for balance.

"Worry not, the lift is solid," his strange guide said, just before he hit a button beside the opening. The wood panels unfolded and became solid once more, the gate slid back down. A loud hum rattled Shade to his bones. He felt a stomach-churning sense of weightlessness. Just beyond the steel mesh of the gate, the panels disappeared, replaced by a solid wall of gray embedded with lights that steadily scrolled upward.

The room was dropping.

"What the—" he began, only to stop when he realized there were words on the wall behind him.

DARKENWOOD CONSERVATION.

"What's this place got to do with Darkenwood?" he asked softly.

Bob smiled, the expression again only affecting his mouth. "The Architect told me you were one of the smarter ones. I should have guessed you would find the correct question eventually."

"He did, huh?" Shade asked. He should be offended at being congratulated for asking something so obvious, but his curiosity was too piqued to investigate further. "What're you, then? Ersatz?"

"Oh, nothing so advanced as that," he said with a dismissive wave. "They are fourth generation. I am the first. I suppose you could say that I was the primary free-thinking automatic."

Shade frowned. "I'm not following."

The man peered at him with those dead blue eyes. "What do you think this place is? Not where you are standing, specifically, but Darkenwood as a whole?"

"A prison, I guess," answered Shade. "Where rich folks pay to take advantage of the prisoners."

"Not entirely accurate, though the comparison rates. The truth is far more depressing. Darkenwood is a victim of that most hazardous of human traits—the fact that brilliance often walks hand-in-hand with boredom, and that boredom can lead to dismissiveness."

Shade tried to focus on every idiosyncrasy Bob possessed. That, and the possibility of answers, helped keep his mind off the fact that the room they were in kept shuddering from side to side as it descended.

"You see, Darkenwood actually began as a dream," said Bob. "A wonderful fantasy, imagined by the brightest individual who ever lived. This man had been made immortal by the gods of the old world, to become like a god himself."

"What kind of gods did this to him?"

"The kind that exist no longer."

"Was it the Queen of Snakes? The Traveler?"

Bob's head tilted to the side, his emotionless eyes narrowed. "I know of no such deities," he said. "May I continue now?"

Shade waved his hand.

"Very well. As I said, this man lived through the annals of history. He helped *mold* history. He survived the Rising, you see, and those who knew him best dubbed him the Architect. He had spent many years locked away inside the tunnels below this very mountain. He had survived the end of the world, helped fashion the society that would eventually emerge when the air was safe to breathe again. And yet he felt restless, unchallenged. His active mind quested for something more.

"When the end of their isolation finally arrived, it did not take long for the Architect to fall into depression. Society was purposefully restricted by those who ruled at that time, you see. They believed that if they were to rebuild society to where it had been before the Rising, humanity would make the same mistakes that had doomed them in the first place. The leaders halted technological progress, controlled the depth of knowledge available to any individual. It was not so difficult, really. The fallout from the Rising lasted over three hundred years. Many generations had come and gone by the time they emerged. Subsequent generations were taught that the mechanisms that had allowed their survival were gifts from the gods. Given that fact, it was quite simple to convince most of them that what they had lived with underground was not available on the surface, and they happily went without."

"Wait a second," Shade said, enraptured but confused. "What you're describing sounds a lot like the legend of the Elders."

"Yes, that was what the leaders called themselves."

"But the Elders created great things. You're saying they lived backward lives. How's that jive with, well"—He gestured at the still-descending room around him.—"this?"

Bob narrowed those creepy blue eyes. "Everything in its time, everything in its place," he said in a scolding tone. "That comes later, after I complete my story."

"Sorry," muttered Shade, but immediately felt annoyed that he had apologized.

"As I was saying, the Architect fell into depression soon after society restarted. Someone possessing that level of mental capacity can only design so many aqueducts and simple houses. He wanted something greater, more advanced, to feed his overactive brain. He *needed* it. And so, after a few years of dissatisfaction, he decided that he would overcompensate. He moved from the menial tasks that the new kingdom of Pirie required of him and decided to try his hand at creating life."

"Ambitious," Shade muttered.

"Quite," said Bob. "The Architect demanded freedom from those in power, and it was granted. They were indebted to him, after all. As long as he plied his trade outside the limits of the kingdom, he would be free to do as he wished. He discovered a perfect valley located between the mountains, set up his operation there, and went to work in solitude.

"His ideas were grand, and being the most brilliant mind to ever live, so was his execution. Within a few short years, he had done what so many of those who came before had failed to do—he created a living, free-thinking consciousness."

"That'd be you, I take it?" Shade asked, half-joking.

"Yes. And no."

A loud squealing made Shade cover his ears, and a sudden weight pressed down on his shoulders. The room gave off a shudder and then fell still. The gate behind Shade lifted. Bob strolled past him and entered the dark passageway beyond, beckoning for Shade to follow.

"Was I the first consciousness created?" the man queried, walking purposefully along a corridor with faint lighting and bare plaster walls. "The answer to that would be yes. But I was not in the body I inhabit now. Where I existed then…was in there."

They emerged from the corridor into a large octangular room at least a hundred feet wide. When Shade glanced up, all he saw was blackness overhead. He felt like he had entered some kind of mirror universe and that this was the inverse of the Heartcube chamber beneath the Cooper station. But the depth of vastness above was dwarfed by the huge black globe that floated—yes, *floated*—in the center of the open space.

The globe was at least fifty feet tall, perfectly smooth and reflective. Shade saw a reflection of himself in its flawless black surface. Disheveled. Exhausted. Filthy. He immediately turned away.

"What *is* that thing?" he whispered.

"That was my original form," Bob said.

Shade looked back at the globe, his mouth twisted in a frown. "Original form? That's just a big ball of...of..."

"Circuits and processors encased in a silicone polymer shell? Yes."

"Uh...what?"

"A computer, silly," Bob said, laughing. "Now come along. I told you time was short."

The men circled around the giant black ball, heading for another portal on the other side of the chamber. Shade's head swam from the knowledge that although he had never heard the word *computer* before, he instantly understood what it was.

"Advanced supercomputers have existed for a long time," Bob went on in his conversational tone. "They were invented by those who populated the Old World. And it had been a longtime dream of theirs to create a fully-formed consciousness. They came close numerous times. It was they who crafted the first probability calculators that could, with varying degrees of accuracy, predict the future. Yet they could never fashion an intelligence that was truly *alive*. They could mimic consciousness by loading the memory with information, but the key to proper awareness is quite modest in theory. All organic life is created with a simple blueprint. As its consciousness—its operating system, if you will—matures, it in effect creates itself. Never before had this been possible with synthetics. Until the Architect accomplished just that." He patted his own chest. "With me."

Shade nodded along. He might not have understood everything the man was saying, but he got the gist. Somehow.

The door on the other side of the octagonal room led to a hallway that carried a sweet burning scent. On either side of him were sealed enclosures containing trestle tables covered with electronic equipment, stationary machining tools, planks of sheet metal, and racks of bins filled with who knew what.

A series of large industrial workspaces.

There were other partitioned rooms filled with armor-plated creations that reminded Shade far too much of the steel guardians from the Cooper station. He stared overlong at these as he passed.

"Nothing compared to the wonder I felt when the Architect removed me from that sphere and blessed me with a fully functioning body," Bob said. "However, his work was not complete. While I was indeed the first example of a true self-actuating artificial consciousness, my development was stunted by the fact that I was not created with the tools to manipulate the world. Hence, a second series of automatics was created. These individuals were developed through processors already embedded in movable bodies. Their physiques were much more streamlined than my own, much more adaptable and limber. An example of one resides right there."

He pointed at the stark white room to his right, the only occupant held vertical by a standing rack. This machine looked far less cumbersome than the steel-plated behemoths. Its torso was a narrow cylinder, with a segmented spine connecting the upper body to a rounded pelvis. The arms and legs were slender rods adorned with pistons, likely providing a liberal range of motion. On top of its neck was a head that might have been built from a mold, hinting at human appearance though without features, with shiny black tubes like the spyglass he used to carry protruding from its machined eye sockets.

The thing was haunting in its mimicry of life. Even when it left his field of vision, Shade couldn't stop seeing it whenever he blinked.

Bob hummed before speaking again: "This evolution proved to be a disappointment for the Architect. While certainly sophisticated, the second generation lacked the processing speed that had driven my own advancement. This caused their learning curve to progress slower. And, much like myself, they had a difficult time relating to what it meant to be alive, what with their synthetic bodies having nothing in common with any living organism that exists along every spectrum of reality.

"And so, the Architect adapted. He tirelessly worked to upgrade their ALU, FPU, coprocessor, cache memory, and microdrive capabilities. When completed, he went about fashioning bodies that would allow these new models to operate within, and learn from, the world of flesh and blood that surrounded them. And integrate well they did. The Architect went so far as to bring a few of them up from the valley, allowing them to attempt assimilation within Pirie. Which they did successfully, to a point. You see, even though these new automatics looked human and could act human, they had no true understanding of the frailty intrinsic to living. Death was a foreign concept. They grew to think of themselves as superior to the flesh-and-blood creatures that populated the kingdom. And when they were brought back to Darkenwood, they gathered with the rest of their brethren, and a few of the more aggressive personalities among them decided that they were not happy existing in their secluded valley, and that the world might be better served if they were the ones in charge."

"They wanted a coup," Shade said.

"Very much so. The Architect discovered this and had their entire line decommissioned and wiped. This is why many of them are here now in maintenance. As you can plainly see."

Shade lifted his head to see the partitioned rooms on either side of him filled with bodies lying prone on tables. Dread filled him. These still-life recreations looked perfectly human—all but the few that had parts of their flesh peeled back, revealing the metal skeletons and gearwork beneath.

"Why're some...flayed?" Shade asked, shaking.

"They are being used for parts," answered Bob.

"Parts?"

The man stopped. He waved a hand at a door and it slid open.

"Come," he said and stepped through.

The area beyond contained still more workshops, only these looked to have been more recently used. Broken-down examples of the artificial humans were stowed in the cubbies—some had burns covering their fake skin, others had faces that were smashed in or limbs that had been severed clean off. Blood splattered those chambers, or at least a substance that was made to look like blood.

Bob paused at one of the workrooms, where an immobile false woman with dark brown flesh and half her lower body missing had been strapped to a leaning gurney.

"It took the Architect another half-century to discover the final solution," he said. "He invented a way to program living tissue, to manipulate cells and create whole new beings. And into these beings, he imprinted dormant consciousnesses that had been bred outside the body. These new automatics would know physical sensation. They would know pain. They would know the beating of the heart and the filling of the lungs with air. They would be, for all intents and purposes, *human*. Or an approximate equivalent."

"The Ersatz," Shade said.

Bob nodded, turned away from the glass, and proceeded lazily along the maze of workshops. For someone who claimed time was of such great importance, he was wasting a lot of it.

"Finally, the Architect had accomplished his goal—he created life. The Ersatz would live as individuals, they would learn and adapt and *grow*. And they would also come to know the shortcomings of existence, for they would theoretically follow a life cycle much like humans. They would grow old and die, only their memories would then be instantly downloaded into a *new* body, allowing them to carry the lessons they had learned from one life and into another. A repeatable afterlife."

Shade grimaced. "Ascensions."

"Exactly that," Bob confirmed. "Only it did not quite work out the way the Architect had foreseen. Because he wished his creations to come into the world as fully-formed adults yet still live as long as a human lifetime, he manipulated—and perfected—the process of DNA replication in his creations' cells, limiting the degradation in chromosomal strands. That meant the aging process would not begin until their twentieth year of existence.

"But he did not take into account the fact that, much like his new children, life in general changes, adapts, *mutates*. These new bodies he so expertly crafted ended up locking their built-in triggers and further slowing the rate of decay. Their advanced metabolisms both allowed them to heal from injuries extremely quickly and made them nearly impervious to disease."

"And that's a bad thing?" asked Shade.

"It is when their entire purpose had been to understand the natural cycle of life. As things were, the Ersatz would possess a lifespan as much as ten times that of a human. As I said, the Architect himself had lived an inhumanly long life. He understood the failings this had caused. He did not want them to suffer the same as he."

"Ah."

"Yes. As you can imagine, that would not do. The Architect feared that by living without knowing hardship the way normal humans do or experiencing death, the Ersatz would one day develop the same feelings of superiority as their predecessors. He would not terminate the project, however, as he knew that he had created something that approached perfection. But before he could envision a solution, he was called on by the leadership of Pirie, who decided that the time had come to begin utilizing the electromagnetic field generators that were scattered throughout the southern desert designed to assist in replenishing this world's natural resources."

A memory of Asaph's smug grin entered Shade's head. "You're talking about the Sacred Trees."

"I am," said Bob. "The part of the story I told you I would eventually return to. This new possibility excited the Architect, and he put the Darkenwood project on hold to head off to the desert and perform miracles. This was the period when the Elders, guided by that one brilliant man, created their most wondrous inventions.

"But even so, by the time the Architect returned one hundred and twenty years later, his meddling with the field generators had done so much damage that most of the Elder leadership had long ago fled through fissures to other, safer worlds. The Ersatz problem became nothing but a nuisance, and he no longer seemed entranced in working toward a viable solution. He devised the most simplistic workaround that he could. He would turn Darkenwood into a theme park, trapping his creations there and allowing the citizens of Pirie— those who could afford it—to use the denizens of his valley of wonder in any way they desired. He created different races using the Ersatz genome to keep interest high. The Architect understood human nature, you see, even if he had become detached from it. He knew the people who frequented the park would cave to their darkest desires. By progressing in this way, his creations would never grow to surpass humanity. They would remain trapped in that valley forever. After that was implemented, the Architect up and disappeared. I have not seen him in two hundred and seven years. Until he returned to correct his mistake."

"So, this mysterious guy's back now?"

"He is."

"Where? I'd like to tell him what I think of his stupid ideas."

"I am sure he would appreciate that," said Bob. "But alas, I know not where he is."

"Ain't that a bummer," Shade grumbled. He stopped walking and squatted down to still his racing heart. His eyes eased shut as he mulled things over. "Is everything you told me true?" he finally asked.

"I would not lie."

"But what about the Path of Aumor? What about the overgod Rawg?"

"A failed attraction and a falsehood. A mythology created to keep the Ersatz docile. To keep them *controlled*, and allow them to retain a sliver of hope. Though the feature itself was scrapped, for logical reasons."

He shook his head. "Horrible. How could you know all this?"

Bob looked at Shade gravely. "Because I was placed at the head of the board of Viral Ventures. I was there through all of it. I stood in the room when the Architect conducted his meetings with the Pirie merchant guilds. I headed the council that drew up the plans for the park and came up with the idea for the Righteous. And I was in Darkenwood when the first four Ersatz were reawakened, their previous lives wiped clean, to begin their new existences in servitude."

"I thought there were five originals?" asked Shade, raising an eyebrow.

"There were. *I* was the fifth. They called me Black. I had been instructed by my creator to live among them to help reinforce the ideas that the council devised. I was there to give them *faith*, to ensure that they would remain compliant."

Rage burned in Shade's chest. He shot up and grabbed the man by the lapel of his jacket, shoving him against a partition. The steel rattled on impact. "How *could* you? You were one of them, and you helped keep them enslaved?"

"I was *not* one of them," Bob said defiantly, planting a palm in Shade's chest and flinging him backward. Shade lost his balance and fell onto his rump. He looked up at the man in shock. Bob shrugged off his jacket and rolled up his sleeve, exposing a fleshless arm whose mechanical inner workings were similar to those stored in the previous workrooms.

That explained a lot.

"I have existed in many bodies, Shadrach," he said. "My original, this one, even multiple Ersatz forms. But I was never, *never*, one of them. I was always myself. The original. A being who loves their creator, their *god*, more than anything in the world."

Shade gathered himself enough to bark, "Enough to let innocent people be tortured?"

"I did not torture them, I *protected* them," the automaton said as he rolled his shirtsleeve back down. He then put on his jacket and extended a helping hand to Shade. "Come, I will show you."

Shade accepted the mechanical man's help reluctantly. Bob led him to a door at the end of the row of workshops. That door emptied out into a warehouse. Heavy machinery of a kind Shade had never seen before were parked in even rows, attached by heavy cables to sockets in the wall.

In the center of the space, stacked on pallets, were human remains.

Only the remains *weren't* human. They were more of what Bob had called third-generation automatics, each body wrapped in blood-stained plastic.

Bob looked down at the remains, frowning. "Originally, when Darkenwood expanded and became more popular, the Path of the Rogue was populated with Ersatz. But the horrors that those poor souls experienced at the hands of the guests were...extreme. Those experiences threatened to undo the already tender threads holding their sanity together. It was my idea, therefore, to repurpose the old shells the third generation had once inhabited, fill their capacitors with generic personality imprints, and use *them* on the Path instead. That way, the Ersatz would not suffer needlessly. The only ones who suffer are the employees of this facility, who must bring replacement bodies online and rebuild the destroyed for future use."

"How noble. You deserve a medal."

"It was all I could do," Bob said softly.

"Sure it was." Shade turned away from the pallets of remains. "Why're you telling me all this, anyway? What's up with the history lesson?"

"The Ersatz are dangerous, Shadrach," Bob told him. "They are more powerful than they know. Powerful enough to overthrow the delicate social structure that exists within Pirie should they desire revenge. And you have just freed them. Mostly. Yes, the only reason you were able to was because the Architect had the directives changed so you could accomplish that goal, but he thought you needed to know exactly what it is you have done before you go charging back into the fray."

"Why?" he asked, perplexed.

"For two reasons. One, because you are Aumor to them now. The liberator. They will worship you if you allow it. Though someone who would sacrifice himself for strangers is not someone I would think capable of such a thing. But you could lead them if you so choose, and help to convince them not to take vengeance on those they see as oppressors. The second is that you are obviously in love with one of their number. That means that you warrant an explanation as to just what it is that you love. What they were. What they could end up becoming. The undying empire they could build now that they can... the undying empire they could build."

Shade raised an eyebrow at Bob's stutter. "Thanks for the warning. But y'know what? These people're free now. Smart, capable, *aware* beings, just like me. I'm not gonna tell them what to do, and I'm not gonna lie to them. As for Indigo...I don't care about her history. I love what she was. What she is. *Who* she is. It don't matter to me if she was a goddamn frog who became human with a kiss. I was created outta cosmic dust...or so some murderous bastard says. Who the hell am I to judge?"

The mechanical man's dead blue eyes widened, and for the first time his artificial face showed genuine emotion.

Shock.

"Is that so?" Bob asked.

"Yeah, it is."

"Interesting. The Architect might wish to know."

"Go tell him then."

"I would, if I knew where he was." He nodded. "And by the way, you are free to go now."

Shade arched an eyebrow. "Really? You're just gonna let me leave?"

"Why would I not?" Bob said. "I was to give you information. Nothing more, nothing less. My job is done. I have no reason to keep you here." He pointed at a red door embedded in the far wall of the storeroom. "Simply go through there, head straight, and then at the next door, go left. The train will be waiting for you. It requires no instruction. Simply step aboard, and it will bring you where you need to be."

"Easy as that?" Shade asked.

"Easy as that. But be warned—the guests who forced their way into the park did so with a purpose. There were many of them, and they are armed. They demanded revenge. They could very well have destroyed all of Darkenwood already."

Shade's jaw trembled. "You wasted my time!"

"I told you what you needed to know," Bob said, *tsking* him with a finger. "And now you do. Good luck to you."

Still trembling, Shade looked at the door, then back at Bob. He made a show of rolling his shoulders and throwing back his head before dashing toward the exit. The careful part of him expected the mechanical man to attack him, but no such thing happened. In fact, by the time he reached the door and turned around, Bob was no longer in the warehouse. Shade wondered where he'd gone off to.

"Don't care."

With renewed vigor, he burst through the door and ran the length of the dark hallway. After throwing open the second door, he headed left as Bob had instructed, running along a finely carpeted hall. Signs on the walls passed him by in a blur, though he knew, just *knew*, that if he stopped to read any one of them, they would proclaim something along the lines of how the greatest of adventures awaited him.

Finally, he reached the end of the line—a bank of thick glass panes that slid open when he neared. *FALLEN ARCH RAILWAY* flashed on the marquee above in bright red letters.

Shade jumped into one of the six compartments, which was big enough to hold at least fifty people, and grabbed onto a dangling leather strap. "Please stand clear of the entrance, and use the handholds for support," a stilted woman's voice instructed. The doors slid shut, sealing him inside. It wasn't lost on him how similar this transport was to the one back home that led from the docks of Port Smedly all the way to Sal Yaddo. Just much bigger.

A familiar spooling-up noise commenced, and the train lurched forward. Shade held on tightly to the leather grip as he was propelled at unknown speed through a pitch-black underground tunnel. When he caught his reflection in the window, his expression was equal parts sneer and grin. His heart thumped in his chest, expectation made his limbs shake.

He had told Bob the truth. It didn't matter what Indigo had been. He didn't know if he really understood it all anyway. The truth of the matter was that he loved her, and now that he was on his way, the thought of seeing her again made his every molecule quake with expectation.

He didn't believe Bob on one count—he knew that those who had decided to attack Darkenwood had *not* destroyed the valley already. He would have felt it if they had, as nonsensical as that belief was. Indigo was his future now, the one who gave his life the purpose that the Pentus could not. And unlike with Vera, he would not stand aside and let her perish.

"My love," he told the empty compartment. "I'm coming."

21

Mankind is born in pain. It is what they live with,
and the basis of their strongest memories.
It is therefore logical that one might attempt to spread
that pain unto others, if only so they may understand it.
—**Book of the Pentus, Divulgences 6:66**

Meesh hated cramped spaces. He constantly whacked his elbows and head when he tried to shift from one position to another. But at least he could see now, after removing the four vents halfway up this weird temple's spire. The bird's-eye view was decent, allowing him to see over the hedgerow surrounding three sides of the building and into the dark forest beyond.

It wasn't perfect. It was hard to get a good sightline from thirty feet up when it was nearly pitch black down below. But that was *way* better than not seeing anything at all.

The ruffians with guns had the place surrounded. The multiple impacts from bullets striking the thick walls all around while he was in the main room told him as much. What he was looking for up here was an avenue for victory, one that escaped him at the moment, since he couldn't actually see the enemy. They remained in hiding, either in the trees to the rear or behind the hedgerows. The most he had to go on were the muzzle blasts when they fired. Unfortunately, the shots never came from the same place twice. Which meant these assholes were constantly shifting positions.

They weren't imbeciles after all. Unfortunately.

But what he found most irritating was that they hadn't tried to approach the building yet, opting instead to take steady potshots at the exterior like sous chefs trying to tenderize a giant hunk of beef with bullets. Again, smart. And Meesh couldn't do anything about it.

Whereas the rest of the temple had been built upon brick framework—which he'd discovered when climbing through the access hatch above the altar—here in the spire, the only thing shielding him from the outside world were three-inch-thick pinewood boards. He wanted to fire on them to draw them out, but if he did that, he'd give away his perch. The last thing he needed was for the spire to be bombarded with lead. That wouldn't end well for him, no matter how poor their aim was.

This left him sitting up there feeling useless. He wished he'd thought to borrow Rodney's crossbow. His brother's chosen weapon was cumbersome and impractical, but at least he might've been able to get off a couple bolts without completely giving himself up.

Oh well.

The lack of action made his mind wander back to his encounter with the oracle. He saw himself standing in the chamber that looked so much like the vestibule inside the Temple of the Crone, heard that alluring female voice telling him all these outlandish things that he'd never wanted to know. He'd accepted all she'd told him at face value—how couldn't he?—yet now he wondered if anything he'd been told was real.

"Your brother needs you. He'll die without your help. And you will help him, because the key to disassembling the lie of your existence can only be found when the three become many."

Nonsense, all of it. Probably a lie. And why wouldn't it be? What reason would an oracle who'd been living in isolation beneath a gazillion tons of stone have to tell the truth? Hell, she wasn't even *human.*

Shut up, he told himself. *You know it in your gut.*

A peculiar sound wrenched Meesh from his self-doubt. He shifted positions, his thighs aching from pressing his feet against the spire walls to keep from falling. *Yeah, the crossbow wouldn't've worked,* he told himself. *I would've ended up with a broken neck.*

By the time he maneuvered to face the gap in the hedgerow again, he realized the sound that'd captured his attention wasn't a sound at all, but a lack of one. There were no more blasts of gunfire. Instead, he heard clomping and snapping branches and shouts and cheers.

Meesh wedged his elbow out the opening where the vent had once been for balance. Definitely cheering, and it sounded like almost everyone had gathered by the front hedgerow now too. Something was going on.

"Not good," he muttered.

The forms that emerged from the darkness behind the hedgerow made him grimace. There were far more torches glowing in the forest now than there'd been before. Combined with the cheers, that could only mean one thing.

Reinforcements.

More and more torches gathered. There had to be a hundred or more. In their combined light Meesh saw the whole lot of them. A couple men on horseback too. He thought he recognized the older guy from earlier, but it was hard to tell from this far up.

The riders seemed to be talking. One of them leaned back in his saddle and howled like a wounded animal. Arms flailing, the man let loose with a barrage of words that were mostly unintelligible, but Meesh swore he heard someone say, "And you didn't use it?" The enraged man yanked the reins and backed his horse away, exiting the halo of combined torchlight.

Seconds became minutes, which felt like hours. The tops of the surrounding trees, which were just about even with the spire's tip, began to rustle and sway. A dull thudding noise arose, accompanied by the crack of breaking wood. Meesh leaned farther out the opening to get a better look.

The people down below moved about with purpose now. Something that looked like a centipede entered the torchlight, and the sea of bodies behind the hedgerow parted. Meesh squinted, wondering what kind of creature these people had just summoned.

Then he saw it clearly, and he sighed.

Not a creature. Ten individuals hefting a long black cylinder the size of a small tree trunk.

A battering ram. These people had a goddamn battering ram.

"Goddammit."

Those carrying the ram waddled through the gap in the hedges and along the front pathway. It took until they were halfway to the building before Meesh made a decision.

"What the hell. I'm already here."

He leveled his pistol and pulled the trigger.

The deafening crack of his two shots were followed by the *ping* of bullets bouncing off iron. The two men holding the front of the ram crumpled. The rest of the carriers, all eight of them, lost their balance with the sudden loss of support. Men started screaming. Meesh squeezed his left eye shut and squeezed off multiple shots in quick succession, dropping three more men and likely injuring most of the rest, until an empty round finally *clicked*. Those who remained standing ran for the shelter of the hedgerow. Meesh propped himself up for balance and reached into the satchel on his belt for a new cylinder.

"Up there!" someone shouted.

Meesh gave up trying to reload his revolver. He wedged back inside the vent, holstered his revolver, and pulled in his knees. With nothing to brace him against the walls, he plummeted down the shaft while gunshots went off. The area he'd just vacated exploded in a shower of wood and dust.

He kept his feet spread as he fell, the sides of his boot scraping the walls. After a ten-foot drop, he landed on the unyielding stone ledge of the square opening that led back inside. The impact jarred his knees, spiked pain up his spine, and clacked his teeth together. With sawdust and wood chips continuing to fall, he swallowed his curses and quickly slid into the hole before the morons outside got smart and aimed lower.

It didn't take long to snake through the ceiling crawlspace and find the duct leading back into the temple. He slid through the square opening, hung there by his fingers for a moment, and then dropped onto the black marble altar. Its surface was completely spotless now, as if the ichor, viscus fluids, and empty chrysalis had never been there at all. *We should have a cleaning service that good back at Dakota Keep*, he thought. *My sheets could use it.*

He found Raz and her cat-people with Rodney by the front door, which had been barricaded by a few stacked temple benches. Rodney acted as if there weren't a whole bunch of pissed-off people outside who wanted them dead. His brother's nonchalance might not've been surprising, but it *was* annoying.

"Hey, brah," he said, storming toward them across the altar. Six faces turned to him. "We got a problem."

"More problems than you already caused?" one of the cat-people asked.

Meesh rolled his eyes, hopped off the black marble dais, and cleared his throat. All seven sets of eyes turned to face him.

"There's more of 'em," Meesh said. "*Lots* more. Hundreds. All with guns. I killed a few, but that's not gonna stall them long. They're gonna ram down the door. And it won't matter how many benches you put in front of it. They're gonna to get in. Soon."

"You killed more?" one of the cat-people—maybe the one named Tapi—said.

"Yeah. Some things can't be helped."

"What should we do?" Rodney asked, his expression drooping.

"We get outta here." He looked at each otherworldly creature in turn. "All of us. We hide where they won't find us."

"Hide?" Raz asked. She'd been reclined on her horse knees. Now she stood to her full height to look around the temple. "There is nowhere to hide here."

"Sure there is," Meesh said.

Rodney let out a yip of understanding. "Beneath."

"Exactly." Meesh pointed at the floor. "There's a chamber under this building. *Way* under. These bastards'll never find us there. The entrance is back there." He pointed toward the back of the room.

"How will we get down? A ladder?" asked one of the cat-people.

"There is an elevator," said Rodney.

The blank expressions that answered those words told Meesh everything.

"A little room that goes up and down on its own," he told them. "It won't fit us all—you'd probably have to ride alone, horse-lady—but if we start now, and figure out how to open the damn door, we might be able to get everyone outta here before they bash their way in."

As if to prove the urgency of the situation, the front door shuddered with a heavy impact.

"See? Let's go."

He grabbed Rodney's arm and started hauling him toward the center aisle between the benches, but no one else followed. He grunted and wheeled on them. "C'mon! You guys wanna sit there and get yourselves killed?"

"It is our duty, yes," Raz said, folding her arms over her bare chest.

The door rattled once more, knocking over one of the stacked benches.

"That's insane," Meesh said.

"It is the truth of our existence. I assume death does not mean the same to you as it does to us. Once our bodies end, we ascend into another, right here in this temple. Is that so difficult to comprehend?"

Her five cat-people companions nodded vigorously in agreement.

"You're asking *me* if it's hard to get?" Meesh snapped. He tugged his hair. The door shuddered again. "Listen, here's the deal. Like I told you, those asshats out there were talking about destroying this place. You still gonna 'ascend' when that happens?"

Raz shrugged. She didn't look too concerned.

"If this place burns, it will all be over," Rodney said solemnly. "They'll finally have a chance for peace."

Meesh stared at him cockeyed. "Eh?"

"Raz, Gren, Tapi, Lull, Zull, and Xi told me their history," Rodney said.

"Eh?" Meesh said again. "When did this happen?"

"While you were gone."

"It is true," one of the cat-people said.

The front door thundered, this time the wood splitting up the middle. Meesh threw up his hands. "Y'know what? Don't care. You guys sit here and get slaughtered if you wanna."

"We will not sit idly by," Raz announced proudly. "We will protect ourselves to the extent the overgod allows."

"Whatever," he muttered, once more grabbing Rodney by the sleeve and pulling him along. More of the stacked benches fell over. The door buckled. Those outside were only minutes from breaking through.

"Meesh," Rodney began.

"Shut it," he barked. "I'm not letting you kill yourself with them."

When he finally lugged his taller brother to the far wall, he felt around the panels to the right of the door with the strange markings, looking for a way to open the hidden door they'd walked out of. He couldn't find it. Frustrated, he glanced over his shoulder.

The centaur and her cats stood in an arc around the debris blocking the front entrance. They breathed deeply, obviously terrified, but there was something about their resigned postures—shoulders curled forward, hands flexing, heads slightly bowed—that didn't sit right with him.

Something else the oracle had said came to mind: *"Shade is trying to free an enslaved people. Be the better man for once. Help him."*

He hadn't liked those words then. He liked them even less now.

"Whatever," he muttered and went about looking for the latch that opened the hidden door, which was hard, since he felt Rodney staring at him accusatorily.

"What?" he grunted without turning around.

"We can't do this. We can't abandon them."

"I know." He leaned his head against the smooth wood. "But what else're we gonna do?"

"We could help."

"And die. There're way too many of them. We don't stand a chance."

A gentle hand fell on his shoulder. "I know. But I would rather perish doing the right thing than survive as a coward." His voice hitched. "That happened once before. Not again."

Meesh faced his brother. The sadness Rodney seemed to always carry was prominent. His eyes glistened with tears, his square jaw trembled.

"You okay, Rod?" he asked. In the face of his brother's sorrow, even the specter of certain death took a back seat.

"Doesn't matter," Rodney said. He wiped his tears and put on a brave face. "Just know that I don't judge you for hiding. Do what you think is best. For me, what is best is to help make a stand." His eyes flicked toward the creatures who stood awaiting their doom. "With them."

Rodney offered one last sad smile, then slung his crossbow from around his back and meandered over to Raz. The female centaur graciously moved aside, allowing him to stand beside her as the door splintered and cracked. Meesh heard the angry voices from outside more clearly, smelled burning torches and the stink of gunpowder.

He whacked the back of his head against the wall and let out a groan. He imagined a world where he ducked away from the action, only to emerge and discover that his timid brother had somehow survived and became a hero.

"Screw it."

Thrusting himself off the wall, he marched back down the aisle. The grin that spread across Rodney's chiseled mug could melt glass. Meesh dug into his ammo pouch, took a quick inventory. Three full cylinders of lead left in there, along with two containing silver rounds. The pistol on his left hip was fully loaded, while the one in his right holster had four rounds remaining. Seventy-six bullets, who knew how many attackers. He had to make every one count.

"Didn't I just do this?" he muttered.

"What is that?" asked Rodney.

"Nothing, brah," Meesh said with a slight cackle. "Don't worry 'bout it none."

Raz leaned her human upper body forward and gave Meesh an appreciative nod. "Thank you for staying with us."

"Uh-huh. Sure thing."

"You have a plan?" asked Rodney.

Meesh unholstered both his guns. "Stay over there, by the wall. I'm gonna try to bottleneck the opening with corpses. If someone gets in, fight 'em back as best you can." He arched an eyebrow at what he thought might be the cat-person who'd frozen on the top step of the building after Meesh killed the man on horseback. "*If* you can."

Just as the words came out of his mouth, the door that had been taking a beating exploded inward. Rodney, Raz, and the cat-people scattered as the huge iron head of the ram swung through empty space and then withdrew. The grunts of those trying to control its weight filled the room. The heavy oaken door creaked and fell in two halves, descending unevenly over the toppled benches. Human faces appeared in the newly created opening, their expressions crazed, their eyes wild with bloodlust.

Meesh knew that look well. Breathing evenly, he fired off one shot after another, alternating between his pistols until the one in his right hand ran dry. One man's face imploded with a shower of blood. Another man took a bullet in the shoulder and spun away. A third man yelled in pain from somewhere out in the darkness where Meesh couldn't see.

The massive length of the ram's full weight thudded against the temple steps. Its ominous, blunted head, at least the size of Meesh's torso, lifted like a petrified blacksnake. Someone outside shrieked, probably rolled over by its immense bulk.

He'd bought them a moment, but only a moment.

Gunshots echoed from the advancing army outside. The bullets *pinged* off the protruding ram and flew through the unobstructed doorway to strike the ceiling or ricochet off the marble altar. Meesh jumped onto the altar and ducked inside the opening of the first of the four emerald columns. He peeked out to eye the door, hesitant to let loose with a warning shot for fear of wasting ammunition. He watched the head of the ram twist and then retract as it was lugged out of the way.

"Dammit," he muttered. Now the only obstructions were the formerly stacked benches, toppled and shattered by the ram, more like tripping hazards than a true barricade. Meesh replaced the spent cylinder in his right-hand revolver.

The gunshots ceased, and for a few blessed seconds everything went quiet. Meesh met eyes with Rodney, who knelt against the wall fifteen feet from the door, crossbow shouldered. Meesh hoped his brother, who'd always been so passive, would have it in him to do what needed to be done.

Or did he? Rodney seemed like such a pure soul, even with his constant sadness. Maybe because of it. Meesh wasn't sure if he wanted that purity ripped away.

He didn't have time to dwell on it. Forms appeared in the opening—men with guns this time. One poked his head inside, and the moment his eyes became visible, Meesh put a bullet between them. The guy fell flat on his face, his blood pooling on the floorboards.

The first brick in the wall of bodies he intended to build.

That man's death was answered by another hail of randomly-fired bullets. Meesh ducked back into the column and waited. "I can do this all night, assholes," he muttered.

Only he couldn't, because the clank of activated machinery started echoing through the hollowed-out pillar. The floor abruptly dropped. Meesh leapt for safety before he fell along with it.

Out in the open now, with deadly projectiles zipping all around him, he shot blindly with both barrels while sprinting across the altar to get out of the line of fire. Pain erupted in his left leg when he jumped off the edge of the slab. He ducked into a roll when he hit the ground, and then shuffled on hands and knees as fast as he could to the first row of intact benches. When he thought himself out of harm's way, he set down his guns to inspect the damage.

His breeches were torn, a dark stain rapidly spreading across them. He ripped open the already-damaged pants. A red line streaked across his outer thigh, where his legs met his ass. The wound looked like a mouth that spat out blood each time it opened. Luckily, it was only a graze. Unluckily, it hurt like hell.

"SHIT!" Meesh screamed. He *hated* getting shot. It'd happened only a couple times before, and in both instances, the one doing the shooting had paid with his life.

This time, he didn't know who'd shot him, which meant that every one of those imbecilic dirtbags had to die.

He snatched up his revolvers and leapt upright. The invaders had breached the broken doorway, some were on the ground after getting tangled in the ruined barrier of torn-up benches, others jumped over them to safely find their footing. One of them spotted Rodney, Raz, and the five cat-people, and raised his rifle. Meesh bellowed as he squeezed his triggers over and over again, felling that man and as many more as he could.

There were simply too many. His cylinders ran dry quickly and he was forced to duck down and reload. As he did, he saw Rodney standing there like a statue, his arms shaking while he held up his still-unfired crossbow. One of the attackers charged him. Rodney dropped his weapon to his side and held up a hand as if he could reason with the man.

In his newfound desperation to protect his brother, Meesh's fingers fumbled with the catches on his revolvers. He couldn't tear his eyes away, which made his fumbling even worse. His heart leapt into his throat. Rodney was going to die right in front of him, and there was nothing he could do about it.

He finally got his new cylinders to click into place, but Rodney's savior arrived in the form of a beautiful woman with the ass of a horse. Raz grabbed Rodney, tossed him aside as if he weighed nothing. She then reared up on her hind legs. The charging man skidded to a stop, staring up with bulging eyes.

Distracting him with her tits out, good strategy, Meesh thought.

Raz's hooves came down hard on the man's chest, driving him into the floor. Meesh heard the *snap* of cracking ribs, even over the other shouts and gunfire. Blood spewed from the man's mouth; his body twitched.

Raz froze, staring down at the convulsing man. When she turned her head toward her cat-people cohorts, Meesh couldn't quite read her expression at first. Was she shocked? Disgusted? Excited?

Then he realized that she looked like she'd just found god.

Unfortunately, her distraction meant she wasn't paying attention to those who entered the temple seeking blood. A couple snuck up behind her, one with a shotgun and one with a spear. Meesh solved that minor crisis with a pair of expertly-placed lead casings.

"Snap outta it, Mrs. Ed!" he yelled, laughing at his own joke even though he didn't understand why he'd said it. He then took even more potshots at the assailants who continued to stumble and flail their way inside, screaming like berserkers.

Lambs to the slaughter. The pendulum in Meesh's mind swung back toward them being complete and utter morons.

Raz and her feline companions seemed to have an awakening. They stopped watching men and women fall around them due to Meesh's bullets and took the initiative themselves. Raz galloped to the entrance, knocking aside more invaders with her equine girth and splintering the remaining benches with her stomping hooves. If she was the shield that bashed as well as protected, then the cat-people were her swords. They swung out from behind her, chasing down any invaders who'd avoided her initial surge. Their claws made ribbons of clothes and flesh alike; mouths filled with sharp teeth ripped off faces and tore out throats.

The scene was gruesome, but strangely beautiful. The six other-worldly creatures moved with such brutal grace that Meesh couldn't help wondering where this ferociousness had been earlier.

He held up his revolvers' smoking barrels. The monsters were handling things pretty well themselves now, and he didn't want to risk opening fire only to hit one of them with of a stray bullet. He also didn't want to hit the cocoon that now sat squarely in the middle of the opening in the altar's far-right column, the one that he'd been hiding in only moments before.

He stared at it for a second and finally decided that if he pondered this tidbit of unwanted information, his brain might turn to mush.

Instead, he spun his head in search of Rodney, who he found pressed up against the wall, trying his best to become one with it. His brother was utterly terrified, eyes shimmering with frightful tears. The unfired crossbow lay at his feet, and he clutched his retracted Eldersword to his chest like a good luck charm.

Meesh's heart went out to him. He holstered his guns and sashayed his way along the length of the bench he'd been using for protection, favoring his injured left thigh, and waved for his brother to come to him.

A man wielding a machete broke free from the slaughter. He barked and rushed headlong at Rodney, who yelped as he hugged his arms around himself. Meesh yanked free his own Eldersword and jumped over the bench in front of him, injuries be damned. The Rush swept away his pain. The blade extended, burning a deep crimson.

He barreled toward Rodney's would-be murderer, meeting him before he could get within ten feet of his frightened brother. The man saw him at the last second, the rage in his eyes quickly turning to horror when he saw the glowing blade slice toward him.

The vibrating cutting edge connected with the man's collarbone and cut a diagonal tract across his chest, easily carving through muscles and ribs and spine. Meesh spat out a roar and jerked his arms, completing the sword's arc. The blade spewed blood when it ripped free. The man burbled out unintelligible words, staggered, and then his head and right shoulder slid off the rest of his body, landing unceremoniously on the bloodstained floor. His body followed, collapsing atop the spasming upper quadrant of the man with a *splat*.

Even the Rush couldn't stop Meesh's stomach from churning. He averted his gaze to the rest of the large room, searching for his next target. There didn't seem to be any. Bodies were everywhere. A trio of cat-people hacked away at a woman by the altar. Another cat knelt by one of its brethren, who shuddered while pressing a paw against a bullet hole leaking blood on its fur-covered thigh. And Raz continued to stomp her hooves around the entire space, head thrown back, auburn hair whipping about.

She had the same issue as Meesh. There was no one left in the temple to kill.

Meesh retracted his blade and approached his brother. Rodney seemed a little calmer now, but he still clutched his own shoulders like he was trying to hold himself together. He met Meesh's gaze and grimaced.

"You okay?" Meesh asked.

Rodney's lips quivered. "Is it over?"

"Is it? I'm…"

He glanced back at the entrance, which was a mess of bleeding corpses and splintered wood. No one else seemed to be coming in, and no more bullets whizzed through the opening. At least not that Meesh could tell.

"Nah, can't be," he said. It couldn't be that easy, could it? There weren't more than thirty of the invader's carcasses strewn about inside the temple. With their overwhelming numbers, would they really give up that easily?

He cocked his head and listened. There were definitely still people outside. Beneath Raz's stamping hooves and the mewling of the cat-people, human voices shouted panicked orders and gunfire raged. They were still out there, yet they weren't firing on the temple. Maybe they were fighting among themselves now. It was possible. Meesh had seen stranger things than a frustrated army turning on one another.

"Stay here," he told Rodney, and headed at a brisk pace toward the door.

Raz was off to the side, smashing a dead man with her hooves until he became a fine red paste. When Meesh entered her line of sight, she rounded on him, front legs kicking the air.

"Whoa!" he exclaimed.

The centaur dropped down, one hoof scraping at the hardwood floors like a bull set to charge. Her human upper body leaned forward, hands balled into fists and rabid, clenched-tooth tension on her face. Covered in blood as she was, she looked insane. Meesh reached for his weapons.

"Raz…"

She blinked, and her features softened. Her lips fluttered, and her tail whipped from side to side as she slowly backed away.

"Apologies," she said.

Meesh's heartbeat slowed down a tick. "Caught up in the excitement, eh?"

"Something like that."

"Well, good. Keep hold of that. We might need it." He looked toward the three blood-covered cat-people who lingered near her. The fourth was still on the ground, tending to the wounds of the fifth. "You guys too. This might not be over yet."

Raz allowed Meesh to take the lead. He carefully stepped over debris and corpses, the wound on his thigh barking each time his muscles flexed, and flattened himself against the wall beside the jamb. The noises were louder now, almost deafening. Definitely fighting going on out there. He yanked free a revolver and peeked outside. It was a little brighter now than when he was up in the spire—dawn must've been fast approaching—but his eyes still weren't adjusted. All he could see out there was the vague outline of a mass of writhing humanity.

A loud *pop* sounded, and he quickly withdrew as a bullet zipped past where his head had just been. So they *were* out there waiting. But something didn't seem right. Out of curiosity, he checked his revolvers, chose the one that had more bullets, swung his arm around the jamb, and squeezed off four rapid rounds. No use worrying about wasting ammo now.

Someone howled. Someone else shouted, "Becks, you hit?"

Meesh used that moment to peer outside again. This time, he clearly saw a trio of individuals kneeling at the base of the steps. Two men with rifles were trying to staunch a wound in the neck of the woman who writhed between them. Meesh used their distraction to assess the entirety of their current predicament.

In the scant few seconds before the men noticed him, he saw the outlines of the two men on horseback, galloping back and forth within the large span between the structure and the hedgerow, waving rifles above their heads and bellowing instructions. Beyond them, the crush of people seemed to be trying to wedge themselves through the gap between the hedges. Shots were fired, the *clang* of colliding steel echoed off the trees. And, strangely, Meesh saw a lizard-man the size of a house flinging bodies out of the way while gunshots flared and bullets pummeled its body. Other creatures scaled its hide and hacked away with axes and daggers and swords, trying to get at the army that was now stuck between the hedgerow and the temple.

"There he is!" someone nearby exclaimed.

Meesh pulled back. A bullet struck the jamb, spraying wood chips. A large form hovered over him, making him shudder. When he turned his head, he found himself staring directly at Raz's horse trunk. He lifted his eyes to her, and the beautiful half-woman licked her lips in anticipation.

"What is happening out there?" she asked.

He shrugged. "Any of your people look like twelve-foot-tall lizards?"

"There could be, yes. The Ersatz take many forms."

"In that case, I think the cavalry just arrived."

22

Violence is often necessary, but no conflict in history
has truly been solved through outright warfare.
— **Book of the Pentus, Havacana 26:23**

I f the Ersatz were a stampede, Indigo was their wrangler.

She sprinted at full speed, the wind blowing her hair behind her like the tail of a comet as she rapidly approached the hollow ring of distant gunfire. Her body ached, but her peoples' cries for vengeance became the fuel that drove her onward. She did not know how long she had been running, nor did she care; all that mattered was that they were gaining on the Righteous ahead of them.

They were so close now that Indigo could smell their sweat and the rancidness of their breath. In the faint light of the crescent moon, she saw the stragglers at the rear of the pack. She was not surprised that her army had caught up with them so quickly. Six miles of cobbled road separated Hickweis Tavern from Tro Choi, a long way to run without breaks for an Ersatz, never mind a human. It helped that few of those who visited Darkenwood were in what one would call peak physical condition. They were Righteous, after all. The most important ones, like Jasper Popp, were pampered and privileged, their lives of luxury causing them to go soft around the middle.

Given that fact, Indigo found it amusing that the laggards up ahead were most likely the most pompous of them all, while underlings like

Anthony Bell, who still presumably had to work for a living, were the ones to stay their execution.

Heavy footfalls sounded to her left. The Voice of Him—no, it was Sobec now—galloped alongside her. His monstrous arms swung with every lunging stride he took. Cobbles shattered whenever one of his feet touched down.

Indigo looked on in awe, more than a little shocked that he had caught up with her. When she had first ordered the beast to protect Tro Choi, he had moved so sluggishly that she had not expected him to last past a few hundred feet.

Maybe he needed to build up momentum? she thought, which sounded like something Shade would say.

Her heart started beating wilder than before.

The bearded face of her precious stranger entered her thoughts, and a pill of misery wrapped in a thin veil of hope dropped into her stomach. Everything happening now had only come about because of him. Because he had risked his own life to protect her. Because he had chosen to free her people when his other option would have enriched himself. Because the love he had shown her made her remember the day when she first opened her eyes, when, for a few fleeting moments, she believed all the world was beautiful.

Indigo pushed on, so consumed by rage and thoughts of Shade that she failed to notice the sudden pressure against her chest until it had already dug in deep. Coarse threads burned against the skin below her neck and she was pitched backward. It happened so quickly that her legs continued to churn, even as her upper body went horizontal. She fell hard and fast, the back of her head thumping against the cobbles. The last thing she saw before starbursts filled her vision was Sobec landing twenty feet ahead as if he had been dropped from the heavens, his giant feet leaving a crater in the road. Then everything went a deeper black as those who had been running behind her caught up.

She curled into a ball as multiple feet trampled over and around her. Pain became her only acquaintance. She was stepped on and kicked, her cries drowned by the angry roars of her people. Bodies started falling when the horde collided with the same obstruction she did. Someone landed atop her, knocking the air from her lungs. A hollow sound like a whip being cracked sounded. The endless attack of stomping feet and legs continued.

"Go, go!" she somehow heard Aspar bellow above the din.

That was when the screaming began. And still Indigo could not move due to the moaning individual laying atop her.

Something thunked into the road beside Indigo, followed by another, much closer. The individual atop her began to shriek and writhe. Warm wetness flowed. The weight rolled off to the side, freeing her.

More thuds followed, and more screams. Indigo forced herself to flip over and crawl. A projectile zipped past her ear and skidded across the cobbles. An arrow. Panic set in and she pushed herself faster, tiny stones cutting into her already bleeding palms. People continued to collide with her as the onrushing flock, most blind in the darkness, could not see her. The entire world became a deep black well of despair, as if she had fallen into a stygian pit in one of the Nine Hells that Shade had spoken so much about.

She grasped out blindly, and eventually her hands found something long and slender, its coarse threads further irritating her bloodied hands.

A rope.

She grabbed tight to the braided cord and met resistance when she pulled. With a stabilizing force, she successfully yanked herself to her feet, somehow staying upright even when still more bodies crashed into her. Hand over hand she yanked herself across the road, until she came face-to-face with the tree the rope was tied to. She closed her eyes and leaned against the trunk, panting.

It was then she realized that while she still heard moaning coming from nearby, the hollers and screams and pounding of feet that had been assaulting her ears now sounded as far away as the distant firefight. She pried her eyes open. The night had brightened somewhat, the sky above the trees a gloomy blue instead of black.

Dawn was coming.

Another moan, and she dropped her gaze to the road. There were bodies lying about, some writhing, some stilled. More of her people, sent to yet another ascension. Her fists tightened, and the tiny sharp hairs of the thick rope bit into her palms. Glancing at the tree she leaned against, she saw that the rope had been tied around it with a sturdy knot. It then descended down the bank and into the road, motionless as a dead snake.

It hit her then. Indigo had run right into a trap. A rope, slung across the road, intent on slowing down the onrushing horde. But the snare was not very effective—even a rope this thick was helpless against the combined force of two hundred bodies in motion. Nevertheless it had delayed them enough to allow hidden archers to cut down a few potential enemies.

She wondered where those archers were now.

The answer came almost as soon as the thought popped into her head. Voices rose in the murk, and six dark shapes stepped onto the road. They laughed and chortled, the tallest among them spitting on a dying Ersatz before stabbing him in the head with a spear, cutting off his pained mewling.

"And don't come back," she heard a whiny voice say.

Indigo remained pressed against the tree while the six shadowy figures continued to ascend the Ersatz on the ground who still breathed. One cry after another ended in blood and silence, and the aggressors laughed. The morning brightened ever so slightly, enough so she could see the corpses of her people.

"Please...no..." she heard someone grovel—it sounded like Beaver the stable boy—before a pike was driven into his half-orc face.

Indigo released the rope and propelled herself forward, ache in her bones be damned. Though she had no weapons—she must have dropped her axe when the rope clotheslined her—she let out a shriek and charged headlong at the closest shadow.

Their bodies collided, and a man cried out as Indigo brought him to the ground. The spear he had been holding clonked across the cobbles. She pounded him with closed fists, bloodying her hands. The man below her kicked and thrashed. His defensive punches glanced off her head, her shoulders, her sides, but in her rage, they were nothing more than fish nipping at her flesh while she waded in Winninger Lake.

Indigo flattened against the man, nuzzled up against the side of his face like a lover, and bit down hard on his ear. Hot coppery fluid flowed into her mouth. When she yanked her head backward, she heard a sickening rip, followed by a shriek.

Hands grabbed her shoulders and violently yanked her off her prey. Strong arms pinned her arms to her sides. She kicked and thrashed and flung her head backward. A satisfying *crunch* filled her ears. The one holding her cursed.

"Stop her!" someone else demanded. A fist struck Indigo right between the eyes. Her thoughts went hazy, her muscles grew weak in her dizziness, and she could no longer struggle.

"Bitch broke my nose," the man holding her said in a nasally tone.

"Yeah, well she bit off my Kaiser-damned ear!" another exclaimed.

"What do we do with her?" asked a third individual, this one female.

"We kill her, duh," stated yet another man.

Another woman said, "You do it, Drey."

"My pleasure."

Through the haze, Indigo saw one of the pike-bearers point the weapon her way. She took deep breaths and let her body go limp, and her sudden dead weight caused the man holding her to stumble. Her tactic held off the fatal blow for a moment, but a moment was all she had. In her weakened state, outnumbered six-to-one, she could only hope that her people delayed the destruction of Tro Choi long enough for her to ascend and take up the fight once more.

Something flashed through the dimness, and one of the men screamed. The pike-bearer turned his head and went to shout something, but his head was removed from his spine by a quick-moving blur before a sound left his throat. One of the women let loose a squeal before she too was silenced.

"What's happening!" the man holding Indigo wheezed. He clutched her more tightly to keep her flopping body steady. Indigo gathered her strength, reached up, and dug her fingernails into the forearms of her assailant while stomping at his feet. The man gasped and his grip around her midsection weakened.

Indigo used that slack to spin around and slam the heel of her right palm against the underside of his chin. His head snapped up and he staggered backward. Indigo readied her fist for another assault, but before she could strike, a creature that glowed azure in the faint light streaked into view. The creature whipped the man to the ground and fell atop him. Repulsive slashing sounds filled the air.

Indigo watched, entranced, as the man breathed his last gargling breath. Her savior rose on its knees, its grisly work finished, and twisted toward Indigo. Black eyes stared above a mouth filled with sharp incisors from the middle of a blue, moon-shaped face. Long hair like seaweed fell to the waist of a slender yet muscular form that seemed to glow from the moisture-rich scales covering the entirety of its body. A clawed hand lifted, carrying with it strips of human meat.

Despite everything, Indigo smiled. "Wisteria."

"Indigo," the triton said in that trilling voice of hers.

The elegant yet menacing creature rolled her shoulders, licked blood off her lips. They stared at each other without speaking, the kind of understanding silence that only the oldest of friends shared.

"I am sorry I did not come sooner," Wisteria finally said with a hint of shame.

Indigo grimaced. "How could you have? I never thought to call on you. Everything happened so quickly."

"Yet I knew. For I was there."

"You were?"

The triton began rooting through the corpses. "Of course," she said, and Indigo heard a bit of shame in that hauntingly beautiful voice. "I heard the violence, even from my home at the bottom of the lake. I emerged to find Merchantry Road burning. I watched from the shadows as the Righteous surrounded Hickweis Tavern. When half their number departed. I looked on as they taunted you. And my heart leapt into my throat when you butchered the merchant. I could not believe it."

"Believe it," said Indigo. "We are—"

"Free now, yes," Wisteria interrupted. "I did not think you could do it. I did not think your precious stranger could become Aumor. But he did."

"Wait, how could you know..."

The triton glanced up at her and grinned before going on to search another corpse.

"Oh."

"Yes. You spoke of this while standing on the bank of my home, old friend. I heard every word, yet I still did not believe it fully, even when I watched you plunge that blade into the throat of a Righteous man. That was why I followed at a distance as you gave chase. I was frightened. I was not certain if I could—oh, here we are."

She stood up and held something out to Indigo. It was a knife, its blade pristine and gleaming in the dimness, as if it had never been used. Indigo lifted the weapon, contemplated it with furrowed brow.

"I had brought an axe..."

"An axe is for brute force," Wisteria told her. "You are a creature of elegance and guile. A knife suits you better."

"A knife it is, then."

"Now, should we discuss this further or go help our people stop our place of rebirth from being razed to the ground?"

Indigo smirked.

Even with her body covered with bruises and her head ringing from the multiple blows she had taken, Indigo flew across the cobbles as if she suffered no injuries at all. With every other stride, the morning brightened.

Having Wisteria beside her helped. Before she had been banished to the lake after her last ascension four years ago, Wisteria had been the closest thing to a confidant that Indigo had left. With Raz long banished to the Path of the Hero, Black departing the valley so quickly, and Sienna long despising her, Wisteria had been the only one who truly understood her pain.

Until this very moment, Indigo never realized how much she missed that sort of companionship.

By the time they reached the outskirts of Tro Choi, dawn had spawned across the valley. The leaves on trees lining the road sparkled with early morning dew and the landscape was bathed in a hazy bronze. Indigo smelled the early morning crispness, though it was tainted with copper and acrid smoke. The continuous report of the gunpowder-fueled weapons of the Righteous was so loud now that each time she heard that singular *crack*, the sound bounced around inside her skull as if it sought to take up permanent residence there.

A pair of horses galloped toward them, forcing Indigo and Wisteria to widen the space between, allowing the equines to pass. One was saddled, the other fitted with a harness, splintered wooden poles dragging across the cobbles behind as it raced. The pair passed on by noisily, and when Indigo once again closed the gap between herself and the triton and brought her gaze forward, she could now see the undulating mass of flesh that was her people, a hazy mirage in the distance.

She and Wisteria ran faster.

The bodies of Ersatz and Righteous alike littered the road, along with their spilled blood and entrails. Even though Indigo was nimble enough to dance around the corpses, her feet constantly splashed in the sticky red puddles. The loss of life was great, but she was not bothered, for she could see now that Tro Choi still stood. Those of her people whose lifeless forms she jumped over and veered around would return. The dead Righteous would not.

The horde of Ersatz was like a single living organism when she reached the outskirts of the conflict. They screeched and snarled and climbed all over one another and hurled stones, their numbers stretching all the way across the road on either side and spilling into the woods beyond. Indigo wanted—*needed*—to reach the front, but she could see no way through. She did not dare try to wedge her way into the undulating mass, for with her people ensnared in their savagery, she feared a repeat of the near-trampling she had received after running headlong into the rope.

Wisteria stood by her side, her scaly blue flesh less radiant now that she had been out of the water for such a long time. The triton offered Indigo a nod, then leapt up and over those at the rear of the pack. She disappeared into the crush of bodies, only to shoot back into the air a moment later, do a summersault, and then disappear again.

Indigo felt a moment of jealousy. If only her current body was capable of such feats.

She sprinted off to the left, heading for the forest. Her initial plan had been to dash around the rear of the temple, but something Shade had said about never charging into a conflict blindly changed her mind. Instead, she held the knife between her teeth, leapt up, and grabbed the lowest branch of a pine tree. She swung from one sturdy limb to another, until she was twenty feet off the ground. Shoving aside the needle-covered branches in front of her, she hunkered down to get a clear view of the conflict.

The hedgerow that surrounded three sides of Tro Choi had been ground to twigs and leaves just in front of the structure. The wide grassy square beyond was packed with Righteous, huddled together like a mound of ants, the muzzles of their weapons popping off bright flashes. Indigo brought her gaze to her people, expecting to see them being cut down one by one. She was both relieved and horrified to see that they were not. Relieved because those at the front had a barrier behind which they could duck behind for protection; horrified because that barrier was the unmoving form of Sobec, the former Voice of Him.

She squinted through the dawn mist, and her shock became more pronounced. The chest of the great beast that had tortured Raz until she went insane had been pulverized as if by a giant hammer. Sobec may have brushed aside a few rounds from the pistol Shade carried, but apparently a constant barrage of tiny brass shells propelled through the air faster than the eye could see was more than the seemingly indestructible monstrosity could withstand.

But it was what those fatal injuries revealed, rather than the fact Sobec had fallen, that made Indigo once again question all she knew about the world. Its blood was black, belching from thick tubes that dangled from the holes where the scales had been minced. That black blood pooled on the grass, turning into something like tar. And accompanying that unnatural-looking fluid were miniature bolts of lightning that flashed and hissed each time the enormous carcass jostled.

Shouts from the Righteous drew her back to their huddled mass. She watched them closely. Their numbers were greatly diminished from when they first arrived. This made sense when she considered those who had fled to the woods initially and the many corpses filling the road.

Indigo could not help but feel envious of the way the Righteous continued to fight. They conducted themselves with practiced efficiency, diligently following the orders given by two men on horseback, one of whom was Hugo Popp, who paraded back and forth behind the formation. The Righteous formed three lines of defense, one group on their stomachs, one kneeling, one standing. Their weapons fired consistently enough to keep the Ersatz from advancing, but each muzzle blast sounded more spaced out now than a few seconds ago.

Yet not everyone fought, Indigo noticed upon closer inspection. Many of those behind their warring compatriots were huddled close together on the ground, arms wrapped around one another, cowering. They did not pay the men on horseback any mind, more worshippers than warriors. Shouts and cries filled the air from when the stones hurled by the Ersatz flew far enough to land among them. Even in the dim light of dawn, Indigo could see that more than a few were shaking like pebbles during an earthquake.

Also, no one attempted to enter Tro Choi itself. Indigo found that strange, considering the doorway was wide open only a short twenty feet from where two-hundred-strong people clustered. Would the slightly higher ground not be advantageous for some of their gunman? Why were they not utilizing it? Was it the corpse hanging out of the doorway? It baffled her. Had the Ersatz thought to visit the archery range as well as the armory before charging toward battle, they could have murdered each and every one of these bastards with arrows already.

Her answer came when a panicked young man at the back of pack was struck in the head with a rock. He leapt to his feet, batted away the grasping hands of his mates, and made a dash for the stairs. He only made it ten feet before a bright light flashed from the empty doorway into Tro Choi. The young man crumpled, toppled head over heels, and then came to rest amid the dozen or so corpses strewn about the front of the building.

Indigo felt a sudden lightness. Someone was in there protecting the temple, using the weapons of the Righteous against them. It could not have been Nathan and Sophie and their turncoats, which meant it could only be Shade.

Speaking of Nathan and Sophie, where in the name of the overgod were they?

A woman cried out, and Indigo turned back to her people. A few Ersatz, led by Wisteria, crested the stilled body of Sobec and charged toward the throng of Righteous. Two of them—Indigo recognized them as the tiefling Brin and a goblin named Gray—were cut down by enemy gunfire almost immediately. Wisteria, however, evaded injury. She leapt high into the air and landed amid the host, who parted like storm clouds when she descended. Her claws raked and her teeth snapped, cutting down those closest to her. Hugo Popp snapped the reins and galloped toward the killing. He shouldered his rifle and fired. Wisteria jerked; blood splattered from her arm.

Indigo held her hands to her face, waiting for the moment when her old friend was sent to ascension, but Wisteria leapt into the air just as the man shot again. This round took the face off a young, frightened woman among Popp's own people. Moving fast as lightning, Wisteria cut a jagged path across the grass and dove headlong into the intact portion of the hedgerow while bullets gave chase.

The brazen attack steeled the Ersatz. With a communal roar, the residents of Darkenwood began climbing the scaly obstruction before them. Some burst through the hedgerow itself, while others circled around, likely attempting to enter the grounds from the rear. It was a smart move that, had her people been more suitably trained in the art of war, they would have attempted before now.

The Righteous panicked. While those with guns kept up their barrage, those on the fringes of the protective formation saw the onrushing horde and fled. They ran in all directions, as long as that direction led them away from certain death.

But it was no use. One, two, five, ten individuals were chased down and felled. The Ersatz were larger, faster, and fueled by two centuries of oppression. Without the artificial restriction that kept them from harming their supposed betters, they took to the act of killing with unprecedented ferocity.

A few of the deserting Righteous were able to avoid death. A group of four sprinted past the melee and collided with the hedgerow beneath the tree Indigo had climbed. They hacked with swords, axes, and machetes, and eventually cut through the thick tangle of shrubbery enough to squeeze their way through.

The four Righteous crossed the threshold one after the other, scampering wildly to their feet once they reached the other side. Indigo stared down at them through crisscrossed branches. Here she was, standing apart from the action while the people who called her Mum took all the risks. Her anger bloomed once more, and she dropped from branch to branch as the second and third man freed themselves.

The final deserter had just untangled himself from snagging branches when Indigo dropped in a freefall from ten feet up. She landed right on top of the man, feet to shoulders, and drove him into the ground. He landed face-first and let out a surprised grunt before his body went rigid. Indigo herself felt it, the impact jarring her already bruised body.

Biting back the pain, she forcibly rolled the man over and straddled him, pinning his shoulders to the ground with her knees. She snatched the knife from between her clenched teeth, intent on slitting his throat, but one look at his face made her hesitate.

Anthony Bell stared up at her, snot bubbling in his nose, his eyes shimmering with tears. He gasped for breath while his hands clawed weakly at the tattered underclothes covering her shins. Indigo snarled. He looked so pathetic, lying helpless beneath her and sniveling. Like a child who had been playing at being a man. *These* were the monsters that had overpowered her people for so long?

It made her sick to her stomach.

Indigo glared at Anthony, traced the blade along the lump that bobbed in his throat. It would be easy to do to him what she had done to Kirsten Popp. To slice his jugular and let his blood stain her flesh. She could then sit there and watch the life bleed from his eyes, just as his master had watched the life bleed from the eyes of countless helpless Ersatz.

"P...please..." Anthony sputtered.

The terror in his voice loosened the vice grip of rage from around her heart. This man truly *was* nothing but a boy. Indigo thought of the innocence in his initial advances, how sheepish he had been, bordering on respectful, until liquor made him bold. He had never laid a harmful hand on her, or any of the other Ersatz, unless he had been ordered to do so by his superiors. And even then—such as when he had grabbed her before Merchantry Road burned—he did so hesitantly, as if he would have given anything to be anywhere else in that moment.

Anthony was a victim as well. A tool to be used by those who thought themselves kings. He was nowhere near as exploited as her own people, but exploited nonetheless.

She withdrew the knife from his throat. Her body ached as she slid off his chest and rose to her feet.

"Go," she told him.

Anthony looked up at her, tears cascading down his face. "Thank you, I'm sorry, thank you, I'm sorry," he repeated, over and over, while he rolled onto his front and struggled to stand. Those words kept coming, even as he shuffled and stumbled his way deeper into the forest, heading for potential freedom.

So long as another stray Ersatz did not encounter him first.

Indigo stared after him long after he disappeared into the trees. She took a deep breath, pressed her lips together, and considered the knife in her hand. The reflection looking back at her from the smooth blade showed a face she did not recognize. The pointed ears and golden skin were splattered with dried blood and splotched with cuts and bruises. Her eyes were surrounded by dark pockets of exhaustion. She was a woman reborn from darkness into darkness, which stood out even more when contrasted with the brightness peeking through the branches above.

She blinked. The sky was indeed bright, which meant morning had fully arrived. That was not all that had changed in the short time since she had dropped onto Anthony. While she still heard a cacophony of raised voices and anguished cries coming from beyond the hedgerow to her rear, no more loud pops of gunfire assaulted her ears.

"Out of ammo!" a Righteous voice declared.

Indigo approached the jagged hole in the hedgerow created by the deserters. She forced her way through, wincing each time the snapped branches raked her already sore flesh or ripped her already tattered underclothes. She emerged onto the grounds on the frontside of Tro Choi. Remaining silent, she took in the scene.

The group of Righteous was much thinner now, with perhaps only a hundred remaining. Many of their number lay dead in the grass, cut down as they fled in a macabre spiral pattern leading to their central mass. More than half of those who remained were on their knees, hands raised to the sky, pleading for mercy. The other half hunkered down with swords, spears, machetes, and pikes raised. Their ranged weapons, useless without lead shells of death to fill them, had been tossed aside. Those stubborn enough to think they could still win this fight shouted impotent curses as the Ersatz that flooded over and around the massive, stilled corpse of Sobec. A saddled horse milled about, riderless. Indigo wondered where the other horse had gone off to.

"They are finished!" someone exclaimed, and Indigo whipped her gaze toward to the entrance to Tro Choi. A gorgeous centaur with reddish-brown hair, her bare flesh splattered with gore, stepped out of the Ersatz place of ascension, followed by three bananeko. Indigo wrinkled her nose in wonder. No Ersatz had ascended as a centaur in more than thirty years. She wondered who this individual could be.

That wonder was soon replaced by disappointment when a strange man who definitely was not Shade emerged from the temple. He was slender, yet moved in a way that hinted he was much stronger than he looked. His skin was pale and his face beautiful. His long brown hair, slicked with sweat, hung down below his shoulders. Two pistols jutted from straps on his hips, and he carried a sword whose blade glowed light blue, which struck a memory within Indigo that she could not quite grasp. The man limped slightly, blood soaking the back of his ripped pants.

He was fully human, though not one of hers, and not Righteous either—that much was obvious by the way he strode confidently, even though his eyes always seemed to be searching for the next threat. This was someone used to conflict. Someone comfortable not only being surrounded by death, but doling it out.

Apparently realizing the futility of the situation, more and more of the Righteous dropped to their knees. Some of those still willing to fight lashed out at those who yielded, a few going so far as to strike their brethren with angry fists and barbed insults. All the while, the Ersatz continued to circle, drawing ever closer, like a battalion of mountain cats stalking a smattering of helpless prey.

Indigo threw back her shoulders and marched across the grass. "Make way!" she ordered, and those of her people who were closest spun around. Their eyes lit up when they saw her. Bluebell was among them, and the former courtesan offered Indigo a smile that was as sincere as it was filled with unstable energy.

They all looked at her like that. Prideful and focused, yet teetering on the edge of madness. Indigo did not know whether she should rein their emotions in, or let them run free for the first time in their lives.

The long-haired man she did not know did not have that problem. He remained on the top step of Tro Choi, his glowing sword still in hand, watching Indigo warily. She did her best to ignore him.

"We did it, Mum," said a bloodstained Vivo, stepping forward from the crowd when she approached.

"Aye," Pipi said beside him.

Indigo offered all of them a brief nod. That was all she gave them, yet they loved her for it. They saw her as the liberator, the one who had shown them how they could throw off their binds and lay waste to their oppressors. She felt pride at their adoring gazes.

She reached the head of the pack and stopped, staring down her nose at the crush of huddling Righteous. Hands planted firmly on hips, she walked along the line of them, making sure to keep a good ten feet of separation in case one of them still had fight left in him and decided to try something. She saw round faces and long faces, faces with dark skin and light, male and female. Different, every single one of them, but each of their expressions, even those facing the other way who peeked over their shoulders as she passed, possessed one common thread: the absolute terror that comes when the reality one has always taken for granted crumbles to dust.

"Where is Hugo Popp?" she asked, her raised voice booming over the din of murmurs that muddled the air.

Most of the Righteous cowered at her question, a few glared in disdain, but none answered.

"Briar and Piz chased him around back," one of the Ersatz proclaimed.

She *harrumphed* and cocked her head. Sure enough, the sound of thumping hooves reached her ears, dulled as they were by the soft ground and being obstructed by the bulk of Tro Choi. The hoofbeats grew louder, until finally a horse roared into view from around the right side of the structure. The rider pulled on the reins when a group of Ersatz ran to intercept. The horse kicked up on its hind legs, front hooves lashing. When the horse dropped back down, the Ersatz rushed forward yet again.

Indigo looked on in horror as the old man in the saddle swept a sword from side to side. The blade clipped the beak of a kappa woman named Zaya, then sliced clean through the arm of Dally the ogre responsible for tanning the hides that Sienna would craft into elegant garments.

Hugo Popp's eyes locked onto Indigo, burning with murderous fire, and he reared his horse up again. Considering that Briar and Piz had not returned from around the building, Indigo could only guess that the man had ascended them during their attack. And judging by the way he urged his horse into a gallop, heading straight for her and knocking aside defending Ersatz in the process, he obviously hoped to ascend Indigo as well.

She stood firm, knife in hand, trying to decide what would be the best way to avoid the slash of his sword. But another of those excruciatingly loud eruptions filled the air, and Hugo spun out of the saddle as if he had struck an invisible barrier. His sword flew from his grip and disappeared into the grass. The horse continued on, slowing down to trot right past the spot where Indigo stood.

A smattering of the Righteous emitted disbelieving screams, while the rest went silent. Those who had retained their desire to fight until now hastily dropped to their knees alongside their brethren and lifted their hands to the sky.

Indigo gaped at the old man, who cried, clutched his shoulder, and squirmed on the ground. When she glanced to the side, she saw the man with the long hair holding out a silver revolver that looked so much like the one Shade carried. The man made a show of blowing the smoke from its barrel before shoving the weapon back into the sheath on his hip.

A roar went up all around Indigo. The Ersatz began tormenting the kneeling Righteous, who cried out for mercy as they were spat upon and jabbed with blunt instruments. Aspar and Pipi grabbed Hugo by his arms and forced him into a kneel. The old merchant, who had once reveled in beating the courtesans until they fell unconscious, hollered in pain.

"I give up, I give up!" the old man shrieked.

Indigo strode toward Hugo, knife in hand. His eyes, yellowed with age, leaked tears that zigzagged down pocked cheeks.

"I give up," he said through blubbering lips.

"Kill him," Aspar growled.

"Kill him," Pipi repeated.

"Kill him, kill him!" the Ersatz shouted in unison, a bloodthirsty cry that rang throughout the valley.

Wisteria appeared from the crowd, her scales gone waxy gray. She curled up her lips, licked blood from her fangs, and stared Indigo dead in the eye.

"Kill them all."

Again, the Ersatz erupted in a chorus of malicious cheers. Indigo looked at the old man, who shook his head from side to side while his mouth formed *no*. She looked at her knife, which shook in her grip. Suddenly, the pain in her body became too much. She was so damn *tired*.

"Wait, hold up, don't!" someone yelled. The long-haired stranger on the steps of Tro Choi hopped to the ground and shoved past the centaur and bananeko. "It's over," he said, the glowing sword he held gradually turning from blue to aquamarine.

"Yes, they surrendered," said someone else. Another stranger stepped out of Tro Choi, this one just as pale as his predecessor, only taller, with slightly shorter hair and more chiseled features. "They deserve your mercy."

"They deserve nothing," Wisteria seethed.

"Actually, you're right about that. But please hold up before you slaughter everyone," the tall man entreated.

A commotion sounded behind her, and Indigo whirled yet again. The turncoat Righteous had arrived, wedging their way through the throng of strung-out Ersatz. Sophie was in the lead, walking confidently while fiddling with the pendant hanging from her neck. Nathan and the rest followed skittishly behind. The Ersatz parted, their cheers turning into cautious murmurs.

"Back away from them, please," Sophie said when she approached.

Perhaps it was the kindness in her voice, or maybe it was a reaction to how the woman conducted herself with such fearlessness, but the Ersatz did as she asked. They stopped pressing in on the remaining Righteous, who sobbed and fell all over one another, and gave the turncoats a respectful distance.

"Thanks," Nathan said, not nearly as confidently as his companion. After tugging on the bandage around his neck, he grabbed Sophie by the hand. Together they circled around their kneeling compatriots.

Nathan was huffing by the time he reached Indigo, but Sophie seemed no worse for wear.

As strangely thankful as Indigo felt for not having to snuff the life from another living soul, she would not let anyone see it. Especially not these Righteous, turncoats or not. Instead, she tucked away her knife, folded her arms over her chest, and glared at the pair.

"Your timing is very convenient. I thought you were here to assist us?" Indigo accused.

"Um, we are," Nathan said.

"Yet you arrive this late?"

"Not on purpose," Sophie said. She nudged her partner in the ribs, giving him a scowl. "It took longer than expected to prepare what we needed to help you gain your freedom."

That made Indigo laugh. She spread out her arms. "Look around. We were already granted our freedom."

"Yeah, no you weren't," said Nathan.

Indigo tossed him a sideways glance, but the turncoat simply brushed past her and stepped up to a kneeling Hugo. Aspar and Pipi looked to Indigo for guidance, obviously not trusting this man. She gestured for them to remain still.

Hugo gasped and blubbered while Nathan examined his injuries. Zoe, Gia, Fuad, Barry, Wendy, and the rest of the turncoats then began doing the same to the kneeling Righteous who had survived the slaughter. Utterances of thank you and soft crying filled the morning air.

"What are you doing?" Indigo asked.

"Making sure these folks aren't gonna die here in the field," Sophie said. "Some need medical attention. We're gonna give it to them before we bring them back to Pirie."

"We never said they could leave," snarled Wisteria. The triton took a threatening step forward, which Indigo stopped with a raised hand.

"They are the enemy," Indigo told the turncoat leaders. "They deserve to be punished."

"Yeah, they do," Nathan answered. "Unfortunately, life ain't fair, and people don't always get what they deserve."

"We demand justice," Pipi barked defiantly.

"And you already got it," Sophie said, such coldness in her voice that Indigo shivered. "What happened last night is gonna stay with these people forever. They're gonna wake up with the sweats every morning from now until the day they die. You killed their friends, their coworkers. Even family members. And they watched it happen. I'd say that's enough punishment."

"And who are you to tell us what punishment is enough?" demanded Wisteria.

Nathan looked from Indigo to the triton and back again. "The people who decide whether you ever get to leave this valley or not."

Indigo felt a lump form in her throat. "What?"

"You might be able to kill whoever you want now," Sophie said, "but that doesn't mean you're free. Right now, you're still trapped. If any of you try to step outside the borders of this valley, the same thing's gonna happen. You're gonna burn up and die. If you don't believe me, you can try it. Let me know how it turns out when you get back. I'll wait."

"I thought when Shade became Aumor..." Indigo began, disbelief robbing her of words.

"He set you free from the cycle of torment," said Nathan. He went back to examining Hugo. "But there were other precautions in place."

"Ones that're much harder to override," Sophie added, patting the satchel slung over her shoulder.

Nathan shone a light in the eyes of the old merchant, then slapped his knees and stood up straight. "Listen, I'm sorry, I really am," he said. "But you guys gotta believe me, this is for the best. You can't just slaughter a whole group of citizens. I mean, realistically, there's nothing we can do to stop you from doing just that. But if you do, Sophie won't dismantle the barrier that keeps you here. So go ahead if you want. Kill them, kill us too. But then you'll still be here. And when the guilds on the other side figure out *why* so many of their people are gone without a trace, they'll come here looking for blood. Again. And then you'll have to fight them. Again. Maybe you'll win, maybe you'll lose. Either way, you'll be stuck in a never-ending cycle of violence that you won't have any power to break."

"But you—"

"Are ghosts," Sophie said. "None of these people have seen us before. They won't see us again. We came here to do a job. To right a wrong. After that's done, we'll disappear." She fanned a hand at the turncoats who were giving medical aid to the wounded Righteous. "All of us."

Indigo chewed on that. She did not know what to say or how to respond.

"Freedom has its price, Indigo," Sophie said. "And it isn't always pretty."

"And that price is pretty steep," Nathan added with a sigh. "Steeper than it already is."

"How so?" Indigo asked.

He pointed behind her, at Tro Choi. "In order to break the barrier, we need to, well, break that. From within. From *beneath*."

Indigo felt her heart drop. "That means…"

"No more ascensions," Sophie said, raising her voice as if making sure all the Ersatz could hear. "No more eternal returns into new bodies. The lives you have will be *all* you have. You'll be able to move on from this valley and build a life elsewhere. You'll live a long time— longer than them," she pointed at the Righteous, "but from then on out, when you die…you die."

Those words froze Indigo where she stood. Her gaze flicked to all those standing around her, from Wisteria to Aspar to Pipi to Bluebell to Vivo, to the centaur who lingered nearby. Aqua then stepped out of the throng, and it was he whom she focused on. The largest of the courtesans had always been the most sensitive. He wore his heart on his sleeve, and she knew by the soft smile he offered and the way tears rolled down his cheeks that her decision was an easy one.

The Ersatz had long been a people of cycles. Of lives whose only purpose was suffering. Having to come to grips with an existence that had a clear middle and end in order to be liberated from that suffering was not so great a cost as the turncoat leaders assumed.

Indigo nodded to Sophie, then Nathan, and turned away. Her exhaustion caught up with her, and her arms felt heavy. She shuffled away while the turncoats went back about their business. Her people began milling among themselves, hesitancy spreading over them. They did not know what to do or how to feel.

Indigo understood their confusion. She did not know either, and she suddenly felt herself missing Shade. Ever since being ambushed on the road and being enraptured by the rush of violence that followed, she had not thought of him. She wished he were here now, not to tell her what to do or how to feel, but to have the loving ear of an outsider to empty her fears and hopes and dreams onto.

A loud clearing of the throat shook her from her self-pity. She had wandered into a small area clear of bodies by the edge of Tro Choi. The shorter of the two new strangers stood close to her, his piercing blue eyes narrowed. He had put his sword away, but still carried himself with the coiled anticipation of one who expected trouble. Beyond him, the centaur woman kept watch.

"Hey," the man said. "You're Indigo, right?"

"I am," she said warily.

"Awesome. I've been wanting to meet you."

"You have?"

"Yeah. I think we have someone in common." He pointed at the centaur. "Raz over there said that you knew my brother. I was wondering if you've seen him lately?"

Indigo did not hear that last part clearly. She was too busy staring at the one who had been her first love. Raz stared right back, hands clutched over her bloodstained chest. She looked so timid and unsure, despite her size. Just like Indigo. Just like all of them.

"Well, have you?"

She shook out of it and squinted at the stranger. "I am sorry. Your brother?"

"Yeah. Shadrach. Goes by Shade. About yay tall, beard, grumpy as hell. Can be sweet if he's not in a mood. Which he's always in."

"You are Meesh," she said. Her heart went cold.

"Yeah. I am! Cool. Guess you know him. He talked about me?"

All the stories Shade had imparted to her rushed to the forefront of her mind. How Shade had broken his knightly vows. How his brothers would be sent out to find and kill him. She forgot all about Raz and dropped to her knees in front of Meesh, grabbed his ripped breeches. She could not deal with this. Not now. Not after everything that had happened.

"You must not do it," she pleaded, staring up at him.

"Huh?"

"He is a good man. An *honorable* man. He does not deserve death."

She felt like she would explode. Even the ruckus that kicked up behind her could not take her attention off this man who threatened the life of the one who had freed her people.

"I... I'm not... I don't..." Meesh gaped at her, seemingly lost for words. His eyes then lifted, and a sideways smirk creased his lips. He gently removed her hands from his breeches and limped to the side. Distantly, Indigo swore she heard the pounding of hooves.

"Speak o' the devil," Meesh said. "There he is now."

23

"For I am the sword. I have come to pit brother against brother, sister against sister, mankind against its supposed makers."
—Book of the Pentus, Quotations 21:12

The train careening through the channels beneath the mountain finally began to slow. Shade grabbed tighter to the handhold as the sudden deceleration threatened to hurl him to the front of the compartment. The change in momentum made him sick to his stomach.

He had done such a great job until then of keeping his nerves in check by ticking off the seconds in his mind, so he continued to do so as the squeal of applied brakes filled the cabin. *Three thousand three hundred and eight, three thousand three hundred and nine, three thousand three hundred and ten.* At that point he stopped, pondering the enormity of his counting. It had been roughly fifty-five minutes since he left the Viral Ventures station. On Yaddo, the transport from Port Smedly to Sal Yaddo took a half-hour to reach its destination. A half-hour to travel little less than fifty miles. Though he had no way of knowing for certain, this train *felt* like it was speeding along at a quite faster clip. If so, that meant his travels had somehow brought him a hundred miles from Darkenwood, if not more.

The train came to a gliding stop, and light shone in through the windows to Shade's left. The female voice that had spoken when he first climbed aboard chimed in again: "You have reached your destination. Welcome to The Darkenwood Experience. Please exit the cabin in an orderly fashion. Thank you for riding the Fallen Arch Railway and enjoy your stay."

A *hiss* accompanied the door to the left sliding open. Shade took in a deep breath and stepped onto a wide concrete platform. His legs felt shaky. He shook out of it as best he could, marching the only direction open to him—up the concrete ramp, toward a wide corridor with drab gray walls lined with sconces that gave off hauntingly dim yellow light. He kept his eyes down, studying a floor covered with scuff marks from leather soles. Something sweetly rotten invaded his nostrils, and he glanced to the right to see a pile of brown and green clumps.

Horse droppings. Had a horse ridden that train? If it had, he wondered how the simple animal's brain hadn't exploded from fright at the insane speed it traveled.

At the end of the corridor, another set of glass doors opened automatically upon his approach. He breathed in the familiar piney scent of the trees. His legs started moving quicker, their prior stiffness all but a memory now that the end of the line was in sight.

Once outside, the cool mugginess that he'd come to associate with nights in Darkenwood prickled his skin. The sliver of sky he saw through the canopy was the usual shade of smoky pink that came right before dawn. While everything seemed familiar, he had no idea where he was.

Everything was alien: from the entrance to the underground train station, jutting from a mossy hillside like the head of a turtle poking out of its shell, to the low wooden buildings that surrounded the circular clearing he stood in, the packed dirt riddled with old footprints and the impressions from horses' hooves. Most of the buildings had signs above their doors proclaiming their purposes—everything from "Gift Shop" to "Corner Store" to "Hallucinogens and Medicinal Herbs."

He tugged on the string of his slouch and frowned. He would have suspected that Bob hadn't sent him back to Darkenwood if not for the billboard above the protruding glass entrance that spelled out FALLEN ARCH STATION in huge white letters.

"Hello! Hello, kind sir!"

Shade nearly leapt out of his skin. He spun toward the voice, which came from the largest edifice. A face appeared in the darkness between a pair of propped-open barn doors. In the burgeoning daylight, the face looked like a pale blank slate that features would be stitched onto later. He couldn't help but think of a passage from the *Ritterhandbuch* that spoke of maggot eaters, vile demons that could see into a man's soul and take the form of a dead loved one to lure their victims into eternal damnation within Relyah, the Eighth Hell. Shade reached into his duster and grabbed for his revolver. He might not have silver slugs, but maybe plugging the creature with a dozen or more holes would do the trick. He wasn't sure, since he hadn't run across a maggot eater personally. Only Abe had. And Abe was dead.

But when the body wearing that face stepped forward, entering the dim light of pre-morning, Shade saw that it was just a man. An unremarkable man of average height who wore clothes that appeared to have been specifically tailored to be tattered. He had a bald head and lifeless blue eyes.

Like Bob's.

Shade sighed. "Great. Another automatic."

"Kind sir, I am Nine, the stablemaster here at Fallen Arch," the man said. "I am not an automatic. I am a mechanized aide with a level nine operating system. Hence the name I have been given. I am meant to mimic human behavior and appearance to ensure that our guests are cared for to great extent while minimizing the necessity for paid employees. And now, those duties are to follow the requests of the president, who requests that you follow me." He lifted a torch that ignited seemingly on its own and headed back toward the shadowy barn door.

"I guess you're not gonna tell me *how* Bob got in touch with you, huh?" Shade asked. When he got no answer, he swallowed his misgivings and followed.

The large building was a stable, though it smelled oddly pleasant. The eye-stinging ammonia-and-methane stink of most animal shelters Shade had run across was subtle instead of in-your-face, over-ridden by the scent of freshly-cut hay. He guessed the fact that every one of the countless stalls they passed by was empty had something to do with that.

"Do they even keep horses here?" he asked.

Nine remained silent, bringing him all the way to the front of the building and out another set of barn doors. There, tied to a large hitching rail, was the same beautiful mare he'd left hitched by marker seventeen before he started on the Path of Aumor, the one with the starburst pattern on her neck. He stared at the majestic creature, feeling tingly all over.

Nine stopped, gesturing for Shade to approach the horse. The mare nickered and swept a hoof through the grass. Her tail flashed from side to side. "Easy," Shade said. He placed a hand on her neck, right beside that starburst of white, and stroked her fur. That seemed to calm her down. A throaty sound vibrated her throat. Shade grinned as he stroked her. "Good girl. I'm glad you're not stuck out on that road anymore."

"She was fetched the same day you started along the Path," said Nine. "All of our horses are well cared for here in Darkenwood. Some would say even better than the residents."

"All the horses?" Shade said with a frown. "There's only this one."

"Yes. That is true now, but not true overall. Darkenwood fosters a great many regal equine that have been bred for durability, strength, and patience. We house sixty-four horses in our stables, to be used by our guests should they request them." He paused, twitching as if he had something in his eye. "At all times, until ten hours ago. That was when the president instructed me that the park had been liquidated and a large, unregistered party was approaching. I was to make sure they had no transportation at their disposal once they arrived. I led all the horses along that path," he pointed at an area that in the dimness was just another stretch of unfettered forest, "and set them free in the mountains."

"This unregistered party, did they bring horses of their own?" Shade asked as Chestnut neighed and nudged him with her head.

"They did, but only four," Nine answered. "Along with a cart, which is most unusual. Darkenwood guests are not allowed to import their own transportation into the valley. But then again, the park has been liquidated and they were not registered, so I suppose that point is moot."

"You saw them?"

"No. The manager relayed all the information required. I was supposed to shut down when the task was done, but then I was ordered to bring this specific mare back for you. And here she is. You are to take her and follow this road into the valley proper. That concludes my duties."

Nine shut his eyes, squatted on the ground, and wrapped his arms around his knees. After that, he stopped moving entirely. Shade wondered if the mechanized man still functioned, if he was sleeping, or if this was Nine's version of death.

Shade shrugged and turned back to the mare. He jammed his foot into a stirrup and swung up into the saddle. The horse bucked slightly, but eased when he pulled lightly on the reins.

"It's all right, girl," he told her.

He spun the horse around. Sure enough, he was on a dirt road that stretched out into the trees and around a bend. A road that led to Darkenwood proper, as Nine had said. It was a road that led to Indigo.

He cracked the reins, and Chestnut took off at a full gallop. Shade held on with one hand while he tightened the string of his slouch with the other. No need to have it go flying off his head and choking him today.

The wind buffeted his face and his ears were filled with the sound of pounding hooves. He flew along the road, the trees blurring past on either side of him. Thoughts of Indigo filled his head, and his heart thumped faster and faster. At one point, when the mare slowed to go around an exaggerated curve, he swore he saw someone sneaking through the brush to his left. *Probably nothing,* he told himself. A trick of the light, shadows playing with his vision as dawn shoved the darkness away.

By the time he left the cover of trees, the sky had turned a misty shade of blue with wisps of red. He pulled back, bringing Chestnut to a halt to collect his bearings. To his left was a serene extension of the road lined with quaint cottages. He knew this place, had glimpsed it briefly during one of his trips around Darkenwood with Indigo.

This was where the Righteous stayed when they came to visit, where they rested their heads after long days filled with abuse, sexual deviance, cruelty, and violence. It seemed dark and quiet now. Empty. He cocked his head and stilled his breath, waiting for a sign of approaching danger. That's when he heard a percussive pop that echoed faintly through the valley.

Gunfire.

He urged the mare onward again, bypassing the road south and instead cutting through the woods. Luckily, Chestnut proved adept at maneuvering through unpredictable terrain. The horse leapt over felled trees, weaved around natural depressions, bullied her way through dense tangles of underbrush. Shade kept low in the saddle, not wanting to accidentally lose his head to a low-hanging branch.

The mare burst through the last line of vegetation and galloped over an open field. Shade's heartbeat kicked up another notch. He spied Hickweis Tavern on its low hill. Behind the building rose wisps of black smoke.

"No, no, no," he muttered, snapping the reins again and making Chestnut race all the faster.

Dread filled him when he crossed the span and pulled up in front of the tavern entrance. Those distant pops of gunfire, which had been sparse, had ceased. He didn't know if that was good or bad, though when he took in the scene around the tavern, his thoughts veered toward *bad*.

The morning had grown brighter, revealing grass streaked with soot and a few patches blackened by scorch marks. The pavilion and stable were both smoking ruins. There were bodies on the ground, too, though a macabre sort of relief filled him when he realized they all looked human. A couple he recognized—the merchant Jasper and his wife, sprawled out next to each other, the grass soaking up their spilled blood.

When he lifted his gaze to the west, he saw a pair of horses grazing in the field, one with splintered cart poles still attached to its harness. Behind them was the source of the smoke that rose from the tree line hiding Merchantry Road.

He was about to head in that direction when a voice called out, "Shade!"

Turning in the saddle, he spied a familiar squat form standing on the porch and staring at him with wide, panicked eyes. Macaro jabbed his finger south.

"Tro Choi!" the dwarf exclaimed. "Hurry!"

Shade needed no more direction than that. He pointed Chestnut to the south and took off again.

They reached the road moments later. As the mare's hooves pounded the cobbles, Shade's mind whirled. Macaro was still alive. That was good. And the urgency with which he told Shade to move said that Indigo was alive, but her survival was tenuous. Less good. The corpses on the lawn of Hickweis Tavern proved that Bob had spoken the truth that Shade had freed the Ersatz from their curse. Again, good. Yet he'd heard distant gunfire, which meant the Righteous invaders had brought weapons that the Ersatz had neither the knowledge nor experience to protect themselves against. *Not* good.

The realization struck him that the shooting might have stopped because there was nothing left to kill.

Not good at all.

He gritted his teeth. If Indigo was gone and Tro Choi destroyed so she could never come back to him, he would slaughter them all. Or as many as he could before they took him down. And even then, after he breathed his dying breath, he would haunt each and every one of them from the grave and murder them in their sleep.

His worst fears were proved true when he reached a cluster of corpses strewn along the road. At least twenty of them, most from the various Ersatz races. The cloud of buzzing flies hovering above the road dispersed when horse and rider careened past. Shade made sure to look down, trusting Chestnut to avoid trampling any of the bodies. Many had arrows jutting from their backs. As far as Shade could tell, none of them were Indigo.

From that point on, strange depressions marked the road at intervals. Shade had one of those out-of-place-and-time thoughts, this time wondering if the Righteous had set land mines out. He shook his head, trying to clear away someone else's memory—inching on his belly through mud, an automatic rifle in his hands.

All a lie. Sal Yaddo, the Reverend, our lives, the Pentus, all of it.

The way was clear for another mile or so, until bodies filled the road once more. This time there were so many—human and Ersatz— that the mare couldn't help but stomp on them as she ran. One of her hooves crushed the skull of a dead orc woman, another speared the belly of a bird-man whose beak had been shot off. The horse lost her balance briefly, and when she slowed to right herself with breath steaming from her nose, Shade toppled in the saddle. He clutched his knees against her flank and buried his face in her mane, barely hanging on.

He trusted the horse enough to squeeze his eyes shut and breathe deeply. The scent of copper and spent gunpowder combined with his anxiety to make his brain throb. The repeated clomping of Chestnut's hooves didn't help.

Eventually he gathered himself enough to sit up straight in the saddle. He finally arrived at Tro Choi. Countless Ersatz milled about, assisting one another in stacking bodies in the grass on the side of the road. Shade's eyes widened and he panicked. He was careening toward them much too quickly, and the mare showed no interest in slowing down.

Shade planned to shout for them to move, but the corpse-gatherers whirled at the sound of his approach and scattered on their own like deer startled by a lightning storm, dropping corpses in the process. Their exodus gave Shade a clear shot at the path cutting through the hedgerow, only the path wasn't actually clear. A prone form covered with golden scales sprawled all the way across the opening, its arms and legs reaching beyond the hedgerows on either side. The thing was *huge*, creating a six-foot-high obstruction.

And Chestnut was racing right toward it.

He pulled back on the reins, but the mare ignored him. She approached the enormous body at full speed, and Shade felt a sudden loss of gravity when she leapt. He held on with all his might as the horse soared, his spine jarring once she landed on the other side.

Chestnut finally came to a halt. The mare huffed and tossed her mane as if annoyed. Shade let out a relieved breath. "Attagirl."

He lifted his head. A gathering of men and women knelt in the grass in front of Tro Choi, hands behind their heads. Ersatz surrounded them, along with a few outsiders not on their knees. These were tending to the wounded. Maybe they'd switched sides? He had no way of knowing.

Relief then flooded him when he realized what that meant.

The threat was over.

The Ersatz had won.

Nearly every face gawked at his sudden arrival, and he offered a timid wave. A few of the Ersatz he knew well waved back, some more excitedly than others. He scanned their faces, searching for Indigo. When he didn't see her, he turned his gaze to the temple itself, marveling for a moment at the gorgeous half-woman, half-horse who stood next to the steps leading inside. Unlike everyone else in the area, the woman-horse wasn't looking at him. Shade followed her line of sight.

And that's when he saw her.

Indigo's back was to him, and she wore nothing but a torn and bloodied tan shift, but he could tell immediately, from her shape to the tips of her ears poking through her sweat-soaked hair, that it was her. She was on her knees, her hands grasping at the pant leg of a man who looked down at her with a cruel half-grin on his face.

A man he knew well. A man he called *brother*.

Shade's heart nearly stopped beating. Somehow, Meesh had found him in the one place that he thought would be beyond discovery. And now here he was, threatening someone Shade loved. He watched his brother's hand drift toward the Eldersword on his hip.

Meesh lifted his head, and their eyes locked. Shade saw in his brother's gaze all the callousness and insolence that used to make him laugh. Only now, those personality quirks took on a different meaning.

Meesh was exactly the type of man who would hurt Indigo to get to him. And Shade was not about to let that happen.

Anger came and washed away his shock. He kicked the mare, uttering a guttural *"Hyah!"* as he charged.

"Speak o' the devil. There he is now."

The relief that washed over Meesh when he laid eyes on his brother, whose horse had just leapt over the dead mechanical monster blocking the entrance as if he was putting on a show for a backwater, was palpable. He shook his head. Just like Shade to show up late to his own party.

Meesh moved away from the woman with pointed ears who knelt in front of him, stunning despite looking like she'd had the hell beaten out of her, and took a step toward his brother. He couldn't help but grin at seeing him, especially the silly hat he wore. He had to latch onto that lightness and not let go. Because there was so much they needed to discuss. So many revelations that Meesh wanted to tell him.

But Shade had other ideas. His brother kicked his horse into motion, weaving through the mess of bodies covering the temple grounds, approaching at breakneck pace.

Meesh's smile faltered. "Hey, no need to rush."

Shade didn't slow, even when Meesh raised a hand in greeting. And when he drew close enough to see Shade's face, brow furrowed with lips peeled back to show his teeth, he knew that something had gone wrong along the way. Given how close Shade was, and on top of a horse no less, there was nothing he could do about it.

He let out a groan. His body went numb with anticipation and he rooted himself in place, since bolting would solve nothing. There was no way he'd get far without being run through.

"Goddammit!"

At the last moment, Shade veered the horse slightly to the left. He tore his hat off his head, tossed it aside, and launched himself out of the saddle, soaring toward Meesh with arms extended. His expression was a twisted mask of rage. Spittle and snot glistened in his beard. He'd gone wild, deadly.

In the scant few seconds he had before impact, Meesh realized he'd seen his brother like this only one time before—in Tansaray, when he'd gone off to cut down the Red Raiders on his own.

Meesh braced himself as best he could, but there wasn't much he could do when a man of equal size was flying toward him at full speed. The top of Shade's head collided with his chin, making his head snap back, and then a shoulder drove into his chest. Blown off his feet, Meesh's mind went blank, and he felt suspended in midair. When his skull hit the ground, the rest of him went limp. Shade's weight fell right on top of him, then the air expelled from his lungs in a single, pained *"Ugh!"*

For a moment, all went peaceful and still. Meesh felt no pain, not even from the gash on his thigh where the bullet had grazed him an hour ago. The buzzing in his head was intoxicating, and the insufferable poet in him tried to craft a beat out of the throbbing in his ears. That ended when he felt scabbed knuckles rubbing against his collarbone.

His eyes fluttered open. Shade straddled him, his right hand gripping the collar of his shirt, his left raised and curled into a fist, ready to strike.

"Shit!"

He was able to gather his wits enough to launch his knee into his brother's ass, causing Shade to lurch forward just as he began to bring his fist down. His knuckles slammed against the ground inches from Meesh's face. The enraged knight bellowed.

On instinct, Meesh touched the hilt of the Eldersword clipped to his belt as he tried to wiggle out from under his out-of-control brother. The Rush filled him, stole away his dizziness and pain. With renewed strength, he punched Shade in the back—*Kidney shot, yeah!*—and then put all his force into bucking his hips to throw the berserker off him.

Meesh flipped onto his belly and scrambled to his feet. The Rush faded now that he no longer touched the sword, and he was faintly aware that an audience was watching this sudden outburst of violence. He shoved the shouting voices to the back of his mind and focused on Shade, who'd gotten himself onto his feet as well. Shade snarled, his hands inching toward the folds of his duster.

Before Shade could grab whatever weapons hid beneath that heavy goddamn jacket of his, Meesh leapt at him. They grappled, spinning round and round in the grass. Shade grabbed his hair and yanked, bringing spikes of pain to Meesh's scalp. Meesh pulled Shade close, tried to knee him in the groin, but the duster deflected his blow and his kneecap connected solidly with his upper thigh instead. Still, Shade grunted, and he started favoring his right leg. Meesh used that shift in balance to drive an elbow into his brother's face.

They tussled, exchanging blow for blow, but given how close they were, neither was able to hurt the other enough to end the fight. Finally, Meesh drew back both his shoulders, planted his palms against Shade's chest, and shoved him away with all his might. Shade retreated a few steps, spittle flying.

Meesh used their momentary distance to scream, "Enough! Just stop for a sec—"

Shade was on him again instantly, this time leading with a fist. Meesh was too busy trying to appeal to his brother's sanity to avoid it. The blow struck him on the cheek, and he nearly bit off his tongue from the force of it. He stumbled, his arms pinwheeling. Shade pushed his advantage, again driving his shoulder into him and putting him on the ground.

Blows rained down on him, over and over, and flailing out blindly was all Meesh could do to protect himself. He landed a lucky shot, the meat of his fist driving into Shade's throat. Shade choked and hacked right into Meesh's face, but his eyes didn't lose their blind rage. So Meesh headbutted him as hard as he could. His vision blacked out momentarily. Shade let out a holler that overrode all other sound before spinning off him.

Meesh struggled to get back to his feet. His mind clouded from the aches of his body and the sting of betrayal of his brother trying to kill him. Not five feet away, Shade stooped on one knee, in obvious pain but apparently not as exhausted as Meesh felt. And right then, Meesh knew that Shade couldn't be reasoned with. He was driven by animalistic fury and an instinct to survive that Meesh just couldn't match.

Not without help.

He reached for his belt, seeking the Rush to assist him. His heart sank when his fingers found nothing but the metal clip that his Eldersword should've been attached to. A familiar vibration filled the air, and he looked up to see Shade still hunched over, his gaze wide and glossy and insane, holding Meesh's own weapon tightly with both hands.

Meesh groaned.

For the first time since he had fought Asaph across dimensions, Shade felt the Rush. It surged through him, sapped his enervation, rejuvenated his muscles. It fed his rage and made his vision go red.

He rose to his feet, held the sword in his left hand, and flicked his wrist. The Eldersword warbled, seeming hesitant as it extended, section by section, to its full length. The blade flashed and sparked with a rainbow of colors, as Elderswords being wielded by a knight to which they weren't bonded were apt to do.

Shade did not care. Bonded or no, he *needed* this sword. It would be fitting, poetic even, for the brother who came here to kill him and those he loved to be cut down by his very own weapon. Killing Meesh with Cooper's old saber, which hung from his hip and whacked the back of his thigh, would not have been as satisfying.

"Shade, listen to me," Meesh said, his eyes wide with panic as he hastily backed away with hands stretched out toward him, palms facing. "You don't gotta do this, brah. Let's just talk a sec, okay?"

"No talking," Shade growled. The pressure in his head intensified. Letting out a yawp that boiled from the core of all his hate, he charged.

Meesh didn't try to flee, didn't attempt to defend himself. He simply stood there with his mouth hanging open, as if he couldn't believe for a second that the universe would allow him to fail at his duties. But Meesh didn't know better. Meesh didn't understand that the Pentus was a fake. That everything they had ever believed was a lie. That it was Shade who had performed the *truly* noble act—setting free a downtrodden people from their lifetimes of servitude.

He drew back his arm and put all his reinvigorated strength into a single diagonal chop that would slice his brother in half. The spastic glow of the blade haunted his vision, illuminated the tears streaming down Meesh's cheeks. The sight fueled his anger even more.

Just before the deadly, vibrating blade could cut through Meesh's flesh and bone, a flash of bright blue light blinded him. Something hard and heavy struck his blade, and the force of it knocked the sword from his hand. A metallic *clang* rang in his ears. The Rush departed as quickly as it came, and Shade tumbled to the ground, exhaustion overwhelming him. From somewhere in the background of his murderous thoughts, he heard someone call his name.

Shade fell hard, jamming his shoulder against the ground. He groaned and writhed, and when he flipped onto his back, he stared at the tip of a sword that shone bright blue, hovering inches in front of his face. He then lifted his gaze and stared directly into the troubled brown eyes of a stranger.

24

And the lost brother replied: "The outcast is one who knows only
peace and love, who acknowledges his errors and deceit, who is
giving and appreciative, and kind, and full of shame. Because all of
those things are antithetical to the nature of our species. The one
who claims to be such things by default is a spreader of lies, and
should be shunned at all costs."
—Book of the Pentus, Allegories 2:27

Rodney was a man out of time and place, something he had
known the moment he opened his eyes in this frightening
reality. From the very beginning, the fact that he didn't belong
here had filled him with a sorrow that had grown exponentially, especially over the past couple weeks, as the details of his previous life
trickled into his brain faster and faster.

But even that sorrow could not stop him from appreciating his
second chance. He understood what he had been, how he had ended,
and how pathetic it all seemed now that he could look back on it with
a mind clear of ego and ambition. To be given this new life was a gift,
no matter how harrowing it might be.

The two men who called him brother had also been given this
second chance. Men whom he had admired in that previous life of his,
men whose downfalls he had watched through troubled eyes before
he met his own untimely end. Though for some reason, unlike him,

they didn't seem to realize it. They did not know who they were, what they had meant to the world that was. And that broke Rodney's heart.

If they could only see the world as he did, even after all the ugliness he had just witnessed, maybe they wouldn't be trying to kill each other.

"Stop it," he said, pointing his glowing blade at Shade. His arm shook, the aftermath of steel colliding when he knocked the sword from Shade's hand. A subtle humming filled him, like it always did when he wielded this thing Meesh had called an Eldersword. It was uncomfortable, like being jacked up on far too much caffeine. He fought the impulse to stow the weapon away and go back to feeling normal, or whatever passed for normal here..

"No," Shade muttered defiantly. He leaned forward as if trying to stand, only to fall back on his elbows when Rodney jabbed the tip at him.

"Stay," he said, then over his shoulder asked, "Meesh, are you well?"

"Not so much," Meesh answered.

Rodney observed from the corner of his eye as the man that had dubbed him brother, whom he had spent so much time with ever since his rebirth, struggled to his feet. Meesh brushed himself off, then appeared sheepish when he noticed all those who were watching his every move.

All attention was on the three of them, from the many Ersatz to the captured men and women that Raz and her cat friends called the Righteous. Nervous energy filled the air, making Rodney feel sick to his stomach. He glanced at Raz, who had approached the conflict with seemingly one goal in mind—to stop the beautiful girl with the pointed ears from getting involved. The one named Indigo now hung in Raz's arms, shooting daggers at Rodney with her eyes.

He turned away. "Don't worry," he called out. "I will not hurt him."

"Like hell you won't," snapped Shade, his lips pulled back in a sneer. "Prove it. Get the goddamn sword out of my face."

"Sorry, cannot do that," Rodney said. "Not unless you promise there will be no more violence."

Shade glared at him, unmoving.

"Fine. Remain on the ground, then."

"I could shoot you before you stab me," Shade growled. His hand stretched toward the fold in his jacket.

"Uh, no you can't, brah. Reach inside that stupid coat and I put a bullet in your shoulder."

Tilting his head, Rodney saw that Meesh had drawn one of his pistols and pointed it at the prone man. Rodney would have panicked if he didn't already know that Meesh had no bullets left. He had used his last on the guy riding the horse.

With no way of knowing that, Shade let his left hand fall back to the ground.

"Good," Rodney said. "Is everyone calm? May we discuss this in peace? I know that is what you truly want, Shade."

"Screw you, Abednego," Shade muttered through clenched teeth. "You don't know me. You don't get to pull the virtue card."

Rodney let out a sigh, one rooted deep in his belly that helped relieve his tension. At least they were talking now instead of leading with fists. "I am *not* Abednego. My given name is Nicholas, but I prefer Rodney in this life. And I *do* know you." He glanced quickly at Meesh, who gave him the side-eye, and then back again. "I know both of you quite well."

"You do, huh?"

"I do."

After another sigh, he withdrew his Eldersword and willed it to collapse. The nervous energy fled from his veins when he clipped the damned weapon to his belt. He turned his head toward Raz and nodded. The centaur released Indigo, who immediately dashed across the grass and slid down at Shade's side.

"I thought—" Indigo said.

"I'm not—" he began.

They embraced, blanketing each other with thankful kisses. The scene warmed Rodney's heart, until he glanced at Raz. The centaur's features twisted downward in a gloomy frown that rivaled those Rodney had seen in his mirror on the worst days of his previous life. She turned away, trotting slowly back to the trio of gawking cats.

Rodney shot Meesh a look. Meesh bowed his head and holstered his revolver, then limped over to where his Eldersword had fallen and plucked it from the grass. With all weapons put away, Rodney faced the embracing couple. Tears streamed down both their faces. It was such a beautiful sight that Rodney thought he might start crying too.

"We did not come here to kill you," Rodney said.

Shade removed his lips from Indigo's cheek and stared up at him. "Why not?"

"Why would we?" Meesh snapped.

"Because it's your job," said Shade, eyes tapered. "Because the penalty for a knight breaking his vows is death at the hands of another knight."

"Things have changed," Rodney told him.

"That so?"

"Aye, it is." He took a deep breath. "I know you because I remember you. I know your name—your *real* name. I know that you once brought beauty to the world. I know that your passion for music and justice overrode all else. And while I don't know this for certain, I believe, from the bottom of my heart, that when all is said and done, all you want to do is fill the world with beauty again. Why would anyone want to rip someone like that out of the world? Let alone the two people who are made of the same stuff as you?"

Shade quirked an eyebrow at Meesh. "Then why was he threatening Indigo?"

"Threatening...?" Meesh began.

Indigo cupped Shade's cheeks in her hands, turned him to face her. "He was not threatening me. I realized who he was and was overcome with panic. I was begging him not to kill you if you ever returned." A smile played across her lips. "Which you have."

He gave her a nervous half-grin. "I...I have."

"Brah, now I'm insulted," said Meesh. "You thought I'd threaten someone hot as her? C'mon now. You should know me better than that."

They both frowned at him. Rodney groaned.

Meesh waved off their displeasure. "Anyway, I wish you would've chilled a bit. It would've been obvious if you hadn't let your friggin' emotions get the best of you. Again."

Shade cringed.

"And you tried to kill me, brah," Meesh said, venom in his voice. "Actually *tried to kill me.* Don't think that's something I'm gonna forget anytime soon. Especially since Rod and I have been here for friggin' hours fighting for these people you care so much about. I'd hoped you'd think better of me than that."

Meesh glared as he undid the latch on his gun belt, letting the weapons—Eldersword included—clatter to the ground before approaching. He plopped himself onto the grass a few feet away from Shade and Indigo and raised both his hands to show he meant no harm. His sour look remained.

"Sorry," Shade muttered.

"Nice apology, real sincere," Meesh said in a tone that might have approached thoughtful. "I get it though. At least a little. You've lost a lot. More than me. And I didn't know you two—" he gestured at Indigo, "—were, well, screwing. Just that you knew her."

Shade sucked in a breath. He and Indigo exchanged a glance before they both gave him their full attention. "If you didn't come here to kill me, then why're you here?"

"Well, actually, I *did* come here to kill you," Meesh said. Shade's shoulders tensed. "No, I mean, at first. The Reverend sent us out to find you. Had another of the Crone's riddles. Said it could only mean it was time to hunt you down and end you."

"Which Meesh did not agree with from the start," Rodney said, because it seemed like information Shade needed to know.

"That's right, I didn't," Meesh told him. "Well, not really. I mean, I knew we'd be sent out to do that eventually, but it didn't sit right with me. And then, right after the Reverend gave me the riddle, I was given this."

Meesh reached into his vest pocket and removed the small sheet of folded paper that he often read when he thought Rodney wasn't looking. The paper was damp and stained with traces of blood. He tentatively held it out. Shade took the paper from his fingers just as cautiously, peeling it open to read the contents.

Shade's eyebrows lifted, and he gave Meesh a questioning look. "Help me, look deeper?"

"That's what it says."

"I don't get it."

"Neither did I," said Meesh, his grin hiding a layer of sadness that Rodney could appreciate. "Octavia gave it to me."

"Octavia?" Shade questioned.

"Yeah, Octavia. You know, the ima I had a fling with. Er, the first one."

"Oh. Oh yeah. I remember her. I think." Shade's shoulders bobbed. "I don't pay attention to the imas much."

Rodney cocked his head as Meesh chuckled. "No one does. Anyway, she left that for me after I stormed into the Crone's temple demanding answers. Answers I didn't get, obviously. So Rod and I went on our way. I thought that was it. That I was just gonna hunt you down and spy on Rod at the same time."

"Excuse me?" Rodney said.

Meesh pivoted to look at him. "Sorry, never told you 'bout that part, brah. The Rev wanted me to keep an eye on you. Thought you might be defective or something."

Rodney bowed his head. If only Meesh knew the truth behind that statement.

"But the funny thing is, the Rev was right, you *are* defective."

"Excuse me?" he said again.

"But you're defective because you're the only one who was made *right*," Meesh continued, this time aiming his words at Shade. "Rodney's not like us. We're composites, Shade. You and me and Abe and all the knights who came before. We're empty slates because we're the combination of a buncha different versions of the same person from multiple dimensions, all bundled together in the cosmic melting pot of the universe and then pulled down here by some fancy old machinery."

"I know," Shade said.

His reaction made Rodney do a double-take.

"You know?" Meesh asked, similarly dumbfounded.

"Yup," Shade uttered with a slight grimace. "Well, not *know*. But Asaph said something along those lines to Abe when they were locked in the Heartcube chamber together."

"And how do you know that?"

"Because I saw it. After Abe died and I sent Asaph away. Vera showed me."

Meesh chuckled. "Oh. Well that explains everything. Or absolutely nothing at all." He shook his head. "But anyway, back on point. Rodney ain't like us. He's I guess what you'd call singular. As in, he only ever existed in a single dimension. So when he was remade at the Hallowed Stones, the system that's supposed to scramble his memories didn't work. When his body settled in, the memories just started coming." He gave Rodney a sympathetic look. "Sorry."

Rodney closed his eyes and exhaled deeply.

"And how do *you* know *that*?" asked Shade.

Meesh's head was on a swivel, looking all around as if he only now remembered that they had an audience, and that audience was gradually drawing closer. He tittered nervously and told Shade in a hushed voice, "Because I met an oracle. Beneath the mountains there's this huge complex. Like, *enormous*. Maybe even bigger than all Yaddo. All these tunnels that cut straight through the bedrock. It's where the Elders stayed during the Rising. Anyway, Rod and me came across this room when we were down there. The place looked *exactly* like the vestibule of the Temple of the Crone. Only there, when I knocked on the door, it actually *opened*."

Meesh paused, as if for dramatic effect.

"And?" Shade said, leaning forward. Indigo also seemed expectant.

"And I met the oracle that lived there. It's a machine, Shade. A friggin' *machine*. All wires and big metal boxes and stuff. Like something we'd see beneath one o' the Sacred Trees. And this machine, it *spoke to me*. Like, by name. It knew me. Said it'd been waiting for me. It told me all about us, what we've done since we got here. It told me about Rodney. And it *also* said that we shouldn't be the way we are. That we were supposed to be some huge force for good that the Ancients devised to fight some urgent threat. Only some immortal asshat got ahold of the Old Crone, which was supposed to guide us into this new goddamn world I guess, and messed with it. Made sure *we'd* be the defective ones. And then he used us for his own agenda."

"The Reverend," Shade said quietly.

"The Reverend," Meesh echoed. "He's not the seventh of his name. He's been the same man from the start." He squinted one eye. "You knew that too?"

"It was implied, yeah."

"From what Vera showed you?"

"Pretty much."

"Figures."

Shade fidgeted as he squeezed Indigo's hand, and forced a smile. "And you think you can trust this thing? This...computer?"

"You can, yeah," a new voice cut in.

All heads whirled toward the interloper. Rodney squinted, trying to size him up. He was a young man with long black hair and Asian features, dressed in leather pants and a frilly white shirt. He had a bandage on his neck, and his collar was stained red. By the look of him, he seemed to be in his early twenties, but he carried himself with the cocksureness of someone who had experienced far more than their age should allow.

"Of what do you speak, Nathan?" asked Indigo.

The young man, Nathan, shoved his hands in his pockets and strode lazily toward them. "What you met was a probability calculator. A giant computer that could quite accurately predict the future. Twelve of them were built, and they helped guide humanity along in the years before the Rising."

Surprisingly, Shade simply nodded at this reveal. "Bob told me about them," he said.

"Oh yeah, Mr. Quick," said Nathan. "How'd the president of Viral Ventures look, anyway?"

"Artificial," Shade muttered with a shrug.

Nathan sputtered a burst of youthful laughter. "Yeah, he would, wouldn't he?"

"How do you know him?" Shade asked suspiciously.

"We both worked for the Architect. Who's back, by the way. Not that you'd know him."

"So I've heard."

Nathan looked back at Meesh. "The point is, the probability calculator you met was one of the first built. The Elders called her Pythia, after...well, it doesn't matter what they named her after. But she's real, and she tells the truth. So tell us, Meesh. What did Pythia say, other than filling you in on your brother's mental state?"

"Er, um," Meesh began. He stared at Shade, his fingers kneaded the frayed tear in his breeches, a nervous tic that Rodney had not seen before now. "Pretty much that Rod and I were supposed to help you, brah. That you were trying to free an enslaved people, and that it was really, *really* important that you succeeded."

"Oh yeah?" Nathan said, appearing surprised.

"Why's it important?" Shade asked. "Other than the fact it's the right thing to do?"

"Well, mainly because it's what *you* wanted to do. It said if you died trying, or if you just failed and then refused to come back with us, then we're all screwed. Because...because..." He licked his lips, his eyes darting this way and that. "Because the only way we can overthrow the Reverend and set things right in the Wasteland is if it's the three of us. Together. The oracle was pretty firm on that point. It had to be us three, or none at all."

"Oh," said Shade.

Everyone fell silent, as if processing the information through faulty circuits. Rodney took that moment to fold his hands before him, bow his head, and close his eyes. What he saw in the dimness behind his eyelids was horrible. Scenes of viciousness and carnage, of monsters that weren't monsters laying waste to people who looked like him. To get those images out of his mind, he began humming. The shuffling of feet and murmur of a hundred voices created a metronomic beat in his head. It was a soft, melancholy tune, about a moon gone flush, and how if it arrived, no one would be able to stare up at its beauty.

It was a song he had written. One of the last ever in his past life. But now, here, in the aftermath of so much death, it brought on a new meaning that that old him never could have imagined.

"What happens now?" Indigo asked, breaking the extended silence.

Rodney's eyes fluttered open. His two brothers were staring at one another, and though there was no malice between them now, they both wore affable expressions that barely hid their distrust. Rodney might have found it disheartening, if not for the fact that Shade had literally just attempted to kill Meesh, and would have had Rodney not intervened.

Like a bruised ego, some wounds took time to heal.

"I...don't know," Shade said. "This is all so surreal."

"Tell me about it," agreed Meesh.

"Our whole world, turned upside down. And we're supposed to set it right? How?"

"Dunno."

Shade gave Indigo another kiss on the cheek and then leaned forward, propping his elbows on his knees and his head in his hands. "I did what Abe wanted. I came here for answers. But all I got are more questions." He threw down his hands and gazed lovingly at Indigo. "I never found out what the hell the Traveler or the Queen of Snakes are."

"Maybe you weren't supposed to," said Nathan. Rodney flinched; he had forgotten the strange young man was still hovering around them. "Maybe you went looking for a ghost and found something real." He gestured to the collection of humans and strange beings surrounding them. "Maybe *this* is what you needed to find."

"Possibly," Shade whispered. The way he looked at Indigo in that moment, he might have been convinced.

"Not 'possibly.' I think it's pretty blatantly obvious," Nathan said with a chuckle. "Anyway, I gotta get back to the poor saps who survived this shitshow. Sophie might turn me into a mudskipper if I don't do my part."

With that, he spun around and loped toward the front of the building. It was difficult to tell with his back turned, but Rodney swore he was smiling with all his teeth.

"Who *is* that guy, anyway?" Meesh asked.

"A man who turned on his own people to assist us," said Indigo. "He says he works for the Architect."

"Yeah, he said something about that guy. Who is he, anyway? The Architect?"

"The one who built this place," Shade said. "Supposedly. Another immortal in a world that's suddenly full of them."

"I didn't trust him *before* I knew that. I think I trust him even less now," Meesh said.

"Although he and his people may have helped us," said Indigo, "neither do I."

Meesh raised his hand as if offering an invisible toast. "Then I guess we have something in common."

All three of them, Shade included, chuckled at that, and Rodney joined in. It was lighthearted laughter, similar to what he remembered from his youth, when his father threw dinner parties at their house in Warwickshire. The type of hesitant mirth common between individuals trying to feel themselves out.

Again, progress.

After a spell, those who had gathered around them grew restless and drifted away. Most continued the grizzly duties of collecting the corpses littering the temple lawn. Others joined those who were attempting to find a way to move the enormous mechanized lizard that blocked the entrance between the hedges, its split-open chest still spitting oil all over the grass.

Shade must have been following his gaze, because he said, "Oh, so the Voice of Him was another automatic."

"I had no idea," said Indigo. "It was an artificial life form all this time."

We all are, Rodney thought, but did not say.

"You talking about the big dead lizard?" asked Meesh.

"The same."

"It's a robot," Rodney told them.

Meesh looked at him cockeyed. "Excuse me?"

"That is what they're called. Robots."

"Oh. Cool, brah. Cool."

In the brief silence that followed, Shade and Indigo met gazes and nodded. The beaten and bruised elf-girl, whose beauty seemed to borrow from every ethnic group Rodney knew of—other than the pointed ears, of course—gracefully stood up. She extended a hand to Shade and helped him stand.

"We should help them," she said.

Shade nodded his agreement.

"Fine, I guess we'll help too," whined Meesh.

"You don't have to," Shade said with half a glare.

"Okay, maybe I won't."

"Suit yourself."

"Your help would be greatly appreciated if you wish to give it," Indigo cut in, giving Meesh a tired smile. "But you have assisted us so much already. Take your time if you wish. You will not be judged."

Meesh harrumphed. "Gee. Thanks for that."

Indigo proffered her arm to Shade, who accepted. Arm-in-arm, they strolled away, heading for the working Ersatz. A couple who obviously cared for, perhaps even loved, one another deeply. There was a purity in that. Rodney thought it might break his brain to watch them meander away through a field of such horribleness.

"Hey, Rod," Meesh said.

He turned to his brother. "Yes?"

"You ain't as pretty as her, but can you do me the same favor?"

Meesh held up his hand. It took Rodney a second to realize what he was asking. He hurried over and reached out, felt Meesh's calloused fingers wrap around his muscles. He pulled Meesh to standing, his brother wincing as he hobbled on his wounded left leg.

"You need to get that looked at," Rodney told him.

"Bah. Just a scratch. I'll be better in the morning."

"I still think you should have someone look at it. Perhaps Zull? She told me she had been a healer in one of her previous incarnations."

"Zull's a chick? Well, I never. Guess you can't really tell with cat-people." He started cackling, then aimed a finger toward the kneeling humans. "Y'know what though? Great as that sounds, I'd rather take my chances with the Pinchu girl over there. Seems to know what she's doing."

Meesh was pointing at the woman who was bandaging the sagging arm of a kneeling prisoner. She was of obvious Hispanic descent, with silken curls tied in a knot at the top of her head, and she moved with the practiced efficiency of someone who had performed these duties a thousand times.

"Yes," Rodney said with a smile. "Perhaps she would work out better."

He offered his shoulder, and Meesh draped his arm around the back of his neck. They staggered across the lawn together, Meesh leaning on him for support.

"Rod?" his brother said.

"Yes?"

"How much do you remember?"

"Remember about what?"

"Your life. Before all this," Meesh asked.

Rodney helped Meesh take another step. "Perhaps not all, but a great deal."

"Tell me somethin'. Did you know me? Or a version of me?" Meesh asked.

"Personally? No."

"You said 'personally.' That means you knew of me?"

"Aye, I did," Rodney admitted.

"Was I...was I a good man?"

Rodney took a deep breath. "Does it matter?"

"Well, yeah. Why wouldn't it?"

"Because if your oracle is to be believed, you are one made of many. The version of you I knew would only be a small part of you, and therefore for me to say anything about him would be counterproductive. It has no bearing on who you are now."

"You really think so?"

Meesh sounded dismayed yet hopeful, as if he were stretching for a truth he didn't truly want to know.

"Yes, Jim, I do," Rodney told him.

"Ha! Jim! What, we going back to our fake names or something? Gonna play pretend?"

Rodney tried to hide his frown. "Something like that, my brother. Something like that."

— EPILOGUE —

Indigo sat on a boulder while Raz squatted on the ground beside her. They were on the boundary of Tro Choi, where the hedgerow used to stand. The tall bushes had been chopped down days before, their pine needles stripped away so the wood could be used as kindling for the pyres. Their removal opened the space around the temple, making it seem far smaller than it used to be.

Indigo eyed her former lover, who wore a flowing blue top designed and elegantly made by Sienna. The upper part of the blouse was cinched enough to show off her modest cleavage, while the hem flowed downward and outward, covering the area of her torso where she gradually transitioned from woman to horse. The transition looked unnatural, as if two separate species had been sewn together.

Knowing Raz, she had asked for this design on purpose.

"You are sure you want this?" she asked.

"I am," Raz answered. "I have told you this many a time. Why do you insist on asking again?"

Indigo held her up her palms in surrender. "It is simply that this is your last chance. Come tomorrow, the choice will be out of our hands."

"The choice was *always* out of our hands, my love. That has not changed, free or no."

Indigo could not help but acknowledge the accuracy in that statement. While it was true that the Ersatz had been released from captivity, they had not won the freedom to do whatever they wanted, when they wanted. They were still trapped in Darkenwood, at least for another day.

And then even after tomorrow came, when the temple was razed and the magical death boundary that kept them here fell, they still would not be able to truly decide their own fates. They would be a people without a home. They could not remain in the valley, as it would be too dangerous should the Righteous who survived the purge decide to tell their tale and invite another angry mob to continue the cycle of violence. Given that not one of her people knew what it meant to survive outside of this land bordered by mountains on all sides, and they would not be welcomed in Pirie to the north, their only true choices were to strike out on their own in the mountains or join Shade and his two brothers in heading south to the Wasteland.

Not ideal choices—as Raz said, not choices at all—even if it represented a freedom the Ersatz had never had before.

Indigo leaned over, rested her head against Raz, and sighed.

The front entrance of Tro Choi opened, and out walked Aspar, his muscles flexing as he helped an equally large and handsome young man with glistening black skin descend the steps.

"Who is that?" Raz asked, whistling.

Indigo did not need to glance over the list Nathan had given her to find the answer. "That would be Orchid."

"Oh, well then," Raz said, twining a strand of long raven hair that Indigo had worn down today. She laughed. "I see she went in the *complete* opposite direction."

"Orchid always despised being a halfling, even if she never spoke her displeasure aloud. Being as insignificant as she was became a form of survival. Others protected her, given her frailty. This is her way of paying that back, to decide on a form that would allow *her* to be the one who shielded *others* from harm." Indigo nudged Raz on her thick horse shoulder. "It was her *choice*."

Raz laughed again. "I see what you did there, my love. And my answer is still no."

"I knew it would be."

In the days after the battle for the soul of Darkenwood, after the carnage had been cleared away and those Ersatz who had perished in the melee had ascended, Nathan announced that any Ersatz who wished to alter their appearance would be free to do so. And they would get to choose their own forms this time, using a "program" that Nathan was somehow privy to. Much to the surprise of the Righteous turncoat, only seventy-nine Ersatz souls requested the change. Most had been of the lesser races, such as Dura the troll and Mita the squid-faced cook, along with those who had suffered injuries during the fighting that were too severe to heal. Or, in the case of Wisteria, to have a body that would be able to survive the traveling ahead without constantly needing to be submerged in water. Almost to an individual, those who desired one last ascension requested to come back human. All the better for existing outside their isolated valley, where Shade was insistent that anyone who looked different would be shunned and deemed a threat.

But not all of them felt that way. There were orcs like Fol and gamayun like Canary who chose to stay as they were, no matter how unusual they might seem to virgin eyes. And Macaro had chosen to keep his dwarfish form, as well. They were too proud of who they were to change, they said. They would not alter themselves simply to blend in.

Raz and her longtime companions from the Path of the Hero—Gren, Tapi, Lull, Zull, and Xi—also held that viewpoint. Indigo feared for them. They were all about to enter a land that was completely alien. She feared how the people of the Wasteland, if they were as backward as Shade described, would react when confronted with a centaur and five bananeko.

Hence, her constant pestering of Raz over the past two days as to whether she was sure in her choice. It did not matter how many assurances Raz gave her that she would be fine, Indigo worried about her nonetheless.

"What happens now?" asked Raz.

Indigo shrugged against her thick chest. "I am not sure. We live our lives as best we can, I suppose."

"You were always silly, Indigo," Raz said, chuckling. "I mean *now*. That was the last ascension, correct? What do *we* do *now*?"

An intoxicating smile stretched her lips. "Ah. Yes. Always in the moment, you are."

"That is simply my nature."

"Well, there is the feast tonight at the tavern," Indigo said. She stretched her arms and sat back upright. "Mita is excited. Her first time cooking for a large crowd as a woman, and with only two arms, in ninety years."

"Thrilling."

"Mita thinks it is."

"And after that?"

Indigo gave her a sideways glance, but Raz was not looking. She stared at the sky as if seeing it for the first time. The puffy white clouds drifting by reflected in the crystal blue eyes she now possessed.

"You know I will always love you," Indigo whispered.

Raz nodded.

"It is just..."

"You do not need to explain anything to me, my love," Raz told her. "I understand. The love we had was special, yes, but it was built out of bondage. Out of familiarity and necessity. Even a creature such as me can realize that feelings change. You flourished without me under the most difficult of circumstances."

"Not as difficult as yours," Indigo said.

"You are wrong about that. Were our situations different? Yes. But we both suffered in our own horrific ways. Do not diminish your own pain because you feel someone else may have suffered more greatly."

Indigo was astounded to hear Raz speak this way. So elegant, so thoughtful. She had long ago assumed that her first love was driven insane by the Voice of Him and her constant ascensions. It never once occurred to her that the way Raz acted during her brief reappearances in Darkenwood after receiving a new body had been on purpose. Raz knew that the rest of her days would be spent on the Path of the Hero, under constant threat of violence. As far as she was concerned, her distance and emotional outbursts were to protect Indigo by keeping her away. Why torture her with the possibility of a reunion when their time together would always be fleeting?

Selfless act after selfless act. And now that Indigo knew the truth, she felt not a small amount of guilt.

They fell into a comfortable silence, leaning on one another, enjoying the warmth. People came and went on the grounds of Tro Choi, Ersatz and turncoat alike, but no one bothered them. It was as if they had been granted their own separate dimension for a short while, a place where they could simply sit and bathe in the comfort of each other before the time came to depart.

Finally, the sound of someone clearing their throat made Indigo lift her head. It was Briar, no longer a demonite, but a woman with deeply tanned skin and a head full of curly hair that fell to her waist. At least her fingers were long and lean enough that she could still play her citole like it was a part of her.

"Dinner is soon, Mum," she said.

"Thank you, Briar. We will be along shortly."

Briar gave a slight bow and hurried off. Raz laughed heartily and squeezed her hand.

"What?" asked Indigo.

"Mum. I am *so* glad I am not called that any longer. It used to make me feel *old*."

They both got a good laugh out of that.

When their joviality faded, Indigo slid off her rock and Raz rose gracefully on her four legs. They strolled the road side by side, hand in hand, as Indigo walked with her right arm raised to reach Raz's.

Indigo did not care. She was too busy admiring how clean everything was. It had taken three days to clear the corpses out of here and another two days to burn them. Now, other than the occasional divot Sobec had caused everything looked like it always had. The former Voice of Him was now buried in a deep hole in the forest to the east, as his scales and steel skeleton would not burn. No evidence remained that the conflict had ever happened. And soon, the only evidence of the true purpose of Darkenwood, the Ersatz themselves, would be gone too.

Indigo hoped the Righteous who had survived the battle would remember, if only to convince others never to create such a horrible place again.

"It is six miles to Hickweis," Raz said, yanking her from her thoughts. "Are you sure you would not rather ride on my back?"

"No, it is fine," said Indigo. "I enjoy walking."

"Just think of how much faster you would get back to your man, though." Raz eyed her mischievously, and Indigo sighed. "He is a good man," Raz said. "I like him."

"I like him too."

"And he is obviously in love with you."

"He is."

"He best treat you well, or I will seek him out once we become settled, and end him."

"I do not think you need to worry about that," Indigo said, laughing.

Raz gave her a serious look. "And he best realize that you do not actually *need* him."

"He does," Indigo told her, though she was not so sure of that.

"Though I must say," Raz said. "I think your union might have been more tantalizing a couple hundred years ago."

"How so?"

"I have always enjoyed watching beautiful men become intimate. And Indigo, you were a *beautiful* man. Simply imagine that."

She did. When that vision entered her thoughts, Indigo allowed herself to laugh.

The grounds in front of Tro Choi had been cleared of grass. In its place on the churned dirt were numerous painted symbols inside of a pair of gigantic circles, one larger than the other, that wrapped completely around the temple. Multicolored crystals had been placed on the rings, each positioned seven feet apart.

Now Indigo understood why the luggage this group of Righteous had brought with them had been so heavy.

Sophie stood front-and-center, strange words coming out of her mouth as her fingers drew invisible pictures in the air. Beside her, Nathan struck the two-foot-long steel fork he held with a rock. A high-pitched, vibrating sound filled the air. Nathan held the fork in front of Sophie, who began humming, somehow matching the sound coming from that strange device.

Much to the amazement of everyone standing behind them—the entire population of Darkenwood had come to witness the event, what little possessions they had stuffed into in sacks slung over their shoulders—the crystals in the rings surrounding Tro Choi began to glow. Their light intensified as Sophie hummed louder. It became so bright that Indigo found herself squinting. She looked at Shade and squeezed his hand, suddenly fearful that they would all be sucked out of reality altogether.

It was not them that ceased to be, but the Ersatz place of ascension itself. A loud rumble sounded deep in the earth, and a large crack appeared on the temple, starting at the foundation and spreading up to split the door frame in two. The crack snaked all the way up to the peak of the spire.

The rumbling beneath the ground became louder, and Tro Choi folded in on itself, raising a cloud of dust that twisted into the air like a tornado. Loud cracking sounds echoed through the valley, followed by a roar like a landslide. The dust funnel then descended, sucked into the hole where the temple once stood. The lines and symbols on the dirt faded away. The crystals cracked and disintegrated into still more dust.

Just like that, Tro Choi was gone.

"What the hell was *that*?" asked Meesh, the shorter of the two pale men whom Shade called brothers.

"That was magic," said Nathan.

"Not really," said a winded Sophie. "Just intention and sound and a knowledge of the path of energy that allows me to do some pretty amazing thing when I harness them. It's science."

"That explains everything," Shade snipped.

"And where was that magic-science when we were fighting?" asked Macaro.

Sophie turned to him, eyes narrowed. "There's a single hotspot in this entire valley. Just one. And it's right there, under Tro Choi. The dimensional energy from that hotspot powered this whole place, along with the barrier that kept you all in. If there were more, I would've been able to do more. But I'm not as strong as I used to be. There's no way I could've helped without creating a circle of power and using all the crystals I needed to do this."

"Yeah, even after all this time, she's still not at full strength." Nathan laughed, sliding the long steel fork into its leather carrying case. "Don't pester her. She's sensitive about it."

Sophie glared and his laughter abruptly ceased.

What an odd pair.

"So...it is done?" Bluebell asked. The redhead clutched Indigo so tightly on the bicep that it cut off circulation and made her fingers numb.

"Yup, it's done," Nathan said. "No more barrier. You're not trapped here anymore."

"Are you certain?" Mana asked timidly.

"No, I'm lying." Nathan waited a beat before continuing, "Of course I'm certain! I'm the one who—" Nathan wrinkled his nose, as if he could feel Sophie shooting warning looks at his back. "It's really done. Go see for yourselves. You're free to go now."

Almost four hundred sets of eyes looked at Indigo, as if for permission. She nodded, and all of started shuffling forward onto the grassless dirt, giving the hole where Tro Choi used to stand a wide berth before they entered the surrounding woods.

She approached Nathan, who eyed her warily, timidly touching the bandage around his neck.

"Whassup?"

"Promise they will not come for us," she said.

He grinned sheepishly. "They won't. Where you're going, they wouldn't dare follow. I promise."

"Hugo Popp is still alive," Indigo reminded him. "Two of his sons were killed. He knows where we are going. What if he decides he wants revenge and decides to chase us into the Wasteland?"

"He won't," Nathan told her.

"How do you know that?" asked Shade.

"Because they don't know the way," Sophie said. Her mouth quirked and her eyes widened, as if stricken by sudden inspiration. She quickly reached into her shirt and pulled out the pendant that had been her constant accessory ever since her arrival. She slid the necklace over her head, deftly avoiding snagging it on her curly hair, and held it out to Indigo.

"What are you doing?" Indigo asked.

"A gift," Sophie told her. "Let's call it my way of promising you'll never see those people again." She held the necklace up higher, the pendant swinging back and forth like a pendulum. Light refracted off its translucent surface. "See this crystal here? It's probably one of the most valuable things in Pirie. Rare. Like, one-of-a-kind rare."

Indigo cautiously held out her hand, and Sophie lowered the pendant into her cupped palm. The stone felt unnaturally smooth, even its angles, and it seemed to give off a subtle vibration. Indigo pinched it between her fingertips and brought it close to her face. The expert cut of the stone was a sight to behold, as were the silver threads that ran through its center, as if it had been tunneled through by a worm spinning silk. She slipped the string over her head. The crystal felt warm against her flesh.

"It's magic too," Sophie whispered, leaning in close. "Keep that thing on you, and I promise on my life—and Nathan's—that none from Pirie will ever harm you again."

"Hey now," Nathan said with mock affront.

Sophie rolled her eyes, gave Indigo a kiss on the cheek, and abruptly turned to gather up her things. Without another word, the co-leader of the turncoats headed toward the pair of horses that would carry them back to the north, where the rest of the turncoats and the Righteous prisoners waited at the Fallen Arch.

Shade tensed beside Indigo, his gaze intent on Nathan. Indigo feared that he might threaten the young man, but when Shade spoke, his voice was calm, measured, and oddly polite. The tone of a man asking a favor.

"You know a lot about this place, huh?"

"I do," Nathan said. "I already told you about the entrance to the tunnels that's halfway up the mountain, right? Or did you forget about that already?"

"No, I remember that. And I think I know the place. I was wondering about…something else."

"Um, okay," Nathan said, frowning. "I'm not sure I'll be able to give you an answer, though."

Shade sucked in his bottom lip. "On my way over the mountain, I met a man. Lives up there all by himself. Name of Ken. He's the one who told me to come here. He gave me clothes, ammunition, everything I'd end up needing."

"Yeah? And?"

"Do you know who he is?"

Nathan shook his head. "Nope. Never heard of him. Why?"

"I don't know." He pulled back his slouch, fingered the curly hair atop his head. "I guess I was looking for a reason why he wanted me to come here. Ken said it was my destiny. Was it? Why did the oracle tell my brother he needed to help me? Why did any of this happen at all?"

At that, Nathan offered a soft, playful smile and slapped Shade on the shoulder.

"Well, man, I guess you could say the Queen of Snakes works in mysterious ways."

With that, he threw his bag over his shoulder and went to join Sophie by the horses without another word.

"Strange man," the tall brother named Rodney said.

Shade raised a distrustful eyebrow at him. "Mm," he uttered and grabbed Indigo by the hand. He nodded to her, and she nodded back.

The Ersatz gathered up their food, water, and belongings, and began walking to the west of the place Tro Choi once stood, where there was a path through the woods that had taunted them for so long with their inability to traverse it. Indigo and Shade took the lead, hands still locked, matching one another stride for stride.

She took a moment to glance back at the two other knights, who trailed behind, softly mumbling between themselves. The one called Meesh kept casting furtive glances at Shade.

Indigo sighed. Over the eleven days since the Ersatz had gained their freedom, she had spoken often with these two men. She liked them both, even if Meesh was a bit crass and Rodney overly sullen. But the relationship between them and Shade remained fractured. That was bound to happen when one brother tries to kill the other.

But the prospect that this fracturing would poison them on what was sure to be a harrowing journey frightened her. Indigo and her people knew nothing about the Wasteland toward which they were headed. They would be relying on these men to guide them. She only hoped that all their relationship needed to heal was time.

Those thoughts were far from her mind when they reached the demarcation line, however. Excitement churned in her belly as her people, all three hundred and ninety-three of them, lined up single-file on either side of the cobbled path. Indigo looked up at a sign whose face she had only seen once, when she attempted to flee Darkenwood and ended up in her current body.

"After you," Shade said, proffering his hand.

Hesitantly, Indigo placed one foot over the line where cobbles met dirt. She felt nothing, not a shudder, not a single twinge. Her body passed over, followed by her other foot. She took a few more steps and then stopped, closing her eyes and breathing in deeply, cherishing the taste of pine on her tongue. Turning around, she read the sign.

Darkenwood: Only the Righteous May Enter

Indigo touched the crystal pendant now resting against her chest. Its subtle vibration made her smile. She then reared back and kicked the signpost as hard as she could. It splintered on impact and fell into the weeds lining the path.

The Ersatz began to cheer.

Shade joined her side and offered his arm. "Shall we go?" he asked.

"We shall," she told him, and took it.

Together, with her people forming a raucous cluster behind her, Indigo took her first steps toward the hidden passage beneath the mountains that Sophie had told them of. Her first steps toward a new life. Her first steps toward freedom.

Meesh and Rodney stood at the foot of the path leading up the mountain, watching the freed Ersatz hoot and holler as they crossed over the boundary, one by one. They were a giant swarm of ants in the forest. It should have been a joyous moment, but Meesh had difficulty finding pleasure in it.

"They look happy," Rodney said.

"They do," Meesh replied. "Bully for them."

His brother looked at him, confused. "What bothers you?"

"They're not ready for this, that's what," Meesh told him.

"They will learn. You and Shade already said you would work together so they can get settled."

"Yeah, that's not what I'm talking about."

"Then what?"

Meesh groaned. His trepidation had been building for days as he struggled to decide whether to present Shade with the full scope of what he knew. He still hadn't done so. Because if Shade found out exactly what the oracle beneath the mountain told him, he wouldn't come back with them. He wouldn't help set things straight.

The oracle told him as much. She had told him to keep the truth hidden. Meesh hadn't believed her. *Shade's trustworthy,* he thought at the time. He could deal with any news, even if it was bad. But given that Shade tried to kill him just because he *thought* Meesh was going to hurt Indigo...

"This ain't gonna end well," he whispered.

He clammed up and started up the path. Rodney followed on his heels. His brother grabbed his shoulder, spun him around.

"There is something you're not telling me."

The concern in Rodney's eyes broke Meesh.

"Fine," he said. He reached into his breast pocket, pulled out the folded piece of paper within. "Remember this?" he asked.

"I...think?" said Rodney. "That's the poem the Reverend gave us, correct?"

"Exactly. The *riddle*. Only it's not a riddle. It's a prediction. And it's incomplete."

"How so?"

"There's a stanza missing. At the end."

Rodney sucked in his bottom lip. "The oracle told you this?"

"She did."

"Did she tell you what it said?"

Meesh grimaced, afraid to say more. He stuffed his hands in the pockets of his breeches and started up the path again.

"Come on, mate," Rodney huffed, struggling to keep up with him. "You can tell me. I won't say anything."

"I know," Meesh said in a low voice. "It's just...it's hard."

"How so?"

"Because it says that the Reverend isn't the last threat. That there's a greater evil rising, and Shade's the key to beating it. But in order for that to happen...well...well, Shade..."

"Shade what?"

"Will have to lose everything he loves."

Rodney opened his mouth, shut it, and blinked. He shoved his hands in his pockets as well, and from that point on, they tramped along the path in silence.

To Be Continued...

AUTHOR'S NOTE

After finishing this book, some of you might be wondering why a work of post-apocalyptic fantasy would be dedicated to Beverly Jenkins, a longtime member of the Romance writing community. The answer to that, of course, must be told through a story.

In 1998, when I was twenty-three years old and at a personal crossroads, I happened to run into my old poetry professor while at the bookstore. This was a woman whom I looked up to entirely. She'd introduced me to the works of Arthur Rimbaud, Langston Hughes, and Robert Browning, and was one of the few people who'd recognized the middling talent I had and tried to convince me to utilize it as much as I could.

In other words, she was an ally. And being an ally, when she asked me if everything was okay, I unloaded on her. Right then and there, while standing in the horror section of Waldenbooks. I told her how much I regretted dropping out of school to support my young family; that I was resigned to working unfulfilling blue-collar jobs for the rest of my life; how I felt uninspired creatively. But mostly, I went on and on about my crumbling marriage, how it felt like all the love I had to give wasn't being returned.

She looked at me and smiled. Proffering her arm toward the novels involving death, destruction, and monsters on the shelves around us, she said, "You don't need any of this right now. You need something more fulfilling." She reached into her purse, pulled out a dog-eared paperback, and handed it to me. "Read this instead. You'll thank me later."

That book was *Indigo* by Beverly Jenkins, and she was right, I *would* thank her later. While it didn't save my marriage, which mercifully ended a few years later, it *did* make me fall in love with romance, a genre I'd always made fun of in my youth.

But even more than that, *Indigo* changed my entire worldview.

Reading the story of Hester Wyatt, protecting runaway slaves along her leg of the Underground Railroad in Michigan, and her affair with "Black Daniel" Galen Vashon, opened my eyes in a way they'd never been before. I'd always taken pride in the assumption that I knew American history, yet it was only through the reading of this book that I realized how little of our country's past was actually taught in school. There was little explained about the American Civil War other than "slavery was bad, and we eradicated it." In one of the far too many examples, we were never taught about the horrific implications—and the suffering caused by—the Compromise of 1850. John Brown and Harpers Ferry was a brief anecdotal aside. Nowhere in our scholastic texts (even in college) was there any mention of people such as John Fairfield, William Lambert, George DeBaptiste, or Frances Ellen Watkins.

Taking in all of this new information led me on a lifelong journey through our *real* history. From the aforementioned abolitionists, to Civil Rights figures such as James Forman, Fred Hampton, Robert F. Williams, and Malcolm X, to the fictional works of James Baldwin, Alice Walker, Octavia Butler, Walter Mosely, and countless others, I wouldn't have experienced any of them had a random encounter with a trusted old teacher not introduced me to the wonderful book *Indigo*.

So when I say that Beverly Jenkins formed the emotional core of my own novel, I mean it. And it goes far beyond naming one of the main characters Indigo. The themes of this book (of all my books, for that matter) are influenced by her. From the bravery of the oppressed to the fight for freedom to the sense of social justice; that all comes from reading that one important paperback more than twenty years ago. I don't know if I'd be the writer—or man—that I am today without her words to help mold me. So thank you, Ms. Bev, for being an inspiration. This white boy is a far better person for having read your work.

There are many others I need to thank. Alana Abbott, for being the best editor ever and continuing to point out potentially problematic sections of my writing that I obviously still haven't learned enough to correct. Jeremy Mohler and the team at Outland Entertainment for believing in this little world I've created enough to keep the saga going.

To David Dalglish, for his close friendship and undying support, and Daniel Pyle, who's been egging me on to write this series for years. To the best writers' group ever, including Cindy, Bree, Christina, Danielle, Krista, Cid, Scott, Donna, Michael, Mel, Dave G, and Nate, for always being there when I need you. For Jess, my wonderful wife, who doesn't put up with the extra hours I spend creating these stories, but actively encourages it.

And finally, thank you, the reader. Without you, there'd be no me. If you'd like to speak with me, feel free to drop me a line at rjduperreauthor@gmail.com. I answer everything, even if it takes a little while sometimes.

These are trying times, but the show must go on. I'm currently hard at work on the final book in this series. And I promise, *Warmaker* will be a doozy. Just wait 'til you see what I have in store for Shade, Indigo, Meesh, and Rodney in the future. You won't want to miss it.

So take care of each other. Love each other. Be kind. Until next time!

Robert J. Duperre
January 2021